She Who Comes Forth

Other Books by Audrey Driscoll

The Herbert West Series

Book 1. The Friendship of Mortals
Book 2. Islands of the Gulf Volume 1, The Journey
Book 3. Islands of the Gulf Volume 2, The Treasure
Book 4. Hunting the Phoenix

She Who Comes Forth

a novel

Audrey Driscoll

She Who Comes Forth
by
Audrey Driscoll

Published by Audrey Driscoll

ISBN 9781999424015

And at the last from inner Egypt came
The strange dark One to whom the fellahs bowed;
Silent and lean and cryptically proud,
And wrapped in fabrics red as sunset flame.
Throngs pressed around, frantic for his commands,
But leaving, could not tell what they had heard;
While through the nations spread the awestruck word
That wild beasts followed him and licked his hands.

Soon from the sea a noxious birth began;
Forgotten lands with weedy spires of gold;
The ground was cleft, and mad auroras rolled
Down on the quaking citadels of man.
Then, crushing what he chanced to mould in play,
The idiot Chaos blew Earth's dust away.

"Nyarlathotep" (XXI from H.P. Lovecraft's *Fungi from Yuggoth*)

The Chapter of Experiencing Departure and Disappointment

Luxor, Egypt, September 27th, 1962

My hair flopped into my eyes—again. I tried to blow it out of the way, but that never works. I pushed it behind my ear for the hundredth time that day, my dirty hand adding to the accumulated grime on my face. Sighing, I turned back to the pile of rocks in front of me. Check for inscriptions. Check for chisel marks. Attempt to discern shape. Sort and classify.

The clink of tools on stone and the murmur of voices blurred into a distant hum, joined by the drowsy buzz of flies. Even in the shade of the tarp stretched over the sorting area, it was hot and getting hotter.

"Hello, Miss America!" The Grinner arrived with another basket of rocks. His thin body jiggled under his grey *galabeya* and his eyes squinted under his faded blue turban. "It is beautiful day! *Very* happy to see you!" He was smiling so hard I thought his face would split and the top of his head would fall off, turban and all.

"Hello," I said. I couldn't remember his name. Ali? Omar? I couldn't keep them straight. To me, this one was "the Grinner," and I couldn't call him that to his face.

"Please put that here." I pointed to a spot next to the basket I was working on. "Thank you. Very much." I turned back to my current rock, hoping he would take the hint and leave.

"His name's Mustafa," Hank said from behind me. "It's no hardship to remember the workers' names, France. Just like I remember yours. They appreciate it."

Great. Another mini-lecture from Hashish Hank. I squinted up at him, brushing the hair out of my eyes yet again. "But my name isn't 'Miss America.'"

Hank grinned. "That means he thinks you're pretty."

"I'll keep that in mind." Even my sarcasm-producer was weary.

"And you'd better step it up." He gestured toward the new basket of stone fragments that had joined my half-full one. "The Boss wants us to get this section done today, so there's lots more to come."

"All right." I blew a raspberry at his departing back and picked up a rock. Check for inscriptions. Check for chisel marks. Try to discern shape. Sort. Classify. Wipe sweat, push hair behind ear.

Shit, it's hot!

Archaeology, Egyptian style.

If only I'd known.

****

Providence, Rhode Island, two weeks earlier

"You're really going."

I turned from the gaping suitcase on my bed to look at Alma, who stood peering at the pile of papers on my dresser — passport, proof of vaccinations, letters of invitation and introduction, plane tickets and itinerary.

"Yes, of course I'm going. You knew that."

"Knew but hoped you wouldn't. Even though I admit if I were you, I wouldn't let anyone convince me not to." She smiled, which made me feel guilty.

"Don't worry about me," Alma said, as though she had read my mind (which I often thought she could). "I'll be fine. The young should leave the nest. The old can look after themselves, and if they can't, it's time they kicked the bucket." Her hearty tone failed to contradict the sadness in her eyes. "Come along for a drink when you're done or need a break."

Her voice faded as she escaped down the hall. Alma hated anyone to see her cry, so I didn't follow her, but went back to packing. All the new clothes I'd bought—cottons and linens for a hot climate—were safely stashed. I was in the final stages now, dithering over an extra blouse or two, wondering how often I would be able to do laundry, so were three dozen pairs of panties enough? And what about those Bermuda shorts? Totally appropriate for an archaeological site, but would shorts, even tailored ones, be considered indecent in Egypt? I tossed them in anyway.

Egypt! I was hit by another one of those bolts of excitement and nervous fear. I was really going to Egypt. My tickets were bought, my seat on the plane reserved for departure in exactly three days.

The trip was a gift and a celebration, a generous graduation present from Alma and Charles. Everything had come together about the time I graduated from Brown University with a BA in Ancient History. I applied for and got a job as assistant to Dr. William Stanton, an archaeologist conducting excavations in Luxor, Egypt, the site of ancient

Thebes. And my legal change of name was finalized in time for me to obtain a passport.

I picked up the passport—new and pristine, but not for long. The picture was too serious, of course, but it made me look older than twenty-one, which was a good thing. France Leighton—a new name for my new life. Much better than Francesca Willett.

I sighed, thinking of the obligatory side trip to visit my mother, followed by another, to see the man who was my father, whether he liked it or not. Once that was out of the way, a hop across the Channel, train to Paris and then to Marseille, and another boat, across the Mediterranean to Alexandria. Just me, alone (except for Eudora, of course).

Another bolt—of pure excitement this time. I picked up Eudora and did a little dance with her before grabbing my bow and sitting down to play the opening of Bach's first cello suite, sloppily and too fast. I switched to one of the *Sarabandes* instead. Eudora's vibrations matched the current of excitement running through me. "We're going on an adventure," I said, laying down the bow. I gently plucked her strings. "What do you think of that?"

Dark chocolate notes and contented rumbles. Happy sounds.

Since Uncle Charles's death five months before, Alma had taken to having afternoon tea in a remote room on the second floor. "It was Charles's study, back in the old days," she said. "And it's nice and cozy."

Well, maybe she thought it was nice, but I didn't. The room was full of old books, and the furniture looked like it belonged in a junk store. Alma always kept the curtains closed and turned on the lights, even on bright, sunny days. If I were Lucy or Andre, I would have complained about the extra work it took to lug the tea-trays up there, but they didn't mind. Of course, they'd worked for Alma and Charles since what she called the "old days."

By the time I arrived, they'd been and gone, leaving a plate of sandwiches and another of iced cupcakes beside the teapot and cups. Alma was sipping what was probably her second glass of Scotch.

"Dig in and have a drink," she said, putting down the magazine she was reading. "Tell me again what you'll be doing in Egypt." She lit a cigarette. "You'll be this professor's secretary, is that it? Or are you going to look after his kids?"

"No, no! The kids are in school somewhere. I won't be a secretary, either. I'll be keeping records of the excavation, listing finds made every day, taking pictures, making sure everything is recorded properly. Dr. Stanton said there's a chance of finding a tomb, just like King Tut's, so it's a fabulous opportunity. I guess I might have to type a few letters, but mostly I'll be in charge of documenting the dig."

"Hmm. Sounds like you'll be a secretary. Okay, okay, don't get upset," she said, laughing. "I'm sure it'll be interesting, and at least you'll be using some of the stuff you've been studying the last four years."

"Exactly. Just think, I'll be in the land of the pharaohs. I'll walk in their temples and touch things they made and used. I'll *experience* ancient Egypt, not just read about it in books."

"You're a romantic, just like Charles."

Three days later, Andre manhandled my two heavy suitcases down to the front hall. I followed him with my overnight bag and Eudora in her case.

Alma emerged from the office she had shared with Charles. "Francesca, surely you're not taking the cello!"

"Why shouldn't I? She's mine. If I don't take her, I'll forget how to play."

"But you'll be living in a tent or something. Think of the dust! And the air is really dry in Egypt, especially where you'll be. The wood will crack. It's almost two hundred years old. And I doubt you'll have any time to play."

I put my arm around the case. "I won't be in a tent. There's a dig house. I told you about it. Uncle Charles gave her to me. I don't want to leave her behind."

Alma waved her hand and turned away. I thought she was about to cry again. "Too late to argue with you."

Charles had given me something else not long before he died. The day after my birthday, he summoned me—yes, "summoned" is the only word that fits—into the office.

"I have something for you," he said. "You're twenty-one now, so it's time you had this. It's not a birthday present, though, but a legacy." He reached into a pocket and placed a ring on my outstretched palm.

It was a big, clunky ring, made of pale gold with engraved designs and an emerald. It wasn't pretty. It didn't suit me.

"It's… Why are you giving me this? What do you mean, it's a legacy?"

"You're meant to have this ring, Francesca. That's all you need to know."

He looked tired, and I was pretty sure he was hoping I wouldn't argue or ask any questions. But I had to.

"Where did it come from?"

"I don't know. It's very old. Put it in a safe place. Keep it. That's all you need to do. You don't have to wear it. In fact, it might be best if you didn't. Just keep it."

"Where did you get it?"

Charles closed his eyes for a second and took a deep breath. "From your grandfather, Francis Dexter."

That made *me* want to close my eyes and sigh. Grandparents were supposed to be simple and reliable, not messy and complicated.

Charles and Alma became my legal guardians when I was twelve. I knew Alma was my grandmother and Francis Dexter, who died years before I was born, was my grandfather. But to me, Alma's husband Charles was my grandfather, even though I called him "Uncle."

As if this wasn't enough, my father wasn't married to my mother, because he already had a wife. I was illegitimate. And after my mother married Alfred Willett and had two more kids, she didn't want me around, so I was exported to America. Which was just fine with me, actually.

I was glad to be getting away from all these complications. In Egypt, I would be whatever I could make of myself—France Leighton—and not anyone's mistake or unwanted loose end.

I didn't want Francis Dexter's ring. But Uncle Charles was dead serious, and he didn't look well, and I loved him.

"Okay," I said, "I'll keep it safe."

Packing for my big trip, I dug the ring out of the bottom of my jewelry box and tucked it into a secret pocket inside my overnight bag. To remind me of Charles when I was far away in the land of the pharaohs.

****

The Cairo train station was huge and busy, full of people hurrying in all directions, bumping into each other, their voices echoing and mingling. I was the only one standing still, because I didn't know where to go. How would Mrs. Stanton recognize me?

Fortunately, there weren't that many tall, blond Americans in the crowd. A few minutes later, I heard my name called, and saw two American-looking people emerging from a huddle of dark-suited Egyptians.

"France Leighton?" The trim, brown-haired woman held out a white-gloved hand. "I'm Adele Stanton. At least your train was on time. This is Hank Dykstra, our excavation lead hand. He'll deal with your bags. What's that, a guitar? Oh, a cello. All right, give it to Hank. Come along, both of you."

She led the way quickstep through the crowd, not bothering to check if Hank and I were following. I looked at him helplessly, and he grinned.

"Better do as ordered," he said, his voice muffled by the voices and echoes all around. "When Adele speaks, everyone jumps."

The taxi from the train station took us through the colourful melee of the city. Poring over articles about Egypt in the *National Geographic*, I had concentrated on pictures of archaeological digs, rather than urban scenes. The streets were full of men in *galabeyas* and turbans, men in western suits and fez hats, men, men, men. There were a few women in traditional loose black outfits that made them almost invisible, and even fewer wearing modern clothes. Egypt was a man's world, despite a billboard showing a sophisticated woman drinking Coca-Cola.

We ended up at a hotel, not quite as cool and tidy as the one in Alexandria, where I had spent my first night in Egypt. At this point I was no longer Miss France Leighton, independent traveller paying her own way, but an employee of the Stanton Temple Precinct Project.

I was dazed by the rapid transitions of the past several days. Train from Providence to New York City, transatlantic flight to London, a prickly visit with my mother, followed by a rather chilly one with Nicholas Leighton. And then the train through France, southward and southward; the Mediterranean crossing to Alexandria, and finally another train to Cairo.

Mrs. Stanton and Hank carried on a conversation while we had supper in a restaurant near the hotel. The waiters spoke Arabic or French. I didn't know Arabic at all, and it felt like my college French had been lost on the trip, so I was glad Mrs. Stanton took charge and ordered for me. Hank was quite the conversationalist, jabbering away to the waiters and making them laugh. I couldn't tell if they were laughing at him or with him. He looked American, even with his dark suntan. I guess it was the light brown curly hair and the straightened teeth.

I kept quiet and listened to their talk, which was mostly about supplies and meetings with different people in government offices and museums. No one said anything about what I would be doing once we got to the dig site, and I didn't want to ask. Dr. Stanton's letter of appointment had been encouraging but vague.

The next day, Hank toured me around while Mrs. Stanton went off to do business. Cairo was a confusing mixture of old and new. We jostled through narrow alleys between ancient stone walls, with tall buildings visible in the distance. Hank was a real help in carving a way through the crowds and bargaining with people selling things. I bought postcards and some glass and enamel beads.

In the afternoon, the three of us went to the Egyptian Museum. Statues of pharaohs near the entrance welcomed me to their country. I didn't have time to linger near them, because Hank steered me toward a set of stairs, while Mrs. Stanton went off somewhere, saying she would see us later.

"Let's go up to the Mummy Room," Hank said.

I wondered if he was trying to test me. Maybe he thought I would faint at the sight of ancient dead bodies. I decided I wouldn't, no matter what, but I did feel a bit queasy looking at the dry, leathery skin clinging to the skeletons and flaking off in spots, and the ropy shrivelled muscles.

"How did they get this way?" I asked. "I mean—they used to be wrapped in those linen bandages, didn't they? Like in that movie, 'The Mummy.' Why are they lying here naked?"

Hank laughed. "For the sake of knowledge, of course. Egyptologists have been unwrapping mummies for decades. In the old days they used to have unwrapping parties."

Now I did feel a bit sick. "But it's... indecent. When they were bandaged and put in tombs, it was supposed to be forever."

"Well, tomb robbers didn't think so. And without studying the mummies, we'd know less about how they lived and died. It's science now, not like before. And they're treated with respect here."

I didn't want to argue. "I think I've seen enough, if you don't mind."

Gold funeral masks from various tombs should have been a relief but weren't. Not as directly disturbing as the human remains, but I couldn't help thinking about how they must have been carefully placed over the swathed faces of the mummies. Now they were displayed in one room, while the mummies were in another. I thought about the curse of the pharaohs and wondered what I would do if the excavation I'd be working on found an unopened tomb.

Leaving the room of masks, I noticed one I hadn't seen before. The eyes—black irises on white enamel, outlined in black—looked right at me out of the golden face. The full lips almost smiled, as though he was thinking, "Ah, there she is!"

I wanted to linger, to get acquainted and savour the welcome, but Hank was halfway down the hall.

We arrived in Luxor at dusk. The air smelled of smoke and dust, but I was happy to leave the stuffiness of the train. Hank picked up my bags and directed me toward a big black car. It was fully dark by the time we were ready to go. After a short drive along a bumpy road we stopped.

"Home sweet home," said Hank, getting out and shouldering my cello case.

"I can carry that," I said, determined to bring Eudora into her temporary new home myself, like a bridegroom carrying his bride across the threshold. Besides, Hank would have to lug my suitcases.

"Okey-dokey. This way, please. And be quiet, everyone's probably asleep."

"Already?" I was tired from the trip, but it was barely nine o'clock.

"Breakfast's at five, and everyone's on the job by five-thirty. The early bird beats the heat." He waved at a closed door. "Girls' Dorm in there. You'll be okay with the overnight bag? I'll leave these out here then. Good night."

An unfamiliar voice is more effective than any alarm clock. "I guess this is the new gal, France Leighton. Odd name—France."

"Do you think we should wake her up? You know how upset Mme Stanton gets when someone's late." This one had a French accent.

It was pretty awkward waking up in a strange place, with total strangers looking me over when I was half-awake and had to pee. Rising to the occasion, I excused myself, found the washroom again, peed, had a quick wash and returned to the scene prepared to meet and greet.

The others were gone. Being on time, it seemed, was more important than meeting the new gal. I hauled my suitcases from where Hank had left them and dug out what I hoped was an appropriate outfit—khaki linen skirt, white cotton blouse, blue neckerchief for accent. Then I went to find the rest of the crew.

That, believe it or not, was the best part of the day.

When he interviewed me back in Providence, I thought Dr. Stanton was kind of handsome, for an older man, but at breakfast he looked untidy and frazzled. After a fleeting handshake he didn't spare me a glance. Right after the meal, Mrs. Stanton summoned me to an office on the second floor of the house. She wore an olive-green dress with brass buttons and pocket flaps, almost military. It suited her.

"Miss Leighton," she said, "I'm not quite sure what we're going to do with you."

I felt my jaw starting to drop and clamped my mouth shut.

"You see," she continued, picking up a letter opener from her desk, "I wasn't aware my husband had hired you until a few days ago, when he informed me of your imminent arrival in Cairo."

"But he interviewed me at Brown University, back in May! I sent in an application in response to an advertisement for someone to keep records of the excavation." I hated that my face felt hot, and sweat was breaking out in my armpits.

Mrs. Stanton laid down the letter opener and held up a hand. "Oh, I'm sure you did. And of course he interviewed you. He never hires anyone sight unseen. Young women especially." She moved her lips in what must have been meant as a smile. "I don't expect he told you that *I'm* in charge of documenting and record-keeping. Or that I already have a competent assistant. But here you are, so we may as well use your talents, whatever they are."

What followed was another interview, way tougher than the one by Dr. Stanton. That had been no more than a pleasant chat. Dr. Stanton had encouraged me to burble on about my interests and aspirations, all the while listening and smiling benignly. He certainly hadn't quizzed me about my knowledge of Egyptian hieroglyphs (nil), modern archaeological theory (minimal), statistical analysis (less than nil), and Arabic (also nil).

"So," Mrs. Stanton said, pacing around the room, slapping her palm with the letter opener, "you have a B.A. in Ancient History with a couple of courses on Egypt and the

Middle East. You have some French and a nodding acquaintance with Latin and Greek. You're weak in math, have no experience of fieldwork, and speak no Arabic."

She turned around and gave me that tight smile again, pointing the letter opener right at me. "But you're young, you're attractive and, I'm sure, fairly personable."

I scraped my self-worth off the floor and organized my thoughts. "Mrs. Stanton, I applied in good faith for a position described as 'excavation assistant.' I was given to understand by Dr. Stanton that I met the requirements for that position. On that basis, I travelled here at my own expense. I'm ready to work in whatever capacity Dr. Stanton intended me to."

"I'm sure you are," she said, laying down the letter opener with a sharp click, "and now that both you and Dr. Stanton understand the situation, we must find a role for you that won't waste your time, or anyone else's."

That role ended up being "unskilled excavation assistant," or, more accurately, "rock sorter." Under Hank's supervision, I examined the stone fragments dug up by the Egyptian labourers and passed some of them on to those with more expertise. Hank gave me a quick course on the basics of archaeological fieldwork, in the hope that I would become more than marginally useful before the end of the field season.

And of course, there was the unspoken but perfectly clear understanding that I would under no circumstances find myself in a compromising position with Dr. William Stanton. I didn't bother pointing out that wasn't totally under my control.

2
The Chapter of Experiencing Insult and Injury

The Stanton Project's dig house, just outside the Karnak temple complex, was a big, shabby stucco building, sort of a tan colour with patches of yellow and faded orange. Besides the kitchen and bathroom, the ground floor had four main rooms—the combined dining/meeting room, a workroom/office and the two dormitories, labelled "Men" and "Girls." There were three of us "girls" in residence—Mrs. Stanton's assistant Meg Elliott, visiting art historian Louisa Dufour, and me.

The Girls' Dorm was smaller than my bedroom at home. Thin curtains hung between the three narrow beds. There was *no* private space, unless you counted the bathroom, but lingering in there wasn't an option, even if I'd wanted to. Each of us had a tiny chest of drawers and a couple of pegs on the wall to hang stuff. The shared closet was miserably small and a total mess.

I kept most of my clothes in my suitcase, which I pushed under the bed, but I had nowhere to play my cello. Poor Eudora languished in her case, also under the bed. After supper my first day, I opened the case and lifted her out. I stroked the smooth, dark wood of her neck and plucked her strings. They thrummed so faintly I thought she was dead, but when I touched her tuning-pegs, she came alive and whispered.

Oh, we're far away, far away from all that's familiar. We're lost, we're strange, we need to find the right road...

"Shh, Eudora. It's okay, I'm here, we're still together. Let's play."

I screwed in the endpin, picked up my bow, and drew from her strings the familiar chanting drone, the reverberation of life in hollow air, song of heart and soul. The irritations of the present withdrew, faded away, vanished.

"What the *hell* is that racket?"

Meg Elliot stood in front of me, red hair bristling, a pencil and ruler clutched in her fists.

"It's J.S. Bach. His first cello suite."

"Well, that's great, but I'm trying to finish a report. I need to *concentrate. Must* you do that *now?*"

Well, yes, I must. "You're working in the office, though, aren't you?"

"Which is right next door, in case you hadn't noticed. That *noise* you're making is quite penetrating." She didn't bother waiting for me to say anything else, just stomped out.

I decided to be a good girl and consulted Mrs. Stanton the next day, but she wasn't sympathetic. "This is an archaeological excavation project, Miss Leighton, not a summer camp. If playing your cello is so important to you, you may wish to reconsider your priorities. In the meantime, how about if you do your practicing out in the courtyard? In your spare time, of course."

Later, hearing Mrs. Stanton and Meg talking. I was sure I caught the words "Providence princess." I didn't stick around for more.

The courtyard was a paved space under a gnarled tree, with a roofed-over extension of the kitchen to one side. I had an audience of the Egyptian kitchen staff—the cook and her two helpers. They smiled politely but I didn't think they really appreciated my efforts. At least they didn't complain.

Eudora was my best gift from Uncle Charles. He bought her for me soon after I came to live with him and Alma at age twelve.

Alma wasn't impressed. "An eighteenth-century cello for a kid? And it's way too big for her."

"She'll grow into it," Charles assured her, and he was right. I grew up with Eudora. I'd had violin lessons in England, when my mother decided that was the thing to do. Or maybe they were my father's idea. He would have paid for them, but of course he didn't live with us, and the funds were diverted to other uses when my half-brother arrived.

In Providence, lessons resumed, and soon I was able to make music with my "beautiful gift." That's what "Eudora" means, in Greek. Charles suggested the name and I thought it was perfect. We played together sometimes, but Charles wasn't much better a pianist than I was a cellist.

My being left-handed made everything awkward. My teacher, retired from a brilliant career in Europe, insisted I bow with my right hand. "Otherwise you will be impossible in the orchestra. You will knock the elbows. Bow with the right, finger with the left, that is the way."

I was a disappointing student. My fingering wasn't bad, but it took me a long time to train my right hand to use the bow. At times I rebelled and played the wrong way around, which didn't help my technique. I was good enough to play for my own amusement, but never disciplined myself to achieve mastery.

In spite of all this, I loved the instrument. I loved embracing her to play, the rich smoothness of her wood, her immediate response to my touch with fingers or bow, the deep, thrumming voice that seemed to come from hidden depths.

Eudora became my friend and confidante, the instrument—literally—of my emotions. Through her, I expressed joy, sorrow, and anger, and found comfort and peace.

Now, in this friendless place, I missed my sessions of communion with Eudora at bedtime. I was too intimidated even to take her out of her case with my dorm companions asleep nearby, even if they sometimes snored quite loudly.

"We've finished mapping the west precinct wall, and the inventory of finds is up to date."

Meg Elliott, Mrs. Stanton's super-competent assistant was displaying super-competency. Too bad I had missed most of it, except for her odd habit of over-pronouncing multi-syllabic words. "Mea-sure-ments." "Ar-ti-facts." "Par-a-met-ers." She reeled off masses of facts and figures. Her voice blurred with the sound of the fan and acted on me like a sleeping pill. This was my first all-staff meeting. There were more to come. *Oh joy.*

The members of the Stanton Temple Precinct Project sat, slouched or slumped around the long table like members of an archaeological Last Supper. Mrs. S. chaired the meeting from one end of the table. Meg sat at her right hand, along with several specialists (architecture, ceramics, metals, epigraphy). Across the table were Louisa Dufour, visiting art historian, Hank, the Excavation Lead Hand, and France Leighton, superfluous rock sorter. Dr. Stanton occupied the other end of the table, opposite his wife.

Concentrate. I was falling asleep again. I kept nodding off and waking up with a jerk, hoping no one had noticed. *Concentrate.* Meg Elliott's voice rose and fell, enumerating artifacts catalogued, square centimetres of wall reconstructed, texts transliterated. Every now and then, the crisp crinkle of a page being turned interrupted the drone, and the "whup-whup" of the overhead fan provided a subdued continuo.

Continuo. I hadn't played Eudora today. Or yesterday. She must be feeling neglected. *Concentrate.*

A barrage of page-ruffling snapped me out of my semi-doze. Meg folded up her maps and straightened the typewritten pages of her report. I thought I detected a glance of contempt cast my way as she sat down, tucking her curly red hair behind her ears.

"Thank you, Miss Elliott," said Dr. Stanton. "Our current season of fieldwork here at Karnak is well under way. I'm sure you're all eager to do your parts to further its goals, under the expert eye of Mrs. Stanton. In the meantime, I will be exploring possibilities for starting a new project next year, in the Valley of the Kings."

"We've agreed we're not ready to proceed with that, Bill." Mrs. Stanton's voice cut through the remaining fog in my head and made me sit up. Next to me, Hank stopped doodling and became alert. I couldn't help noticing that his doodles included a surprisingly good sketch of Mrs. S. cracking a whip over Dr. S., who was ogling a well-endowed young woman. I was trying to decide if she was Louisa or someone else when Dr. Stanton replied.

"If we want to apply for a permit anywhere near the Valley, we have to get our act together at least one field season in advance." His face had taken on a pink flush that didn't look good on him, and his jowls shook slightly as he spoke.

"Exactly," said Mrs. Stanton. "It's a complicated process, which is why I think we should concentrate on wrapping up the Temple Precinct Project before we even think about a new application. The authorities don't like unfinished business, as you know quite well."

Dr. Stanton looked ready to argue further, but his wife, who was chairing the meeting, stood and glanced around the table. Most of us appeared to be studying our notes, except for a few who had perked up like hunting dogs on a scent.

"That's all for now, folks. Does anyone have any final thoughts or questions?"

No one did, except probably Dr. Stanton, but he wasn't going to get a chance to voice them. Meg gathered up her notebooks and papers and followed Mrs. Stanton from the room. Hank and I waited until everyone else had filed out, clearing the narrow space between wall and table.

"Another meeting of the Stanton Temple Precinct Project staff fades into history." Hank folded up his doodled-upon sheet of paper and stuffed it into a shirt pocket. He turned to Louisa and me. "How about a stroll, ladies? Let's go out and watch the death of the day."

"Okay, 'Ank," Louisa said. "I would like to go out and breathe *l'air frais*."

"France?" Hank looked at me. "I'll bet you could use some *air frais* too. You were bobbing in and out of snooze-land most of the meeting."

I had to smile. "At least I wasn't doodling, like someone I know." I wondered if he'd asked me only to be polite, and if I'd be a fifth wheel. But I wanted to go out and see something besides the Project's house and the site. Louisa was all right. She could get a bit carried away and start gushing on and on about Art, but at least she didn't bug me, like Meg. "Sure, I'd love to go."

We "girls" stopped by our dorm to freshen up and grab our purses, and met Hank by the outside door.

"Where are we going?" Louisa wrapped a sheer pink scarf around her smooth dark hair. The scarf matched the lipstick she had just applied.

"Downtown," said Hank. "The throbbing heart of Luxor. Through the *souk* to the corniche. A meeting of east and west. Come along, ladies." He stuck out both elbows, and Louisa and I took an arm apiece.

We left our walled compound attached to the backside of Karnak and joined a tide of other walkers, guidebook-clutching tourists slung with cameras and local Egyptians wearing *galabeyas*. I found myself thinking a *galabeya* might be pretty comfortable for lounging but scrapped the notion quickly. Louisa would never wear anything like that. She stepped along smartly in her dirndl skirt and cork-soled, wedge-heeled sandals. But then, she was French.

Hank obviously knew his way around. We were in a street of what looked like apartment buildings or small hotels and shops of various kinds. "Where are we going?" I asked, and then remembered he had already answered the question.

"With the flow," he said. "No need to ask the Nile, is there? It goes where it flows. And so do we."

"Oh, 'Ank, you are teasing us, aren't you?" Louisa laughed and reached into her purse for a package of cigarettes and a lighter. She paused briefly to light up.

"What will we do when we come to the Nile?" I said. "Hop on a boat and float away?"

"Float on a boat." Louisa giggled. "Let's do it."

"Not tonight, girls." Hank sounded stern. "Tomorrow's a school day, remember? We must rise before Ra and return to the salt mine."

Behind us, an amplified voice was describing the glories of the Karnak temples to a group keen to see the pillars and pylons illuminated by floodlights and spotlights for a dramatic effect. We heard this spiel every night as we got ready for bed, along with the call to evening prayers at the mosque. So far, I hadn't had an actual tour of the temples, just looked around a bit on my own.

In the glare of the day, it was too hot to appreciate anything but shade, but now the sun had vanished behind the hills on the Nile's west side. A fresh breeze enhanced the cooling effect as we reached the paved walkway along the river, called the corniche. It was definitely the place to be as day turned to night, for tourists, locals and in-betweens like us.

"*Monsieur et Madame* Stanton, they are not *en accord*, I think?" Louisa remarked, as we strolled along. "I was surprised when they argued in the meeting."

"Well, it was the first general meeting since we've been fully staffed," said Hank. "Mrs. S. thinks it's important to set the right tone by presenting a united front so everyone starts off on the right foot."

"But Dr. Stanton, doesn't? Or he has other ideas?"

Hank grinned. "He's full of ideas, not all of them practical. He'd love to be the American Howard Carter."

"Do you think there are any more intact tombs out there?" I asked. "Like King Tut's?"

Hank cleared his throat. "Miss Leighton, it's not 'Tut,' but 'Tut-ankh-a-mun.' You are standing on the ground he trod. He was a king, the son of the gods. You must show respect."

He sounded so much like Meg Elliott at her most sanctimonious that I had to laugh. "No, seriously," I said. "I thought all the good tombs have been found already."

"Oh, I wouldn't assume that." Hank stopped by a railing at the edge of the walkway and looked out over the Nile. "It's not a simple bit of ground over there. Who knows what might be hidden in those valleys?"

Beyond the black mirror of the river, spangled with the bright lights of tour boats and the firefly glow of feluccas, the irregular pyramid shape of el-Qurn rose like a stage-set of black cardboard, crisp against the luminous blue of the sky.

I'm here. Let it begin. Something inside me spoke to something in the black pyramid across the Nile, where someone waited for me, eternally patient. *What kind of notion was that?* I shook my head and brought my attention back to Hank.

"The Valley of the Kings winds through limestone and shale," he said, as though talking to himself. "The different layers vary in thickness and permeability. You would think nothing ever changes over there, but sometimes there are flash floods that move tons of sediment. Yes, floods." He responded to my unasked question. "It hardly ever rains, of course, but when it does, it—"

"Pours," said Louisa, with a smile. "I know that idiom. 'When it rains, it pours,' meaning too much of a good thing." She clutched her elbows and shivered. "I'm getting cold. 'Ank, do you know a good café close by? A cup of coffee would be nice. Maybe at that hotel?" She pointed to a large, fancy building that looked anything but Egyptian.

"The Winter Palace? Not my style. I know a better place."

We followed him through the crowds, past hotels and shops, into the *souk*, threading narrow alleys packed with merchandise. Hank discouraged overly pushy vendors with brief phrases in Arabic, but a few times he had to indulge Louisa and me when we wanted to look at the wares on display. There was so much to see—brass vessels and bright scarves, carpets, jewelry, replicas of statues and sarcophagi, powders and herbs in a multitude of jars. And food—fruits and vegetables artfully arranged, looking so delicious I started to feel hungry and hoped we were getting close to Hank's café.

As we traversed a maze of dimly lit streets on the far fringes of the *souk*, I thought how in a short distance we had gone from the twentieth century to the middle ages and might even slip back to ancient times. What if we were to find the temples new and intact, their colours bright, and rituals being performed by linen-clad priests? Instead of tourist spiels, I could almost hear chanting, the bray of horns, a blare of trumpets and rattle of sistrums...

"Here we are. *Entrez*." Hank's voice interrupted my daydream, or whatever it was. Evening dream? He ushered us through a doorway with a lamp hanging over it. A sign next to the door had Arabic writing as well as "Bennu Bird Café," along with a picture of a long-legged bird like a heron.

The interior of the café was bright, compared to the street. Besides the electric lights, candles flickered on the tables. It smelled of coffee, spices and tobacco.

A man wearing a fez came toward us. "Mr. Hank! Good evening. Ah, you have a lady friend. No—*two* lady friends. Very nice."

He conducted us to a table near the window. The back of the room was full of men who barely looked up from their newspapers and gurgling *hookah* pipes. A woman bustled over, possibly the proprietor's wife. She wore western-style clothes, makeup, gold hoop earrings and the tallest beehive hairdo I had ever seen. I was so busy wondering how much back-combing it took to hold it up, that I didn't realize Hank had ordered for me.

The coffee came in little metal pots, along with a plate of sticky-looking flaky pastries.

"*Café turc*," said Louisa. "*Very* strong."

"This is *café égyptien*," said Hank. "Lots of foam, I see. The foam's the thing. Try it, France."

I was used to ordinary coffee with cream and sugar. There was no sign of a cream pitcher, but I suspected it wouldn't do to ask for some. I took a careful sip. Hot and sweet, it was perfect with the honey-oozing pastry.

"Mm. Good," I said. "Say, Hank, do you come here often?"

"Yeah, I like this place. It's a compromise between East and West. They're open early and late, do a nice breakfast—with 'American coffee'—and it's cheap. Just ask Meg." He smirked.

As if I'd ask her anything. "Well, thanks for sharing it with us."

"Of course. I was brought up to share. Good socialists, my parents. Right now they're busy campaigning against nuclear weapons. With the Americans and Russians threatening each other, I suppose they have a point."

"People in Canada involve themselves with such matters?" Louisa asked. "That's where you're from, isn't it?"

"Oh, yes, Canada is full of conscientious types."

"What part of Canada?" I asked.

"Vancouver, British Columbia," said Hank. "And you, France? Not from France, I'm thinking."

"Providence, Rhode Island."

"Really? I thought you were English. British? I never know which is right."

I sighed internally. "Well, I was born in England, but I've lived in Providence since I was twelve. I guess my accent is a mixture of New England and old England." I finished my coffee and got a mouthful of grounds. At least the spluttering that followed saved me from further explanation.

"Oh, oh, I should have warned you about that." Louisa handed me an extra napkin. "Actually, you're supposed to pour out the grounds and get your fortune read."

"Maybe getting a mouthful is actually a good omen?" said Hank. "Like when a bird poops on your head."

"The Bennu Bird," said Louisa, lighting up another cigarette. "It's the right symbol for getting up early and staying out late. Burning at both ends."

I must have looked puzzled. "You know," she said, "the bird on the sign outside. It may have been the original phoenix, the bird that burns in its nest and rises out of the ashes."

"As we will have to do, way too soon." Hank pushed his chair away from the table. "Time to go."

On the way out, I looked at the sign by the café's door. "I'm sure I've seen this bird, or one just like it, in pictures of ancient Egyptian art."

"Yes," said Louisa. "He's everywhere. The tomb paintings are full of bennu birds."

"Have you been inside any of those tombs?" I asked. "In the Valley of the Kings?"

"*Mais oui.* You have to see the originals to fully appreciate the details."

"I've never been there." I didn't realize I had spoken aloud, but Hank and Louisa looked at each other.

"No problem," said Hank. "You must see Seti's tomb, at least. Pharaoh Seti I. It's the best of the lot, isn't it, Louisa?"

"*Bien sûr.* I never get tired of seeing those paintings."

"We'll make an expedition, then. On Sunday."

"Okay!"

"Deal! KV17, look out!"

Despite the coffee, I had no trouble falling asleep, but woke up way too early and couldn't get back to sleep. Finally, I threw off the blanket and sat up. The illuminated dial on my watch glowed twenty after four. My heels bumped against Eudora's case, which didn't quite fit under the bed.

Eudora. I scrambled into some clothes, found my sandals and pulled my cello from her ignominious hiding place.

"Let's go play in the temple." We had a half-hour before reveille.

One of the privileges of being part of an official archaeological excavation in the Karnak temple complex was backdoor access to said complex. We could come and go as we pleased, provided we exercised common sense, such as leaving things as we found them and not bothering tourists or tour guides.

I paused long enough to filch the flashlight kept near the door for nighttime visits to the bathroom. Quietly, I opened and closed the outer door and switched on my stolen flashlight, wrapping my fingers around its end to confine the beam. I picked my way toward the gate in the precinct wall that I used every day to go to my rock-sorting job. Skirting the familiar excavation area, I headed toward the towering pillars of Amun's temple, hoping the god wouldn't mind my uninvited arrival.

By the time I reached the Hypostyle Hall, the light was bright enough that I switched off the flashlight. I stuck it into my skirt pocket, where it made an awkward lump.

I was in a stone forest. Tall pillars rose all around me, their tops flaring out to form a kind of canopy. Or a thicket of giant papyrus plants, which is what the pillars were modeled on, according to Louisa. Dawn light filtered among the trunks of stone, illuminating some and leaving others in shadow. Instead of bark, they bore dense arrays of hieroglyphs and carved figures—striding pharaohs, seated gods, submissive slaves, grovelling prisoners, and animals of all kinds.

Standing there between darkness and light, I imagined a procession, with drums and percussion instruments accompanying chanted words in praise of Amun-Ra, whose temple this was. *In this place we shake the sistrum, we pacify the god with our sweet voices...* Immersed in the atmosphere of ancient reverence, I hoped the god would welcome and accept my gift of music.

I seated myself on a pillar's projecting base, opened Eudora's case and lifted her out. Her wood gleamed in the soft light. I screwed in her endpin and placed my bow by my side.

"Hello, darling," I said. "Here we are, in this ancient, sacred place. This is what I wanted, but I'm so unhappy! I miss Providence, and Alma, and especially Charles. I don't belong here, with all these smart, nasty people. Well, I'm okay *here*, in this temple, but at the dig, they all think I'm stupid and useless. I should give up and go home."

I ran my fingers over Eudora's strings, drawing forth a sweet, low thrumming. Bending down, I listened closely.

No, not yet. It's not time. Those two—Hank and Louisa—they seem all right. This is where you need to be. And don't you want to see that tomb? Besides, do you know where "home" is?

Good question.

"Home," to most people, means a mother and a father, perhaps brothers and sisters, all living in the same house. I remembered Hank and Louisa's casual references to parents, and how I had remained silent because I didn't want to start explaining my situation. Yes, I was born in England, but didn't live there, with my parents. My mother had been happy to send me to America, and my father...

Well, Nicholas Leighton had certainly showed me what he thought of his illegitimate daughter, his little mistake, his by-blow.

****

I wrote to him weeks before my departure from Providence. A reply arrived, sent by his secretary—a card stating the time of my "consultation" with Mr. Leighton, complete with the address of his Harley Street consulting rooms.

The hall was panelled in dark wood, the carpet also dark and thick enough to muffle my footfalls as I approached a door with a brass plate, on which was engraved "N. St.-Geo. Leighton, MBChB, FRCS." I stood there looking at it, while part of me wanted nothing more than to turn around and beat a retreat to my hotel room. I was on my way to an exciting job in Egypt; why torture myself with this visit? But in the end, I pressed the button next to the door.

To the receptionist who opened it, I gave my name and the fact of my appointment with Mr. Leighton.

"Oh yes, Miss... Leighton?" My name became a question, followed by a sharp glance at my face. She recovered her composure. "Please wait here. I'll see if Mr. Leighton is ready to see you."

The few minutes I waited were sufficient to pace twice around the reception room, looking at the no doubt tasteful décor without really seeing it.

"This way, please." The receptionist escorted me to the door of the inner sanctum.

My father rose from behind his desk and came toward me, hand outstretched. "Hello, Francesca, it's good to see you. You look well." He took my hand, pressed it briefly and let it go.

"I am well, thank you." I tried to compare him to distant childhood memories, but my dim impressions of an occasional tall, blond presence didn't stand up to scrutiny. Nicholas Leighton, successful neurosurgeon, looked older than 44, his hair golden-grey, his face lined. But there was a practiced elegance and a distinct resemblance to photographs of Francis

Dexter in Alma's house. And I thought I could see a resemblance to me.

He must have been as uncomfortable as I, and somehow that made me better disposed toward him. He invited me to sit and asked the expected questions about my trip so far and its intended destination. "What an opportunity for a young person. I'm sure you'll find it worthwhile." His grey eyes met mine as I responded, but then his glance fell to the papers on his desk.

"And how is... Alma?"

"My grandmother. Your mother. She reminded me of that little detail before I left Providence." The bitterness in my voice surprised me, and I looked at my hands, clasped together in my lap. "Alma's okay, I think, but she's well up in her seventies, you know. And she misses Charles dreadfully, even though she tries not to show it."

"I'm sure she does. News of his death was a shock to me. But Alma—she's not deteriorating, I hope? Her health, that is."

"I'm not sure." I looked at him squarely. "She drinks more than is good for her."

He sighed. "It's been years since I've seen her."

Almost a decade, in fact. "She kept hoping you would come. So did I."

"I was too busy. Yes, I know that's a poor excuse. I suppose I ought to make one more visit."

"She'd like that." I smiled. "You know, even though it was a surprise when she told me, some years ago, that she was my grandmother, it didn't change anything between us. We've always been friends."

"That's good to hear." He smiled too, and it made him look younger.

"Alma also mentioned the man who was your father—Francis Dexter."

The smile vanished. His brow creased and he turned his head toward the window. "I can't tell you anything about him. I know no more than you, perhaps less. Alma managed to convince me that, technically, he was my... progenitor. But my father, as far as I'm concerned, is Norbert Leighton. He brought me up and gave me his name. Francis Dexter is nothing to me. Why do you even ask me about him?"

I neglected to point out that I hadn't asked him anything. "Well, it's natural to be curious about someone you never heard of, who turns out to be your grandfather."

"I suppose so. I'm sorry I can't be of help. I met the man only once."

"You did? When? And where?"

A brief, ironic smile. "At a party in Provincetown, just before the war. Full of inebriated eccentrics and artistic types. I must admit, I was somewhat inebriated myself. We had a nice little chat. I was a student at the time, so we talked about that. Of course, Alma hadn't yet told me who he was, so I didn't mind..." He paused, looking uncomfortable.

"Didn't mind what?"

"Oh, his... manner. Not my style. I didn't really take to him, if truth be told. Look, I really can't tell you any more. Alma would be the logical person to ask about him, don't you think? After all, she must have known him quite well."

I said nothing, just sat and watched him fiddle with a fountain pen.

"You changed your name," he said, after a few moments of silence. "'France Leighton.' I admit I'm a little flattered, but I hope you realize it would have been... awkward to introduce you into the family."

"'Awkward'? I'll bet it would have been." An angry laugh escaped me. "Did you even consider it?"

"I acknowledged my responsibility for you and provided for your upbringing." His knuckles whitened and I thought the pen might snap.

"From a distance, though," I said. "Both you and my mother were happy to see me off to America. You were lucky Alma and Charles were there to take your places."

My father dropped the pen onto the desk and gave me a wintry stare. "All right, Francesca. You've made your point. Is that what you came here to do?"

"Well, no," I said. "I was actually hoping we could get to know each other, but I guess this isn't the right time. I'd better go."

He sprang up, looking relieved. "It's been... good to see you, Francesca. France, I mean. My apologies."

"That's okay. Thank you for my name. And my life. I'll make no more demands of you. Goodbye."

"I deserve that, I suppose." He stepped out from behind the desk and held out his hand again. "Goodbye, France." He hesitated, holding my hand. "Write to me if... if you want to."

I pulled my hand away. "Goodbye."

****

"Awkward—that's me," I whispered to Eudora. "I was awkward in Providence, as Alma and Charles's sort of granddaughter. I'm awkward here—an unskilled rock sorter. I guess I'm a 'sort of' girl."

Wiping tears from my eyes, I grabbed my bow and drew it across the strings, making a discordant groan, and then another. With the edge of my anger dulled, I fumbled out a phrase from the Albinoni *Adagio*, found the melody, and played it again and again, the music bleeding out of me, grieving, sobbing.

A hand touched my shoulder. I jerked violently, dropped the bow, nearly dropped the cello, and shot to my feet.

"Miss Leighton, I'm sorry, I thought—"

Dr. Stanton, pipe in hand, mouth open in surprise. "Are you okay?"

"No! No, I'm not okay. I hate it when people sneak up on me."

"I heard you playing. I was smoking in the courtyard and heard music somewhere in the temple. So beautiful. I had to see who it was." He bent, picked up my bow and handed it to me.

Could he tell I'd been crying? I didn't have a hankie and dabbed at my eyes with my fingers, but my nose was running too. My legs gave out and I slumped back onto my seat. "I was just... I couldn't sleep..." *Geez, talk about awkward!*

Dr. Stanton grasped my elbow and pulled me to my feet. "Let's get you back to the house. A good breakfast is what you need."

I was still clutching Eudora in one hand and my bow in the other. "Yes, but I have to pack up my cello first." I set the bow down, unscrewed the endpin, dropped it, scrabbled around and found it, put Eudora into the case, with the endpin and bow in the correct spots. I fastened the case's clasps and straightened up, discreetly wiping my nose on my sleeve.

"Here, I'll carry that," said Dr. Stanton, picking up the case. "You look a bit shaky. Sure you're all right?" He slid his arm around me and steered me toward the perimeter wall, which wasn't nearly as far away as it had felt when I had picked my way here in the dark.

"I'm okay," I said, pulling away from him. "I didn't sleep well, and then I was feeling a bit homesick."

"Quite understandable." He replaced his arm around my back. His cologne tickled my already irritated nose. I was edging away from him again when his hand cupped my breast.

I jerked away, politeness be damned. "Dr. Stanton!" I wanted to bonk him over the head with the flashlight but I had lost it somehow among the stones.

"Excuse me, my dear. No harm done, I'm sure."

He was smirking! I made to grab the cello case from him and flee but caught my foot on the irregular surface of the path and turned my ankle. "*Shit!*"

"Such language, Miss Leighton." He laughed and grabbed my arm. "I've got you safe, young lady. Just hold on and we'll be there in no time."

Now I really couldn't walk unaided, but I clamped my fingers firmly around his forearm to make sure his hand would support my elbow and nothing else.

And, of course, the first person we met as we entered the house was Meg Elliott.

3
The Chapter of Entering the Tomb of a King

Meg's eyes got big and round, and a sly little smile flickered over her lips.

"Good morning, Dr. Stanton," she said, the smile giving way to a grin. "*And* Miss Leighton."

"Miss Elliott, good morning." Stanton didn't seem the least bit disconcerted. "Good thing you're here. Miss Leighton sprained her ankle wandering around in the temple area. Perhaps you could help her. Strap it up or whatever. In time for breakfast, hopefully. Oh, and please take this, if you will." He handed Eudora to Meg and took off.

What a jerk!

"You sprained your ankle?" Meg stood there, holding Eudora but making no move to help me in any way. "What were you doing?

Trying to get away from that lecher. But I didn't say it. "I was playing my cello in the temple, and I twisted my ankle on the way back. Dr. Stanton happened to be out there too and… helped me." Even as I spoke, I realized how phony it sounded and felt my face getting hot.

"Well, weren't you lucky? Can you walk as far as the dorm?"

I nodded, gritted my teeth and hobbled the six yards to my bed, where I sat down with a suppressed groan. Meg laid Eudora next to me and began rummaging in the closet.

"There's a roll of elastic bandage in here somewhere," she muttered. "Ah, here it is. Okay, let's see that ankle."

Watching Meg's red curls bobbing as she wound and crossed the bandage around my injured joint, I had a totally different picture of her than when she was holding forth at the staff meeting.

"I didn't know it at the time, but Girl Scouts was great preparation for archaeology," she said, fastening the end of the bandage. "Try wiggling it. Not too tight? Okay, that should do it for now. But you'd better ask Hank to check it officially."

"Hank? Why him? You did a great job on it. Thanks, by the way."

"You're welcome," said Meg. "Hank's our official first aid attendant. He's had special training, apparently, and gets paid extra. But if you'd rather I re-do the bandage later, just ask."

"I guess this means our Valley of the Kings expedition will have to wait." Hank wiggled my foot, eliciting jolts of pain from my sprained ankle.

"You're right. Darn, I was looking forward to it. Is there a lot of walking involved?"

"Well, we'd take a taxi from the ferry to the tombs, and it's only a short stroll to KV17, but there are a lot of steps going down, and the lighting isn't great in there, so it's best not to take chances. Give it three or four days."

He went over to a calendar on the wall of the workroom. "Let's see, Louisa'll still be here. She takes off next week."

I had overheard Louisa mention her departure but hadn't found an opportunity to ask her about it.

"Will it be getting cooler soon?" Every day, as the sun hoisted itself over our site, I was quelled by its power. Temperatures regularly hit the nineties. The heat sapped my strength and enthusiasm, even under my canvas shelter. I was used to the humid warmth of Providence summers, but the intense, relentless light of Egypt pressed upon me like a sheet of white-hot metal. I couldn't imagine a whole day of hiking up steep paths under its glare.

"Maybe a little." Hank smiled. "France, you haven't acclimatized yet. Give it a chance. Think about next April, when we're getting ready to wrap up the season before Luxor turns into an oven."

"I might have to quit before that."

"Hang in there." He held out a hand and helped me up. "Let me see you walk."

My ankle must have been getting used to its infirm state. I left the workroom with barely a limp.

"Hmm, humm, himm, thrmm, humm." Eudora emitted soft, low, significant suggestions. *More than you know, more than you think, it's here, here, here.*

The first coolness of evening crept into the courtyard. In the kitchen area, the cook and her helpers were finishing up their post-supper cleanup and getting ready to go home. In my usual corner by the wall, I strummed Eudora's strings and wondered if I would feel worse returning to Providence in defeat or staying here and struggling with heat, glare, fractious coworkers and creepy Dr. Stanton.

"*Salut,* France, how's the ankle?" Louisa pulled a chair over and sat.

"It feels a lot better. I can actually walk without limping, if I don't try to go too fast. Say, I heard you're leaving soon."

"Yes. I am unhappy to say it, because I would like to remain longer, but *Maman* is ill and *Papa* needs help." She shrugged. "*C'est la vie.* So I'm leaving in one week. But we will make a visit to Seti's tomb first. It's closed to public viewing right now, but I have permission to take photographs."

"Yes! I've been reading *The Egyptian Book of the Dead* to get into the right mood. Hank lent me his copy. I can hardly wait to see the tomb and the paintings. The real thing."

"The day after tomorrow? Your ankle will be okay by then?"

"It will." Even if it kills me.

"*Bien.*"

I thought she was about to go, but she turned back after a few steps. Glancing around, she sat down again, pulling her chair closer to mine. "One thing—I heard you were alone with Dr. Stanton when you hurt your ankle."

"No, I wasn't! At least, I didn't want to be. I woke up early and couldn't get back to sleep, so I went into the temple—the Hypostyle Hall—to play my cello." I clutched Eudora's neck and gave her a little shake. "Suddenly, there he was, right next to me. Talk about startled! I dropped my bow and everything."

"And that's when you sprained the ankle?"

"No, that happened later, on the way back here, when I was trying to get away from him."

"Ah, I thought so. What did he do to you?"

"He... put his hand where it had no business." I couldn't say the word "breast" for some reason, but I touched the spot.

Louisa nodded. "I knew it. France, that man is *un débauché*, a creep. He tried that with me the second day I was here. I think he tries something like that with just about every young woman."

"Even Meg?"

She smiled. "Ah, Meg, she is *formidable*. I don't think he would have dared. But you, France, you should be careful. People might think you're too friendly with him."

"Too *friendly*? That's stupid! Where would they get that idea?"

"Well, he seems to be near you quite often."

"Not by my choice, that's for sure." I started to pack Eudora back into her case. "I'm going to avoid him like poison ivy. But he is the boss around here." I busied myself with the fastenings of the cello case, too mortified to look at Louisa. If *she* thought I had encouraged Dr. Stanton's attentions, because I was either loose or stupid, I might as well give up and go home.

Louisa touched my arm. "France, *mon amie*, I'm not saying you are at fault. I'm just warning you to be careful. As for who is the boss of the dig, it's Mme Stanton."

A light breeze bellied the sail of the felucca. I sat between Hank and Louisa on one of the wooden benches lining the hull. A gaggle of tourists aimed binoculars in every direction, exuding odours of different brands of suntan lotion. A knot of Egyptian passengers huddled in the stern, talking among themselves.

"Amazing how fast these boats get across the river," said Hank. "You don't think you're moving at all, and then, surprise—you're there. These fellows really know how to work their sails and use every breath of wind."

"Oh, it's lovely out here! Nice and cool." I was glad to get away from the dig and the house, the close quarters and the heat. I checked my beach bag for my emergency supplies— spare set of sunglasses, jar of zinc oxide ointment, bottle of aspirin. The canteen Hank had given me was too big to go in the bag. It was also heavy and rusty, and I suspected it leaked.

"Oh, it'll heat up soon enough," said Hank, raising a hand to the sun. "Hail to Ra! But in the tombs, you'll be in the domain of Osiris."

"And the domain of Meretseger, don't forget," said Louisa. "The cobra goddess who lives on the mountain and protects the tombs. 'She Who Loves Silence,' that's one of her epithets."

"Are there cobras here?" I asked.

"There are, but don't worry about them," said Hank, which didn't reassure me much. "Meretseger protected the tomb workers as well as the tombs. She struck wrongdoers with blindness but forgave the ones who begged forgiveness."

Louisa was busy organizing a couple of cameras and bags of equipment. "I hope I remembered everything," she said, unzipping and rezipping pockets and pouches and fastening straps. "Lots of extra film and flashbulbs. I hope Alain has all the lights set up."

"Alain?" The name was new to me.

"My friend from the French excavation over here," she said. "He's working in KV17 today, so it's a perfect opportunity for me to get some last photos. And for you to see the tomb, of course."

By the time the boat was made fast to the dock on the west bank, the light had changed from dull orange swathed in misty purple to a harsh white glare, bleaching the colour from the cliffs and slopes ahead. I fished out my jar of zinc oxide ointment and applied a fresh coat to my lips and nose.

"There's Omar," said Hank, waving at a man standing next to a beat-up car with a handwritten "Taxi" sign on its roof. The fellow waved back and hurried toward us, smiling.

We disembarked and headed for the car. Hank introduced the driver, and the two of them deposited our gear in the trunk while Louisa and I got into the back seat. Hank sat up front with Omar. As we rattled past green fields toward the bare, stony hills, the two of them carried on a conversation in a mixture of English and Arabic. The words "jeep" and "topographic" jumped out from the jumble of sounds.

We screeched to a halt near a modern-looking building with a number of footpaths leading away from it. I got out of the car and collected my bag and canteen. Louisa slung her cameras around her neck and an equipment bag over a shoulder. I offered to carry another bag whose shape suggested a tripod. Hank and Omar were still talking, their conversation punctuated with vigorous hand gestures. Groups of tourists passed us, led by lecturing guides.

"So what's the plan?" I asked, when Hank finally came over to us. "Are we going to see the tomb, or what?"

Hank and Louisa looked at each other. Maybe I sounded crabby. Well, I was crabby. The sun striking the buff-coloured stone made an oppressive glare. I could feel a headache coming on. Why were we standing around doing nothing? I found my aspirin and washed down a couple with rusty-tasting water from my canteen.

"We are going to the tomb," Louisa said. "You and I, anyway. 'Ank, you said you have something else to do?"

"Yep. Something came up." He looked toward the pyramid-shaped hill behind the tomb area. "I'll come and find the two of you at KV17 in a couple of hours. That okay with you?" He glanced from Louisa to me.

Well, it had to be okay with me, didn't it? But I felt I had missed something important, and that bothered me. I started getting that fifth wheel feeling again.

Shit, I should just pack up and go back to Providence.

But I wanted to see an honest-to-God ancient Egyptian tomb. Even more—the tomb wanted me to see it. I couldn't very well turn down a pharaoh's invitation. I took another swig of water and turned to Louisa with a manufactured smile. "All right, I'm ready. Let's get going. Where are Seti's digs?"

She thought for a moment and laughed. "*Digs.* Very good. This way."

We followed a wide footpath around several rock outcroppings. I wouldn't have noticed the tomb entrances if it weren't for signs drawing my attention to squared lintels over black holes leading into the earth. The sight made me shiver with mingled excitement and dread.

Louisa waved at a slight, bearded guy who stood smoking in front of a tomb whose entrance had a closed gate of metal bars with a heavy lock. He waved back, snuffed out his cigarette on the heel of his boot and came to meet us.

"Alain!" said Louisa. "Here we are, *enfin*. This is one of my colleagues from the Stanton Project, France Leighton. France, this is Alain Brossard. He's working in this tomb today, so he'll let us in."

Alain shook my hand. "May I carry your bag, *Mademoiselle*?" I gave him the tripod case and the three of us trooped over to the entrance of KV17, the tomb of Pharaoh Seti I.

"I'd like to get some photos in one of the small rooms off the burial chamber," said Louisa, while Alain unlocked the gate. "I can give you a quick tour of the tomb *en route*, France. You must see the burial chamber. It's *magnifique*."

I couldn't wait to get into the tomb, no matter what attractions it held, as long as it offered relief from the burning light of the sun.

Steep steps led downward, illuminated by a string of electric lights near the ceiling. A wooden handrail had also been added, to my relief, as my ankle was still a little shaky. I stepped carefully downward, relishing the blessed coolness and shade.

"This is the longest and deepest of the tombs, France," said Louisa, assuming her role as guide. "More than one hundred metres."

I took off my hat and sunglasses and stuffed them into my bag. Once my eyes got used to the relatively dim light, I saw the walls were solid with pictures and hieroglyphs arranged in vertical columns. At the bottom of the steps a figure opened blue wings in welcome, with two other winged beings in profile beneath it.

"This tomb is painted with a number of funerary texts, starting with the Litany of Ra in this first passage. In other parts of the tomb, we have the Amduat, the Book of Gates, and in one little room, the Book of the Heavenly Cow."

"Holy Cow!" I said. "That sounds like a joke to me."

"Oh no, it's not a joke, France!" Louisa wasn't smiling; her sense of humour didn't extend to her professional interests, it seemed. "*Le livre de la vache du ciel*. It's a myth that tries to explain suffering and death. Humanity rebels against Ra and he puts the sky goddess Nut—in the form of a cow—between earth and heaven. Eventually, Ra sends the goddess Hathor to kill the rebellious humans, but then he has to make her drunk on beer so she doesn't kill all the others too... Oh, well, perhaps it sounds ridiculous, but really, it's like the story of the flood in the Bible. And the painting of Nut the Cow is *magnifique*. You'll see."

We followed Alain down another set of steps into a square room with four square pillars. More hieroglyphs on the walls, and figures painted on the pillars. More steps, another passage, another set of steps. Each series of steps was shorter than the last, but even so, I felt I was being absorbed into the underworld.

Whether it was the presence of a fellow French speaker, or because she was thinking about her research project, Louisa began using more French words as we went along. I thought about interrupting but decided to let her carry on about *la perspective* and *le symbolisme* and *les couleurs vives* while I soaked in the ambience.

Seti I of the Nineteenth Dynasty. Three thousand years ago, his dead body was brought to this place hollowed out of solid rock especially for him. These rooms and pillars, reliefs and paintings had been created for him. Rituals had been performed, verses chanted, the tomb sealed up, to keep him safe. Safe? Not really, because Seti's mummy and whatever else had been here was gone. Only the pictures remained.

"Say, Louisa," I said, interrupting her lecture. "How about if you go take your photos and let me look around a bit on my own? See, I have a flashlight."

"Are you sure you'll be okay? The lights are only in the main rooms and passages. Don't go into any that are dark. Do you have extra batteries?" Her forehead wrinkled and she glanced back toward Alain, who was disappearing down yet another set of steps.

"All right, here we are at the burial chamber. Everything is in a line. You won't get lost if you stay out of the side chambers. And I'll be in this room here."

Brighter light shone out of the room she indicated, where Alain was bustling about with cables and lights. On the back wall was a large painting of what must have been the Heavenly Cow. She was huge and brown, with long horns and a gang of small humans under her belly, one hanging onto her tail. Interesting, but I didn't want to get in Louisa's way.

Alone in the burial chamber, I stood and looked around. The electric bulbs overhead did not cast enough light to reveal details, so I shone my flashlight here and there, spotlighting sections of the walls and pillars.

The domain of Osiris, Hank had called the tombs, and here I could see what he meant. The mummiform figure of the god of the underworld was everywhere, with his green face and hands holding the crook and flail. With him were figures standing in boats, or lined up like they were waiting for something, or sitting like passengers on the bus to eternity. Animal-headed deities consorted with Osiris on every pillar.

Snakes were everywhere too—cobras and really long serpents that could not possibly represent any kind of reality, tangled together in figure-eights. Below them, bearded guys tended furnaces full of orange flames.

Those ancient Egyptians were crazy!

The arrangement of pictures and hieroglyphs reminded me of comic books I had read in my room at Charles and Alma's house in Providence on rainy afternoons—superheroes, Nancy and Sluggo, Little Orphan Annie, Dick Tracy, and the Great Illustrated Classics. But these stories were obscure to me and utterly bizarre. Snakes had legs and arms, human figures had animal heads, animals had human heads. Disembodied arms rose in ritual gestures or supported solar disks or giant beetles. Boats sailed along a subterranean Nile, bearing mysterious objects, eggs and insects.

As I walked slowly around the pillared chamber, I recalled what I had learned about ancient Egypt's religion and mythology, things Louisa had said about the motifs and the funerary texts, and passages I had read recently in *The Egyptian Book of the Dead*. It was all about the soul's journey from life to death, the weighing of the heart and a triumphant return to life in a world beyond death.

I looked up at the vaulted ceiling. Far above me was a dark blue firmament studded with stars, and fantastic creatures painted in gold. A row of thin human figures balancing spheres on their heads, a lion with stars on his back, a horned bull—or possibly the Celestial Cow?—a hippopotamus with pendulous breasts mounted by a crocodile.

Crazy!

I leaned my head right back, pointed the flashlight upward and gazed, turning in a circle. Dark blue paint, night sky, or water? Dark water, in which drowned stars glimmered and coalesced into a stream of light that whirled around me and lifted me off my feet.

I heard chanting, faint but growing louder—no, not louder but stronger, accompanied by the rattle and jingle of sistrums and a thrum of stringed instruments (Eudora, is that you?). I saw a row of flickering lamps, each with a clear, soft flame, and human shapes swaying. A deep voice intoned words I did not recognize, but whose meaning I understood…

"Be at peace with me and let me behold beauty, may I journey forth on earth. May I see Horus as steersman, with the god Thoth and the goddess Maat, may I grasp the bows of the boat of the setting sun."

The line of lights divided into two, and they moved to either side of me. Behind the lights bobbed heads of humans, of animals, of monsters? They moved with deliberation, in time with the chanting.

The words had power. Their reverberations in this stone hollow made fast the structures of time and the land, made sure the sun rose, set, and rose again, the moon waxed and waned, vanished and returned. The Nile rose and fell, flowing eternally, bearing the boat of the gods, ferrying souls to the Land Beyond.

"May Ra grant my soul to behold the sun and moon every day, and may my soul come forth and walk where it will. May my name be proclaimed and may there be made ready for me a seat on the boat of the sun, and may I be received into the presence of Osiris in the land of victory."

This was why the stone was cut, the pigments ground, the sacred texts and images painted. Gods and their servants, kings and queens were manifested in glory, acknowledging the essence of existence. Every flake of stone, handful of dust, drop of wine, water, and oil had its place. The soul united with the flesh and the spirit of millions of years prevailed in glory and peace.

"I am the girdle of the robe of Nu which shines forth light into the darkness. I have opened the way, I have made light in the darkness, I have come forth, having made an end of the darkness, which has become light."

Light broke and splintered above me, jabbed my eyes like shards of glass.

Millions of years, millions of years, millions of years...

"France, are you all right?" Louisa shook my arm, her flashlight jittering.

I raised a hand and tried to push the light away, but I couldn't reach it. I covered my eyes and became aware of the rough, gritty surface on which I lay.

"Are you all right? What happened? Can you sit up?"

I sat up, provoking a jolt of pain in my head. "I'm fine. Just a headache." So why was I on the ground?

My flashlight lay beside me, still shining. I shook my head. "I don't know what happened. I guess I fainted or something."

"We have to get you up into *l'air frais*. Wait, I'll get Alain." Louisa started to get up.

"No, no, no!" I said. The last thing I wanted was to be ejected into the sizzling light outside the tomb. I hoisted myself to my knees. "I'm all right. Just give me a hand up, please."

Louisa probably weighed twenty pounds less than I did, but she managed to help me to my feet. "Did you get all your photos?" I realized I had no idea how much time had gone by. "If you need more time, that's okay with me. The air in here is fine, really." I bent and picked up my flashlight.

She looked at me, frowning. "I'm almost done. Just have to pack up. Do you know how long you've been lying here?"

"Well, I don't know exactly how long I was on the floor. I spent quite a bit of time looking around." Looking around and... what? Dreaming? Hallucinating?

"I remember looking at the ceiling," I said, pointing upward, "and I guess I got dizzy, that's all. We should be meeting Hank pretty soon, shouldn't we? Or is he going to come down here?" Anything to divert her from me.

"Well, yes, we should go up. He has to wait for us by the entrance, because it's locked, remember?"

"All right, let's get your gear and go," I said, intent on showing her how well, how truly okay I was.

Louisa's cameras, tripod and other things were still set up in the small room off the burial chamber, dominated by the Heavenly Cow and her retainers. "Were you in here the whole time?" I asked, folding up the tripod and stuffing it into its bag.

"*Mais oui!* Where else would I have been?" Louisa coiled up a cable with what seemed like excessive vigor.

"And you didn't hear anything?"

"What sort of thing?" She stood frowning at me, the cable forgotten in her hands.

Music and chanting. "Well, I don't know—me falling down, maybe? The flashlight hitting the floor? Never mind. I was overwhelmed by it all and lost it for a few minutes."

Once we were packed up, Louisa went to summon Alain from some other part of the tomb, to open and re-lock the gate after us. By the time we had climbed the final set of steps, my ankle was twinging and I hoped it would hold out for the rest of the day. Hank lounged by the tomb entrance, looking quite comfortable and puffing on one of his smelly cigarettes.

"How long have you been waiting?" Louisa lit up as well.

"Not long. Half an hour or so. How did you like your first look at a pharaoh's tomb, France?"

"It was great. Really impressive. Having it practically to myself was special—the tomb, the pictures, the rituals. I mean, I tried to imagine the rituals. What about you? What were you doing? I thought the plan was for all three of us to see the tomb."

"Yeah, but Dr. Stanton asked me to do something for him over here." His glance bounced off the rocks behind me. "I'm sure Louisa was a good tour guide."

"Oh yes, she was."

Louisa interrupted. "'Ank, she fainted down there. I found her on the floor."

I interrupted right back. "It was nothing. I'm fine now. Is Omar going to take us back to the ferry?"

"He's probably waiting for us. Are you sure you're okay, France?"

Hank insisted on taking my pulse and peering into my eyes. As if that would tell him anything.

I took a final glance backward as we left the tombs. Someone stood farther up the path—a tall figure in a black *galabeya* and turban. Not a tourist, maybe a guide? He must have seen me, because he slowly raised a hand as if in greeting or farewell. I almost returned the gesture, but instead turned and followed the others.

The brown water chattered against the boat's hull as a southerly breeze helped the current bear us toward Luxor.

I looked back at the receding shore. "How many tombs are there, anyway?"

"Hundreds," said Hank. "Tut's tomb is KV62, and there are about a hundred in the Valley of the Queens. Plus the Tombs of the Nobles and any number that haven't been found yet."

"Are they all like the one we saw today, Seti's? Painted and full of stuff like Tut's?"

"At one time, but of course most of them were looted, either by actual robbers or by the early archaeologists." Hank grinned. "That's why Tut's tomb was such a big deal. When you consider that he was a pretty minor king, you can imagine the treasures that must have been in the tombs of guys like Ramses II or Thutmose III. They must have been fantastic." His eyes narrowed slightly.

"Think of all the work they did over there," I said. "Digging all those tombs, hundreds of them. The place must be honeycombed."

"They were symbolically re-creating the dead person's world," said Louisa, "so he could enjoy the same things in the afterlife that he did before. They even made servants for them—the *chaouabtis*. Little mummiform figures. You must have seen some of them in museums."

"*Shabtis*," said Hank. "That's what we call them at the Stanton Project. Well, some of us say *shawabtis*. We have arguments about which is right all the time. Thousands of them were made. There were seven hundred in Seti I's tomb alone, and I think there are even a few sorry specimens in the workroom. I'll show them to you if you like."

"All right," I said, "but the point is that all these things were made and assembled, and the mummified dead person was put in his coffin—or hers, for that matter—and special words spoken. And then the tomb was sealed up for eternity. Isn't that what they thought?"

"'Millions of years,'" said Louisa. "I guess that meant forever."

"But now it's all been undone!" A few nearby tourists looked at me. "The mummies are lying naked, on display, their servants—those *shabtis* or whatever—are in museums and the tombs are tourist attractions. It isn't right!"

"Whoa, France!" Hank put a hand on my arm. "Valid points, but you have to admit that at least we're learning all kinds of things by studying the tombs and their contents. It's not treasure-hunting any more."

He and Louisa looked at each other. I knew that look. I was used to it. All my life, eventually, people would exchange that look. "There she goes again. Better rein her in." Well, I would save them the trouble.

"It's been a long day," I said, pushing my hair back from my face and resetting my hat. "I didn't realize seeing that tomb would be so... intense."

"It's okay, France," said Louisa, patting my arm. "We're almost home now."

Not me. I don't have a home. But I didn't say it.

There was no one in the Girls' Dorm when we got back. Louisa and I freshened up and changed out of our creased and dusty clothes. She went into the workroom to write up some notes, and I sat down on my bed with Eudora.

"Tell me, what happened there, in the tomb?" I whispered. "I didn't faint, I just... went somewhere else. Or something came to me. The past? Did I really see Pharaoh Seti's funeral? Or was I hallucinating?"

Fingers caressing strings, I bent so my hair touched them and heard a faint susurration followed by deeper throbs and thrums.

Don't worry, it's all right. Don't you understand? You're meant to be here. You have something important to do. Be patient. For sure you will learn what it is in good time. It will be shown to you.

Girlish voices approached. I packed Eudora away and unpacked my public face.

The next morning, as breakfast ended and we prepared to disperse to our jobs, Mrs. Stanton approached me.

"May I see you for a moment, Miss Leighton? Upstairs in my office, please."

She didn't stop to make sure I was coming, just set off up the stairs, back straight under her crisp linen shirt. Taking her place behind the desk, she motioned toward the chair I had occupied during the grilling she'd given me the day after I arrived.

"You've been here a week," she said, "and I gather you're struggling a little."

"Struggling? I'm not sure I understand you, Mrs. Stanton."

She picked up that darned letter opener and started slapping her palm with it. "Well, you find the climate uncomfortable, and you had some sort of accident—sprained ankle, was it? And yesterday you had a fainting spell in one of the tombs in the Valley of the Kings. Do you have any health problems I should be aware of?"

I felt like slugging her, or telling her exactly how I got that sprained ankle, but I restrained myself. "I can cope with the climate. I admit I find the heat and sun a bit wearing, but I can manage. My ankle is fine now. I'm not accident-prone. In the tomb, I was looking up at the ceiling and got dizzy. I don't know who told you about that, but I was out for only a minute or two, I'm sure. Louisa helped me up and I was fine."

"Where was Hank? I thought the three of you went together."

"He had to do an errand for Dr. Stanton."

"Hmm. Which tomb were you in?"

"Seti I's. KV17."

"I see." She turned to the window and stood clutching the letter opener. She set it down on the desk and produced a smile. "I actually asked you here for another reason."

She moved a pile of newspapers toward me and began to riffle through papers that had been under them. A headline caught my eye: "Soviet Union Says No Missiles to Cuba."

Mrs. Stanton picked up a piece of paper. "Ah, here it is. The Egyptian Department of Antiquities is organizing a cultural evening ten days from now for all the archaeological teams working in or near Luxor. It's a bit of a nuisance, to tell the truth, but cooperation may benefit future projects, so everyone plays along. And 'plays' is the word. They need musicians and I happened to mention that we have a cellist among us. I'm hoping you'll be able to contribute your talents. I'd really appreciate it."

I got the message, loud and clear. As the superfluous rock-sorter, I'd better do anything I could to be useful. Even playing my cello. It was kind of ironic, when I remembered Mrs. Stanton telling me to save it for my spare time.

"Sure, okay, I'll do it. Do you know what kind of music it would be?"

"No idea. I'll get the specifics to you as soon as I know them, and you can practice in the workroom if you wish. I'll let everyone know."

"All right. Thank you, Mrs. Stanton." I started to get up, but she clearly had something more to say.

"That sprained ankle of yours. Would you mind telling me how it happened?"

"I had an idea the acoustics in the Hypostyle Hall would be interesting, and playing before dawn wouldn't bother anyone. I guess Dr. Stanton must have heard, though."

She smiled a thin, tight-lipped smile. "Yes, that's Bill—a real appreciator of music."

I smiled back the same way—tight lips with a small twitch of muscles. "On the way back here, I made a misstep and turned my ankle. Dr. Stanton carried my cello to the house, where we happened to meet Miss Elliott. She was really helpful and strapped up my ankle."

"Miss Leighton, I don't know if you've realized this. Perhaps you have..." Another twitchy smile. "My husband Bill—Dr. Stanton—can be impulsive. It's part of his brilliance, but not all of his impulses are brilliant." She stood. "We both have work to do, so let's get to it."

Impulsive? I guess you could say so. Okay, Mrs. Stanton, I'll play along.

4
The Chapter of Undertaking a Difficult Task

"What's the story about the Stantons, anyway? There must be one, and I'll bet you know what it is."

Hank and I walked past the Precinct of Mut toward the Nile, on our way to Chicago House. This early, only locals were out on the streets, including two men in dark *galabeyas* some distance behind us. I'd noticed that Egyptian men seemed to like going around in matching pairs.

"Well, I don't know *everything*. But of course there's a story."

"And just now it's hit a bad patch. Am I right?"

Hank paused and wagged a finger at me. "Look out, Miss Leighton, you're treading on dangerous ground."

"I won't tell. Promise." I covered my lips with one hand and made a throat-cutting gesture with the other.

Hank's eyebrows did a little wiggle I had come to associate with indecision. He pressed his lips together for a moment before he spoke.

"Well, everything leaks out eventually. You may as well get the real goods rather than some garbled version. Okay, about ten years ago, Mrs. Stanton was one of Dr. Stanton's grad students at Brown. He was an old Luxor hand by then, and he had a wife and a couple of kids. They stayed in the States while he was out here during field seasons. Mrs. Stanton—the current one, let's call her Adele—was part of the team. Just like you, France. What happened? Well, use your imagination."

I don't have to, actually. "Okay, so they had an affair. I gather that's practically standard operating procedure in the field."

"Sure, but when the season ends, things cool down. Usually. Not this time. A divorce ensued, complete with alimony, followed by wedding bells for Bill and Adele and, eventually, two new kids." He paused. "They're at the American school in Cairo. And Adele's the one that keeps the dig organized, *and* she has plans for a career of her own."

"That's just it." I said. "She's the one who calls the shots at our dig, but the two of them don't agree on everything. What happens to all of us if things get really tense?"

"France, my girl, things are already tense. My money's on Adele carrying on with the Precinct Project, this season anyway. If she can publish under her own name while he goes off on his tangent, that will give her career a leg up. But things could get interesting. We may all have to decide where our loyalties lie."

We were approaching the gardens that surrounded Chicago House, home of the University of Chicago's Epigraphic Survey, where I was to meet the other two members of the impromptu Archaeologists' Trio and find out exactly what sort of music I was to perform with them in just over a week.

"I get the feeling..." I said, and then realized I was thinking aloud.

Hank turned to me with a grin. "Do tell, France. I can keep a secret as well as you. Maybe better. What feeling?"

"Well, I think Mrs. Stanton isn't just carrying on, I think she's following some sort of strategy. Take this musical thing. I can't figure out why she decided to volunteer me for it, but there must be a reason." I shut up. I could think of at least one reason, and I didn't want to discuss it with Hank.

"Exactly," he said. "Everyone needs a strategy. Better work on yours. Here we are."

We went around to the front entrance and up the steps of the sprawling building. "Where are you supposed to meet your musical pals?" asked Hank, as the coolness of the lobby enveloped us.

I was surprised at the transition from the heat and dust of the Luxor streets to the atmosphere of American academia— cool stillness and the library smell of books and sanitized dust. "Uh, I'm not sure. Second floor. Someone's office. Wait."

I rummaged in my purse and found the slip of paper Mrs. Stanton had given me. "The Assistant Director's office. Do you know where it is?"

"No clue. Go up and look. Ask whoever's around. They speak English here, you know."

"Where are you going?"

"Maps and photos. Over there." He pointed down a hallway. "Come and find me when you're through. Or are you going to start rehearsing today?"

I spread out my arms. "You don't see a cello on me anywhere, do you? So I guess not. Okay, see you later." I headed for the stairs to the second floor, secretly glad I had caught Hank asking a dumb question.

At the top of the stairs was a hallway with doors opening off both sides. The air was warmer and the library smell replaced by ordinary stuffiness. Looking from right to left as I progressed, I came to a door with a name on it and "Assistant Director."

Bingo.

The door was ajar, but I knocked before I poked my head inside.

"'*Bonjour*, France!" said a familiar voice—Louisa's friend Alain, who had been in the tomb of Seti I the day we had visited it. I was so glad to see someone I recognized, I felt like hugging him, but restricted myself to a handshake.

"It's good to see you again," I said. "Are you part of the trio? What instrument do you play?"

"Viola," he said, pulling over a chair.

I turned to the other person in the room, who straightened up from his perch on the edge of the desk. This guy was the Assistant Director? He looked too young—skinny, red hair in a brush cut, white shirt, black pants. He held out a bony hand, which turned out to be dry and chilly. "Jack Stark," he said. "And you?"

Alain leaped to amend his *faux pas*. "Excuse me, I forgot myself. This is Mr. Jack Stark. He works with an American group excavating in the Valley of the Kings. Jack, this is Miss France Leighton. She is with the... excuse me, I forget which group you are with."

"Dr. William Stanton's," I said. "The Karnak Temple Precinct Project. I'm pleased to meet you, Mr. Stark."

He waved a hand. "Call me Jack. So you're the cellist." He looked me up and down. "You didn't bring your instrument."

"I didn't think this was going to be a rehearsal." I hated that my face was turning hot and, of course, red.

"We have a performance in *a week*, and you didn't feel the need to rehearse. You must be quite the virtuoso, Miss Leighton." Jack smiled a pointy, evil smile.

"I did not myself bring my viola, France, and I am no virtuoso," said Alain. "Jack is eager to begin playing, but I think first we must decide what to play, *n'est-ce pas?*"

Jack parked his skinny butt on the desk and slumped his shoulders. "We were supposed to be a quartet. We were going to play one of Beethoven's great string quartets. Then the English guy came up with some excuse and the Pole couldn't cut it. Too busy, he said. Quitters, both of them. I would have been fine doing a solo piece, but the organizers want an ensemble, and one violin and one viola aren't. Someone said there was a cellist at another American dig, so I thought, all right, a trio. Beethoven wrote some passable string trios. Opus 9. I'm assuming you have them in your repertoires?" He glanced from me to Alain and back.

Beethoven. I'd never played anything of his.

Alain grinned. "I am *un archéologue*, not a musician. I do not have a repertoire, but yes, I have played one or two of these trios. Some years ago, when I was a student. Which one do you have in mind?"

"Number 3, the G major. I hope *she'll* be able to manage it." He looked at me the way I did when I was trying to decide whether the piece of stone I was holding was an artifact or just a rock.

"Okay," I said, "I'm no virtuoso, I admit it, but—"

"Don't worry yourself, we will manage," said Alain. He turned to Jack. "Do you have the music here?"

"Yes, of course." He picked up a portfolio from the desk.

Of course. Sheet music of Beethoven's string trios—a must-have for an archaeologist in Egypt.

"Wait a minute," I said. "I've never played Beethoven's Opus 9, and I'm not sure I can learn it in a week. How about something by... oh, I don't know—Haydn? He wrote some string trios, didn't he?" I dimly recalled playing one of them at a little concert organized by my music teacher in Providence.

"One of Papa Haydn's little gems." Jack looked at me with sorrowful contempt. "Apart from being too simple and naïve, they were written for two violins and cello. Since our friend Alain here happens to be a violist, they're not an option."

"Well, in that case," I said, "you might have to find yourself another cellist."

Jack looked at me as though I'd declared the earth was flat. "Come on, Miss Leighton, don't tell me you're another quitter. Where's your American can-do attitude?"

I almost told him I had left it at home in Providence, but Alain spoke first.

"Excuse me, Jack. I think Miss Leighton is right. Simple is best. We will be playing for our fellow archaeologists and people from the Department of Antiquities. We don't have to pretend we are real musicians." He looked from me to Jack and back again, as though he was watching a tennis match.

Jack stood straight, like a brave soldier facing the firing squad. "My policy in life is to do everything as well as I am able." He reached behind the desk and brought out a violin case. He opened it, took out a violin, hoisted it to his shoulder, and brandished his bow. Then he played—something. Maybe Paganini; it certainly sounded frenetic enough. Whatever it was, he played it with gusto, with frenzy, with verve. Loudly.

Someone opened the door. An older fellow, bristling with authority. He waved his hands like a conductor. Perfect! I thought, but the guy started shouting.

"Mr. Stark! This isn't a concert hall. And I need my office. Are you quite finished?"

Jack looked a little deflated but recovered quickly. "Yes, we're done, Sir." He reached into a portfolio and removed a sheaf of music. "Here you are, Miss Leighton—the cello part for Beethoven's Opus 9, number 3. Alain, here's the viola part for you. All right? We'll meet here day after tomorrow for our first run-through. Well, not *here*. I understand there's a small conference room we can use." This was directed toward the older man, who I assumed was the Assistant Director and rightful occupant of the office we were in.

"Indeed, Mr. Stark," he said, ushering us toward the door. "I hope you and your friends don't play loudly. This is a place for scholarship and concentration, not entertainment."

Alain and Jack were already out the door. I followed, with an apologetic nod toward the Assistant Director, who shook his head and closed the door behind me.

I caught up with my fellow trio members at the top of the stairs to the main floor. "Where's this performance going to happen, anyway?" I asked. Mrs. Stanton had probably told me but I had forgotten.

"At Metropolitan House, over on the west bank," said Jack, not turning around. "That's where the meetings will be held, and the main hall is perfect for it."

"Why do they want music at all? It seems odd to me. I mean—European classical music in Luxor? At a meeting of Egyptologists?"

I could see Alain nodding in apparent agreement. "I was thinking the same," he said, smiling at me.

Jack stopped so suddenly that Alain and I almost piled into him. "Culture," he said. "Here we are, discovering the great culture of the ancient Egyptians. And modern Egypt is discovering the great culture of the West. We should help them do that."

"By playing Beethoven?"

"What would you suggest? Rock 'n' roll?"

"Well, not with a violin, viola, and cello," I said. "Say, wouldn't it be neat if we could play actual ancient Egyptian music? On ancient Egyptian instruments—sistrums and harps, with chanting. It's pretty impressive, you know."

Both of them looked at me strangely, but I couldn't very well say I'd heard such music in Seti's tomb. "Well, it's an idea." I waved the cello part at them. "Okay, I'll practice this like mad, and hope I can play it with you guys."

The two of them headed for the main doors, now flanked by two men in dark blue *galabeyas* and black turbans. Were they guards or did they just happen to be standing there?

I had a bit of trouble finding Hank. I found the library easily enough but had to ask a staff member where the photographs section was. The woman laughed. "We have more photographs than books. That whole section over there."

Hank was nowhere in sight.

"I was looking for the aerial photos, actually," I said, trying to remember what he had told me. "And maps too."

"Those are in a different room. They're not much use for epigraphy. Over there." She pointed to a distant doorway.

Hank was bent over a table covered with maps and large photographs, his head turning from one to another as if comparing details. I recognized the shape of the Nile in its valley between arid hills. The map of the Valley of the Kings looked familiar, because there was one in the workroom at our dig house, but this one looked a lot more detailed. I waited until he finished writing in a notebook before greeting him.

"Perfect timing," he said. "So, did you get your music program settled?" He began shuffling the maps and photos into separate piles.

"In a way." I held up the music. "Cello part for a piece by Beethoven. I don't know if I'm up for it, but we'll see in a few days. What are you up to here?"

"Just checking some details for Dr. Stanton," he said, pocketing his notebook and pen. "And now, back to our labours in the field. Or are you going to start work on Ludwig van B. right away? Got a special dispensation from Mrs. Stanton?" He smirked.

"Well, she said I could practice in the workroom, but *after* work hours."

"Figures. Roll over, Beethoven. After a lot of rocks, of course."

Halfway across the lobby of the building, a guy came over and started talking to Hank, asking him about hiring dig workers. Hank didn't introduce me, and I wasn't interested in their talk, which went on and on, getting detailed and technical.

A large poster on a nearby bulletin board caught my eye. I went over for a closer look. "Nuclear Power—the Way of the Future: a lecture by Dr. Adam Dexter at Metropolitan House." Even though the lecture had happened two days ago, I studied the photo of the lecturer. Dexter wasn't an uncommon name, but I couldn't help looking for a family resemblance.

There wasn't one. He looked like a pharaoh, with one arm crossed over his chest, except he wore a white linen suit. His sculpted features, his air of calm repose and confidence, aquiline nose and full lips pressed together in a near-smile reminded me of someone I had seen recently. I don't know how long I gazed, trying to remember who and where.

"Ready to go, France?" Hank nudged my elbow. "What's so fascinating?"

"Um, nothing. Have you ever heard of this guy?"

He looked. "Nope. Why?"

"I just wondered."

"Okay, let's get going."

Hank set off toward the main doors and I followed, first taking one more look at the poster. At that face. The two men by the doors must have been guards, since they watched me closely as I exited between them.

I knew it wouldn't be easy, but I never thought it would be so hard. Playing a single part of an ensemble piece is always a strange experience. You need the other parts to interact with before you can tell if you're doing it well. All alone, it's disconnected and absurd.

I didn't, after all, take advantage of Mrs. Stanton's permission to practice in the workroom. I was used to the courtyard, with the old wall, the acacia tree, and the friendly indifference of the kitchen staff.

Eudora was surprised at this return to discipline, after my casual playing and meditative strumming. She rose to the occasion better than I did.

I practiced before breakfast and another couple of hours between supper and bedtime. Even though the weather had cooled, the days were hot enough to require early starts, so I had to wrap things up before lights out at nine. I told myself that Alain and Jack were under similar constraints, but of course I had more catching up to do.

A recording of the piece would have helped, but there was no chance of finding one in Luxor. I fell back on sight-reading and playing the notes as written, trying to identify the parts where I would be most exposed. In a trio is that's just about one hundred per cent of the time.

The point at this stage was to get the notes right. I concentrated on the difficult passages, playing them triple largo at first, gradually speeding up to the tempos marked on the score.

"I don't know if we can do this," I muttered to Eudora, after a session where I felt less competent than the previous one. "Sometimes I think I should back out while I have a chance, even if Jack Stark calls me a quitter. But that's what Mrs. Stanton would think too, and tell me to go home. Except now I don't want to."

Eudora made her usual comforting sounds, thrumming quietly in response to my movements. *It's all right, all right, all right. We'll be fine. This is what we were made for, you and I.*

"Do you like Beethoven?" I asked.

I can sing his songs even though he's younger than I, always looking for something new, asking, wanting. Like you, like you. What do you seek, France? What do you want, what do you need?

Well, those were the questions, weren't they? In the short term, I wanted to master this piece of music. I was pretty sure I could muddle through my part, if the others were at my level of skill, or lack of it. The results would be substandard but achievable. But Jack Stark had more talent and greater ambitions than Alain or I, and in small ensembles it's the violinist who calls the shots. His nationalistic attitude seemed silly, but I wanted to show him up. There was only one way to do that—practice, practice, practice.

I picked up my bow and got back into playing position. "That man who looked like a pharaoh. Adam *Dexter*. Is that a coincidence or something else?"

But Eudora was silent, until I applied the bow to her strings and brought forth a phrase of Beethoven.

I looked forward to our first group practice session, to make this into something other than a solitary struggle. During the day, at work on the excavation, as I handled stones shaped and marked by Egyptians of distant millennia, my mind dwelt among black notes on white paper laid down by a German man a mere 150 years ago. But the Egyptians were nearer.

Mrs. Stanton approached me after breakfast the next day to tell me I would be taking on Meg's secretarial duties for a week, while Meg was filling in for Hank as Excavation Lead Hand. "Hank's taking a week off, so this is an opportunity for both you and Meg."

"I guess it is. Thank you." I was actually wondering if Meg could crack jokes with the excavation workers in both English and Arabic, the way Hank did. But then, she probably had a Girl Scout badge in international relations.

"And how are you getting on with the music?"

"I've been practicing like mad, and we have our first group practice session tomorrow afternoon." And I was nervous as hell about it.

"Good. I'm happy you stepped up for this, France. Anything that makes a positive impression on the Antiquities Department people is worth doing."

The office work was a nice change from my rock-sorting duties. I typed, filed, and sorted the mail in the shade and relative coolness of the workroom, with a fan stirring the air around me. Shuffling through the envelopes, I looked for British stamps, hoping for a letter from Nicholas Leighton. My father had asked me to write him, and I had. So far, though, there was no reply. The only letter for me was from Alma.

I unfolded the typewritten sheets and began to read. That typewriter! It was an old Olivetti Alma had kept from her newspaperwoman days. I had typed out dozens of college papers on it. Seeing the familiar typeface, with its slightly crooked t's and extra dark x's, took me back to late nights in Charles and Alma's office, typing, typing, typing, correcting errors, cursing when there were too many and I had to retype a whole page.

> Dear Francesca,
> Fall has arrived in dear old Providence. People are saying they've never seen the leaves so colorful! The best year ever! And so on. I'm sure you remember.
> I've gone back to the Friends of the Library board, got tired of all their pleas. I guess it gives me something to do besides worrying about how many missiles the Russians have and what they might be doing with them.

A businesslike summary followed, of the board's doings, along with those of neighbours, friends, acquaintances, and the city council. By page three there were more typos and x'd out bits, a few *non sequiturs* and rambling sentences. I wondered how many drinks she'd had, and felt guilt join apprehension and other uncomfortable emotions welling up inside me.

Should I go back? She hadn't asked me to, but I was worried about her. And what could I do, anyway? Play hide-the-bottle?

It's good to hear you've made some friends on the dig. People who are hard to get along with can ruin the best of projects, but if you find a way to work with them, it's amazing how things improve. I certainly hope our officials and the ones in Russia remember that.

Thanks for the pep talk, Alma.

The other day I was talking with Andre and Lucy about your adventure, and Andre came out with the most amazing story. You know he was in Cairo once, and went to see the pyramids.

That picture of Andre on the camel in the front hall — of course!

Well, it seems he's also been where you are—Luxor. He even had a look inside some of those tombs you wrote about in your last letter. It was back in 1935, when he and Francis were on the way from British Columbia to London. He told quite the story about it. Andre can spin a good yarn, as you know.

Well, he never told me that one.

And that reminds me of something else—you may get a couple of visitors. I had a letter from a lady who knew Francis. Her name is Mrs. Amelia Devlin. She and her daughter are on a grand tour and plan to take in Egypt. I mentioned in my letter that you—Francis's granddaughter—are in Luxor, and gave her your address. I hope you don't mind. I'm not sure when they'll be in Egypt, but I would hope she writes to you before they arrive. As I recall, she used to be a medium—seances and so on. I met her just the one time, in Provincetown; can't say I took to her, so I hope I haven't set you up for something awkward.

Thanks, Alma. Just what I need, an oddball visitor. Maybe Mrs. Devlin will give a séance for the crew. Maybe an ancient Egyptian spirit will turn up and tell Dr. Stanton where to find an undiscovered tomb.

I believe the daughter's name is Willamina. Something like that. She must be only a few years older than you; maybe the two of you will hit it off.

Well I'd better close this letter, dear. It's late and I see my typing is deteriorating. Please write soon, and much love.

Alma.

I wondered if Alma was in the same state when she wrote her letter to Mrs. Devlin as when she wrote this one to me. Perhaps the ladies would think twice about dropping in on me.

Jack Stark met me inside the front door of Chicago House. "Change of venue," he said. "They've moved us to a storage room in the basement. Just as well. We won't have to worry about disturbing scholars at work."

He held out a hand. "Want me to carry that?"

"No, thanks. She's not heavy." Actually, Eudora's case weighed more than she did, and together they weren't exactly light. But I wanted to carry her myself. We were in this together, start to finish. "Where's Alain?"

"Down below, tuning up."

The room was small and the acoustics horrible. Instead of the traditional triangle of chairs and music stands, we had to sit in a row in front of a bookshelf with our music propped awkwardly on piles of books.

"Nice cello," said Jack, as I set up Eudora. I thought he looked surprised, as though he didn't expect me to have a decent instrument.

"Thanks," I said. "She—it was a gift from my grandfather. Made in the eighteenth century, in Italy. I can't remember what year exactly."

Jack ran a finger down Eudora's neck. "Better make sure the wood doesn't dry out. I keep my violin in one of the papyrus rooms at Met House. Do you have a climate-controlled room where you're staying?"

"I don't think so," I said. "I guess I'd better find something."

"Sooner rather than later. I've heard of instruments cracking and falling apart." He sat down and raised his bow. "All right folks, let's play."

Everyone's heard the saying, "Chamber music is like a conversation among friends." Well, our first try at Beethoven's string trio was more like a drunken argument. I kept losing the beat, trying to catch up, falling apart, asking for a restart. I felt like I was trying to run a relay race but kept dropping the baton. Again and again.

"Haven't played much lately, have you?" said Jack, nuzzling his violin with his chin and pointing his bow at me. "You're going to have to pull up your socks, France. I hope you're ready for a long session tonight. We have no time to waste, and there's no point practicing by yourself." He grinned with manic glee. "Okay—from the top again."

I had to hand it to Jack—he loved a challenge.

Even though the viola and cello mostly support the showmanship of the violin—and Jack Stark was all about showmanship—they have to do more than saw away in the background. Sometimes Alain or I echoed a phrase; in other spots we provided contrasting textures and tempos. Timing, of course, was really important.

I was okay at the start, but as soon as the tempo picked up, I messed up. To be truthful, Alain wasn't all that great either, but better than me. I made him look good. There's a difference between less than great when you don't care, and really bad when you do. Even though the whole thing seemed silly—archaeologists in Egypt playing music by a dead German to a bunch of bureaucrats—I wanted to do it well. I wanted to show Jack and Alain that I was capable, and Mrs. Stanton, and anyone else who happened to be there. Like Jack, I wasn't a quitter—no siree!

For what felt like the hundredth time, we started, kept going, sounded pretty good—and then I crashed and burned. Again.

"Wait, stop. Please, let's stop!" I held up my bow in surrender. "You're right, Jack, I'm not up to par. I can't seem to get into the swing of this."

"What would you suggest?" Jack's face was turning a shade of pink that clashed with his hair.

"Why don't we try singing?" said Alain. "Just this part where we can't put it together? I bet if we get through that, it will go well."

"Singing! What the heck kind of idea is that?" Jack's complexion went from pink to red.

"It's a technique. One of my instructors used to have us sing pieces if we were having trouble playing in ensemble." Alain was quietly persistent. "The idea is each of us sings or hums our part, instead of playing it."

"Let's try it," I said. "It can't hurt. Let's start right here, at the sixteenth bar." I took a breath. "Humm, ha-ha, hum…"

They joined in, even Jack. After a few false starts, our voices mingled harmoniously. Freed from the technicalities of playing my instrument, I was able to keep up with the others and internalize the patterns and rhythms of the music. The pitches were wrong, of course—unlike the cello's, my voice was higher than the other two—but that didn't matter. After three or four vocal run-throughs, we picked up our instruments and played better than we had up until then.

"Well, it's still rough, but we made progress, didn't we?" said Alain, as we packed up our instruments and music.

"Sure, but at this rate it'll take too long," said Jack. "This is only the first movement. There are three more, and—believe me—the final one is tough."

"But we're only playing the first movement, right?" I was appalled at the thought of slogging through the rest of the piece.

"I think one movement will be sufficient," said Alain. "Don't forget, everyone is going to be interested in archaeology, not music. They probably won't even listen to us."

"Exactly!" I said. "Jack, all we need to do is inject a bit of culture, not bore them with it. Look at it this way—one movement played well is way better than four done badly. Besides, has anyone checked with whoever is organizing this thing about how much time we have? What else is on the program? Let's find out before we kill ourselves on this." The room was hot and stuffy and I wanted out. Working at the Stanton Project suddenly seemed like fun and games by comparison.

"I agree with France," said Alain, clicking his case shut.

"Stop right there," said Jack, holding up his palms. "Don't even think we can get away with just the first movement. I've heard it won't be just archaeologists at this meeting. There's a rumor going around that some kind of scientific group from the U.S. is coming too. One of them's a big shot nuclear physicist."

I stopped in the middle of closing up my cello case. "Did you see him? What did he look like?"

Jack grinned. "Bald-headed and glowing. No, I didn't see him. It was just a rumor."

"Hey, France," said Alain, as we climbed the stairs to the main floor, "did you realize you were singing 'millions of years, millions of years' in Egyptian?"

"What do you mean? I was just... vocalizing. Humm, heh, ha-hum, he-hum. That's all."

"Well, 'heh' means 'eternity,' or 'millions of years.' It can sound like heh, ha, huah, or hahu."

I laughed. "Well, didn't I say we should be making ancient Egyptian music instead of Beethoven?"

"I think Beethoven will make a better impression," said Jack.

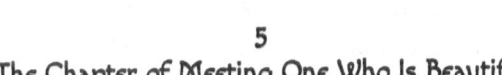

5
The Chapter of Meeting One Who Is Beautiful

Hail, thou god Temu, grant unto me the sweet breath which dwelleth in thy nostrils! I am the Egg which is in Ķenķenur (i.e., the Great Cackler), and I watch and guard that mighty thing which hath come into being and with which the god Seb hath opened the earth. I live; and it liveth; I become old, I live, and I snuff the air.

I shut *The Egyptian Book of the Dead* with a bang. "Shit!" I said, and then, "Sorry, Meg. Blame it on Mr. Budge and his crazy book."

"Still reading old Budge?" Meg Elliott looked up from her magazine. She always read *Time* or *Newsweek* before lights out. I wondered if all the bad news ever gave her nightmares. The cover of the magazine in her hands showed a huge mushroom cloud. "Nuclear Armageddon?" blared big red letters underneath.

"Yep. I get through a couple of pages every night. It's as good as a sleeping pill, except when I'm fed up with it, like tonight. I don't get it—all those gods, all those weird references to eggs, and places that might be real or might be the afterworld or underworld. And the Great Cackler? Give me a break. Is it just bad translation, or were the ancient Egyptians a really strange bunch?" I thought of the bizarre pictures in Seti's tomb.

"Well, it's a matter of dispute, of course," said Meg. She laid down her magazine and took a sip of tea. "Recent translations are supposed to be better than Budge's. They're a pretty dry read, though. Some people prefer his biblical style."

"You're right about biblical—makest, dwelleth, cometh. I can handle that, but the images the words conjure up are beyond bizarre."

"Oh, that's symbolism. You have to remember, the Egyptian religion was based on the cycle of the agricultural year, the rise and fall of the Nile, the passage of the sun across the sky, through the underworld, to rise again the next day. 'Coming Forth by Day'—that's what the soul does, after its passage through the underworld."

"You make it sound simple." I rolled over onto my back and sat up. "But the details contradict each other. Like the god Set, or Suti—that's another thing, the gods have half a dozen names—he's supposed to have killed Osiris, or maybe Horus, but they come back to life, and Set is actually honoured in some of the chapters—and it just seems nutty."

"Well, Dr. Stanton is very knowledgeable about the funerary texts," said Meg, with a mischievous smile. "He loves to quote them. You should ask him for his interpretations. I'll bet he'd be delighted."

"I think I'll skip that," I said, putting the book on the floor next to my slippers and pulling the curtain between our beds. "Good night, Meg."

I had already heard Hank's ideas on *The Egyptian Book of the Dead*, the E.A. Wallis Budge version. "Goes better with a pipe, actually," he said. "Hash opens it up somehow, so you plunge into the tableaux experienced by all those souls—Ani, Nu, Nebseni. They're always "triumphant," as I recall, meaning resurrected. You just sail along with them, rejecting filth, fighting serpents and dog-headed critters, until you come to the Field of Reeds, where you eat cakes and drink ale..." His eyes took on a faraway look.

"Except I don't actually smoke hash, Hank."

"Easily remedied, Miss Leighton. Just say the word."

I wondered if sharing Hank's indulgence might help with my struggle to master the Beethoven trio. I was still shaky and unreliable, despite practicing alone and with Jack and Alain in the basement room at Chicago House. Maybe I cared too much, and that made me stiff and hesitant. Hank was so casual and untroubled. People liked him, from the Egyptian labourers at our dig to scholars and bureaucrats. Even Mrs. Stanton had a soft spot for him. He was right at home in Luxor, almost like he'd turned himself into a local, not a visitor like the rest of us. Unlike the Stantons and their grad students, he wasn't striving for anything, just enjoying life as it came.

But could that be explained by his use of a drug I knew almost nothing about? I had no idea what it might do to me, and right now, when I was trying to make Mrs. Stanton think I was worth keeping around, while avoiding awkward situations with her husband, I didn't think it was worth the risk.

Sorting mail in the workroom the next day, I picked up a two-foot-long brown paper mailing tube with a return label from the Egyptian Geological Survey in Cairo, addressed to Mr. Henry R. Dykstra. The name didn't register at first, but then I realized it was Hank. I was wondering about the contents— maps, maybe?—when I became aware of an unwelcome scent. English Leather, Dr. Stanton's cologne.

Shit.

"Any mail for me, my dear?"

I had already set aside his and Mrs. Stanton's mail, intending to run it up to their office. I picked it up and handed it to him, flashing an artificial smile.

"Thank you." He gestured toward the mailing tube. "What's that?"

"Something for Hank."

"I'll bet it's from the Geological Survey, and it's actually for me," Dr. Stanton said, picking up the tube. "I asked Hank to order it."

"Um, are you sure? I thought it might be for his uncle. He's a geologist, isn't he?" Hank had taken a week's leave to accompany his relative on a sightseeing trip.

"Nope," Dr. Stanton said, tucking the tube under his arm. "It's definitely for me." Instead of leaving, he stood in front of me, radiating English Leather. "I hear you're deep into *The Egyptian Book of the Dead*." He smiled.

"Who told you that?"

"Little bird. Are you enjoying it?"

He's a professor. Talk to that part of him. "It's certainly different from Christian religious texts. And yet, in a way, it's similar. I suppose there's a fundamental unity among such works."

"I gather you're finding it a little obscure, though. Not relating to the symbolism?"

Who told him that? Meg? I'll kill her! Except Meg wasn't particularly chummy with Dr. Stanton. Hank—it had to be him.

"Some of it's a little bizarre, I suppose," I said, trying to sound casual. "I keep reminding myself it's a translation from an ancient language, so there are bound to be bits that aren't clear to us—to me."

"Sure, but it speaks directly and poetically across the millennia." He cleared his throat, looked up at the ceiling, pressed one arm to his chest and dramatically extended the other, like an amateur actor about to deliver Hamlet's soliloquy.

"'Those who dwell in Annu bow down their heads unto me, for I am their lord and I am their bull. I am more powerful than the lord of time, and I shall enjoy the pleasures of love, and shall gain the mastery over millions of years.'"

I hoped he didn't realize I was trying not to laugh. "Wow. Impressive. What a memory."

A small cough sounded from the doorway. Mrs. Stanton. "Oh, there you are, Bill. Quoting the 'Transformation into Ptah' for Miss Leighton's benefit? I think she has work to do, and so do we. Were you on your way up to the office?"

I bent my head so my hair would swing forward and hide my grin. Dr. Stanton's cheeks had turned a guilty shade of pink.

"What's that?" asked Mrs. Stanton, as they turned to go. She pointed at the mailing tube from the Geological Survey.

"Oh, just something for Hank that came in today's mail. I thought I'd put it in his mailbox and save Miss Leighton a step or two."

Right.

Taking a break from my next practice session, I picked up *The Egyptian Book of the Dead* and opened it at a page I had marked with a slip of paper.

My heart, my mother, my heart, my mother! My heart whereby I came into being! May naught stand up to oppose me at my judgment; may there be no opposition to me in the presence of the sovereign princes; may there be no parting of thee from me in the presence of him that keepeth the Balance!

I murmured the opening words again. "My heart, my mother, my heart, my mother." How was my mother? This was the first time I'd thought of her in weeks. What did that say about me? Of course, she hadn't given me much thought either. And Alma—was she all right? She wasn't my mother, but I felt more for her than for the woman who gave birth to me. Why was my life such a mess?

Bending over Eudora's hollow body, I stroked her strings. "...may there be no parting of me from thee... May you come forth into the place of happiness..."

Next thing I knew, I was crying, dripping onto Eudora's polished wood.

"Sorry. I'm sorry," I said, mopping up the tears with a tissue. I dabbed at my eyes, blew my nose and strummed Eudora's strings again.

Oh, France—you silly girl! You have opened the door. Great things are coming. Remain steadfast, keep your ears and eyes open. This is the land of Khem, old beyond memory. This is where you will come forth into a new day.

Even Eudora was starting to sound like the *Book of the Dead*. "All right, enough of that. Back to Beethoven."

I wondered if anyone had tried setting the texts to music. For the first and only time, I wished I could write music as well as play it.

Hank showed up the next day, accompanied by an older man, whom he introduced as, "Dr. James Henry Dykstra, otherwise known as my Uncle Jim."

Uncle Jim was wiry and weathered, with tightly curling grey hair clipped short. He wore one of those bolo ties I associated with cowboy outfits, but he wasn't a cowboy, despite coming from the Canadian province of Saskatchewan. He was a scientist, and his interest was uranium. At supper that evening, he was the guest of honour.

"Why are we making such a fuss over this guy?" I asked Meg. Not that I expected her to know, but she happened to be nearby. "He's not an archaeologist, never mind an Egyptologist. Just because he's Hank's uncle?"

"Archaeology is changing, you know." Meg gazed at me through her glasses, her expression saying she thought I was displaying wilful ignorance. "It's the new paradigm. Data must be gathered scientifically from as many sources as possible."

"I thought that only matters in prehistory, where there's no written record."

Meg's expression didn't change. "Data are data. Sure, there are written records here, and a wealth of artifacts. But information about the physical environment is valuable. For example, a geologist could analyze sediments from a site to get an indication of the climate at the time the artifacts were created. And there's the new carbon 14 dating technique. Prof. Dykstra probably knows about that."

I had made my point, such as it was, and didn't bother to argue. "Okay, fine. I just hope he isn't an old bore."

Despite these reservations, I found myself listening to Dr. Dykstra's after-dinner anecdotes. I knew almost nothing about geology or uranium, and cared less, but his slow, rambling way of talking was like a train. I got on board and rode along.

Uncle Jim taught at a university in a place named Saskatoon, and did field research on the distribution of uranium deposits. The government of Egypt had engaged him as a consultant. Perhaps he was supposed to provide advice on prospecting, but the fact that Saskatchewan was becoming a major producer of the radioactive metal seemed more than coincidental.

"Egypt's modernizing fast, and they're gonna need energy, lots of it," said Uncle Jim. "Now they've started building the dam at Aswan, but they know nuclear power is the future, so they'll want to exploit that resource too."

"We were in Aswan yesterday," said Hank. "It's pretty impressive."

"But won't damming the Nile change the whole way of life in Egypt?" I said. "They built their culture around the river for thousands of years. What will happen to the annual flood?"

"It'll be *managed*, young lady." Uncle Jim looked at me with red-rimmed blue eyes that blinked about as often as a lizard's. "Right now, Egyptian farmers are at the mercy of the Nile. Oh, sure, the inundation is called a 'gift,' but that's the romantic view. If the flood fails, they get drought. If it's too high, they're flooded out. The dam will fix that and supply hydroelectric power too."

"But what about those temples that will be submerged? Does Egypt really want to lose them just so it can control the Nile? It doesn't seem right. Why can't people just leave things the way they are?"

"Ah, the romantic attitude of youth," said Dr. Stanton, with an oily smile I pretended not to see. "The temples will be relocated. A feat of modern engineering to equal the ancient one of building them."

"Won't that be terribly expensive?" I had heard a lot of discussion about this already, but with an outsider present, I felt more confident to voice my opinions.

"A modernizing nation needs energy," said Uncle Jim. "That means making hard choices. You can't make an omelet without breaking eggs, and if you want the eggshells put back together, well, it'll cost you."

I was about to say that huge monuments weren't comparable to broken eggs, but Meg changed the subject.

"Dr. Dykstra, have you seen anything interesting here in Luxor? As a geologist, I mean." Her face was a couple of shades pinker than usual.

Uncle Jim laughed. "It's impossible for geologists not to see interesting things, wherever we go. When you can read the record of landforms and sediments, the world is an open book, full of the fundamental tales of Mother Earth." He smiled a satisfied smile, and I wondered if this was one of the lines he trotted out when lecturing in his faraway university on the Canadian prairies.

"The Nile, of course, is the main engine of landform creation here," he continued, "but the materials on which it works were laid down much earlier. You can see them in that pyramid-shaped hill on the other side."

"El-Qurn," said Hank. "The royal tombs are very close to it."

"Exactly." Meg pushed aside her teacup and leaned forward. "The tomb builders must have known something about the geology of the place. Okay, they didn't call it that, but they had to recognize the different kinds of stone, didn't they?"

Uncle Jim beamed at her. "You've got it right, young lady. Those fellas back then knew their rocks."

Meg picked up her teaspoon and tapped the table with it as she spoke. "So could someone look at the landforms in the area and predict where more tombs might be found?"

Was I imagining things, or did Dr. Stanton and Hank dart glances at one another? And Mrs. Stanton, who had been reading and making notes, raised her head and looked at them sharply over her glasses.

"Oh yes, that would definitely be worth trying," said Uncle Jim. "Whether you're looking for uranium ore or buried ancient Egyptians, being able to read the geological record can certainly help your search. In fact—"

Dr. Stanton spoke up. "So, Dr. Dykstra, I hope you're doing something besides work while you're here. How about some sightseeing? Hank knows where all the good stuff is."

"Of course!" said Hank. "We're going over to the west bank tomorrow. I'll give him the grand tour—temples, tombs, and everything."

They set off soon after breakfast the next day, when the rest of us were starting work. Alain Brossard and I followed in their footsteps later in the afternoon, carrying our instruments and music. We were going to our final rehearsal before the concert, which was two days later. Jack had insisted on a practice session in the space where we were to perform—the great hall at Metropolitan House.

"We'll need to figure out just where to position ourselves. I'm not sure how the acoustics work, what with the dome and all the open space. I've tested my fiddle there, but I want to hear us together."

There was no arguing with Jack, so off we went. Beethoven and I still weren't the best of friends, despite

Eudora's and my efforts. I kept telling myself, "In a couple of days it'll be over, one way or another." But I always came back to the fact that the ordeal was still before me.

We had to wait for more than half an hour before the man running the ferry felt his boat was sufficiently full to cast off.

"Jack won't be happy about this," I said. "'Rehearsal at 5 p.m. sharp.' Isn't that what he told us?"

Alain shrugged and took a puff on his cigarette. "He knows how things work in Luxor."

As well as the usual huddle of tourists, the passengers this afternoon included a group of young Egyptian women, clearly locals. One of them noticed me staring. Embarrassed, I smiled at her, hoping she didn't think me rude. She smiled back, showing a flash of teeth, and I realized Eudora had attracted her attention. Not many tourists carried large musical instruments around. I put Eudora into an approximation of playing position, case and all, and mimed playing with an invisible bow. Alain saw what I was doing and reciprocated with his viola.

The woman grinned and jostled her companions' elbows, pointing at us. "You play music?" she said.

"Yes," I replied. "We'll be playing at Metropolitan House."

"Okay, very nice," she said, and must have relayed this information to her companions, who stared and giggled.

As the boat was being docked, I saw Jack waiting for us, bouncing up and down on his toes, a frown creasing his face. As soon as we disembarked, he hustled us toward a nearby car, yet another of the beat-up Mercedes-Benzes that seemed to be standard equipment at Luxor dig houses. He jumped into the

95

driver's seat and took off at high speed, barely giving me time to close my door properly.

"What took you, anyway?" said Jack. I gave Alain a "told you" look but got only another shrug in response.

"The ferry took forever to fill up," I said. "You know how it is."

"No. *You* know how it is, so you should have left earlier."

I thought it best to remain silent.

Metropolitan House was truly impressive, with its domes and arches, but Jack didn't give us any time to look around, never mind a tour. As he led the way through the cool, tiled vestibule into the main hall, I thought I detected an unsettled atmosphere, as though a transition was under way. Cartons stood near one wall, along with a couple of book trolleys like those used in libraries.

"Looks like someone is moving in, or out." Alain's observation echoed my thoughts.

"Poles," said Jack, cryptically, as a smiling man came toward us, hands extended in apparent welcome.

"Come in, come in! I apologize for our disorder, but I assure you, all will be ready in time." He spoke with a Slavic accent, which helped me put two and two together. A Polish group must be moving into the house, to the annoyance of all-American Jack.

The welcoming man introduced himself, as head of the Polish mission to study and reconstruct the Temple of Hatshepsut at Deir el-Bahari. His name was so bristly with consonants and sibilants that my ear refused to admit it. He didn't stay to converse but swept an arm around the room and departed with a bow.

"Filthy Slavs," muttered Jack, and I hoped no acoustical quirk had transmitted his comment beyond our group. "They'll probably wreck the place. The Egyptian government bought it from the Metropolitan Museum, and the Department of Antiquities decided to rent it to the Poles."

Jack paused, as though waiting for commiseration, but Alain and I just looked at him. Muttering something else that sounded like "cabbage soup and perogies," he turned toward a piano at one side of the hall.

"Is that for us?" I asked.

"No, silly girl—we don't need a piano, do we? You haven't seen one at any of our practice sessions, have you? But it gives the right atmosphere. How about if you guys get set up." He pointed to a group of music stands. "I managed to scrounge those up too, so at least we'll *look* professional." This directed at me, of course.

Alain and I got ourselves unpacked and organized. Of course, it took me longer, what with screwing in Eudora's endpin. Meanwhile, Jack hoisted his violin into position and produced a volley of bravura flourishes.

Show-off.

"Sounds good, doesn't it?" he said. "The dome has great acoustics. You guys ready? Okay, let's get started."

I would love to say that the great acoustics, the extra space, our correct positioning, the music stands, and the presence of the piano made my performance good, rather than mediocre, but that didn't happen. I was still too slow in the *presto* sections and came in too late at crucial points.

Jack stopped playing, jumped up, and slashed his bow down. "Too sloppy, France," he said. "For God's sake, it's two days before we're on, and you're making us sound like a bunch of incompetents. The group is only as good as its weakest member, and you're it."

"So count me out. I'm finished!" I shot to my feet, clutching Eudora, and almost flung my bow at him, almost snatched the music off my stand and crumpled it up. My muscles twitched with eagerness to act out my anger.

But you don't drop your instrument. You don't throw your bow. Ever. That was ingrained in me from my first lesson. I choked down my rage and stood glaring and bristling.

Alain stepped between us. "How about *une pause*, a time-out?" His voice was soft, the suggestion delivered so mildly, I almost laughed.

Jack blew out his cheeks and sat down.

I had to do something helpful. "All right, I seem to have lost ground since last time. I don't know why, but give me a break, Jack. Once I mess up, I keep doing it, so let's go back to that first spot I missed and count it out slowly. That usually works for me."

"Welcome back to Square One," Jack muttered.

"Let's do it, Jack," said Alain. "Count and sing, like we did when we started. Just those twelve bars."

"Okay, fine. You guys sing, I'll count. Let's go—one, two three…"

We attracted a small group of people who must have thought we were performing an *avant garde* piece featuring vocalizations. But the counting and singing made a bridge that got me over the rough spot. After a couple more tries, we played together without a hitch—one complete run through and then another—before we called it a night.

As we sounded the final notes, applause broke out from the far side of the room. Some of the Polish Mission folks, I thought; and then I recognized Hank and his uncle, and a tall man in a white linen suit. My heart leaped. He was my mysterious stranger, the man on the poster I had seen at Chicago House.

Hank came up to us, saying something enthusiastic I didn't pay attention to, because I was watching *the man*. The tall, slender, graceful man, who was talking with Hank's Uncle Jim like they were old pals.

"Who's that?" I asked Hank, not caring if I interrupted him.

"Oh, him," said Hank. "He's a scientist of some sort. I don't know why he's here. Probably part of an effort to modernize Egypt. He seemed to like the way you guys played."

The men were moving toward us, still talking. Uncle Jim was talking, anyway. The other—he was looking at me. A little smile played over his shapely lips, his eyes narrowed with secret amusement. "I know you," his expression said to me. "And soon you will know me, and the world will change."

Then they were standing in front of me, and Uncle Jim was saying, "Miss France Leighton, I would like to introduce Dr. Adam Dexter."

"How do you do, Dr. Dexter," I said, forming the words with stiff tongue through rigid lips. I put out my hand, and he took it in his. His skin was deeply tanned, or perhaps he was naturally dark-complexioned. His eyes were the colour of raw copper.

"Miss Leighton. I'm happy to meet you." He held my hand, and I was happy to leave it in his grasp. "And your cello as well." He nodded toward Eudora. I had forgotten I was still holding her with my left hand.

"I'm sorry I missed your lecture," I said. "By the time I saw the poster at Chicago House, it was too late." My hand was still in his.

"…we'll have to work on those problem spots, so make sure you get here on time, France. Good night!" Jack's voice, distant and receding. He vanished down a hallway, pushing Alain, who was looking back at me.

Disconcerted, I pulled my hand away from Adam Dexter's. "Oh, I'm sorry. I have to go. I have to pack up. Jack, Alain, wait! I'm coming!"

"It's all right, France," said Hank. "You can go back to Luxor with us."

"May I offer you a ride to the ferry landing?" Dexter's voice was smooth as good coffee. "Dr. Dykstra?"

"That would be kind of you," said Uncle Jim. "Thank you very much."

Hank waited with me while I packed Eudora into her case and gathered up my belongings—music, purse, jacket. We followed Uncle Jim and Dr. Dexter outside. No beat-up Mercedes for Dr. Adam Dexter. He showed us to a shiny black sedan with a uniformed chauffeur and a second man, also in uniform, waiting to help us inside. Uncle Jim, Eudora and I climbed into the back, facing forward, while Hank and Dr. Dexter, their backs to the driver, faced us.

"And how was your tour of the necropolis, Dr. Dykstra?" asked Dexter. "Are you weary of tombs and temples?" The question was directed to Uncle Jim, but his eyes were fixed on me. "You and I," those eyes said.

Hank let out a laugh and replied before his uncle. "Tombs and temples, nothing. Sure, we visited them, but Uncle Jim wasn't interested in statues, inscriptions, or paintings. Rock and stone, that's what got his attention. Granite, diorite, limestone, schist—I heard all about them."

"Occupational hazard," said Uncle Jim, not a bit perturbed. "Those Egyptians knew their stone. I have to hand it to them, they were masters at working the stuff, especially when you consider they didn't have power tools or motor transport."

At the ferry landing, Dr. Dexter helped me out of the car and carried Eudora to the dock. "I understand you and your colleagues will be playing at Metropolitan House again soon," he said. "I hope you don't mind if I attend. I was intrigued by your performance tonight."

Oh no! Oh yes! What is it about him? Is he related to Francis Dexter? To me?

"Please do. I'll look forward to seeing you." Clutching Eudora to my chest, I turned and scrambled aboard the boat. My feet tangled together and I would have fallen if Hank hadn't put out a steadying hand.

"That was quite the car," said Uncle Jim, as dark water opened between boat and dock.

"Maybe the government laid it on," said Hank, "but driving it all the way out here seems above and beyond."

"Well, they certainly never offered me anything like that." Uncle Jim eased onto the hard seat with a sigh.

"I guess Dexter has more nuclear power than you," said Hank.

He and Uncle Jim sat on either side of me, as though they thought I needed propping up or protection. Their talk—about Cuba and the Russians again—passed over me as the evening breeze pushed the boat along. I had nothing to say, but a lot to think about.

What kind of scientist was he, exactly? Was he a professor? Did he teach, do research, publish papers, go to conferences? What was he doing here, and why was he interested in me?

"Who is Adam Dexter?" I blurted out the question without thinking.

There was a short silence, as though my companions had to shift mental gears before replying.

"Nuclear physicist, I think you said, Uncle Jim?" said Hank. "Could be energy production or could be weapons."

"He says he's with the International Atomic Energy Agency," said Uncle Jim. "Its mandate is the peaceful use of atomic power, but Dexter talks about Los Alamos as though he's familiar with the place. I've seen his name in the literature, but this is the first time I've met him. He's good at talking without saying much, so I think he might be involved with top-secret stuff."

"This seems like a strange place for him to turn up," said Hank. "No nukes in Luxor, although these days everyone's talking about Russian missiles and the end of the world. You uranium-obsessed folks have people spooked."

"'End of the world.'" Uncle Jim sounded testy. "Come on, Hank—you know what a resource nuclear power is. It's just a matter of applying it to peaceful uses. Hiroshima and Nagasaki—those were aberrations."

"Russian missiles fired from Cuba would be one hell of an aberration."

They thrashed the subject over for the rest of the ferry ride. I clammed up. There was no way I wanted to tell them about the effect Adam Dexter had on me, because I didn't understand it myself. And they probably wouldn't care, anyway.

As I trudged wearily into the Stanton Project's dig house, I remembered I hadn't heard what time Jack had told me to turn up at Met House on the day of the concert. A final practice session was a good idea, though. I would have to try and telephone him or Alain. And, of course, I would have to practice like mad. Practice and pray.

I'm late. Really late. I've got to go, even though I'm not sure where. I grab Eudora's case and race down endless flights of stairs. The airport is here somewhere, isn't it? Oh shit! I forgot my music! Run back, find the stairs. They're gone! I run down a long hallway. People hurry by, so fast I can't see their faces. They don't want to look at me; they know I haven't practiced enough, and I can't play anyway, because I left Eudora's endpin at Metropolitan House, in Egypt, on the other side of the world.

I'm in a washroom. Dozens of sinks, dozens of stalls. Puddles of water on the dark blue floor tiles. I push open a stall door. Ugh—the toilet is plugged and overflowing, full of shit and toilet paper. I try another one. Same thing. I can't find the door I came in through. I've lost Eudora. I'm all alone.

Alone and lost. Pillars all around me, as far as I can see, a forest of them. Huge, fat stone pillars, crawling with inscriptions I can't read. Every time I try, the images shift and fade. A passage opens, a wider space between rows of pillars, square ones this time, of plain, dark grey stone, without writing or images. I walk between them, on and on.

This is a place of peril, even though nothing moves except me. The danger is everywhere, in the pillars, in the stones on which I walk. It thrills in the air like an electrical charge. A figure stands in the distance, a dark vertical, waiting. For me. I can't keep from walking toward it, despite my fear, now grown to terror. I must turn around. Too late! Its voice speaks within me. "I am Yesterday and Today, and I have the power to be born a second time."

Now the world changes.

Dim light. I was lying down. Lying in my bed. Safe in bed. In Egypt. In Luxor. In the dig house of the Stanton Temple Precinct Project. I could hear Meg's breathing through the curtain between our beds. I recognized the wavy pattern in two shades of red printed on the curtain's fabric.

It's okay. I'm all right. It was only a dream.

I reached down and felt Eudora's case under the bed. I knew where everything was—cello, endpin, bow, music. All right.

A couple of hours later, after finishing that day's filing, typing and mail sorting, I filched a sheet of notepaper and wrote.

> *Dear Alma,*
>
> *I hope you are well. I worry about you, thinking you might not be looking after yourself. If you want me to come home, just write and say so.*
>
> *I met a man yesterday at a rehearsal of the trio I told you about—a nuclear physicist named Adam <u>Dexter</u>. He's about 35, I think, or maybe a bit older. I wondered if we might be related but didn't get a chance to ask. Do you know if Francis Dexter had any relatives?*
>
> *Much love,*
>
> *France.*

I read over the note and nearly crumpled it up. I could rewrite it, leaving out the part about coming home if she asked me to. But then I folded it, put it in an envelope, addressed it, stuck on a stamp, and tossed it onto the pile of outgoing mail.

6
The Chapter of Intoxication, of Tardiness, and Triumph

On my last day of helping out in the dig's office, Mrs. Stanton asked me to join her after supper, in the private office upstairs she shared with her husband. Dr. Stanton poked his head in the door, apparently on his way out for the evening.

"Don't wait up for me, Adele. Have fun, ladies."

Mrs. Stanton waved at his departing back and asked me to sit down, first pulling the usual visitor's chair to her side of the desk.

"I want to say how much I've appreciated your work in the office. You kept things running smoothly with minimal help from Meg. I'm proud of you both." She went to a small cabinet behind the desk, from which she took out a bottle and a couple of glasses. "How about a drink to celebrate?"

A bit surprised, I nodded. "Sure. Thanks." Watching her pour an amber liquid into each glass, I wondered why she hadn't asked Meg to join us, and then guessed the two of them had already had a debriefing session. Had drinks been part of it? Surely Meg was a teetotaler. Wasn't clean living part of the Scouting code?

"I hope you're okay without ice," Mrs. Stanton said, handing me a glass. "And is Scotch okay? I should have asked you already, but it's that or nothing."

I laughed. "No ice is fine. Whisky and water, that was Uncle Charles's drink of choice. He made a point of initiating me to it when I turned twenty-one. 'You add a few drops of water, but not too many. Just enough to open it up, not drown it.'"

"Uncle Charles?" She slid a carafe of water toward me and propped her feet on an open desk drawer.

"Well, he was actually my grandfather, sort of. My grandmother's husband." I poured a careful amount of water into my glass. "My family's kind of complicated."

She didn't take up that thread, but after a brief silence, she said, "I hope you're finding your experience here rewarding, France. Have you made plans for next spring?"

"Not exactly," I said. "I suppose I'll go home to Providence, but I haven't decided what I'll do there. Get a job, maybe, or travel some more. I'll probably stop in England on the way home, to see my mother. And then my father," I added.

"'Complicated,'" Mrs. Stanton said, with a sympathetic smile. "I hope you don't think I'm being nosy, asking about your plans. As your employer, I feel responsible for you. You're at a stage of life where it's crucial to make the right decisions. Young women today have a lot of opportunities, but often they don't realize that until they've boxed themselves in."

She took a sip of her drink, set her glass down and sat looking at something behind me. For a second, I thought Dr. Stanton had come back early, but then I realized she was thinking.

"Are you engaged, France? Or maybe you have a steady boyfriend?"

"No. No, I don't. Not yet." I wasn't about to expand on my romantic experiences in college, which consisted of uncomfortable negotiations in car backseats and darkened rec rooms in frat houses. Boys were attracted to me like wasps to a picnic, but actual *men* were scarce as unicorns. Too old for me or married, often both. Except Adam Dexter. *I wanted to leave my hand in his.* My cheeks grew warm and, I knew, pink. And not from the whisky. "Mrs. Stanton—"

"More nosiness. I'm sorry, France. I'm sure you think I'm being presumptuous. And maybe I am, but not from idle curiosity. What I'm getting at is I hope you will continue your education before you commit yourself to marriage and children."

"Why? Do you always take an interest in the life choices made by your staff members?"

"Just the women. Young women with potential to change the world. I've had enough experience to offer advice."

I thought for a moment. "What about Meg? Do you give her advice?"

"Meg's career plans are quite detailed, and yes, I am advising her. But you—well, I get the feeling you're in a state of indecision."

"I am, sort of. But I decided to come here. To Egypt, to Luxor. At first, I thought it was a mistake, but there's so much here, all that history lying around underfoot. And it's not all dead stones. In the Hypostyle Hall or in one of the tombs in the Valley of the Kings, I can almost see the ancient Egyptians, as though the present is a curtain I could brush aside if I knew how…" I stopped, thinking again of Adam Dexter.

"That's exactly the effect Egypt had on me," said Mrs. Stanton. "Except in my case it was amplified by infatuation and lust." She reached for the whisky bottle. "Ready for a refill?"

I held out my glass. "Lust?"

"Yes, lust. It's a powerful force, and not just in men. Ten years ago, I was thrilled to be shown the wonders of ancient Egypt by William Stanton. He used to quote bits of the texts to me back then. He thinks it's a sure-fire way to impress young women, and maybe he's right. It worked on me when I was your age. I heard him trotting out one of his favourites to you the other day."

"I have to say, it didn't quite do the trick." *Should I tell her he did more than quote?*

"Good for you, France. Anyway, to make a long story shorter, I fell into the 'grad student marries her professor and becomes his slave' trap. By the time the glamour wore off, I had two kids and realized I'd have to work three times as hard as any man if I wanted a career in Egyptology. And I really wanted that."

I set my glass down on the desk. "Do you think that's what I should want? A career like yours? Because I'm not ready for that right now."

Mrs. Stanton waved a hand. "No, of course not. A decision like that is yours alone. I'm just saying you have to think about these things, so when opportunities arise, you don't let them slip away. And beware the power of lust. It can lead to poor decisions."

I decided to ignore that. "Is your career working out the way you want it to?"

She sighed. "It's a slow process. I hate to admit it, but I'm still riding Bill's coattails. I haven't published much on my own yet, but I'm really close." She held up a hand with crossed fingers. "The Temple Precinct Project is technically his baby. If he goes racing off on a tangent, it'll upset our joint apple cart."

I started to laugh, my mirth provoked by the mental image of Dr. Stanton galloping along with a cart full of apples, and Mrs. Stanton frantically trying to gather up the ones falling off as the cart bounced over rocks and potholes.

My laughter ended in a coughing fit. "I'm sorry, Mrs. Stanton," I said, as it subsided. "I know it's not funny, but that apple cart image..." I composed myself. "I've heard a rumor that Dr. Stanton wants to find an undiscovered tomb."

"Please call me Adele. Yes, Bill wants to find another Tutankhamen."

"But why is that such a bad idea? Apart from being a distraction."

She sighed again. "It's definitely a distraction. We're funded to reconstruct parts of the Karnak Temple Precinct, and to produce useful data about it. We can't arbitrarily start on a totally different project. That would involve a new research plan and funding applications. I know for a fact Bill hasn't done the necessary background work to write a credible grant application. And it's not just funding. The Egyptian government must issue a permit for every archaeological investigation. It's unlikely any one archaeologist would be given more than one permit at a time."

"I see." I sat and thought about all this, while Adele refilled our glasses. Adding water to mine, I wondered if another drink was a good idea. *Why not? This could be the only time she opens up like this. Make the most of it.*

"But aren't you excited at the possibility of finding another tomb? Look how famous Howard Carter became after finding Tut."

"That was another era. I'm interested in building a career and ensuring a future for my children. That means finishing my current project, not taking off on a treasure hunt. Bill doesn't have any real evidence for his idea." She frowned. "At least, none he's willing to share with me."

She took a gulp of her drink. "Okay, it *would* be a big deal to discover a new tomb. I can't disagree with that, but the chances are slim, and that's not where my research has taken me. I have to build on the foundation I've started." She smiled. "I'm sure you'd love to be involved with finding a new tomb."

I shrugged, realizing my nose was numb, a sure sign I'd had too much to drink. "Well, yes, sort of. It's always a thrill to find something new and wonderful. But I'd have a problem."

"Oh? What problem?"

"Well, I'm not an archaeologist, with a career that depends on publishing, so I guess I see things differently. To me, it seems wrong to open a sealed tomb and take out all the things in it, especially the dead body, if there is one. It's — well, it's no different from grave-robbing." I set my empty glass aside.

Adele stared at me as though I was a newly discovered life form. Her flushed face made me wonder if she was a little tipsy. "In that case, it's a good thing you're working on our project. No dead bodies here." She thought for a moment. "May I ask you a favour?"

"Sure." *Ask away, but don't expect me to go along with it.*

"I know Bill finds you attractive." She raised a hand, stopping the indignant response she must have seen forming on my face. "Relax, France, I'm not accusing you of encouraging him, just saying something we both know. What I'm asking is that you act as though you appreciate his attentions. Up to a point. Get him pleased with his ability to charm an attractive young woman. For sure he'll spill the beans about his exciting plans. I know him."

"But why can't you ask him yourself?"

Her lips twisted into a bitter smile. "He'd lie. Bill thinks he's a good liar, so he doesn't try hard. You heard what he said about those maps from the Geological Survey the other day. He got Hank to order them so his name would be on the package. There's no point my asking him anything until I have enough facts to take things to the next stage." She finished her drink, and I was relieved to see she didn't refill her glass.

"You want me to spy on your husband?"

"If you want to put it that way, yes. Don't worry, France. I'll be doing most of the real spying, but I can use your help."

This has to be a test. "And if I don't do a good job of it? If I miss something important, then what?"

"Then, nothing. You've done a fine job on everything you've been assigned so far. Keep doing that, but if you happen to see or hear anything you think I should know about, just tell me. I'll decide whether to follow up on it."

She put her feet on the floor and stood. "I think it's time we wrapped things up. Tomorrow's your big night, isn't it?"

With a jolt, I remembered the Archaeologists' Trio. Our performance was indeed the following night, and I had intended to spend this evening practicing. And here I was drunk and dizzy.

"It is. Goodnight, Adele... and thanks." I propelled myself toward the door, self-congratulating my ability to maintain an upright posture but grateful for the handrail on my way down the stairs.

Practicing was out of the question, but I managed to get Eudora out from under my bed without waking anyone and

113

sneaked out into the courtyard. If nothing else, I had to make sure of my connection with her.

The courtyard, dark and deserted, was a comforting retreat, with smells of cumin, garlic, and bread dough fermenting for the next day's breakfast. I lifted Eudora from her velvet-lined bed and sat with my arms around her, feeling her familiar shape and the silky warmth of her wood. I laid my fingers against her strings and drew forth the faintest of vibrations, like the purr of a contented cat. The thought made me smile.

"Oh, Eudora," I whispered, "get me through tomorrow night. Please."

You'll get through, France, don't worry. That's not what you need to worry about.

The outer gate made its familiar grate-and-clank noise as it opened and closed, followed by footsteps and — *Oh shit!* — the scent of English Leather.

Don't let him come here, please make him go upstairs!

I heard his footsteps recede down the hall and up the stairs. Relieved, I returned Eudora to her case and beat a retreat to my bed.

The next morning, of course, I had the combination of aching head, dry mouth and queasy stomach that's called a hangover. I couldn't manage breakfast, except for orange juice. Not even coffee was bearable.

Hank was back in charge of the diggers, which meant Meg was restored as Queen of the Office, and I was back at the sorting table. No more lurking in the shade of the workroom, with the fan's gentle "whup-whup." Even under my tarp shelter, I found the heat and glare intolerable, although both were less intense than they had been a couple of weeks earlier. I armoured my eyes with my darkest sunglasses but had to keep pushing them up to see important details on the stone fragments. By lunch time, I felt less queasy, but my headache apparently had plans to stick around for the day. It was almost funny that after all my fretting and preparation, the Big Day of the music performance found me in such a disordered state that I didn't have much energy to spare for worrying.

At least I had assembled and tested my outfit a few days ago. It was pretty easy, because the only garment suitable for the event was the proverbial Little Black Dress. With the proper undergarments and my only pair of high-heeled pumps, I looked all right, if a little naïve. The problem was my hair. I could never get it to hold any sort of up-do; it always slipped and waiting for its downfall drove me crazy. For sure it would collapse while I was playing. But leaving it loose made me look like a schoolgirl wearing her older sister's dress. The only solution was to pull it back and weave it into a fat, loose French braid, fastened with a rhinestone clasp. Along with matching earrings, it would provide the necessary bit of glitter.

Except I couldn't find the earrings. After rifling every possible drawer, case, pouch and pocket, I decided I had probably left them in Providence. My search did turn up something I had forgotten—the emerald ring Charles had given me shortly before his death. The ring I hadn't wanted, thinking it big, clunky and impossible.

I must have been mistaken, though. Looking at it now, I thought it was perfect—large enough to be impressive, but not vulgar. The emerald, dark green with a secret fire in its crystalline depths, rose like a blunted pyramid from its square setting of pale gold. Even the engravings on the metal, almost invisibly fine and strangely intricate, did not appear garish, as I thought before. I would wear it on my right hand, my bow hand. It would catch the light as I played and attract attention. The right sort of attention, I hoped, from the right person.

Freed for the rest of the day by special permission, I went to get ready. At least no one else needed the bathroom, so I didn't have to rush. The shower's tepid trickle was soothing rather than invigorating. I towelled my hair to dampness, combed and braided it. In the arid air of Luxor, it would be dry within an hour.

My dress hung ready and waiting, with undergarments, stockings and shoes nearby. I checked my watch—not even one p.m. I was supposed to meet Alain on the corniche at two, so we could get to Metropolitan House by four. Plenty of time.

My narrow cot with its flabby pillow had never looked more inviting. A little snooze would be just the thing. The aspirins I had taken at lunch time were starting to work. I'd wake up at one-thirty, refreshed and ready for the final effort.

I lay down and closed my eyes.

"France! Hey, are you okay?"

Stop that jiggling, goddamn it!

But the jiggling went on and I had to wake up. Groggy, I opened my eyes to Meg's worried face close to mine, her hand on my shoulder. To make her stop, I sat up.

"Yeah, I'm okay. What's up?"

"I thought you'd be gone by now. Everyone else has left for that event at Metropolitan House. I guess they figured you'd gone ahead."

"What time is it?"

"Ten to five."

Shit, shit, shit, shit, shit!

I leaped to my feet and almost fell over. "I'm late! I'm so late! Oh shit! Sorry." I sat down hard on the bed and leaned over, face in hands.

"When were you supposed to be there?" Meg kneeled beside me.

"At four. Jack'll kill me, and I deserve it." I felt like crying, or maybe throwing up.

"Hold on. We'll get you there. Better late than never." Meg sat down next to me and put a hand on my back. "Just sit and breathe for a minute. Okay? Now, think—what's the first thing you need to do?"

I almost pushed her away but was so weak and shaky I took her advice. "I have to get dressed," I said, pointing at the dress. "Is my hair a total disaster?"

"Looks okay to me," said Meg, lifting the dress from its hanger. Of course, she wouldn't have recognized disaster-struck hair; her own frizzy mop was kept in check with a heavy-duty elastic and a couple of combs. But at least she propelled me through the process. Fifteen minutes later, I was dressed, shod and packed up. I stuffed my wallet and a few other essentials into Eudora's case. I didn't want to tempt thieves by carrying a purse, and little black dresses don't come with pockets. At the last second, I grabbed the emerald ring and stuck it on the fourth finger of my right hand, turning the stone inward so it wouldn't be visible.

"Say, Meg, would you mind phoning for a taxi to get me to the ferry landing?" It wasn't all that far, but I was wearing heels and in a big hurry.

Meg didn't move. "Taxi? This isn't New York City, France. Taxis aren't available on call here. Tourists book them in advance through the big hotels. There are plenty on the west bank, for tourists, but not on this side."

"Shit!" I hadn't done so much swearing in my life. "Well, I guess I'd better run." I looked at my shoes.

"You can't run in those things," said Meg. "Wear your sandals and carry the heels. You can change into them when you get there. Here, put them in this." She handed me a string bag.

"Good idea." I kicked off the pumps, stashed them in the bag and slipped into my everyday sandals. Picking up Eudora, I headed for the door.

"Wait, France! You can't go out like that. Not on the ferry. Not alone. Wear this." She opened a drawer of her bedside table and pulled out a long, black scarf. "Put it over your head and wrap it around. It'll cover your hair and make you less conspicuous." She draped the thing over me, crossing the ends so they hung over my shoulders.

"Okay. Thanks, Meg. Why are you here, anyway? I expected you'd be going with Mrs. Stanton and the others."

Her face turned red. "Well, that was the plan, except Dr. Stanton decided someone has to stay behind. He volunteered me, you might say. Look, you'd better get going. Good luck, France."

Closing the door behind me, she added, "You're gonna need it."

As soon as I was on a paved street, I broke into a trot. Flap, flap, flap went my sandals, and perhaps the sound attracted the attention of a group of young Egyptian guys. "Help you, Miss?"

So much for the black wrap making me less conspicuous. It had slithered off my treacherous hair and hung awkwardly around my shoulders. And my sandals, which worked admirably with bare feet, threatened to go flying off due to insufficient friction with my stockings. I slowed to a walk.

"I help you," said one of the men, grasping my elbow. Another one was trying to take Eudora from my hand.

I stopped. "No! No, thank you. *Laa shukran.*" I finally remembered that useful Arabic phrase. "I don't need any help, really. *Laa shukran.* Goodbye!" I pulled away from them and started walking briskly, hoping my footwear would cooperate.

I headed toward a group of tourists emerging from the main gate of the Karnak Temple, and managed to insinuate myself among them, foiling my would-be helpers. With luck, this group was headed toward the corniche, and could act as unknowing escorts.

I stepped along, just short of running, so as not to dislodge my sandals. The corniche was in sight. But would there be a ferryboat?

I got lucky—one fragment of luck on this fiasco of a day. Not only was there a boat, it was preparing to leave, and— miracle of miracles—it was one of the new motorized boats, rather than the charming but slow feluccas. I paid the fare and flopped into a seat. Hugging Eudora, I anticipated with dread what Jack would say when I finally turned up. Then there was the performance, which I was sure to flub. I closed my eyes and mentally ran through my music, snapping out of my concentration only when I felt the boat nudge the dock.

As I disembarked, I realized I had no idea how to cover the two miles from the ferry to Met House. There was no way I could walk, carrying thirty-five pounds of cello and case, not to mention I would arrive too late. For a moment, I contemplated going right back to Luxor, holing up in a hotel, and arranging a swift return to Providence.

I need not have worried. There were, as Meg had said, a couple of taxis waiting, and—could it be?—Met House's black Mercedes, with Alain leaning against it, smoking a cigarette. Seeing me, he waved, dropped the smoke, crushed it underfoot, and hurried toward me.

"France! At last!" He wore a big smile as he took Eudora from me. I felt like collapsing against him and bawling but managed to restrain myself.

"Yeah, it's me. I finally made it. I'm so sorry!"

"*Ce n'est rien.* It's okay." He opened the passenger door. "Let's go, before Jack explodes over there." He put Eudora in the back seat, and we were off.

"I figured you'd show up eventually," said Alain. "And about an hour ago, someone phoned saying you were on your way. So I decided to come and wait for you. Jack was driving me crazy."

"I guess he's really angry with me." It wasn't a question.

Alain laughed. "Well, he was, but now there are other things to make him mad. You'll see."

Metropolitan House buzzed with activity. People were bustling about, setting up tables and chairs. Smells of roasting and baking wafted through the air, waking up my stomach and reminding me I hadn't eaten all day. Groups of men in suits, with a few women among them, huddled here and there, talking, nodding, laughing.

Alain conducted me over to a couple of motherly-looking women, who hurried me down a number of hallways to a washroom, fortunately not like the horrible one in my dream. I sponged my face, re-did my hair and powdered my nose. I got my high-heeled pumps out of Meg's string bag and put them on. My reflection in the mirror looked surprisingly normal.

All too soon, it was time to face Jack and Beethoven. I turned my ring the right way around. "Uncle Charles, wish me luck," I whispered, rubbing the emerald. I lifted Eudora from her case and screwed in her endpin. Then I picked up my bow and music and went to meet my fate.

Jack was indeed incandescent with rage, but not because of me. He barely noticed my arrival, being engaged in an argument about the arrangement of the room, with a man whose accent was probably Polish. "Impossible!" said Jack, waving his arms. "Barbaric—this is *Beethoven* we're talking about!"

Looking around, I noticed our music stands and the piano had been moved to one side of the room, distant from the dome whose acoustics had delighted Jack. That area was full of chairs and small tables, with larger tables to one side, on which white-clad kitchen staff were arranging platters of food.

The Polish man stood with arms folded, absorbing Jack's invective with no apparent intention to change the setup of the room. It was a matter of how long it would take Jack to realize he had lost the battle.

I decided to join Alain by the music stands and get myself ready. The atmosphere of the place and Jack's discomfiture, but especially the fact that I had managed to get there in time, combined to improve my outlook and even my physical state. My headache was gone, my stomach settled (if empty), my shoes felt right, and I knew the emerald ring was the perfect accessory. I was eager to play.

Alain and I put all three chairs and music stands into place, set up our music and tuned our instruments. "Just remember, France," said Alain, "if you get lost, count the beats. Sing them if you have to—heh, hum, hehum, ha."

I smiled at him. "Thanks, Alain, but I think I'll be fine."

Jack hustled over, muttering under his breath. "Well, well," he said, "I see our Miss Leighton has chosen to join us after all. I hope she hasn't been too inconvenienced."

I didn't bother to reply. I was too busy staring at him. Jack was wearing a tuxedo. It suited him perfectly, although his face was too pink for true sophistication. The wonder was that he had actually brought such an outfit to Luxor. "You look great, Jack," I said, with a grin. "Doing us proud, you are."

In fact, all three of us looked pretty good. Alain's black suit and white shirt, my little black dress, Jack's tux—we almost matched.

A shoal of bodies surged into the hall. An Egyptian man, splendid in dark suit and purple and gold striped necktie, waved his arms from the centre of the room, right under the dome.

"Ladies and gentlemen, your attention please! The first session of the Joint Meeting of Archaeological and Cultural Groups in Luxor has successfully concluded. For one hour you may talk informally among yourselves and partake of refreshments. While you enjoy the excellent hors d'oeuvres and pastries, you will be entertained by a musical trio of archaeologists—Mr. Jack Stark, violin, Monsieur Alain Brossard, viola, and Miss France Leighton, violoncello." He waved one hand toward us and the other at the refreshment tables. The crowd headed directly for the food, except for two uniformed men who stood near the entrance, like guards. A hubbub of conversation began, getting louder by the second.

I never thought I would see Jack speechless, but he just stood there, staring at the spot vacated by the man giving the announcement. His mouth fell open and his cheeks changed from pink to pale. After a second or two, he took a deep breath. Thinking he might be getting ready to scream, I stepped toward him.

"It's okay, Jack. Let's play the Beethoven. It'll be fine. Just think, if I mess up, no one will notice."

Jack raised his bow like a weapon, and his violin too, as though he was getting ready to bash and impale. I prepared to grab his wrists before it was too late. Alain wore his usual little smile, but blinked his eyes as though trying to adjust his thoughts. Probably thinking the same thing I was, he moved closer to Jack.

But Jack's arms fell to his sides. "We should have worked up some little bon-bons and flashy encore pieces," he said, so faintly I barely heard him. "Fluff. Someone should have told me."

"Well, they didn't," said Alain. "Come on, Jack, France is right. Let's play."

Jack stood unmoving for another couple of seconds, during which he must have remembered he was no quitter. He turned toward us, hoisting his violin into playing position. "All right, then. You guys ready? Let's play."

From the very first note, everything felt different. Everything felt *right*, as though a virtuoso cellist had taken over my body. The notes I played meshed with the others' like parts of a precise, finely tuned machine. I didn't feel hurried. I knew what to do, and when to do it—echo, oppose, harmonize, support. For the first time, I lived the music completely. If it wasn't so thrilling, if I had more time to think about it, I would have been frightened.

It's that ring! The emerald ring. Why did Charles say it might be better not to wear it?

Looks of surprise on my fellow musicians' faces turned into delighted grins. I felt my lips forming a grin of my own. We were finally a real ensemble, a true trio.

By the time we finished the first movement, we had a small audience. They stood and listened as we played the adagio, *con espressione* as the composer specified. During the sizzling scherzo, which was where I always messed up, more people arrived, bringing chairs over from the refreshment area. By the presto finale, we really hit our stride, tossing the melodic line among ourselves, our eyes meeting at crucial moments. We built the thing, brought it living into the air, and rejoiced in our achievement. As we played the final note, we jumped to our feet, big smiles on our faces, and bowed to our audience, which by now numbered a couple of dozen.

The applause floated me to the top of the dome, as a great weight slipped away and a bright vista opened before me. Coming back to earth, I recognized some of the faces above the clapping hands. Dr. and Mrs. Stanton, Hank, and—yes, it was he!—Adam Dexter.

The applause died away, and the three of us stood as an ensemble for the last time. "Good job, France," said Jack, holding out a hand to me. "Really good, in fact. I apologize for some of the things I said to you."

"Some of the things"—*good old Jack*. His hand was cold. "Don't worry about that. It was great fun. I'm glad we pulled it off."

Alain threw an arm around my shoulders and whispered, "*Brava*," in my ear. Then he and Jack slapped each other on the back and grinned.

"Miss Leighton?" A soft voice spoke beside me. "A brilliant performance. May I congratulate you?"

Adam Dexter extended a hand toward me. I transferred my bow to my left hand, which still supported Eudora. The emerald ring felt suddenly heavy as I placed my hand in Dexter's. The gem caught the light and sparkled green fire.

"What a beautiful ring," Dexter said. He raised my hand to his lips and kissed it. I felt my muscles turn to water, and almost lost my grip on Eudora.

"Thank you, Dr. Dexter. I'm glad people liked our performance. And that you enjoyed it."

A smile crinkled his coppery eyes. "May I suggest an encore?"

"Oh, no—I'm sorry, we didn't prepare one." I spotted Jack and Alain near the refreshment tables, helping themselves. *Too late.*

"I meant the two of us." Dexter leaned toward me, and I smelled a mixture of incense and sweet resin mingled with something astringent. "I am a competent pianist, and you must have a favourite piece for violoncello with piano accompaniment."

Again, I felt I was a balloon about to float up and up. "*Salut d'amour*, by Elgar," I whispered.

"Of course." He smiled, an interior smile, as though he'd had a bet with himself and won. "A very good choice. Come along."

He sat down at the piano, played some arpeggios, and looked at me with raised eyebrows. *Salut d'amour* was a piece I had played so many times with my teacher in Providence, I could still do it in my sleep.

And tonight, I can do anything. Can't I? "All right."

I played. I drew the correct notes from Eudora, blending them with those from the piano. *We're making music together, he and I.* But I didn't feel the same connection with him as I had with Jack and Alain, the unity of collaboration in creation. Instead, Adam Dexter unrolled a carpet of notes on which I stood and played my cello. I was glad when it was over, especially because Eudora emitted a couple of jarring "wolf notes," real howlers, like an over-tired child who has had too much excitement and wants to go home. That was how I felt too. There was no more air in my balloon.

Dexter got up from the piano, and the two of us bowed to the ten or so people nearby, who may have been listening to and watching us play. Among them were Alain and Jack.

"Thank you, Miss Leighton," said Dexter. "I hope you will do me the honour of dining with me tomorrow evening. I will send my car for you at seven."

I found my voice. "Uh—that would be delightful. I'm staying at the Stanton Project's dig house. Near the Karnak Temple."

"Oh, I know that. I know where to find you. Goodnight, Miss Leighton." He moved smoothly toward a group no doubt headed to the next session of meetings.

But they're about archaeology. What's he doing here?

"Quite the evening you've had, France," said Jack, appearing next to me. "You ace the Beethoven, and then you do a pretty good job on Elgar, playing with a nuclear physicist. That's got to be a Luxor first. But you'd better have a look at your cello. It sounded off just now. The wood might be drying out."

"You may be right," I said. "I've been worried about that."

"It ought to be kept in a climate-controlled room. They have one here, for storing artifacts. That's where I kept my fiddle, up until now. By the way—I need the cello part back."

I grabbed it from the music stand and gave it to him. He tucked it under his arm. "Thanks. Well, I still have some packing to do. Maybe we'll meet again. Goodbye, France." He walked away, his violin tucked under his arm.

"Packing?" I asked Alain, who was hovering nearby.

"He has to leave Met House tomorrow. You see, when the Polish group arrived, everyone who was already here had to leave. That's one of the things that made Jack *dérangé*, so annoyed."

"Oh, I didn't know." I felt small. "Does he have somewhere else to stay?"

"Oh yes, he made such a fuss the Antiquities Department found him another place. And he says he's going back to the States soon anyway. By the way, France, I must apologise that I did not accompany you back to Luxor the other evening, after our rehearsal here. Jack was telling me his troubles, and I was distracted."

"It was all right. One of the fellows from my dig was here, and Dr. Dexter gave us a ride to the ferry landing."

"Dr. Dexter—he was the one you were playing with just now—the Elgar piece?"

"Yes."

"I thought I noticed something a little strange," said Alain. "It was how he played the piano, or maybe didn't play it.

He didn't touch the keys, just held his hands over them and moved them around."

"Really? Could it be a player piano?" We went over to the instrument and I struck a few keys at random. It seemed perfectly normal. "Are you sure, Alain?"

He shrugged. "Well, that's how it looked to me, from back there." He waved a hand at the chairs where he and Jack had been sitting. "I could be wrong, I suppose. Are you ready to go?"

"Yes. No, wait. I have to pack up my cello. I left the case in another room. Do you mind waiting?"

"This time I will wait."

I managed to find the cello case. Laying Eudora into it, I murmured, "We did it, it's over, thank you, thank you."

As I emerged from the room, hurrying so as not to keep Alain waiting, I heard a woman's laugh nearby. A soft, intimate laugh. Peeking around a corner, I saw Adele Stanton in close conversation with someone. Not Dr. Stanton. This man was taller and younger. I caught a glimpse of a purple and gold striped necktie and recognized the man from the Egyptian Department of Antiquities who had made the announcement before the break.

It was possible he and Adele were discussing archaeology, but I didn't think so. Was this the power of lust? And did I recognize it because I was experiencing it myself?

7

The Chapter of Eating and Drinking in a Place of Mystery

Sitting at my sorting table the next morning, I followed my familiar routine (pick up stone, examine for inscriptions and/or chisel marks, place stone in correct basket), but my mind was occupied with Adam Dexter. His interest in me was unmistakable, as was my gut-level attraction to him. A nuclear physicist who was quite a bit older than me, but a real dreamboat. Was it only his looks? I thought back to my first sight of him—a Pharaoh of Old Egypt clad in a present-day suit. Something about him promised a direct connection with the essence of this ancient land.

He was American, not Egyptian. I hadn't noticed an accent when he spoke to me. Might there be a connection between us through my grandfather, the mysterious Francis Dexter? Perhaps I would find answers to these questions this evening. Flutters of anticipation made me shiver.

What would I wear? Unfortunately, the little black dress of the previous night was the only suitable garment. The formality of Dexter's invitation, and the fact that he was sending his car and driver to pick me up, suggested a fancy restaurant, probably at the Winter Palace or one of the other big hotels.

After work, I washed up and got into the black dress and matching pumps. I wove my hair into the same sophisticated (I hoped) French braid, adding the rhinestone clasp. I was inspecting myself in the mirror when Meg came in.

"Hi, France. You missed dinner. Oh, you're going out? Another concert?"

"No, I'm going out to dinner."

"I wondered if you were feeling all right." Her smile (*smirk*, I thought) suggested she wasn't terribly concerned. "You have a date?"

"Yes, actually."

The word "date" invoked a bolt of strangeness. I was going on a *date*. In Luxor, Egypt. With a nuclear physicist who looked like Ramses II. And yes, that was definitely a smirk on Meg's face.

"Who with?"

"Someone I met last night, at Metropolitan House."

"That man you played an encore with."

"Yes. Dr. Adam Dexter." *I wonder if Adele's told her about that Egyptian guy.*

"Well, you look pretty spiffy. Say, do you still have my wrap?"

Wrap? "Oh no! No, Meg, I'm sorry. I must have left it at Met House."

To be truthful, I wasn't sure what I'd done with Meg's wrap. I may have lost it on my frantic run to the ferry landing, or maybe I had left it at Met House. Or on the ferry. "I'll get it back, I promise. Or I'll buy you another one. Did you get it here?"

"No, in Cairo, when I first landed." She frowned and fiddled with a handkerchief, twisting it around her fingers, tying a knot in it and then untying it.

"Darn! How about if we go to the *souk* tomorrow and find you a replacement?"

Meg shook her head and stuck the handkerchief back in her skirt pocket. "Never mind. I didn't use it that much. Have a nice evening."

Was she sincere? I wasn't sure but resolved to buy a replacement for the missing wrap. "Thanks, Meg. By the way, why did you have to stay behind last night? I know how keen you are on anything to do with archaeology. Wouldn't Mrs. Stanton—?"

"Dr. Stanton won that round. I heard them arguing in the office earlier, and then he said I had to stay here, and she didn't say anything. It's not the first time something like that's happened."

"But it wasn't fair!"

"No, it wasn't. But you can't do anything about it, France, so don't worry about it. Enjoy yourself. Good night."

As I was approaching the outer door of the house, Dr. Stanton clattered down the stairs.

"Going out, Miss Leighton?" He looked me up and down. "My goodness, you are lovely, aren't you?" He smiled his oiliest smile.

My first impulse was to get away from him as fast as I could, but I remembered my promise to Adele. If I was going to find out anything useful about Dr. Stanton's doings, it wouldn't hurt to flatter him a bit.

"Thank you. I was happy to see you at Met House last night."

"You were the highlight of the evening, my dear." He came closer to me. I braced myself for English Leather, but he smelled like whisky. It seemed both Stantons enjoyed a drink.

The doorbell clanged, making me jump. I opened the door to a man in a dark blue uniform with gold trim and a matching cap whose black visor shadowed his face.

"I am here for Miss Leighton." he said, in a curiously toneless voice.

"I'm Miss Leighton," I replied.

"Come with me, please," the man said, turning away. "The car is over here."

"Bye-bye." I waggled my fingers at Dr. Stanton and followed the chauffeur.

The car looked like the one I remembered from the night of the rehearsal at Met House. But that had been on the west bank, and there wasn't a bridge. Did Dr. Dexter have two cars at his disposal?

The chauffeur opened one of the doors and bowed. I slid inside, moving from the familiar, smoke-and-supper smell of a Luxor evening into a cocoon of leather and plush, with a whiff of the exotic scent I had noticed around Adam Dexter the previous evening.

The chauffeur closed the car door without speaking and got into the driver's seat. I had yet to get a good look at his face, and I didn't know exactly where we were going. Reaching forward, I tapped on the glass barrier between him and me. No response, but I saw an indistinct dark shape in the passenger seat. A cold lump of fear replaced the hunger pangs in my stomach.

We were moving. Without my realizing it, the car had accelerated to a speed greater than I thought would be possible on any street in Luxor. Out the window was a blur of light and shadow, building facades, vehicles, walls, doorways. I saw no people, nor any familiar landmarks.

I'm being kidnapped. This guy isn't a chauffeur, he's a criminal with an accomplice. He never mentioned Adam Dexter, did he? I was stupid to go with him!

I was wondering how the Stantons would react to a ransom note, when the forward motion of the car slowed, and it stopped. My door opened, and a flickering yellow light revealed Adam Dexter.

"Welcome, Miss Leighton."

Shaky and disoriented, I sat staring at him, clutching my hands together.

"You've arrived," said Dexter, holding out a hand. "Come along, please."

My limbs unlocked. I swung my legs out of the car and took his hand. His grasp, warm and strong, pulled me to my feet.

We stood in a stone-paved yard with walls on three sides. Pillars flanked a set of double doors. Torches flared and flickered beneath the deep blue of a night sky.

This wasn't the Winter Palace Hotel, that was certain.

Dexter took my arm and escorted me between the torch-bearing pillars. The doors, carved with papyrus motifs, swung inward and admitted us into ancient Egypt. Wooden statues of striding deities welcomed us into the dimly lit room. The walls bore scenes of feasting and dancing. Tables and chairs, light and graceful, filled the room.

A man came toward us, smiling a greeting. A *maître d'*? He bowed and led us to a distant alcove. An alabaster lamp cast a warm glow over the table, which was set with modern crystal and china.

The *maître d'* showed me to a chair. He strongly resembled the chauffeur in height, build and demeanour, but wore a white jacket and black bowtie. Could it be the same man? If so, he was a quick-change artist. Or maybe he'd been the passenger?

Dexter spoke quietly to the man and seated himself opposite me, elbows on the table, hands clasped under his chin. The light flattered his features—long nose, full lips, gracefully arched brows that tapered precisely to his temples, reminding me of divine and royal faces in tomb paintings.

"Miss Leighton," he said. "At last."

"Yes," I didn't know what else to say, and felt stupid. "Thank you, Dr. Dexter."

"Adam, please. And may I call you France?"

"Please do."

"Is your name short for Francesca?"

"It's not short for anything. Just 'France.' My mother named me Francesca, but I changed it."

"Why?"

I shrugged. "'Francesca' is old-fashioned. When I turned twenty-one, last spring, I decided to change it."

A pair of waiters appeared, one with a jug of water and a bottle of wine, the other with a basket of flatbreads and small dishes of olives and cheeses. Adam poured the wine and raised his glass. "Congratulations, France."

My stomach rumbled as I touched my glass to his, and I hoped the clink covered the sound.

Engaged in the small flurries of unfolding my napkin, sipping wine and sampling the appetizers, I could not help but notice that the waiters, now departing, appeared to be identical to one another. Moreover, they reminded me of the chauffeur *and* the *maître d'*.

Adam served himself small portions from each dish, but unlike me, nibbled rather than wolfed. "Are you enjoying life in Luxor?" he asked.

I swallowed and wiped my lips. "Yes, I am. I came here hoping to learn about archaeology and ancient Egypt, but there's so much, such a depth of culture and history, and so many ways to experience it." I stopped. *Don't gush, France!*

Adam broke a piece of bread in two and laid both pieces on his plate. "Indeed. Experiences such as playing music by Beethoven and Elgar, to an audience of archaeologists. And one nuclear physicist." He smiled.

"I'm glad you thought my—our playing worthwhile." The restaurant was too quiet. I hadn't seen any other diners when we came in, and I didn't hear any conversations or clinking of cutlery. Surely Adam hadn't reserved the entire place for dinner with me? That would be distinctly strange.

"I'm just wondering... " I hesitated.

"Why I asked you to join me here this evening?"

That wasn't my question, but I nodded.

"Because," said Adam, leaning forward slightly. "I was eager to make the acquaintance of a beautiful and talented young woman. A young woman who has more on her mind than archaeology and history. I hoped we could get to know one another in private."

My face grew hot, and no doubt pink, but I seized the opportunity to ask my question. "It's so quiet. There doesn't seem to be anyone here but us. Do people in Luxor prefer late dinners?"

Adam's brow quirked, as though with annoyance. "Yes, dining late is an Egyptian custom." He turned away for a moment and gestured. The waiters promptly arrived, bearing plates of grilled meats and vegetables. While one of them laid out the dishes on the table, Adam murmured something to the other.

I realized I had not seen a menu, nor been asked what I wanted to eat and drink. But the food smelled delicious. Adam told me about the Egyptian cuisine we were about to eat, remarking on the flavourings and praising the quality of the cooking. "This is excellent. Please try everything."

I didn't hesitate. Between bites, we carried on one of those getting-acquainted conversations. He asked me about my work on the Stanton dig, and how I became involved with the musical performance. In my eagerness, I came close to gushing again and decided it was time I asked a few questions.

"Why are you here in Luxor, at meetings of archaeologists? Is there a connection between archaeology and nuclear physics?"

"Everything is connected," he said, looking into my eyes. "I knew I had to be there, and now I know why."

A murmur of voices started in the main room, along with faint clinks and footsteps, as though a crowd had suddenly arrived. Music joined these sounds, rhythmic pulsations overlaid with the piping of a wind instrument. Part of me wanted to go around the corner and see the musicians, but I hesitated to break the thread of our conversation.

"Why am I here in Luxor?" Adam said. "One excellent reason is it's my home." He picked up the wine bottle and refilled my glass.

"Luxor is your home?" I said. "But you're American, aren't you?" Conversing with him now, I detected a subtle accent.

"Only on my father's side," he said. "From him I got my Yankee surname and American citizenship. But my mother was Egyptian, and from her I inherited my love for this land."

Well, that explains his suntan. "You look Egyptian," I said. He raised an eyebrow. "Thank you, I think."

"When I saw the poster about your lecture, I thought you looked like a pharaoh." I felt myself blushing again.

Adam smiled. "I'm flattered."

The two waiters, whom I now privately called Tweedledum and Tweedledee, arrived with another course. When they left, I faced Adam and took a breath. "There's something I've wanted to ask you since we first met. Do you know... or know of, a man named Francis Dexter?"

A spark of recognition flashed across his face. He pressed his lips together and glanced away from me and then back, his gaze intent and focussed. "I know the name. But what does it mean to you?"

"He's—he was my grandfather."

Adam's eyes widened. "Your grandfather's name was Francis Dexter?"

"Yes, but I never knew him," I said. "He died before I was born."

Another silence, during which Adam leaned back in his chair, elbows propped on its arms, and studied his clasped hands. "I am acquainted with a man of that name."

"When was that?"

"Years ago," Adam said, as though he was talking to his manicured fingernails.

My heart speeded up and the effects of the wine dissolved to nothing. Alma's letter said Francis Dexter visited Luxor in 1935. Twenty-seven years ago.

I almost asked the obvious question, which was, "How old are you?" In the soft light cast by the alabaster lamp, I couldn't guess his age. Thirty-five? Fifty? I suppressed the impulse, not least because I really didn't want to know.

"Is it possible you and I are related?" I asked.

A slow, closed-lipped smile. "Would you like that, France? If I were your cousin, somewhat removed, perhaps?"

My face grew hot again. "Somewhat removed would be just fine," I said, lifting my chin and smiling. *Too forward, France. Cool it!*

I returned my attention to my plate and groped for something else to talk about. Out of the corner of my eye, I saw 'Dum and 'Dee approaching with yet another course. Or perhaps dessert? Percussion instruments joined the music in the main dining room, adding jingling and chiming tones to the rhythms. I thought I heard a spatter of applause and wondered if there were dancers.

"Where did you grow up, Adam? Egypt or America?"

Adam took a sip of wine. "I grew up on several continents. My father was a professor, but we lived in Europe as well as America and Egypt."

"Is that where you learned to play the piano? In Europe?"

"Piano?" He laughed. "Oh, that's something I've picked up recently, to amuse myself. My family wasn't in Europe very long, as it turned out. During the war and after, my father was called upon for his expertise, so we travelled a great deal. And my mother always longed for Egypt, the land of her birth. That was where we spent vacations—in Alexandria, for the most part."

"What was your father's field of expertise?"

"He was an engineer. One who harnesses science for the good of mankind. As do I, although in a different way."

"I see." But I didn't. "Your father's contribution to the war effort... which war was that? And what did he do, exactly?"

Adam frowned. "You have the instincts of a journalist," he said. "An urge to dig out the facts. I don't know what he did, exactly. He never spoke of it to me." His coppery eyes widened, and he leaned toward me. "Do you know, I think he may have been a spy of sorts. A man of mystery."

I could tell he was steering me away from the topic, and I didn't resist. "And Egypt is a land of mysteries."

"Indeed. That's another reason I haven't been able to leave it for long. I come here whenever I need to renew myself. But my work has taken me around the globe, involving matters crucial to the future of the earth."

The shape of his lips as they formed words fascinated me, like watching a time-lapse film of a flower opening, or a butterfly emerging from its chrysalis.

"Really?" I said. "That sounds interesting. Can you tell me about those matters?"

"Unfortunately, no. I am sworn to secrecy."

But you were at a meeting of archaeologists. Surely that's not top secret?"

"You are persistent, Miss Leighton." His sculpted lips shaped themselves into a smile. "I wanted to watch Egyptologists at their work. To observe them in the field, as it were. I'm interested in their attitudes and techniques, as well as the results they obtain. It offers a new perspective on this many-dimensioned land."

"But all that's in addition to your main area of expertise, isn't it? I thought you came here to advise the government about modern energy production."

Adam tilted his head, amusement lingering on his features. "I commend you for your interest in current affairs. Yes, that brought me to Egypt, but nostalgia and sentiment have compelled me to linger. And a certain Miss France Leighton."

Another wave of hot pink. *I wish I could stop blushing.*

"Thank you, Adam. What is nuclear physics, exactly? How does it work, and why are people afraid of it? Some think the end of the world is coming."

Adam laughed. "'The end of the world'! Fortunately, you've asked those questions of someone who is able to give you the right answers, scientifically correct and free of foolish bias.

"You've heard of atoms, haven't you? They're fundamental particles. Everything in the universe is made up of atoms. But atoms themselves are composed of even smaller particles—protons, neutrons, electrons and others. They cling together under the influence of the fundamental forces." He swept an arm in a circle. "Everything—absolutely everything— exists because these particles are held together in a known and predictable way by known and predictable forces. Breaking those bonds releases energy, also in a known and predictable way. Do you understand what that means?"

The dessert was one of those Egyptian pastries I had come to love, an irresistible combination of flakes and sweetness. I stopped in the act of conveying a piece to my mouth and put down my fork, its delicious burden untasted. Adam's eyes gazed intently into mine, his expression serious, the hand he had gestured with tucked under his chin.

"Uh, I think so. It's power, isn't it? Not just electrical power, or how to make a really big bomb, but power over everything."

"Exactly. The power of scientific knowledge, an understanding of primal phenomena. That's why fear is foolish. Nothing has changed in the way the world works, only the extent of our knowledge of it."

While he was speaking, I swallowed my abandoned bit of pastry. "All right, I understand that, but surely this knowledge *has* changed things. Those bombs dropped on Japan in the Second World War. Hiroshima. And nuclear fallout— isn't that dangerous?"

"Fire is dangerous. So is electricity." Adam looked amused. "But science—both discovery and application—is glorious."

"But discovering something doesn't necessarily mean applying that knowledge. Don't you think making atomic energy is a kind of... hubris?"

"Hubris? Why?"

"Well, meddling with those fundamental particles is... fundamental, isn't it? And what about fallout? Some of the people on my dig are really worried about that. They say the next war will be a nuclear one. I don't know much about it, but sometimes I wonder. And I'd love more coffee," I said, indicating my empty cup.

"Certainly." Adam clapped his hands twice, like a sultan summoning a slave, and sure enough, there they came—'Dum and 'Dee. They stood mutely at attention, awaiting orders.

141

Adam said something in Arabic, or anyway not in English, and they hastened to do his bidding.

Adam tapped his fingers on his coffee cup and looked at me intently. "Irrational fear perpetuates ignorance and slows progress. Each scientific discovery presupposes development of the means to manage it. This addresses what you said about knowing and doing. It's true that one of the first uses of nuclear energy was as a weapon, but that does not mean it will be the last use."

"Yes, but aren't new weapons being made? And used as threats? People are afraid of that."

"Fear is another form of energy, France. You can't blame science for that."

I took a breath. "Don't you scientists ever wonder if the consequences of your discoveries aren't... well, *too* big?"

Adam leaned back in his chair, hands clasped together on the edge of the table, a questioning look on his face. "Explain, please."

The waiters returned and poured fresh coffee, one carrying the coffee pot, the other with a linen napkin over his arm, in case of spills, I assumed. As soon as they left, the words I'd been holding back poured from me in a torrent.

"Think of Tutankhamen's tomb—you know, it was nearly intact, that was the wonderful thing about it. Did Carter and Carnarvon ever think whether it was all right to take everything out of it, even the sarcophagus and Tut's body? It was a *grave*. They were grave robbers. The ancient Egyptians mummified their dead king, and put him in all those coffins, and carried all that stuff into a tomb tunnelled into solid rock. They must have performed some sort of ceremony, and said special words, and sealed up the tomb *for all eternity*. 'Millions of years'—that was the phrase they used. Don't you think a *force* was created then? All those objects sat there for thousands of years, just like those particles of yours. Opening up a tomb and taking things out is *wrong*. And maybe splitting the atom is wrong too. You did say everything's connected, didn't you?" My throat was dry and I reached for my water glass.

Adam leaned forward. "If another intact tomb were discovered, would you want to explore it?"

"Yes!" I didn't need his smile to tell me I'd contradicted myself. "All right, I admit it. I'd love to see an untouched tomb. Imagine—everything just as it was placed thousands of years ago, the words of the funeral rites still hanging in the air..." I shivered. "But that would be an impossible experience. The very act of opening and entering the tomb would destroy it."

After a silent second, Adam lightly placed the fingers of his left hand on those of my right, where it lay next to my cup and saucer. My pulse sped up, and I wondered if he could feel it.

"You're not wearing that remarkable ring." said Adam. "I noticed it when you were playing last night."

"That's why I wore it then," I said, "but I forgot to put it on tonight."

Adam compressed his lips and narrowed his eyes. "A pity. Is it a family heirloom?"

"I guess it is an heirloom of some sort. It came from Francis Dexter. My grandfather. Someone who knew him gave it to me. But I have no idea where it was made or how old it is."

Behind his urbane smoothness I detected an inexplicable annoyance. "I hoped to have a closer look at it. I know something of such things. Another time, perhaps."

Did that mean he wanted another date with me? "I'd love to learn more about it," I said. "And about Egypt." I held Adam's eyes with mine. *And about you.*

"We can explore those interests. Together." He stood and held out a hand. "Come with me. There's something I want to show you."

He led me to a paved terrace. Torches made a flickering, uncertain light, with darkness beyond. Adam let go of my hand and stepped forward a few paces. He spread his arms, as though unrolling a scroll. "Tell me, France—what do you see here?"

The Nile Valley stretched before me, bathed in the rich golden light of a rising full moon. The river gleamed like bronze. Upon it rode a boat I had seen only in pictures, a galley with high bow and stern, with banks of oars moving in perfect unison, and a square sail shining like gold.

"Oh, wow, look at that! I didn't know there were still boats like that. Is it for tourists?"

"No," said Adam. "Not tourists." He was near enough to me that his sleeve brushed my bare arm. I caught a whiff of his intriguing, exotic cologne, and wanted to lean against him, to share with him my delight at this magical scene he had revealed.

"I can show you many things you would never see otherwise. I know this place intimately. I can give you the essence of Egypt, to savour, to understand, to *know*."

A second's pause, and then, "Is that what you want, France?"

I turned my head and met his gaze. The light of the pillar-mounted torches reflected in his eyes, but I couldn't read his expression. I was pretty sure he wasn't joking.

"I want to know as much as I can, " I said. "And to feel, to experience the essence, as you said." I thought of my hallucination in Seti's tomb. "How would you do it, though?"

"I know things about this place," he said. "More than your archaeologist friends, more than any tourist bureau or tour guide. With me, you will experience the true mysteries of this land. In fact, you've already begun to do that." He waved his arm toward the distant river, where the galley was passing from view.

Adam slid his arm around my shoulders and drew me toward him. His strength, solidity and warmth enclosed me. I wanted the moment to last forever, but it didn't. "It's getting late," he said. "Come inside for a final drink, and then I'll send you home."

Inside, our table had been cleared, the coffee cups replaced with two glasses and a small jug containing a ruby red fluid. I didn't want more wine, but before I could refuse, Adam filled the glasses.

"Pomegranate juice," he said. "Very refreshing. Think about what I've said tonight, and if you wish to find me again, go to the village of Qurna, in the west bank necropolis. Ask for the one they call 'alyad alyumnaa,' which in Arabic means 'right-handed.'"

He left our alcove and rang a bell. Or at any event, a bell tinkled, and a few seconds later the chauffeur reappeared, uniform and all. Was he one of the waiters? He looked like them, except for the uniform. He bowed and turned. Adam and I followed, his arm around my waist.

In the main room, I saw neither musicians nor dancers. Figures sat at most of the tables, around glowing lamps. There was something about them, though, something strange. For one thing, all of the half-dozen or so women wore the same style of hat, a black velvet pillbox with a bow and a little net veil. How likely was that? But with Adam's arm urging me forward, I couldn't stop to get a better look.

The black car waited outside the entrance, the chauffeur next to it. But wait, hadn't he walked out of the restaurant with us? Oh, of course—there were two of them. One opened the door and helped me inside. Then both he and the driver got in the front seats.

"Good night, France," said Adam. "Until our next meeting." He touched his lips to the back of my hand and let it go.

"Good night, Adam, and thank you." The door slammed shut, and once more I felt I was going on a journey, a much longer and more perilous one than the short distance to the Stantons' dig house.

And again, we were there before I knew it. The chauffeur—or his double—held the door open and I scrambled out and placed my feet on the gritty pavement. Peculiar thoughts roiled through my brain. *Got to find my land legs. Got to get reacclimatized. Feel heavy, so heavy...*

My feet weighed a hundred pounds each, but my head was a balloon tugging on its string. I had no idea what time it was, but it felt late. I groped for the gate's rusty old latch.

Nausea rolled through me like a rogue wave, lifting my stomach, squeezing it and dropping it with a thump. I let go of the latch, lurched a couple of yards along the wall and sank to my knees by a block of stone. Clinging to it, I heaved up my insides. Food, wine, coffee and pomegranate juice ejected in a hot, acrid mess between the stone and the wall.

Limp and exhausted, I hung over the stone, hugging it like it was my last friend on earth. My fingernails scraped its pits and irregularities, the skin of my fingers discerned every sand grain of which it was formed. I rested my cheek on its harsh hide and groaned.

I don't know how long I stayed like that before I found enough strength to stand up and stagger back to the gate. I yanked it open, screech be damned, and slammed it shut behind me, clang be damned.

My first stop was the bathroom, where I rinsed out my mouth and bathed my face. On the way to the Girls' Dorm, I met one of the dig partners, a Brit whose name had escaped me. Roger something-or-other? To my mumbled greeting, he said, "Well, well, Miss L., it must have been quite the party."

"Oh, it was," I said, and clicked the door shut behind me.

I barely managed to get out of my dress before collapsing on my bed.

I slept late the next morning, but considering how sick I had been, I felt surprisingly well and really hungry. Breakfast was over, but I wheedled leftovers and coffee from the cook.

Adele stopped by my sorting table shortly after I settled in to work.

"I heard you were out late last night," she said, after the usual greetings. "With a mysterious stranger. I suppose that explains your late start this morning."

"Yes. I'm sorry." *And you have your own mysterious stranger, don't you, Adele?*

"Not worse for wear, though. Good for you." She smiled and picked up an inscribed piece of stone, looked at it, and set it back down.

"No, not at all. In fact, I feel fine." I squinted up at her, as she stood with the sun glaring over her left shoulder.

"Good. By the way, congratulations on your musical performance the other night. I meant to tell you how much I enjoyed it, but something came up, and then you must have left."

"Actually, I saw you just before I left. You were with that man from the Antiquities Department. The one who did the announcements and introduced Jack and Alain and me."

I watched her closely. A faint pink tinge brightened her cheeks. She tapped her knuckles on the table. "Well, we all have work to do, don't we? See you later."

After work, I persuaded Meg to come with me to the *souk* to shop for a replacement for the black wrap I had lost. We found one easily, and I was happy to pay for it, along with a turquoise scarf I thought Alma would like. Mission accomplished, we wandered through the textiles market, eyeing the wares and other shoppers. A display of *galabeyas* caught my attention.

"I've been thinking one of these would make a good lounging robe," I said. "Sort of like a caftan."

"Sure, but not in public. They're strictly men's garments here."

I bought a grey *galabeya* and a dark blue turban. The wife of the man selling the clothing showed me how to wrap and tie the turban correctly, giggling at the strange notions of tourists.

Carrying our purchases in the ever-popular string bags, we headed for home. Near the Bennu Bird Café, we saw Hank and his Uncle Jim coming toward us. Hank waved, and I raised a bag in response.

"Would you heavily-laden ladies care to join us?"

Meg said she had work to finish, and declined an escort to the dig house.

"Are you sure?" Hank asked. "It'd only take me a few minutes to go with you and come back."

"Exactly," said Meg. "Which is why you don't need to. I'll be fine. I can take your bag, France. See you later."

I had been to the Bennu Bird enough times by now that the place felt familiar and the proprietor greeted me by name. "Hello, Miss France! Welcome, welcome."

Settled with coffee and a date-filled pastry, I turned to Uncle Jim. "It's nice to see you again, Dr. Dykstra, but I thought you'd gone back to the States."

"Well, if I'd gone back to anywhere, it would have been Saskatchewan, Canada," he said, with a smile. "I was in Cairo on business, and Dr. Stanton asked me to come back here when I was done with it. I heard your concert went well. I'm sorry I had to miss it."

"Well, it wasn't really a concert, but it did go quite well," I said, relishing a bite of the pastry.

"And you had quite the evening out last night too, I heard." Hank winked at me over his cup.

Who told you about that? Must have been that Roger fellow I met when I got in. "You might say so." I set my cup down. "Hank, have you ever gone to that fancy restaurant with a view down the Nile? It's on a hill, I think."

"Fancy restaurant? On a hill? Here in Luxor?"

"Yes! That's where I went for dinner last night. With Dr. Dexter, the physicist. There were torches by the entrance, and inside it was like a nice restaurant anywhere. Well, mostly. The furniture and decorations were ancient Egyptian style, and the food was really good." *Until it all came up, that is.*

"Hmm. Must've been at the Winter Palace, but I don't remember seeing any torches there. How much did you have to drink, France? Roger Dunn said you were pretty shaky when you came in."

I ignored that. "It wasn't at the Winter Palace. I'm sure about that. It might have been out of town. There was a terrace with a great view of the Nile Valley."

Hank stared at me, eyebrows raised. "France," he said, "I hate to tell you this, but there's no such restaurant. Luxor's pretty small, and all the restaurants are downtown, where the tourists are." He thought for a moment. "Could it have been a private residence?"

I almost said, "Oh no, there were waiters and everything." But Tweedledum and Tweedledee had been the only other people I'd seen there before we left, except for those vague shapes, some of which had worn identical veiled hats.

"I suppose it could have been a private house," I said. "Adam—Dr. Dexter, I mean—and I went out to the terrace and saw the Nile in the distance. There was a boat on the river, with the moon coming up behind it."

"Moon?" Hank and his uncle looked at each other.

"Yes!" *Do they think I'm an idiot?* "A big, round, full moon, rising over the river."

Hank leaned over the table and spoke slowly. "France, if you were able to see the moon rising over the Nile, you would have been on the west bank. For sure no fancy restaurants there."

I swiped a hand from forehead to chin. Damp. "I just told you what I saw." I pushed away the plate with my half-eaten pastry.

"Forgive me for asking," said Uncle Jim, "but is it possible you indulged in some sort of drug? I know young people like to experiment, and here in Egypt a variety of drugs are available." He aimed a glance at Hank.

"France, you naughty girl!" Hank shook a finger at me. "And here you've been telling me you're a stranger to hashish."

"No, no, no!" I lifted my palms and slapped them down on the table, rattling the cups. "I didn't take any drugs or smoke anything. I had some wine, but not that much, and coffee, and pomegranate juice."

"Pomegranate juice," said Uncle Jim, rubbing his chin.

"Pomegranate juice does not produce hallucinations," said Hank.

"Not by itself, no." Uncle Jim looked at Hank, and then back at me. "Miss Leighton," he said, "you'd best be careful. I don't know Adam Dexter well enough to guess if he'd pull a trick like that, but keep your wits about you if you go on another date with him. Or maybe you'd just better not go."

On returning to the dig house, I took a quick peek behind the stone I had flopped over while throwing up my dinner. There was nothing there, nothing at all, as though both the meal and the restaurant were figments of my imagination.

But Adam was real. Others had met and spoken with him. I would find him again and ask him where we had been.

There was a letter in my mailbox with an Egyptian stamp and a Cairo postmark. Someone signing herself Amelia Devlin had written a terse few lines in a beautiful script, saying she and her daughter expected to be in Luxor soon, and were looking forward to meeting me.

I stared at the letter, mind blank. Who was this person? Then I remembered. Alma had mentioned Mrs. Devlin in her letter. The lady who had known Francis Dexter and wanted to meet his granddaughter.

8
The Chapter of Rising into Air and Falling to Earth

After supper, I took Eudora to my familiar spot under the acacia tree in the courtyard. I lifted her from the case, embraced her, and brought her to life by stroking and plucking her strings. "I'm sorry, dear, for neglecting you. Sorry, sorry, sorry."

Eudora emitted a contented thrumming. A bird called nearby, and another answered from a distance. The soft murmurs of the kitchen staff were punctuated by brief bursts of laughter and the clink of utensils.

Peace.

"What about that dinner the other night?" An agitated flurry of notes under my fingers, the strings tense and taut. "Where was I? And who is Adam Dexter?"

I don't know what Adam Dexter is, but he knows darkness. He knows secrets of Egypt, yes, but he has other secrets.

"Yes," I whispered, plucking at the C string. "I want to know those secrets. Directly, not by looking at chunks of rock and testing theories. He says he can show me, but..."

But? The strings vibrate, the hollow vessel resonates against my heart.

But. But. But.

"But I'm afraid. He's so... different from other men. And I think he's older than he looks. His father was in the First World War, and I'm sure Adam had something to do with the nuclear bombing of Hiroshima. That was almost twenty years ago, so he must be at least forty-five, or even fifty!"

And why should his age trouble you, young France?

My fingers swept the strings. *Agitato.* "Because... because I'm attracted to him. And I hope he is, to me."

A series of plucked notes, repeated. A, D, G, C, C, G, D, A. *And is that what you want?*

"Yes. But maybe not... Oh, I don't know! It's as though he's offering me a wonderful gift."

And you want it, don't you?

"Yes!" I struck the strings, as though Eudora was a guitar, producing a harsh tangle of notes. "Oh, I'm sorry!" I tried to quiet her but a faint buzz persisted.

Why did you agree to play that encore with him? To make me play with him? And Salut d'amour, of all things! Oh, France!

"What? It wasn't such a big deal. We've played that piece so many times. After the Beethoven, I wasn't up for anything hard."

Well, it was hard on me. Remember this, France—I am your instrument, no one else's. Especially his.

And she clammed up. Nothing I did in the way of stroking, plucking or bowing produced anything more than ordinary cello sounds. Eudora's speaking voice, the voice that revealed inner things, was silent.

I laid Eudora in her case like a mummy into a sarcophagus. It was fully dark. The moon peered over the courtyard wall. I remembered what Hank had said about seeing the moon and shook my head. *Maybe Adam Dexter is a hypnotist.*

Too late for an opinion from Eudora. I went to bed.

And couldn't sleep. The regular sound of Meg's breathing was like a ticking clock. Once noticed, it grew louder and more irritating. I got up, made a trip to the washroom, and decided to go back to the courtyard instead of working through another series of uncomfortable positions in my wretched little bed.

The moon, although past full, shone bright and sharp now that it rode clear of Luxor's smoke. Why wasn't the moon as important to ancient Egyptians as the sun? It took me a while to remember the moon-god's name—Khonsu. I would have to find out more about him. Meg or Hank would know. Or Adam?

I was starting to feel sleepy when I heard the distinctive scrape of that sagging gate. The sound was faint, as though someone was taking care to minimize it by lifting up.

Sneaking in, or sneaking out?

None of your business, France.

Except now I was wide awake again, so I might as well snoop. Maybe it was Roger Dunn, coming back from a nighttime adventure. I could pretend to encounter him by chance and ask if he'd had a good time. I climbed onto the bench and looked over the top of the wall.

Dr. Stanton stood with his back to me, his shirt gleaming pale in the moonlight. Watching the moon? Not likely. A small light bloomed in the darkness—Stanton checking his watch with the help of a flashlight.

He has an appointment? In the wee, small hours of the morning? Hmm.

I scrambled off the bench and back into the house. Good thing I was wearing my sandals and bathrobe. My own flashlight in the bathrobe's pocket was a definite bonus.

As quietly as I could, I let myself out the main door and crossed the short distance to the gate. I couldn't see Dr. Stanton, but didn't hear any footsteps, so figured he was still there. I eased open the gate, congratulating myself on making no noise at all.

I poked my head through the opening and peered down the narrow road. Dr. Stanton's white shirt bobbed along, growing fainter with distance. If I wanted to know what he was up to, I had to follow him.

I squeezed through the gate without opening it further and closed it with the faintest of scrapes. Then I proceeded down the alley, hoping Dr. Stanton didn't look behind him, because my baby blue bathrobe was probably as visible as his white shirt. I nearly panicked when he turned on his flashlight again, but he directed it toward the temple precinct wall on the opposite side of the alley. A faint clink told me he had opened the gate into the temple grounds.

Every crunch of gravel under my soles sounded like a gunshot, but I told myself Dr. Stanton couldn't possibly hear it on the other side of the wall. I just hoped he hadn't locked the gate from the inside.

The gate was unlocked. Entering the temple grounds, I saw Stanton's light flickering among the pillars of the Hypostyle Hall, where he found Eudora and me that other time. Who was he looking for tonight?

Did I really want to seek Dr. Stanton out on purpose, in the very spot where he'd taken advantage of me? Alone and in the middle of the night? What kind of message would that send?

But if I wanted to find out if he was up to something irregular, how else would I do it? Especially since it looked like he was meeting someone here. I crept cautiously toward his light. It was no longer moving. Dr. Stanton must be waiting for his date to arrive.

I shone my flashlight a few times to save myself from tripping before I reached the first of the great pillars. There were no obstacles among them, so all I had to do was flit from one to another until I could observe my quarry from a safe vantage point.

I was creeping from pillar number three to pillar number four, and wondering how close was too close, when I heard the shuffle and crunch of footsteps and saw an approaching light behind me. Between me and the gate. Dr. Stanton's date, no doubt.

Thank God for huge pillars! I flattened myself to the nearest one, pressing against the curving stone bulk as though trying to become one with it, and sidling along to keep it between me and whoever was coming.

The new light came closer, moving methodically from side to side. I dropped to my knees and crouched behind the pillar's massive base. A faint murmur of voices, interspersed with occasional harsh coughs, joined the sound of feet coming closer. Two people. Two *men*.

So much for the romantic rendezvous theory.

"I'm over here," said Dr. Stanton, rather redundantly, since he was waving his light around, creating weird effects by lighting up different carvings—a face here, a cluster of hieroglyphs there. I hoped like hell he wouldn't illuminate me. Blue terrycloth bathrobes weren't exactly typical wear for Egyptian gods and pharaohs carved on pillars.

"Okay, Bill, we can see you." Hank's voice.

"You're late. I've been waiting for half an hour."

More like ten minutes.

"Well, we're here now, so just stay put until we reach you."

More footsteps and coughs were joined by the harsh smell of cigarette smoke (which would explain the coughs). A faint thud from Dr. Stanton's direction was followed by an absence of light, grunts, scrabbling sounds and muttered four-letter words. "I've dropped the goddamn flashlight. Hold on a minute."

I was busy suppressing a fit of nervous giggles when a volley of coughs broke out close to me. Really close, like a pillar's thickness away. I froze and huddled back against the stone. *Gods of the Two Lands, save me, please!*

Light returned, also too close for comfort. Dr. Stanton had found his flashlight. All three men were less than ten feet away from me. I held my breath.

"All right now?" Hank sounded his usual cheerful self. "Captain, this is Dr. Bill Stanton. Bill, Captain Hawes."

Muttering, probably over a handshake, followed by, "Made up your mind, have you?" spoken by a fibrous, English-accented voice that must have belonged to Captain Hawes.

"Yes, and I'd like go up as soon as possible," said Dr. Stanton.

"Well, that depends on weather, you know. And early morning's best. Soon after dawn, which is about three hours from now."

"Day after tomorrow?" said Stanton.

"No can do." Cough, cough, cough. "Got business elsewhere. No time like the present, if you ask me. Get your ducks in a row by half past four, and we're in business."

"Half past four *this* morning?" Dr. Stanton's voice echoed among the pillars. Hank must have shushed him, because he continued more quietly. "That's way too soon. It means—"

"It means you'd better hustle," said Captain Hawes, and I was sure I heard a grin in his voice.

"The Captain's right, Bill," said Hank. "What's the point in delaying? We've waited long enough as it is."

"That's only because it took him so long to get organized in the first place," said Dr. Stanton. "'Ducks in a row,' indeed."

A scratch and whiff of sulphur told me the Cap'n was lighting up another cigarette. "Your choice, Professor. Today or two weeks from now. I'm taking the whole rig down to Aswan to do photos of the dam site. Seize the day." A gurgling laugh turned into another coughing fit, followed by a splat of thick liquid landing on stone.

"Two weeks!" Stanton sounded peeved.

"Consider the day seized," said Hank. "Where should we find you, at four-thirty?"

"I'll send a boat to the corniche. A jeep'll meet you on the other side. Not sure where we're launching from yet."

"We'll be there," said Hank, but Dr. Stanton interrupted.

"You can guarantee a good look at the area I specified? I'm not interested in a sightseeing tour."

A moment of dead silence, and then the Captain's voice again. "Professor, didn't you hear what I said? Ballooning is one hundred per cent weather dependent. I can't guarantee anything beyond getting you up and back down. And a great view, of course. I'm sure as I can be that conditions will be favourable, but that's it. If you want a guarantee, you'd better talk to the gods. Lots of them around here."

I wished I could see Stanton's face, but I was more intent on getting myself back to the house without being seen. I had my own ducks to line up.

I remembered the dig crew talking about Hawes, a crazy Englishman who had come to Egypt with his hot air balloon, hoping to set up a business giving tourists aerial tours. I'd been crazy about ballooning since I'd read Jules Verne's *Five Weeks in a Balloon*. This was a once-in-a-lifetime chance, and I wasn't about to miss it.

I managed a kind of slow hurry back to the house, trusting to instinct to avoid using my light. Back in the dorm, I laid the flashlight on my bed and stuffed everything I thought I would need into my beach bag—sweater, hat, two pairs of sunglasses, notebook, pen, scarf, aspirin, my Brownie camera. It was unlikely Cap'n Hawes would supply water or anything to eat. On the other hand, that was just as well, because there would be no washroom facilities.

Over my blouse and Bermuda shorts, I pulled on the *galabeya* I had bought. It was perfect camouflage for a solitary pre-dawn run to the corniche. When it came to the turban, I hesitated, doubting I could wrap it correctly, but then I figured my long blond hair wouldn't go with the Egyptian male garment. I was struggling with the cloth, trying to remember what the woman in the shop had done, when I heard Meg's sleep-fogged voice.

"What the heck are you doing, France?"

Shit. "I was going to write you a note. And one for Mrs. Stanton too."

She turned on a light. "Why? And what's with the *galabeya*?"

"I have to go out. It's a great disguise, don't you think? But I can't get this stupid turban right. What time is it?"

"Three forty-five. Where are you going?"

"Look, Meg, I know this seems nuts, but I have to take off for—I don't know—most of the morning, probably. Hank and Dr. Stanton are about to go up in a balloon, and I'm going too. Want to come? Oh no, wait—you'll likely have to supervise the dig, since Hank won't be there."

Meg blinked like a puzzled owl. "You're crazy."

"Sure, but please tell Mrs. Stanton I'll be back by afternoon, and I'll be doing... the business she and I discussed a while ago. She'll know what I mean."

Meg just sat there, looking peeved.

"Oh, never mind," I said. "Here, I'll write her a note." Scrambling to find pen and paper, I tripped over the loose end of the turban cloth. "Shit!"

"Take that off and let me do it. You have to double it over lengthwise first, remember?" Meg's helpful Girl Scout instincts were waking up and coming to my rescue. She got out of bed, grabbed the cloth and started to manage it.

I scribbled a few lines for Mrs. Stanton. Then I sat on my bed while Meg wrapped the length of blue cloth around my head, tucking the ends in neatly. When she was done, I looked in the mirror. Perfect, flat on top, fat around the sides, no hair showing. "Where did you learn to do turbans?"

"Practice." She grinned, and I wondered what I didn't know about our resident Girl Scout.

I put on my sneakers. No telling where I'd end up, or on what sort of terrain. At the last second, I dug out the emerald ring from its hiding place and stuck it on my finger. Hot air ballooning was a daredevil activity, and if things went really wrong, I wanted something from Uncle Charles with me. I couldn't take Eudora, so the ring would have to do.

It was still dark out, but with a hint of approaching dawn. I strode along the deserted streets, trying to walk like the *galabeya*-wearing men I saw everyday, while keeping my too-white face from showing. The garment was surprisingly comfortable, with inside pockets, as I discovered.

Of course, I had overlooked a fatal flaw in my disguise. Halfway to the corniche, a couple of men in dark garments appeared from a doorway on the opposite side of the street. Policemen? I was dead scared they'd speak to me and expect an answer. A male answer, in Arabic. I'd have to pretend I was deaf or something. I kept my head down and hurried along, hoping I didn't look suspicious. The pair stood and watched me but didn't follow.

The corniche was deserted, except for cats on the prowl. I sat down on a step, keeping an eye out for the two policemen. After a while, I wondered if I had imagined the meeting in the Hypostyle Hall. Maybe I had nodded off after all, and dreamed the whole thing. I was starting to feel like an idiot and thinking I'd better go back to the dig house, when two things happened. A motorboat approached along the river, and I heard voices behind me.

"That must be our boat." Hank's voice was followed by a grunt from Dr. Stanton. It was time to give them a big surprise.

I scrambled to my feet and whipped off the turban and *galabeya*, rolled them up and stuffed them into my bag. My arms goose-bumped with pre-dawn cold, so I rummaged out my sweater and dived into it. I had just finished smoothing my hair when the two arrived.

"Good morning, Dr. Stanton. Hi, Hank." I wished the light was better so I could get a good view of their faces.

"France!" said Hank. "What the—?"

"Miss Leighton?" said Dr. Stanton. "Is that really you?"

"Who else?" I said, as the motorboat drew up to the dock. "And here's our boat. Perfect timing."

"*Our* boat?" A slow grin developed on Hank's face, and he looked at Dr. Stanton.

"I can't believe my luck," I said, picking up my bag and heading toward the boat. "Ever since I first read about hot air balloons, I said I'd go up in one first chance I got."

Dr. Stanton stared at me as though I was a brand new thing in his world. "How did you find out?"

"Little birds," I said, smiling at him. "Three of them. Singing in the Hypostyle Hall." He smiled back.

"This little bird's gonna fly, it seems," said Hank, walking over to help moor the boat.

A taxi pulled up and Dr. James Dykstra climbed out. "Thought I'd be late," he said. "Short notice in the dead of night."

"Couldn't help it, Uncle Jim," said Hank, taking his camera and binoculars and helping him aboard. "Ballooning is one of those 'seize the moment' endeavours."

This trip across the Nile was much faster than my previous ones. We tied up to a dock and were hustled to a waiting jeep that took off with a roar and a cloud of dust. A short time later, we arrived at a flat stretch of sand and gravel. I stood and shivered while a couple of men ran around busily, dragging out an expanse of pale-coloured cloth while Captain Hawes shouted directions.

The balloon looked pretty flimsy, lying there limp and wrinkled, and the crazy contraption that must have been the gas burner didn't reassure me either. Did I really want to do this?

To divert myself, I looked up at the pyramidal bulk of el-Qurn, and at its foot the faint lights of the villages where generations of tomb-robbers were said to live.

Hank came over with—oh joy!—coffee steaming in a thermos cup. "Thanks," I said. "You're a prince, Hank."

"Don't I know it. Really, France, why are you here?"

"Why not? It's probably my only chance to go up in a balloon." I drank the coffee, grateful for its warmth as it worked its way down. "I asked Meg to tell Mrs. Stanton I wouldn't be at work this morning. And neither would you."

Hank eyed me over the rim of his cup. "Thanks, I guess."

"Well, don't you think she'd notice you weren't there?"

Before he could reply, a gout of flame shot into the bottom of the balloon, which was being held up by Hawes's helpers. "Up, dammit, hold 'er *right* up!" he yelled. "Don't let 'er catch fire!"

After a few tense minutes, the balloon took shape, looming over us like an oversized ghost. The crew attached the passenger basket, tightening and loosening various ropes.

"Okay, get yourselves over here. We're ready to launch!" The Captain waved an arm, and the four of us converged on the balloon.

"And who's this young lady?" the Captain asked, looking at me. "You said there'd be three of you."

"This is Miss Leighton," said Dr. Stanton, stepping up next to me. "My assistant."

"Good for you, Professor," grunted the Cap'n, "but the basket holds four, and one of 'em has to be me, so one of you's going to have to stay behind."

"Oh, I'm not going," said Hank, flashing a big smile. "I'll stay behind. In fact, I'm heading back to the site."

"Suit yourself," said Hawes. "All right, Miss, climb aboard. Ladies first."

He and one of his men linked hands to make a step for my foot, and I hoisted myself over the side of the basket, feeling grateful I had worn Bermudas instead of a skirt. Dr. Stanton and Uncle Jim climbed in, followed by the Captain.

"I'll tell Adele that Miss Leighton is safe with you, Bill," said Hank, waving and turning away with a grin. Dr. Stanton opened his mouth to say something, but Hank was talking to one of Captain Hawes's assistants.

What's Hank up to, anyway?

With all four of us in it, along with a massive cylinder of fuel, the basket was pretty snug, and the floorboards felt none too solid. Above our heads dangled the burner, supported by ropes and connected to the fuel tank by a rubber hose.

"All right, cast off," ordered Captain Hawes. The ground crew twitched ropes aside, smiling and waving, probably happy to be staying on *terra firma*. Hank waved and grinned even harder—pleased with whatever he was plotting?

Why aren't we moving? I wondered, and then the ground fell away beneath us. Hank, the other two men, and the jeep grew smaller and smaller as the world broadened out under us.

Dawn broke, the sun swimming incandescent on the horizon and we rose to meet its rising. Below us lay a field of temple ruins; the Colossi of Memnon looked small and ridiculous, like constipated stone trolls on matching stone toilets. Then the vivid green ribbon of cultivated lands along the Nile's sinuous brown length, with feather-duster palms wreathed in mist or smoke, Luxor town small and trivial, brown rocky lands to the east, now lost in the flaming disc of the sun, floating out of molten reds and oranges.

I was winged and invincible. Pressing myself against the side of the basket, I raised my arms. "Hail, glorious Ra! You rise, you shine, King of the Gods!" These words from the "Hymn to Ra," one of my favourite parts of the *Book of the Dead*, rose to my lips and issued forth before I realized it.

"The Lord of Heaven, the Lord of Earth and the creator of those who dwell in the heights and the depths," Dr. Stanton chimed in, stepping over to me. "We dwell in the heights, Miss Leighton." He draped an arm around my shoulders. The basket swayed and lurched.

"Stand still, Professor, for God's sake!" said Captain Hawes. "No moving around. You don't want to unbalance her."

Amen to that.

Stanton moved back to his original spot, and I, feeling embarrassed and silly, rummaged my Brownie out of my bag and took snaps of the sights. Uncle Jim, on my left, was studying something through his binoculars. The early light hit the cliffs above the Valley of the Kings, casting sharp shadows and picking out details.

"It reminds me of the Grand Canyon, sort of," I said, pressing the shutter. "Are those really dried up creeks there, or do they just look that way?"

"Wadis," said Uncle Jim. "They're called arroyos or washes in the desert Southwest, but they're similar features. The Valley of the Kings is a wadi, and there are many others nearby, draining the slopes of el-Qurn. It rarely rains here, but sometimes there are localized heavy showers, and flash floods move a lot of sediment."

"Like all that loose gravel over there, above the steeper parts?" I pointed to the slopes of el-Qurn, drifting by close to us.

"Ah, those are debris cones. Loose sediments slide downhill until they achieve an angle of repose. That's time and gravity at work, slow and steady. Water is faster, but intermittent."

Captain Hawes was busy with his burner, emitting blasts of flame every now and then. A few times he leaned over the side and spat. He must have noticed me noticing. "Reading the wind direction," he said, making me think his phlegmy cough was good for something. "It changes with altitude. Got to keep on its good side."

Uncle Jim turned to Dr. Stanton. "Look for alluvial fans, meaning water action. Some of the tomb entrances—Tut's for example—were buried in flood debris. So you're looking for something like that on the wadi floors. Either that, or spots in the hard limestone above the flood deposits. Those would actually have been better sites, structurally."

"Hmm," said Dr. Stanton. "I'm inclined to think the wadi floors are more likely than the heights. Lugging everything up there would have been a limiting factor."

"Well, you're the expert, but I can't help thinking these were the people who built the pyramids and Karnak. Lifting heavy loads didn't seem to be a problem for them."

We were slowly passing el-Qurn, sailing southward. Beneath us, the great mortuary temple of Hatshepsut looked like a modern architect's model.

"Captain, we need to go back and up, over el-Qurn," said Dr. Stanton. "I told you—I need to see the valleys *behind* the Valley of the Kings."

"Says you," muttered the Cap'n, blasting a shot of flame into the balloon. "Just enjoy the ride, Professor, and let me manage the ship."

"I'd enjoy it better if I could see over there," said Dr. Stanton, pointing behind us and westward.

"Man, how many times must I tell you—a balloon can't be *steered*. It doesn't have a rudder. You have to play the winds, and for that you need the right touch. So settle down and leave me to it." The burner roared again. "All right, up we go."

We rose, in that astonishing silent way. El-Qurn flattened out under us and dark crevices appeared behind its main spur. Hawes shut down the burner, and the balloon glided silently toward the riven surface.

"That's it! Good, perfect!" Dr. Stanton leaned out of the basket and peered down. Uncle Jim had switched from binoculars to camera and was snapping pictures. The balloon slipped lower, tracing a narrow valley with furrowed cliffs to either side. I leaned out, framed a scene, pressed the button, advanced the film, pressed again, trying to capture as much as I could.

From a hollow in the grey, weathered cliffside, a bulging stone eyeball watched me, a flattened spheroid, its colour darker than that of its matrix, tinged with rusty red. "Nice concretion there," said Uncle Jim, as I framed a shot. Snap, advance, snap, advance. And again.

Until I realized I was seeing something strange—red light in a deep cleft below the eyeball rock, bright as the rising sun. Red, I thought. Red, it's *red*, and look there, there, *there*. I snapped a photo, but the film would advance no further. It was full.

Beneath me, the cleft opened, and I gazed into its red depths. Something glowed down there, whose essence was attached to mine. It pulsed, sending up ripples of warmth. I stretched my left hand down to it, as though grasping for an invisible rope. The emerald sparked green fire and the ring warmed my finger. *She's there.* Ancient and eternal, hidden and yet now revealed. To me.

"Going up! *Now!*" Captain Hawes's voice shredded my concentration, my intense and unnatural seeing into the cleft. I blinked and saw a rock wall coming straight toward me, full of intent and purpose.

"Get down!" Uncle Jim yelled, over the roar of the burner. He grabbed my shoulder and pushed me to the floor boards. "Put your arms over your head and stay low."

I felt as though my stomach had been left behind and hoped I wouldn't be sick. A few moments later, the upward motion slowed. We hadn't hit anything. I uncurled and peeked over the edge of the basket. We were skimming over a crumpled, barren landscape that could have been anywhere, including the moon.

"Got to take her down," said Captain Hawes. Cough, cough, cough. Gargle. Spit, spit. "Not where I intended, my friends, but that's the way it is. Wind calls the shots, and we're low on fuel, with all those extra ups and downs."

We were descending again, not majestically but rather fast, even though Hawes kept popping puffs of flame into the balloon. Dr. Stanton's face turned the colour of paste. "I think we're going to crash," he muttered. Uncle Jim was busy stashing his camera in its case and didn't reply. I reached over and patted Stanton's arm.

"Pray," I said.

Rocks and boulders rushed closer, as though they couldn't wait to meet us. The Cap'n was muttering curses and talking to the balloon, or maybe the burner. "You can do it, baby. Come on, you bitch, just a little farther."

Not quite far enough. The basket hit the ground at a steep angle with a jolt that threw me on top of Dr. Stanton. I heard a loud clang, and something hit my head.

I was swinging through the air. *Goodbye, balloon, who needs you?* But why was the ground so close?

Dry dust and the smell of stone in my nostrils. The perfume of the necropolis, of serving at the tombs. Oh, today I'm so tired, my head is so heavy. How will I play, how will I sing the right words?

"No, there. That's good. She'll be all right for a bit. Straight to the hospital from the boat. I'll radio them."

Oh, my head! I won't be able to play. Where's my bow? It broke when we landed, didn't it? I'll have to pluck instead. Pizzicato all the way. Jack'll kill me. Oh, I need to sleep.

"Easy there. You'll be all right, Miss. We had a bit of an accident, that's all."

Where are my legs and arms going? Up, down, sideways.

The river flows, and I float on its back. But I don't remember the Scales or the Feather. And yet I am not devoured. Breath of the god, speed my boat along!

"Be careful! Don't do any more damage, for God's sake. Here we are, Miss. You're in good hands."

I'm going like a rocket! Fast, fast, fast through the tunnel. Whee! But where to? How will I know I'm there?

Hands upon me, touching, grasping. I lie on a table. Are these the sem priests? I should not be here. Let me scream! Give me my voice before I feel the blade!

Who is that? Whose eyes are those, behind the light?

"Answer my questions, please. If you can't speak, squeeze my hand."

I opened my mouth, tried to say something, but only a groan came out. I forced it into the shape of a word. "Can. Yes, I... can."

"What is your name? Tell me your name, please."

"Mer... Meres... Uh, no. France. France Leighton."

"Miss Leighton, can you see my hand?"

The hand that holds the light and wields the knife? "Yes."

"How many fingers am I showing to you?"

"Oh, I dunno... Three. Head hurts. Leave me 'lone."

Hands of my sisters. I am still with them, serving Amun in his temple with my hands and voice. How did I come here from the house of the dead? Homage to thee, Osiris, Lord of Eternity. I rise up to see thee and breathe the air and look upon thy face.

Oh, my head!

I opened heavy eyelids and recognized the cracked ceiling above my cot at the dig house. My head hurt too much to move my eyes, so I closed them again. What a crazy dream. Flying through the air with Dr. Stanton and Hank's Uncle Jim?

My left hand lay over my heart. With my right, I felt for the emerald ring. *Oh good, it's still there.* I pried my eyes open again and wiggled my hand from under the blanket. The ring was unharmed—no nicks or scratches. Unlike the way I felt, which was battered and bruised.

So it must have been real.

"France? Are you awake?" Meg's face loomed over me.

"I guess so. Bad headache. What time is it?"

Meg looked at her watch. "Seven-twenty p.m. You slept all day. I think they gave you a sleeping pill at the hospital."

"Hospital? Really?"

"Yes. You have a concussion. You're not supposed to talk, but if you want, I'll get some tea and a couple of aspirins and tell you what happened."

"Okay. Thanks, Meg."

According to Meg, the balloon had crashed on a hillside near the Valley of the Queens, following a too-rapid descent from above the summit of el-Qurn. One of the ropes supporting the burner mechanism had snapped and part of it hit me on the head. No one else had been injured, apart from a few bruises.

"If that thing had hit you full-force, it would have been a lot worse," said Meg.

"It feels bad enough as it is." I sipped my tea, relishing its warmth and the honey Meg had added.

"You'd better get some more rest now. I've told Mrs. Stanton you're awake. She said she'd come and see you tomorrow morning."

"Is Dr. Stanton okay?" A little imp of curiosity made me ask.

Meg frowned. "You mean not injured? Yes, but if I were you I wouldn't expect a visit from him."

"Oh, I don't. Thanks, Meg, and goodnight." Only after she'd left did I realize I hadn't asked her if she'd given my note to Mrs. Stanton.

"Good morning, France. I'm glad to see you're feeling better."

Did Mrs. Stanton look anxious, standing at the foot of my bed in her military-style khaki dress? Anxious about me, or any liability issues I represented? True, I wasn't injured on the dig site, but I was in the company of the dig's director.

"Thanks, Adele. I do feel much better."

"I think you'd better take the day off and rest."

Without pay, of course. "Yes, I think that's a good idea." At the thought of hours in the sun, even under my tarp shelter, my headache threatened to return.

"Do you feel strong enough to talk?" She pulled up a chair and sat down, so I assumed I did.

"How did I get back here? My memories after the crash are pretty hazy." *The house of the dead, the River, the temple.*

"Well... I wasn't there, of course, but I gather Captain Hawes and one of his crew rushed you to a boat and then to the hospital here in Luxor. The doctor in the emergency ward diagnosed a mild concussion. He didn't think it was serious enough to warrant admission to the hospital, so Captain Hawes brought you here. I asked Meg to keep an eye on you while you slept."

"And Dr. Stanton, did he get back okay?"

"Captain Hawes went back and fetched Bill after bringing you here." She sat and looked at me as though she expected me to say something specific, without having to ask me for it. I gazed back at her, wishing I had something to do with my hands, which wanted to twist together nervously.

Adele shifted on her chair and cleared her throat. "France. No one can blame you for the accident, or for getting hurt. But I wonder what prompted you to be on that balloon in the first place."

"When I overheard Hank and Dr. Stanton talking to Captain Hawes about it, I thought, 'Here's my chance.' All right, it was a bit of a whim, but I might get an idea of what Dr. Stanton's extra project was about. You asked me to, remember?"

She nodded. Only once. Her posture reminded me of the seated deities in paintings and sculptures. "You didn't think it was irresponsible to take off without notice? Just you and Bill in a balloon basket, soaring over the Valley of the Kings?"

I stifled an involuntary giggle. "We weren't *alone*. With Captain Hawes and Uncle Jim—Dr. Dykstra, I mean—it was pretty cozy in there."

"Dr. Dykstra was there too?" The cerise colour her cheeks had acquired began to fade.

"Yes. He was taking pictures of landforms near el-Qurn—alluvial fans and some sort of limestone—and explaining things to Dr. Stanton, recommending where to look for something.

"And anyway," I babbled on, "I didn't leave without any notice. Didn't Hank explain how he decided not to go up, so I could? He said he was coming back here. That was about five-thirty, I think. And I left a note with Meg. Didn't she give it to you?"

Mrs. Stanton stood, frowning. "No one explained anything to me. All I knew was you weren't at work yesterday morning. Then Captain Hawes brought you here, and Bill turned up about an hour later."

The next time I saw Meg, I asked her whether she had passed my note to Mrs. Stanton.

"Note?" she said, wide-eyed. "You didn't give me a note, France. You were in such a crazy rush, maybe you thought about writing a note but didn't actually do it."

It wasn't a point worth arguing, but I did. "I'm sure I asked you to tell Mrs. Stanton I wouldn't be at work."

Again that look, calm but phony. It sure looked phony. "Well, maybe I forgot. You wake a person up in the middle of the night and ask her to remember a bunch of stuff, including how to wrap a turban. Maybe she forgets a few details. You know?"

Maybe I didn't know, but I was starting to guess. *Good old Meg.*

I made myself join the gang for supper that evening, even though turning my head too fast made everything spin. The Girls' Dorm had totally lost its few charms, and I didn't want to get known among the rest of the crew as "that girl who fell out of a balloon." I was there to represent myself, even though I didn't have much of an appetite for stewed chicken with beans and rice. In the usual minor confusion of post-supper dispersal, I sidled up to Hank.

At least he didn't try to avoid me. "Hi, France! Good to see you're okay. That was quite a thump on the noggin."

"It was," I said feeling the tender lump on the back of my head. "Just think—it could have been yours."

He shrugged. "Lucky, that's me."

By this time, everyone had left and the room was empty except for the two of us.

"Seriously, Hank—why did you bow out? Just to do me a favour?"

"In a word, yes." But he shifted his eyes away from me as he said the crucial word.

"I thought you were part of whatever Dr. Stanton was up to."

Hank narrowed his eyes and wrinkled his nose. "A real conspirator," he said. "Okay, I organized the balloon thing, but it wasn't necessary for me to go up. Uncle Jim and Bill were the ones who really needed to."

"So why didn't you say anything to Mrs. Stanton when you turned up for work and I didn't?"

Hank edged toward the door. "I had my hands full with the workers. A couple of them had a running argument going, and I had to supervise them 'til they settled down. And anyway, why would I tell her? Bill isn't too keen on sharing his extracurricular project with her. I was pulling his leg back there when I said I was going to spill the beans."

"Great. Adele thought I was off on a lark with him, until I told her your uncle was there too."

"Uncle Jim as chaperone! He'd love that idea. Look, France, I gotta run. See you later."

"France?"

Deep in thought, I startled at Meg's voice and dropped the hairbrush. "What do you want?" Jolt-induced anger made me rude.

"I forgot to tell you—a couple of women came here looking for you yesterday, while you were asleep. I told them you weren't feeling well. One of them wrote you a note. It's in the office. Remind me to give it to you tomorrow."

Shit, they were probably that Mrs. Devlin and her daughter. "Your track record with notes hasn't been that great lately, has it? Oh, sorry, Meg. I'm still not feeling that well. Sure, I'll pick it up tomorrow. Thanks for telling me."

It took me a while to fall asleep. What did I really see in that valley? And can I find Adam again?

And whom can I trust?

9
The Chapter of Experiencing Unpleasantness and Being Driven Out

Trust was in short supply the next day. It could have been an aftereffect of my concussion, but I thought everyone was eyeing everyone else at breakfast. No. They were eyeing *me*. I didn't hear anyone say, "What's she been up to?" but I was sure they were thinking it. I could see the thought lurking behind the pseudo-friendly smiles and queries after my health. I told everyone I was fine, but I felt shaky, trailing streaks of dizziness when I moved my head too fast.

After breakfast, I followed Meg to the workroom and asked her for the note she had mentioned. She handed it to me without a word—a small, square envelope with "Winter Palace Hotel" on the flap, and my name written in exquisite penmanship on the front. I had seen that writing before, in the letter from Amelia Devlin.

I thanked Meg and was almost out the door when I remembered something. "Say, Meg, have you seen my camera? It's a Brownie. I had it with me on the balloon, but it wasn't with the rest of my stuff when I was brought back here."

"Nope," said Meg, not looking up from the papers she was sorting. "Haven't seen it. Sorry."

"Darn! I thought someone might have brought it here. I guess I'll have to ask around."

The lovely envelope contained an invitation to lunch with Mrs. Devlin and her daughter Willamina at the Winter Palace Hotel in two days, at one p.m. As formal as anything from one society lady to another. After a moment's thought, I used the workroom phone to leave a message for Mrs. Devlin at the hotel, to the effect that I would be pleased to attend. I felt Meg listening intently while I relayed this information.

The missing camera bothered me increasingly as the morning wore on. I doubted I would ever have the chance to go up in a hot air balloon again, and to tell the truth, I wasn't sure I wanted to. The photos would have been a souvenir of the experience, and I hated to lose them. And had I actually managed to get a photo of the strange red glow I'd seen?

Checking a piece of stone for man-made marks, I frowned. I could ask Hank, but somehow I didn't want to. I still wasn't sure why he'd bowed out of the balloon ascent, and he'd been avoiding me since. That left Dr. Stanton. I made a face and tossed the rock into the basket for unmodified stones.

At lunch, Adele announced that she and Meg were going to Cairo on the overnight train and would be away for three days. Those of us to whom this was a surprise perked up for more details, but none were forthcoming. Dr. Stanton and Hank exchanged a quick glance.

Adele pulled me aside as I was leaving the dining hall. "Please sort the mail for the next few days, while Meg and I are away."

"Sure, but what about typing and filing?"

"Oh, don't bother with that. It can wait."

"Even if Dr. Stanton needs something typed?" From my previous experience filling in for Meg, I knew he had a habit of coming up with sudden urgent typing jobs.

Adele frowned. "Well, I suppose, but it's unlikely."

"You think? There might be something to do with his… other project. Like the balloon business."

"Oh, I've already figured out the 'balloon business.' And don't worry about the 'other project.' Forget about it. Just concentrate on your job for the rest of the season, okay? See you in a few days." She flashed a smile and hurried away.

It seemed things had changed. The balloon's hard landing must have done more damage than giving me a bump on the head. I wasn't sure where I stood with Adele any more.

I wondered if this trip to Cairo would include a meeting with the man from the Antiquities Department I saw at Met House—Mr. Purple and Gold Necktie. Maybe Adele had an extracurricular project of her own. I wondered if Meg knew anything about it.

But Meg was in one of her silent moods at supper. Despite my best efforts to charm her into conversation, she said nothing more than, "Please pass the salt," and "Thanks."

Soon after the meal, Adele, Meg, and Roger Dunn—who was on his way back to England and could act as chaperone for the ladies—piled their luggage and themselves into the dig's Mercedes. Hank drove them to the station, and the rest of us carried on as usual.

Without Adele around, the mood of the dig relaxed. Work went on, but at a leisurely pace. The excavation workers took more smoke breaks, laughing and joking with Hank and among themselves.

By now, I knew the names of the three men, and their personal styles—noisy Mustafa, nervous Youssef, and quiet Omar. Delivering the baskets of stone fragments for sorting, they paused to say a few words, crack a joke or two, or ask me how I liked the cooler weather. The slower pace made me more diligent. Feeling less hurried, I took more time to scrutinize the rocks.

About mid-morning, I picked up a chunk of stone and gave it the once-over. It bore hieroglyphs—basket, three vertical lines, and scarab beetle. Looking more closely, I saw a shape like the bottom part of a cartouche—a horizontal line beneath an upward curve. That would indicate a royal name, which meant the fragment should be set aside for special attention by Adele, or, in her absence, Dr. Stanton.

The next fragment I picked up had the curved upper half of a cartouche, as well as the feather hieroglyph and the one I privately called "bed of nails." I tried to fit the two pieces together, but their edges didn't match, even though they seemed to be of the same kind of stone. Either there was a piece missing from in between, or they weren't parts of a single name after all. I filled out the provenance forms and set everything aside for scrutiny by Dr. Stanton.

That afternoon, with field work done for the day, I took my forms and chunks of stone and went looking for Dr. Stanton. He wasn't in the workroom, so I went upstairs to the office he shared with Adele. If he wasn't there either, I'd put the items on his desk and leave, my duty done.

The door of the office stood open and Dr. Stanton was bent over his desk. I hadn't realized how thin the hair was on top of his head. Its waviness hid the bald spot when viewed face to face. At least he didn't resort to the ugly device of the comb-over.

He glanced up. "Miss Leighton, what a pleasant surprise. Come in." A smile spread over his face as he took off his glasses and stood. "You've recovered, I'm glad to see."

"I have, mostly," I said. "A bit dizzy at times, that's all." I held out the two chunks of rock and their accompanying forms. "I found a couple of cartouche fragments today. They almost look like they belong together."

"Really? Let's see." He put his glasses back on. "Sit down and make yourself at home."

I perched on the edge of the visitors' chair while Dr. Stanton peered at the inscriptions. Something on a shelf behind his desk caught my eye—my Brownie camera, or one just like it.

"Well, the stone is similar, but these are parts of two different names. Both refer to Tutankhamen, though. You probably know him as 'King Tut.' One is his birth name and the other his throne name. Come over here and I'll show you."

I dragged my chair to his side of the desk, keeping it a discreet distance from his. But I had to lean over to see what he was pointing at.

"The scarab beetle signifies the 'khpr' sound, and here's the determinative indicating 'many,' but the sun disk 're' is missing, so..."

He droned on, and I half-listened, nodding every now and then, but I was thinking if he'd had my camera all this time, why hadn't he given it back? And why did he have to wear that awful cologne?

I thought I'd better show interest in what he was saying. "So even though they're two different names, and incomplete, they're still important?"

Dr. Stanton looked up. "Oh yes, certainly. Any royal name is notable, especially one that may have been deliberately removed. That would be highly significant."

"Deliberately removed? Vandalism, you mean?"

He smiled. "Vandalism of a sort. You see, to the ancient Egyptians, a person's name was an integral part of them, a vital component of their being. If a name was forgotten, if it vanished from view and speech, its owner would become deader than dead. When a pharaoh fell out of favour, his—or her—name would be effaced from monuments. That was done to Hatshepsut's name by Thutmose III, and to Akhenaten's by Horemheb."

"Okay." I pointed at the stones. "But surely these might have been broken some other way, by accident? I mean, a lot can happen in three thousand years."

Dr. Stanton laughed. "Well, that's what archaeology is all about, figuring out things like that. Given that the name is 'Tutankhamen' rather than 'Tutankh*aten*,' you may be right, but I wanted to explain the thought process one must follow when examining artifacts."

He was giving me a mini-lesson in archaeology, this man who was respected as an expert in the field. For a moment, I felt a bit guilty for my negative attitude toward him. He wasn't a monster, surely, just an old professor. I remembered how scared he'd been when the balloon started to go down.

"Dr. Stanton," I said, "that camera over there, I think it's mine. I lost it when the balloon crashed."

"Camera?" He looked behind him to where I was pointing. "Oh yes, Dr. Dykstra picked it up when we were sorting ourselves out, after Captain Hawes and one of his fellows took you to the hospital. You must have dropped it when we hit the ground."

"I'm so glad it's turned up," I said. "I thought it was gone for good, along with all the pictures I took. They're the only ones I'll ever have of Luxor from a balloon." *Just give me the camera, why don't you?*

Dr. Stanton sat there, smiling in a way I didn't like. "Yes, I suppose those photos mean a lot to you, don't they, Miss Leighton? So, what would you be willing to give me in exchange for the Brownie up there?"

"Give you in exchange? I don't understand." Actually, I was beginning to suspect. I scrambled to my feet, ready to run for the door.

Dr. Stanton stood and put a hand on my shoulder, moving it slowly to rest on the back of my neck. "It's quite simple, France. May I call you that? Such an unusual name. A kiss, pretty girl, that's all I ask."

"You want me to kiss you?" *Do I really need the camera that badly?*

"I want us to share a kiss, that's all. When we've done that, I'll gladly give back your little Brownie, with all its memories of Luxor. Come." He opened his arms.

"All right. One kiss." I took a breath, leaned in, and placed a kiss on his cheek. When I tried to pull back, his arms clamped around me and pulled me close to him.

"No, no, that won't do, my dear. That was barely an appetizer." He pressed his lips to mine and his body to the rest of me and swayed from side to side as though we were close-dancing. "Mmm, mmm, mmm," he murmured, clamping his mouth over mine like a leech.

If he sticks his tongue in my mouth, I'll puke! But I need that film! Endure, endure, endure.

After an eternity of slimy lips and prickly stubble and old-cigars-English-Leather-and-sweat, Dr. Stanton detached from me. "So sweet," he muttered.

"May I have my camera now, please?"

"Of course. *Quid pro quo.* Here it is." He took it off the shelf and held it out, but as I reached for it, he raised his hand and grinned. "One more, my dear, if you don't mind." His left arm sneaked around and pulled me toward him, while his right held the camera over our heads like a prize.

I reached up and grabbed the camera with my left hand, shoving him away with my right. Despite a blur of dizziness, I was out the door before he could say, "Little bitch." He did say it; I heard him as I ran down the stairs.

I almost kept running—outside, down the alley between the dig house and the temple precinct wall, to the streets of Luxor, the corniche—and then where? I stopped in front of the outside door, another dizzy spell spinning the world around me. I headed for the refuge of the kitchen courtyard instead. The cook and her daughters were chopping vegetables and soup was simmering on the stove.

"Hello, Miss France," the cook said, smiling. "You must be very hungry today."

"Oh, I just couldn't stay away. That soup smells wonderful. I'll sit here for a bit, if you don't mind." I made myself stop babbling and smiled at everyone as I headed for my usual spot under the acacia tree.

Come on, France, I said to myself. Don't be such a baby. You knew Dr. Stanton's a creep. All he did was kiss you. *Ugh, that kiss!* You've had fellows on dates come on to you harder than that. At least he wasn't drunk.

Yes, but—but I let him do it. I stood there and let him glue his disgusting mouth to mine and squeeze himself up against me. Now he'll think I'm easy. And maybe I am.

No. Think again. You got your camera, didn't you? That was why you let him kiss you. *Quid pro quo,* like he said. And you didn't let him do it a second time. Focus on that. "Focus"— get it?

Ha, ha, ha, ha, ha! I had to clamp a hand to my mouth to muffle a hysterical laugh. Next thing I knew, I felt like crying. I hid that too.

But I couldn't hide in the courtyard all afternoon. I stopped by the Girls' Dorm to put away the camera and went back to the workroom. It was occupied by the usual bodies, writing up notes or using the reference books, so I felt relatively safe. I deposited mail in the usual pigeonholes and killed the remaining time until supper with minor tidying and a bit of reading. Not that I thought the ancient Egyptian concept of the soul was madly fascinating, but I wanted to avoid the dorm, which would be empty except for me, and whose door had no proper lock, just a flimsy hook and eye arrangement.

Supper was over too soon, with only the prospect of the empty dorm and long night ahead. I didn't think I would ever miss Meg, but her solid presence would have been reassuring. Well after lights out, I was reading in the workroom when Hank came in. The look on my face must have registered.

"You look a bit down in the mouth, France," he said. "Missing Meg and Adele? Too much of the coarse male element oppressing your sensibilities?"

He was uncomfortably close to the truth, but I didn't want to talk about Dr. Stanton. I just wanted to avoid any further encounters with him.

"Care to join me in the smoking room?" asked Hank.

"I didn't know there was one."

"Follow me."

The "smoking room" proved to be a tin-roofed porch around the corner from the kitchen courtyard, on the other side of the courtyard wall. A collection of scuffed and shaky chairs included a pair of Adirondacks that looked homesick and out of place. An equally worn table held a couple of sand-filled tin cans obviously intended as ashtrays.

"That's the best chair," said Hank, indicating one of the Adirondacks, "but it's the best of a bad lot, so be careful." He lowered himself into the other one and proceeded to roll a cigarette, taking tobacco from a pouch and mixing in a brown, crumbly substance from a tin.

"A twenty per cent solution," he said, "since tomorrow's going to be a busy, busy day." He held up the finished cigarette for me to admire, struck a match and lit up. Naïve and innocent though I was, I recognized the pungent smell of hashish mingling with the harsh Turkish tobacco.

"Want to try?" Hank held out the cigarette. "It's training-wheel strength. You'll barely feel it."

Why the heck not? My life's pretty much a mess already. "Okay, but I'm not a smoker. I'll cough and splutter for sure."

"You'll get over it."

I did.

I wasn't sure how much time passed and didn't care. My perspective on things shifted considerably as Hank and I passed the cigarette back and forth. My troubles retreated and a lovely, floating feeling enveloped me. A soft darkness embraced our little corner of the world, dulling harsh edges and turning Hank into a shapeless blur on the other side of the table.

"What're you and Dr. Stanton looking for, exactly? Another tomb, really?" My words drifted slowly between us on a raft of smoke.

"The Unbroken Tomb." Hank exhaled and stretched out his legs.

"'The'? Sounds like an actual, known tomb."

"Oh, it is. To those who believe in it. Capital T, capital U, capital T. Ha, ha!"

He finally stopped laughing and took another puff. "Bill thinks there's a tomb in the heart of el-Qurn—which looks sort of like a pyramid, in case you haven't noticed. It's never been found, either by tomb-robbers or archaeologists. Possibly because it doesn't exist."

"Whose tomb is it supposed to be?"

He buried the cigarette stub in one of the ashtray cans. "Well, there are different notions about that. Some say Akhenaten and/or Nefertiti, which is wildly unlikely. Others say Hatshepsut—a magnificent tomb to go with her magnificent temple at the foot of 'the Horn.' That's unlikely too. Indications are Howard Carter found her mummy in the Valley of the Kings in 1903. Without conclusive evidence, there's room for wild theories, like the one about Nephren-Ka, the Black Pharaoh, who's supposed to be imprisoned in his tomb for all time." Hank snorted and began to roll another cigarette.

"Nephren-Ka? Was he a real pharaoh?"

"Are you kidding? He's right out of the pulp mags."

"Where do you fit into this picture, Hank? Do you believe in this Unbroken Tomb?"

"I think most of it's a bunch of wishful-thinking crap. Not Bill, though. I've been helping him just to keep him out of trouble." He waved a hand toward what I assumed was the west side of the Nile. "There are folks over there ready to take advantage of Americans and other foreigners with money and silly ideas. They sell them fakes at a premium and take them on treasure hunts where anything might happen. I go along with Bill as a kind of buffer since I have a rapport with the locals. And on the other side, I can stop him from doing something to jeopardize the dig here, like piss off the authorities or attract bad publicity."

"But that's not part of your job, is it?"

He thought for a moment. "It's more than that. I belong here. Back home, I'm an oddball, but here I fit right into the cracks between the stones." He waved the cigarette. 'Stones'—ha, ha—get it?"

I didn't, then. "But what evidence is Dr. Stanton's idea based on, exactly?"

"Spoken like a budding archaeologist." Hank struck a match and lit the new cigarette. "Bill has a collection of writings put together by one of those students of the occult—travelers' tales and conflations of mythology and magic. I was surprised he'd fall for stuff like that, but he claims it's backed up by references to texts drawn from secret caches of papyri. Sounds exciting, but when it comes to specifics, it's pretty vague."

"Okay, but what about your uncle? He's all about scientific evidence, surely?" I clasped my goose-pimpled arms together. The evening was growing chilly.

"Oh yes, totally." Hank snorted a laugh. "Bill hasn't told Jim everything—keeping it close to his chest, of course—but I gave him the basic facts. The whole point of the balloon cruise was to spot likely tomb locations in the wadis north and west of the Valley of the Kings. El-Qurn is made of exactly the right sort of limestone for cutting and tunnelling, but aside from a few tombs in the West Valley—Ay's and Amenhotep III's—nothing much has been found outside the main valley. The rationale, of course, is that the Unbroken Tomb is so well-hidden there would be no outwardly visible signs of its presence. Uncle Jim noted a few features in one of the wadis that looked promising, but..."

Hank shrugged and took a puff, blew out the smoke and stretched. "Moon's waning," he said, pointing at the lopsided sphere rising above the perimeter wall, the right side of its face veiled by night. "Khonsu's leaving us." He offered me the cigarette, but I waved it off.

"So that's all there is to it—some old writings and geological facts from your uncle?"

"Yep, that's about it. Well, there's that inscription, but I have serious doubts about its significance."

"Inscription?"

"A limestone fragment with some kind of sketch and a few scribbles. Okay, an ancient Egyptian tomb-worker might have drawn them, but it's just as likely a fake made in Qurna village to sell to credulous tourists. They're really good at that kind of thing. Anyway, this inscription has the hieroglyphs 'mr' and 'mn.' Bill interprets them as 'beloved and hidden.' He's spun himself a story that Hatshepsut's architect and lover, Senmut, created a secret tomb for her, so her nephew and enemy, Thutmose III, couldn't destroy her mummy and obliterate her name."

"Sounds romantic." *Oh yes, romantic Dr. Stanton.* I shivered and pulled my arms tighter.

189

"You're cold," said Hank. "Time to call it a night." He started to get up.

"No, wait—what's your idea about that inscription?"

"Well, if it isn't a fake, I think it might be a tomb-worker's prayer to the cobra goddess, Meretseger. She was the patroness of the workers' village at Deir el-Medina. Tons of limestone fragments have been found there, with all sorts of inscriptions. Some of them are just rough sketches, or even graffiti. I don't think it has any special significance, one way or another. But for Bill, it's like a talisman. Okay, kid, smoking room's closing for the night." He stood and held out a hand to help me up.

At the door of the Girls' Dorm, I remembered something. "Say, Hank, I took some pictures from the balloon. Do you know where I can get the film developed?"

"Oh, I... I can do it for you... someday. We have a darkroom, you know, and I'm pretty good at processing."

"Would you? That'd be great. Well, see you tomorrow, Hank. And thanks."

"For initiating you into the Company of Hashish Smokers? You're welcome." He gave me a quick, one-armed hug. Hank smelled of smoke and dust and tobacco and hashish. Like Luxor itself. "No longer a hash virgin, France," he muttered into my ear. "Good night."

The dig's casual atmosphere in Adele's absence made it easy for me to take an early and extended lunch break. What to wear to luncheon in a grand hotel, in response to a formal invitation? My usual blouse and skirt combination wouldn't do, but fortunately I had brought a dress with fitted bodice and flared skirt, in a blue and white floral print. I even had white shoes to go with it, despite all the dithering I had done before putting them in my luggage back in Providence. Finally, the emerald ring that had brought me luck twice already.

Before leaving, I decided to give my film to Hank so he could develop it whenever he had time. I opened the camera. It was empty. No film.

"That bastard!" I slammed the blameless Brownie onto my bed hard enough that it bounced onto the floor, but fortunately didn't break. Not that it mattered. The film was the important thing, and Dr. Stanton had kept it, no doubt intending to demand more favours in exchange for it.

Not a chance! I'd get it back myself.

I arrived at the Winter Palace a little late, still fuming about the film, but I was impressed by the hotel's grand entrance with its double flights of steps and the magnificent lobby. A uniformed doorman directed me to a restaurant with high, arched windows and chandeliers.

Amelia Devlin was clearly an eccentric, with greying red hair piled high and two or three necklaces slung around her neck, along with a set of half-glasses on a chain. She wore a purple dress, decades out of style, and greeted me with a Midwestern accent that fell on my ears like rubble dumped out of a wheelbarrow.

"France Leighton, here you are at last!" She held out both hands, which confused me. I stuck out my left, although I usually shake with my right, like you're supposed to. Her eyes, amber-coloured and piercing, peered into mine.

"You're left-handed, just like Francis." Beaming, Mrs. Devlin turned to the other person at the table, presumably her daughter. What a contrast—tall, athletic-looking, with dark hair in a jaw-length bob and bangs cut straight across her forehead. Willa Devlin wore a grey linen sheath dress and a single strand of amber and silver beads. Her handshake was brief and firm.

"I would have recognized you anywhere, France," said Mrs. Devlin as we sat down. "Excuse my taking the liberty of calling you by your first name. I feel I know you already. You're the very image of your grandfather, or as close as possible for a young woman."

"Did you know him well, Mrs. Devlin?"

"Not as well as I would have liked. 'France'—what a pretty name. Were you named after Francis?"

"I don't think so. My mother picked out the name 'Francesca' from a novel. I didn't like it that much, so I changed it."

Mrs. Devlin shook a finger. "I can't believe it was only by chance you bear that name. Invisible forces influence our lives, whether we know it or not."

I wasn't sure how to respond to this, but I didn't have to. "The last time I saw Francis was at a party in Provincetown on Cape Cod, in 1939." An expression of pain creased her face. "Only a day or two before his death. I warned him, but he didn't listen." She gazed into my eyes. "All my encounters with him were fated, as is this one, today, with you."

Her intensity demanded a response. "He made quite an impression on you, didn't he?"

"Inevitably," said Mrs. Devlin. "He was no ordinary man. He was known in the World Beyond, even in life. The immortal element within him bonded to mine. From the first moment I met him, we were connected."

The woman is obviously a nut. Just what I need right now.

Aloud, I said, "Francis Dexter died two years before I was born, so I have no personal experience of him."

"No, but you carry his legacy within yourself. You must strive to cultivate an awareness of it."

Our lunches arrived then, saving me from having to respond, and diverting Mrs. Devlin from further uncomfortable questions.

"Are you enjoying your tour of Egypt?" I asked, hoping to steer the conversation into conventional territory for the rest of the meal.

"We are, very much," said Willa, speaking to me for the first time since we were introduced. "Seeing Egypt was my main reason for joining Mother on her travels."

"Have you visited the pyramids? I didn't have a chance to."

"I took a tour while Mother was meeting with... some people in Cairo."

"Camel ride and everything?"

"Oh yes. The complete package." She smiled. "I understand you're an archaeologist?"

"No, just a dig assistant. It's been a real education, though." I reached for the salt.

"Oh! That's the ring!" Mrs. Devlin looked like she had to restrain herself from grabbing my hand. "The very one Francis was wearing the last time I saw him. Did he leave it to you?"

Does she think I stole it? "My Uncle Charles gave it to me, shortly before his death. He told me Francis Dexter would have wanted me to have it, but he didn't explain why."

"Uncle Charles?"

"Charles Milburn, my grandmother's husband."

"Oh yes, Francis mentioned him. A good friend of his, I believe. But that ring… It's very old and has quite a history. Are you aware of its power?"

"Power? Uh, no, I'm not aware of anything like that."

"You probably are, subconsciously. The longer you wear it, the greater its potential."

"Well, if you say so, but I really don't—"

"You're young," Mrs. Devlin said, smiling and patting my hand. "The young have much to learn."

Glancing at Willa, I was sure I caught a brief roll of the eyes, which made me smile. Dessert arrived, just in time. My favourite course, and it meant this lunch would soon be over.

The rest of the meal passed with ordinary talk about the sights of Luxor. I dutifully offered to show them around the Karnak temples.

"No, thank you, France," said Mrs. Devlin, to my relief. "Willa can tell you how much time I need to appreciate a sacred site and absorb its influences."

Willa nodded. "Time and patience, Mother dear."

"Tomorrow we will visit the Theban Necropolis on the west bank," Mrs. Devlin continued. "I've engaged a guide to give us a tour, a man from Qurna village who was recommended by the hotel. He and his family operate a guest house near the Tombs of the Nobles."

Just before we rose from the table, Mrs. Devlin looked at me hard. "I sense that all may not be well with you, France. If you need help or refuge, come to us. We'll be in Luxor for the next week and can extend our stay if necessary."

"Thank you for the thought, but I'm fine, really." *I'd have to be pretty desperate to take up that offer.*

Mrs. Devlin and her daughter headed for the elevators, and I made for the doors on the other side of the lobby. I had nearly reached them when I heard footsteps close behind me and turned to see Willa Devlin.

"Excuse me, Miss Leighton." I stopped and waited. She and I were the same height. The amber beads of her necklace matched her eyes.

"I just wanted to say... don't mind Mother. She can't help getting all metaphysical. It's an occupational hazard. She's a medium, you see."

"A kind of fortune-teller?"

Willa frowned. "Well, a bit more than that, actually. She's psychic, can foretell the future, sort of. It's just that sometimes she gets carried away with the... persona. She's quite sensible and very kind-hearted. I hope you didn't get the wrong impression."

A pair of doormen stood nearby, watching us. Their uniforms were dark blue, not the dark red worn by the fellow I'd asked for directions before. Maybe the Winter Palace colour-coded their staff members?

"Well, I guess I did, but thanks for the explanation, Miss—"

"Willa."

"Thanks, Willa. And please call me France."

A smile. "You're welcome, France."

We shook hands again, and I headed back to the dig house, thinking about how to get my film out of Dr. Stanton's clutches without ending up in them myself.

My chance came the following afternoon. Delivering the Stantons' mail was a perfect excuse to visit their office. If Dr.

Stanton was there, I would simply deposit the letters on their respective desks and leave. If he touched me, I had a scream primed and ready. But if the office was empty, I would seize the opportunity to search it.

I knocked on the door. No answer. I tapped again to make sure. Silence. I opened the door and peered in. The place was dark and deserted. Well, dim and deserted. I placed Adele's mail on her desk and went over to Dr. Stanton's, standing on the very spot where he'd glommed onto me, with no intention of living up to his part of the bargain. *Bastard!*

I dropped his mail on the desk and scanned its surface. My film wasn't there. It wasn't on the shelves behind the desk either. Too obvious. It had to be in one of the desk drawers. Unless he was carrying it around with him, in which case I was out of luck.

I began with the middle drawer. It was locked. Of course. Except—what about that fake Pueblo-style ceramic pot on the desk? I yanked out a handful of pens and pencils. Bingo! One little brass key in the very bottom.

Figured it out, Dr. Stanton. Too bad for you. I unlocked the middle drawer and opened it, revealing the usual jumble of stuff for which middle drawers were created—broken pencils, three fountain pen cartridges, a worn and blackened eraser, paper clips, a ruler, a pencil sharpener, business cards. But no roll of film.

I closed the drawer and turned to the others, three on each side. Okay, left side, drawer number one. Blank note pads and a bottle of ink. No film. Drawer number two. Three rubber bands, a stapler, and an ink stain. No film. Drawer number three. Empty. Right side, drawer number one. Chunks of stone like the ones I handled every day, except all of these had inscriptions. I thought I recognized the two I had found yesterday. No film. Drawer number two. A sheaf of paper with typewritten text. "Inscriptions relating to the priestess Meresamun." No film. Drawer number three was locked.

Shit! How long have I been here, anyway? I had no idea, and Dr. Stanton might turn up any minute.

Well, what about that key? Versatile little thing, it fitted this lock too. I unlocked the drawer and opened it, revealing something wrapped in a handkerchief. Dr. Stanton's handkerchief. Ugh. But it had to be my film.

I picked the thing up. It was flat and heavy, not film. A piece of white stone, probably limestone, with scribbles in black ink. Scribbles, not hieroglyphs, probably cursive or hieratic; I couldn't tell the difference, never mind what they said. But there was a sketch in black and red, faint and faded. Part of a face, hands, vertical lines. Someone playing a harp?

I'll bet this is what Hank told me about, that Dr. Stanton thinks is evidence for his Unbroken Tomb. How about if I take it with me, and when Dr. Stanton notices it's gone, we can do a deal—his hunk of rock for my film.

I set the stone on the desk and took a final look in the drawer. Several sheets of thick paper held together with a paperclip. A note fastened to them said, "Hi Bill, Photos of the Turin Erotic Papyrus. Enjoy 'em!" Fuzzy black and white images of human figures in ancient Egyptian style, except these were engaged in sexual acts. Explicit and adventurous acts involving rather grotesque men and slender, lithe women with Cleopatra hairstyles. My cheeks warmed as I gazed, fascinated and repelled at the same time.

"What the *hell* are you doing here?"

I straightened up with a jerk and almost dropped the pages. Adele stood in the doorway, glaring at me.

"Adele, it's not what you think. Dr. Stanton took a roll of film from my camera—I lost it after the balloon crash, and Dr. Dykstra found it and gave it to him, but he took out the film, and I just thought I'd have a look for it—"

"You're fired. I don't want you here. You've been nothing but trouble since you arrived. Even before you arrived. And now I catch you stealing artifacts. Pack your things and leave immediately."

"I'm not stealing anything! That's not fair! Just listen to me first. Your husband—"

She raised a hand. "I'm not interested in your explanations. You've been playing little games, getting in the way, causing trouble, and I've had it. Snooping into private property in a private office—that's enough. I have too much to deal with right now. You've got until noon tomorrow to leave the premises. I'll get your final paycheque ready by then. This discussion is over."

I decided not to point out that we hadn't really had a discussion. "You might find these interesting." I handed her the photostats and left the room on rubbery legs.

Back in the Girls' Dorm, I flopped onto my bed and stared at the ceiling. My eyes focussed on familiar cracks and stains while my thoughts raced like a machine out of control.

Fired. I'm fired. No discussion. She wants me gone by tomorrow noon. Okay, I'll go back to Providence. Train to Cairo, then what? I'd be going back in four months anyway. Can I use my return ticket on the boat this early? Alma won't mind me coming back. Or I could go to my mother. No! My father? No! He hasn't even bothered to answer the letter I wrote him. I've been fired. Kicked out. That's wrong and bad and unfair. Dr. Stanton stole my film. I was just trying to get it back! I'll tell her about that awful kiss. No, maybe I won't. I agreed to it, didn't I? Oh shit, shit, *shit*!

Eudora! I needed to feel her and hear her voice, needed the calm she brought me. With her help, I could figure out what to do. I hauled the cello case from under my bed (mine for only one more night) and lifted Eudora from hers. I laid her across my knees and stroked her strings.

"What should I do now? Stay and fight? Or go back to Providence? Or to England? I just don't know."

Faint thrums and throbs, weak and half-hearted.

France, you have to get yourself together. Your self— understand? You have resources. Use your weapons—your mind, your heart, your inheritance.

"Inheritance? What inheritance?"

What you've been given by everyone who ever knew or loved you—Alma, Charles, your teachers, your mother. And Francis Dexter. You didn't know him, nor he you, but you carry something of him within you. Forgive me, I'm not what I once was...

Eudora's voice faded to a dim buzz. I found her endpin, screwed it in and set her up. I picked up my bow and played the opening phrases of Bach's first suite—familiar, beautiful, comforting. But Eudora's tone was strange, with a low, buzzing overtone. No comfort there.

I stopped playing, set down the bow and examined my instrument. There was a small crack in the wood below the f-hole on the treble side. Only a small crack, but it looked like it had plans to grow. The dry climate of Luxor had taken its toll.

Eudora was dying.

10
The Chapter of Making a Crossing to the West

I closed the second suitcase and snapped down the latches. Everything else would have to fit into my overnight bag. Good thing I hadn't acquired much extra baggage in my month with the Stanton Project.

The Brownie camera sat on my bedside table. I was leaving it behind. Irrational, I knew, but the camera had acquired a slimy patina in my mind. I didn't want it anymore, but it might be of use to someone.

A cough made me turn around. Meg stood there, hands clasped together.

"I heard you're leaving," she said. "Adele told me. I'm sorry."

I shrugged. "What for? It wasn't your idea." I didn't know if Adele had told her she'd fired me, or why, and I didn't want to get into a discussion about it. "Just think, you'll have the whole dorm to yourself. Spacious quarters."

"Sure, but things will be dull without you," said Meg. "Say, you haven't had breakfast, have you?"

I hadn't wanted to show my face in the dining room. "No, I haven't."

"That means you don't know..." She interrupted herself. "Where are you going to go, anyway? Back to the States?"

"Not right away. I want to see the west bank. After reading the *Book of the Dead*, I figure I have to experience the Theban Necropolis."

"It can be pretty tough travelling around by yourself. Some of the people in the villages over there are friendly to tourists, but you have to be careful. And are you planning to lug all that stuff everywhere you go?" She nodded at my suitcases, boxy overnight bag, and Eudora in her case.

"Well, I don't know. It'll be kind of awkward, I suppose."

"'Awkward'? Try 'impossible.' Wait a minute." She went to the closet and rummaged, throwing out shoes and shoving cardboard boxes aside. "I've got just the thing," she said, her voice muffled. "Here." She emerged, holding a conglomeration of canvas, leather straps and buckles. "I haven't needed it so far, but it should work for you."

"What is it?"

"A rucksack. Perfect for travelling off the beaten path. You wear it on your back, like this." She demonstrated, sticking her arms through the straps with a jangle of buckles. "Pick out the stuff you really need to take—just the basics—and I'll help you pack it. You can leave everything else here until you're ready to go home. Adele won't know."

I stared at her. "Why? Why would you help me out like that?"

"Because I have a feeling you've been treated badly." She raised a hand before I could respond. "Not now. Let's get you packed up, and then we'll go to the Bennu Bird for breakfast— well, breakfast for you. My treat."

She ignored my protests and bewildered questions and opened one of my suitcases. "Need this?" she asked, holding up a blouse.

"Yes," I said, followed by "No" to the little black dress and the blue and white one, and yes to three more blouses and two skirts. Definitely yes to Bermuda shorts.

Less than half an hour later, the relatively small pile of basic, practical garments (including the *galabeya* and turban) was tightly packed into Meg's rucksack. The smaller suitcase and overnight bag were stowed in the closet and the big suitcase was shoved under the bed that used to be mine.

"Shouldn't you be at work?" I asked. "It's after eight." Even by the fall and winter schedule, she was late.

Meg shook her head. "Things are different today. I'll tell you all about it at the Bird. Let's go."

I swung the rucksack onto my back and Meg adjusted the straps. It wasn't too heavy, but I was sure it made me look like Quasimodo. I picked up my beach bag (full of miscellaneous necessities) with one hand and Eudora with the other. "Okay, I'm ready."

"You're not taking the cello, are you?" Meg asked, unknowingly echoing Alma at my departure from Providence.

"Damn right, I'm taking her. There's no way I'm leaving Eudora behind."

"'Her'? 'Eudora'? Okay, I get the picture. Well, at least let me carry that beach bag."

Goodbye, Girls' Dorm. Goodbye, Stanton Project. Goodbye and good riddance, Dr. Creepy Stanton. The main door banged shut behind us, the rusty old gate gave a final screech, and I was headed down the road.

Soon we were settled at a corner table in the Bennu Bird. I relished a plate of eggs, tomatoes, fried eggplant, and freshly baked flatbread. Cups of coffee wafted delightful aromas.

"Okay, Meg, tell me—what's going on at the dig? Why no work today?"

"Well, it looks like Dr. Stanton's taken off with at least half of the Project's remaining funds. That's why Adele and I came back early. When she went to the bank in Cairo and saw the balance in the account, she tried to phone Dr. Stanton. He wasn't here, and Hank's gone too. I guess he was in on whatever Dr. Stanton was up to, wasn't he?"

"I don't know." I took another bite and thought while I chewed and swallowed. "He told me he went along to keep Dr. Stanton out of trouble."

"Well, he didn't do such a great job of it, did he? Adele's fit to be tied. She assumed you were in on it too, after she found you in their office yesterday. And she still resents you because of that balloon escapade."

I made myself ignore her last sentence. "She didn't give me a chance to explain, though, just fired me."

"She was upset, not thinking rationally. They've been going through a bad patch."

"Dr. Stanton *is* a bad patch, Meg. You wouldn't believe what he tried with me." I told her about the missing camera, and what I'd done to get it back.

Meg listened, folding and refolding her napkin, sipping coffee and nodding occasionally. "I'm not surprised," she said when I finished. "That's why I decided to help you out. You may be kind of a princess, but you don't deserve to be treated unjustly."

"Well, lucky me." I started to get up, but Meg put out a hand to stop me.

"No, wait. I'm sorry, I shouldn't have said that. It's a problem I have, talking before I think."

"Okay, but you did think that, didn't you? That I'm a princess—spoiled rotten, I suppose you mean." I sat down again, curious despite my annoyance.

"Well, yes. There I was—working hard, doing real archaeology, trying to build a career as an academic, and then you show up, looking for *fun*. You didn't know hieroglyphics or much about archaeology, and you didn't speak Arabic. Hank's a good time Charlie, but at least he can supervise the local workers. You didn't have anything to offer, so I resented you."

My tongue was getting sore from being bitten. "And now? I can't have changed that much in two months."

"I don't know. Have you? What are you looking for here?"

I wiped my lips. "Maybe you're right. I was hoping for a fun adventure, thinking archaeology was glamorous. Well, now I know better, so I'll play tourist for a while and go home." A thought came to me. "Say, Meg—since you know so much more than I ever will—have you ever heard about a legendary tomb that no one's ever found, in the heart of el-Qurn?"

Meg laughed. "Oh, that! Every archaeologist's dream, and every treasure hunter's too, of course. Yeah, I've heard rumours. 'Legendary' is right, but I guess Dr. Stanton's in the final stages of Tomb Fever. Too bad he went and stole our funds, though."

"So you don't think there's any such tomb?"

"Why? Are you planning to go look for it? Okay, I'm sure there are all kinds of undiscovered tombs over there. Undiscovered by archaeologists, anyway. Those villages—Sheikh Abd el-Qurna and a couple of others—they're built right on top of the Theban Necropolis, which is a huge cemetery. The people who live there are always finding tombs. They've been mining them for centuries. But one special, undiscovered tomb—well that does sound like a legend. Look, France, I'd better get back and see how Adele's doing."

She stood and pulled a couple of envelopes from her purse. "I almost forgot—here's your final paycheque and a letter that came yesterday. Don't try to cash the cheque for at least a week, and don't be surprised if it bounces. The Stanton ship is on the rocks."

"I get the picture," I said, taking the envelopes. The letter was from Alma. Still no reply from my father. "But what about you? Have you thought about leaving the sinking ship?"

"Like a rat?" She sat down again and leaned toward me. "It's like this—in academia, once you're hitched to someone, you stick with them, unless they're going to jail. If you skip out, even for reasons that look good to you, you get a reputation for unreliability. I'm going to make my career in archaeology, even if I have to slog through some… mud on the way. Dr. Stanton's almost a has-been, but Adele—well, you've seen her in action. She's going to make it, and I'll be right there on her coattails."

"Well, good luck, Meg."

I got my stuff together—Meg's rucksack on my back, Eudora in my left hand, beach bag in my right. A final thanks and goodbye, and Meg set off for the dig house, and I to the Theban Necropolis.

I was in no rush, wanting to let my new situation soak in before doing anything irrevocable. In full daylight, with tourists on the streets, there was no danger of being accosted by anyone worse than an insistent tour guide. I strolled down to the corniche and attached myself to a group of Americans waiting for the next available ferry to the west bank. A pair of Egyptian men in dark blue uniforms joined us. Policemen, maybe?

The first boat to arrive was one of the new motorized vessels. By now I knew they charged a premium for speed. Considering what Meg had told me about the dig's finances and my possibly rubber paycheque, I thought I'd better save my pennies. I would wait for the workers' ferry, which was considerably cheaper. I hung back and let the crowd surge ahead of me. As the boat pulled away, the two policemen — or whatever they were — looked back at me as though concerned that I hadn't managed to board. I waved at them to show I wasn't upset.

Settling on a bench to wait, I looked across the Nile at the green cultivated lands punctuated by groups of palms, and beyond them the pyramidal bulk of el-Qurn, shining in the sun of morning. Clusters of buildings were scattered on its lower slopes, like a child's blocks abandoned after a game. A few were brightly painted, their blues and yellows standing out from the earth colours of the rest.

Sitting there with my minimal possessions next to me, and a good breakfast digesting comfortably inside, in the not-yet-hot sun of Luxor, I felt surprisingly carefree, after the shock and anger of the previous day. I had been kicked out of the Stanton dig, but I was still in Egypt, and now I could do what I liked, until my cash ran out. I could explore the secrets of the Necropolis of Thebes, and I even knew someone who could be my guide.

The trouble was, I didn't know how to find him. He had told me to ask for him by an Arabic term I had completely forgotten. Would anyone in those mud-brick villages know him as "Adam Dexter?"

The old-fashioned felucca that served as the workers' ferry approached, and from behind me came a chorus of female voices. Turning, I saw a group of women wearing head to foot black, and younger ones in light colours with bright headscarves. Some of them carried baskets, others had cloth sacks lumpy with unseen contents. As the boat glided up to the corniche, the women quickened their pace and surrounded me, laughing and chattering.

Picking up my belongings, I followed the women on board. Once I had paid my fare and found a place to sit, I noticed one of them looking right at me. I thought I recognized her, and when she pointed at Eudora and mimed playing a cello, I remembered. She had been on the ferry the day Alain and I went to Met House for our final rehearsal.

"You play music?" the woman asked.

I nodded. "Yes, sometimes."

She smiled. "I am Yasmin."

"I'm France."

"Oh, you come from France? *Bonjour.*"

"No, no. My name is France. I'm from the United States. America."

She laughed. "Oh, I see. Miss France from America. How do you do?"

I had to laugh too. "I'm happy to meet you, Yasmin."

"You are going again to Metropolitan House, to play music?"

"No, this time I'm just a visitor, a tourist. Do you live over there?" I waved my hand at the approaching shore.

"Yes. I live in village called Sheikh Abd el-Qurna. My home is there." She gestured at the other women. "These ladies live in other village. We are going home after work."

In the morning? Surely these women weren't "ladies of the night?" "Do you work in Luxor?" I asked cautiously.

"I work in hotel. Clean rooms, make beds, wash dishes. These other ladies, they selling fruit and vegetable in market."

"Oh. You must be tired." I felt a complicated mixture of embarrassment and relief.

Yasmin waved a hand. "I am used to work."

One of the other women said something in Arabic, and Yasmin replied. "She asks what is that." She pointed at my cello. "I tell her you are musician."

"Sometimes I am." Except that Eudora, my hollow wooden companion, my soundbox, was failing.

We were more than three quarters of the way across the Nile. Luxor was starting to look unreal with distance, and the west bank, which had always been "over there" was becoming "here."

Less than a quarter hour later, I disembarked, weighed down by Eudora, rucksack, and beach bag. The day had gone from warm to hot, and the odours of river and farmland mingled with the dry smell of dust. Dust from the Western Peak, the land of the dead.

Noticing the low building of the police station nearby, I remembered I had to register my presence. Only residents of the west bank were permitted to remain overnight. Everyone else had to leave by sunset. Two policemen, maybe the ones that boarded the ferry ahead of mine, stood near the station. The logical thing to do would be to go and introduce myself. But what about people who intended to stay overnight? Did that include me? A trickle of panic eroded my simple enjoyment of the day, and my head started to ache. A weary gloom descended on me. The glare of the dry hills hurt my eyes.

What was I doing here? I had no idea how to find Adam. I looked around for somewhere to sit while I figured out what to do next.

"Miss France!" Yasmin appeared at my side. "Please, you come to stay in our house. We have restaurant. We have rooms for guests. You come, please."

I turned my head. Yasmin's smiling face spun past me, came around again, spun away. *She revolves around me, like a planet 'round the sun. Oh boy...* I squeezed my eyes shut for a second, hoping to stop the dizziness.

"You come, please, Miss," Yasmin said again. "My mother will give you *shai*—tea."

Tea. Comfort. Shade. "Thank you, Yasmin. That would be lovely."

The other women were climbing into a donkey cart that must have arrived while I was having my moment of panic. Yasmin called out to the driver, a boy who looked about twelve, and linked her arm in mine, relieving me of the beach bag at the same time. "He says okay to go with him."

She helped me climb into the cart. I sat down on one of the plank seats, squeezed up against one of the other women. Yasmin handed Eudora up to me and scrambled up, carrying my rucksack. I thought the donkey looked too small and skinny to pull the fully-loaded cart, but the boy gave a command, and we lurched forward. The jolting made my headache worse, but it was better than walking. I put my arms around Eudora and closed my eyes.

Endure. Endure. Endure.

Some jiggling, aching, dust-breathing time later, the cart stopped. Most of the women climbed out, talking, laughing, handing baskets and sacks to one another. Yasmin smiled at me. "Just a little way longer." More dust and rattling; when we finally stopped again, I opened my eyes to a yard with mud-brick walls on two sides. Several children came running over, scattering a flock of chickens. Goats bleated somewhere nearby.

What am I doing here?

Yasmin took charge, ordering a couple of the children to carry my belongings. I clutched my beach bag but was too weak and disordered to protest when one of the kids hoisted Eudora's case and headed for the house. Another one carried the rucksack, figuring out in no time how to sling it onto his back. Yasmin conducted me into a long room furnished with boxy settees and small tables.

"Sit down here, please, Miss France." She smiled and disappeared through a doorway, shouting in Arabic. I leaned back and stared at the ceiling, a map of nonexistent places formed by cracks, peeling patches, and stains scattered among countless shades of pink, blue, buff, and yellow, applied over who knew how many years. The room was open to a paved terrace, where more settees and tables suggested congenial outdoor gatherings.

Yasmin returned, bearing a tray with glasses of tea, a bowl of sugar cubes, and a dish of mint leaves. An older woman followed her, with a plate of honey cakes.

"This is my mother, Layla Mohamed," said Yasmin. The lady smiled at me and said something I didn't understand. I smiled back and said, "*Assalam alaykum, Madaam,*" followed by "*Shukran jazillan,*" which pretty much used up three-quarters of my Arabic vocabulary.

The tea, strong, sweet and flavoured with mint, almost restored me. The cakes looked delicious, but I was afraid to do more than nibble politely. My dizziness linked head and stomach in a way that felt queasy-uneasy. I managed discreetly to take a couple of aspirins, hoping they would appease the head without upsetting the stomach.

Mrs. Mohamed left after a few minutes, but Yasmin kept me company, tucking into the cakes and asking me questions between bites. I told her I was from Providence, Rhode Island, that I was a university student, that I had worked at an archaeological dig in Luxor but was finished with it and touring around before going home.

"Many *archéologues* here," she said. "They like our house, our food. You will stay here tonight, yes?"

"Yes, but I forgot to register at the police station, so they don't know I'm here."

Yasmin waved a hand. "Does not matter. Police know we take care of our guests. You will tell stories about America at our supper."

She probably saw me as an attractive exotic, like a bird or butterfly, that she had brought home to entertain her family and any other guests, while contributing to the family's income, of course. She couldn't know how shaky I felt.

"Yasmin," I said, "I wonder if it's possible… You see, I'm not feeling well. I hit my head a few days ago—an accident— and it aches sometimes. I would like to lie down for a little while." I mimed sleeping, tilting my head sideways over my clasped hands.

"Oh, I am so sorry!" She jumped up, grabbed my bag, and helped me to my feet. "Come, I show you room for sleeping."

We passed a dining room painted bright blue, with two long tables and a multitude of chairs standing ready for diners. I followed Yasmin up a set of steps and through an archway into the open air. More steps continued up the side of the house. A sharp turn took us to an outside corridor, like a motel's. Yasmin opened an ornately made door and showed me into a room like a plaster box, with a bed on one side and a wide bench or shelf on the other. Eudora sat next to Meg's rucksack on the shelf. A jug of water and a bowl stood on a little table, with a folded linen towel. A small window looked over the Nile toward Luxor.

"Sleep here," Yasmin said, indicating the bed. "One hour. I will call you before luncheon time."

I was glad beyond words to be in an enclosed space, alone. The walls, in shades of cream and faded ochre, reflected the light from the window. I was safe here, wasn't I? Sighing, I slipped off my shoes, lay down, and let my dizzy head spin me into sleep.

Part of me must have been listening for Yasmin's knock, because I was wide awake when it came. My headache was gone and I felt better. I just hoped it would last.

On the minus side, to my refreshed senses, the room had lost much of its charm. The cracked and patched plaster, uneven floorboards and sparseness of furnishings spoke of poverty and making-do. Grit lay in the corners, probably blown in from the hillside. How many heads had lain on the flabby pillow? How many bodies had slept on the lumpy mattress? These thoughts raced through my mind, leaving distaste behind. And I had to pee.

"Oh, hello, Yasmin. Yes, I feel much better, but I wonder if you could tell me where the bathroom is."

She pointed to the jug and bowl. "You wash there."

Damn. "I mean the... toilet. Where is that?"

"Oh, I'm sorry. Come with me, please. I will show."

I followed her downstairs, to a rather minimal facility that made the bathroom at the Stantons' dig house luxurious by comparison. Hiding my distaste, I said,

"This is an interesting house. Is it very old?"

"Old, yes. My grandfather, and his grandfather, they lived here. I will give you tour, if you wish, after the luncheon."

What could I say, but, "That would be lovely. Thank you."

When I entered the dining room, washed, brushed and pulled together, there were half a dozen people sitting at one of the long tables, among them Mrs. Devlin and her daughter. Willa saw me first and waved me over.

"I hoped it was you, dear." said Mrs. Devlin. "Our guide mentioned there was a young American woman staying here, and I had a feeling it was you."

"Thank you, Mrs. Devlin. Hello again, Willa." I was absurdly happy to hear they were staying at the guest house.

At least my appetite had returned. Over a meal much like those I was used to at the dig house, I asked the Devlin ladies about their impressions of Luxor and the Theban Necropolis.

"Here, the vibrations are strong and deep," declared Mrs. D. "At Karnak, they are muffled by the hum of the modern, the overlay of history, but here the ancient harmonies may be felt. The Necropolis is a hollow vessel, reverberating with the eternal mysteries."

I glanced at Willa, expecting to see her rolling her eyes at this speech, but she didn't. "Which tombs have you visited?" I asked.

"Oh, we haven't actually gone inside any tombs yet," said Willa. "We came over here yesterday afternoon, and so far have merely sampled the atmosphere. Our guide will give us a complete tour starting tomorrow."

"But we will see a few of the local tombs today," said Mrs. D., turning to me. "They are so near, we can pop over after lunch. The Tombs of the Nobles are almost part of this village. Yasmin has spoken to their guardians already, so they will be expecting us."

"Would you like to join us, France? Or do you have other plans?" Willa regarded me curiously as she spoke. I hadn't explained why I had turned up at the guest house, after telling them—only two days before—all about my job as a dig assistant.

"That's a wonderful idea!" Mrs. D. laid a liver-spotted hand on my arm. "You must come, France. I do believe your presence will enhance the experience for us all."

Well, I didn't exactly have a lot to do, and my nap had restored my equilibrium. "Yes, I'd be happy to join you, but I don't know much about the Tombs of the Nobles, I'm afraid."

"The Nobles were court officials, viziers, scribes, mayors, military officers," said Willa. "I guess they wanted to be near the pharaohs but didn't rate the Valley of the Kings."

"Different neighbourhoods," I said.

She laughed. "You could say so."

After lunch, Mrs. Devlin said she needed a short rest before tomb-viewing. I told Willa about Yasmin's offer to show me around the guest house.

"Sounds interesting," said Willa. "Count me in."

Yasmin took us up to the roof of the house, from which Luxor looked like a distant dream, wrapped in a midday haze.

215

Tables and chairs stood under a shade structure roofed with palm-fronds. Laundry hung on a clothesline. "This is a good place to sit when the sun sets," she said. "Sometimes we have our supper here."

The guest rooms were immediately below this outdoor living room, accessible by the outdoor steps. As we descended, I remarked that they must have been a relatively recent addition to the house.

"Yes," said Yasmin. "My father built this part, to make guest house. He had good fortune when driving taxi. Now we have guests, and Father owns three taxis."

"Good fortune," I said. It wasn't a question, but Yasmin responded as though it was.

"An American man who came here long ago, before I am born, when Father is young. He gave the gold to my father. Now I will show you the old part of the house."

The story of the gold-giving American sounded intriguing, but Yasmin didn't tell us more of it.

Except for the dining room and the one adjacent to it where we had tea, the rest of the house was crowded and primitive. Yasmin hurried us past the family's private quarters, but I caught a glimpse of what must have been the bedroom she shared with her sisters—three narrow beds with clothing and other belongings piled into baskets between them. A passage led to a kitchen that had one wall open to an outdoor courtyard, much like at the Stantons' dig house, except here chickens strolled around, pecking at crumbs. Giant clay water jars, no different from those dug up by archaeologists, stood in a wooden rack along the wall.

"Here are rooms we use for storage and in cold weather," said Yasmin, showing us a passage that had been excavated into the hillside. A kerosene lantern hung from the ceiling. In its dim light I noticed coloured shapes on the walls and recognized the familiar figures of ancient Egyptians surrounded by hieroglyphs.

"Yasmin—" But she and Willa were no longer there. Glancing back at the images, I hurried to catch up with them. They were in the kitchen, where a couple of women were busy washing up the lunch dishes.

"Yasmin, I noticed some pictures in your storage area. They looked like ones I've seen in tombs. Do you know who painted them?"

She stared at me for a second, a small smile forming on her lips. "Maybe the ancient people. Maybe not."

"Do you know… might those rooms be part of a tomb?" I found the idea both appalling and fascinating.

"No one knows," she said.

"I think Mother's ready to go," said Willa, looking down the hall. Mrs. D. was waiting for us, leaning on a cane. She had changed into a skirt and blouse of a type I associated with lady archaeologists of the 1920s. Instead of a pith helmet, she sported an elegant wide-brimmed hat I rather envied, and, of course, a necklace. Only one this time, but of rather large, chunky beads.

I ran up to my room for hat and purse, making sure I had a flashlight, as well as a lot of small change, since Yasmin had mentioned tipping the tomb guardians. Willa carried a camp stool I assumed was for her mother's use.

Away from the cool shade of the guest house, the heat and glare struck me hard, as did the noise and chaos of the village. Donkey carts, goats, chickens and children were everywhere. Small, skinny kids flitted among us, flashing smiles and extending grubby little hands for coins. Yasmin spoke to them and they withdrew a little, standing in a row to watch us go by.

Uphill from the village, bare rock and bare dirt reflected the afternoon sunlight. In the hot, white glare, tomb entrances gaped like rabbit holes, except each one had an iron gate. I could hardly wait to get underground, if only to escape the glare.

Yasmin called out a greeting, and an ancient man emerged from a tin-roofed hut. After a brief conversation in Arabic, she told us the cost of visiting three tombs. "This is tomb of Vizier Rekhmire. You will visit also tomb of Scribe Nakht and Sennefer the Overseer of Gardens. That one is very nice, called Tomb of Vineyards. Please to give small tip to mirror-holders. I must go now. I hope you enjoy, and I will see you at suppertime."

Mirror-holders?

We deposited the correct denominations in the man's wrinkled palm, eliciting a toothless smile and an arm wave directing us toward the first tomb. He unlocked an enormous padlock with an equally ponderous key. Opening the gate, he motioned us inward.

I ducked my head and entered, following Willa and her mother. The wall at the end of the passage was illuminated by a circle of light that wavered and dipped. Looking behind me, I saw the old man wielding a mirror, bouncing a beam of light into the tomb. I remembered a discussion at the dig house about whether the original tomb builders used sheets of metal to direct reflected sunlight into the underground chambers and passages.

Another mirror-bearer, a boy of ten or so, stood at the point where a transverse passage crossed the entrance tunnel.

Tilting his mirror, he caught the light from the old man's mirror to illuminate what would otherwise be a pitch-dark space, showing us important events from the life of the vizier.

I wonder if they'll leave us in the dark if we don't tip. Good thing I brought a flashlight.

Mrs. Devlin's idea of appreciating a tomb was to stand in one spot for a moment, and then turn slowly around without looking at anything in detail. She gestured to Willa, who unfolded the camp stool. Seated, Mrs. D. closed her eyes and seemed ready to stay put.

"She'll be fine for a while," said Willa. "She has a flashlight. Let's look around."

The walls of Vizier Rekhmire's intended final resting place teemed with activity. Every wall showed rows of brown men in white kilts or loincloths, working hard—planting, harvesting, hunting, brewing beer, making things, cooking, eating, or carrying objects from one place to another. In one spot, I was excited to see something different—a couple of women musicians, one playing a harp, the other something like a lute, with a very small body and long neck. I remembered the piece of limestone in Dr. Stanton's office. Strings, hands, a woman's face and hair...

"What's so interesting?" asked Willa. "You've been staring at that piece of wall for ages."

I straightened up. "Musicians. I was wondering how they would have sounded. Especially this one." I pointed to the lute.

"No idea. Not rock 'n' roll, that's for sure. Let's move on. We have to give that kid something else to light up. Make sure he earns his pennies."

The old guardian conducted us from tomb to tomb, along with two boys who held mirrors to light them up for us. "Watch your step," "Please," and "Thank you," seemed to be the limit of their English vocabulary. I wondered if they knew the equivalent phrases in the languages of tourists from other countries.

Entering the holes in the rock and stepping carefully down the narrow passages, we travelled more than a few yards. The real distance was more like three thousand years. It was easy to become disoriented among the multitudes of pictures, worlds full of painted people living their lives. Ancient lives, preserved for thousands of years, until a couple of young American women gawped at them and pointed out details they found amusing.

After Rekhmire, we called on Nakht the Scribe and then Sennefer the Overseer. I noticed more musicians on Nakht's walls, the same harp and lute combo. In one scene, the lute player was naked except for something like a g-string and a collar-like necklace. There were different styles of harp, one played in a standing position, the other kneeling or seated. Did Mrs. Devlin ever hear their music? I would have to ask her.

In Sennefer's tomb, the most memorable feature was grapes. Grapevines were painted all over the irregular ceiling and down part of the walls. Vines and bunches of grapes, and those busy brown men harvesting them.

"So that's what Egyptians needed to be happy in the afterlife," I said. "Wine, women, and song. Just like today."

"There's a party tonight at Sennefer's place," said Willa, laughing.

"And then on to Nakht's. Sennefer has lots of wine, but Nakht hired more musicians."

I lingered in Sennefer's burial chamber. It was time I left, but I was content in the earth's cool embrace. Willa and the mirror-boys were gone. The only light came from my flashlight. I shone it around to find the exit and headed toward it, hoping to catch up with Willa. My light briefly illuminated a face. A face that looked right at me.

Egyptians never painted anyone full-face. I swept the light back. Osiris sat enthroned in majesty, as I had seen him in books and in Seti's tomb. He wore the tall white crown with the two plumes of divinity. His arms were crossed over his chest, holding the crook and flail. His skin was green, signifying death, signifying rebirth. And his face was in profile, the single painted eye gazing at something remote and invisible to me.

Weird. I was sure it was full-face. Is this another dizzy spell coming on?

But I wasn't dizzy. I turned to leave, but something made me look back, directing the beam of light toward the part of the wall where I had seen the Osiris figure.

He gazed at me, with meaning and purpose. He stared through the painted image of the god. It wasn't the face of a living person. Too remote, too still, too pale.

"France? Where are you? What are you doing here?"

I turned, almost dropping my flashlight. I tried to speak, but the only sound I could make was a strangled croak. Willa came over to me, shining her own flashlight, with one of the Egyptian boys close behind. "Are you okay?"

"I'm... I dunno, I guess so. Shine your light over there, will you? At Osiris."

She directed her light to where I pointed. The King of the Underworld looked perfectly all right, except for spots where paint had flaked off. His green face gazed to the left, at the tomb's owner and his wife, who stood with hands raised in the position of worship. "So—what's up?"

"Nothing, I guess. It looked different a little while ago." I shook my head and tried to laugh.

"Oh. I thought you'd gone into a tomb-trance, like Mother does sometimes. Speaking of whom, let's go collect her and get back to the guest house. I think both of you've had enough tomb-touring for today."

Waiting outside were two men wearing dark blue *galabeyas* and black turbans. Maybe they were the mirror-boys' fathers. They looked like brothers, identical twin brothers. They bowed as we exited the tomb and watched us make our way down the hillside.

Finding myself with a free half hour before supper, I decided to read Alma's letter. The fat envelope had two Air Mail stickers and one *Par avion*. After the usual news from College Hill, she wrote (or rather, typed):

> You asked whether your new acquaintance Adam Dexter might be a relative of Francis Dexter's. I have no idea. Francis had two brothers, but their surname was West, not Dexter. (He changed his name; don't remember if I've told you that, and anyway, they were his half-brothers). It's possible his father, an Englishman named Lawrence Dexter, had other children, so there may be some connection. I suggest you look into it next time you're in England. I'll poke around here and see what I can find out.

I asked Andre for more details
about the time he and Francis visited
Egypt in 1935. He told me a long,
rambling story about climbing a hill
near Luxor and getting into trouble
with the locals. I wrote it all down
for you (enclosed). I have to say, it's
a pretty strange tale; at times I
wondered if Andre was exaggerating.

Andre's tale described the Luxor I knew—the Winter Palace Hotel, the ferry, the stony desert around the tombs. His descriptions of rocks, dust and heat matched my experiences. But other elements of his story disturbed me—a tall man who resembled Pharaoh Ramses II, a strange car, and a house that proved to be a tomb. "He has lived here a very long time and knows everything," Andre said about this man. "Sometimes he goes away, but always he comes back."

How long, I wondered, is "a very long time?"

The dining room of the guest house was nearly full that evening. Besides the Devlin ladies and me, there was a party of French tourists led by an archaeologist. He insisted on delivering mini-lectures to his charges throughout the meal, in French, of course. They sat at the other table, but it was near enough to be mildly annoying.

Finished with his lecture, the French professor turned to us. "Your President Kennedy spoke today about the nuclear missiles in Cuba. It appears that matters are very serious indeed, but I assure you France remains your country's steadfast ally."

This remark caused agitated discussion among the Americans present, and urgent questions to the Frenchman, who had listened to the speech on a shortwave radio as it was broadcast several hours earlier. I thought of my family back in Providence—Alma, Andre and Lucy. If a nuclear war started, would I ever see them again?

Presiding over our table was Yasmin's father, Mr. Mahmoud Mohamed, who was also the guide hired by Mrs. Devlin. Probably to lighten the mood, he regaled us with anecdotes from thirty years of experiences with tourists and archaeologists.

Naturally, much of the table-talk was about the wonders of the area, the monuments, temples, and tombs. Fresh from our tour, Willa and I remarked on the vivid pictures of ancient Egyptian life in the tombs we had visited.

"They're more like picture-galleries than tombs," I said, "because everything's been taken out of them. Was that done by robbers or archaeologists? Does anyone know where the mummies and their things ended up?"

"Does it matter, Mademoiselle?" said the French archaeologist. "If these tombs were still sealed, you and your friend would not have been able to appreciate the art on their walls. The contents are in museums now, where they delight many people."

"I know that, but the people who put their fathers and mothers into those tombs expected them to be there forever. They made prayers and spells, and said the dead person's name over and over again, to make sure they enjoyed life in the afterworld."

The Frenchman smiled. "You romanticize the old Egyptians, Mademoiselle. Their time, it is over."

Mr. Mohamed spoke up. "Now, my guests, you will go to our salon, where you will make yourselves comfortable, drink tea and enjoy the sweets."

The wall of the salon was open to the soft darkness of evening. Mint-enhanced tea, figs, and date-filled pastries were a perfect dessert, and the boxy settees were surprisingly comfortable. I sat between Mrs. D. and Willa, within reach of the sweets.

"Miss Leighton was quite taken with pictures of musicians," said Willa, setting down her tea glass and wiping her sticky fingers. "We decided the ancient Egyptians knew how to throw a party."

"*Mais oui,* music was important," said the French professor. "The musicians and dancers for private entertainments were hired for the occasion, but the temple musicians and singers were women of high status."

Mrs. Devlin leaned forward. "Indeed," she said. "Music, especially the singing voice, has enormous power. Because we have never heard the music of the ancients, we cannot begin to understand its uses. But think about choral singing in our church services. Think about chanting in ritual magic. The temple singers invoked the gods, named them, and summoned them and their powers to the rituals."

In the brief silence that followed her words, I thought about my odd experience with the Osiris painting, but before I could say anything, Mrs. Devlin spoke again.

"Willa tells me you're a musician," she said, turning to me.

"Sometimes. I play the cello, but not particularly well."

"Yasmin told us she saw you going to play at the Metropolitan House a few weeks ago." Mr. Mohamed's voice

225

was soft but carrying. "You have your instrument here, I believe. Would you be willing to play a little for us?"

My first impulse was to refuse. I was sleepy and full of supper. There was that crack in Eudora's wood. But I owed these people something. They had been kind and hospitable, far beyond what I expected as a guest. The least I could do was play a melody or two. Besides, I hoped Mr. Mohamed would know how I could get in touch with Adam Dexter, so it wouldn't hurt to comply with his request.

The stairs to the guest rooms were lit only by a flickering lamp in a sconce on the wall. My room was dark, but I remembered where I had placed the cello case. I lifted Eudora out and felt for the crack. It was still there, a thin flaw under my fingers. "Eudora, I'm going to ask a big favour. I hope this won't hurt you. Please forgive me."

I carried her down to the salon, where someone had set up a chair for me. I played "The Swan" from *The Carnival of the Animals*. There was no piano, of course, so my swan didn't have rippling waters to glide upon, but that didn't matter. The slow rhythms invoked a lushness foreign to the desert hills, yet somehow linked in my mind to the vivid lives depicted on the tomb walls. Eudora sang sweetly; I heard no harshness, no prelude to disintegration.

I finished to a spatter of applause and a quiet "Brava," from the French archaeologist. A few people accepted fresh glasses of tea and more pastries, but I took the opportunity to have a word with Yasmin's father.

"Excuse me, Sir, may I ask you something?"

He turned toward me, a smile forming on his lips. "That was beautiful playing. Thank you very much."

"You're welcome. I wonder, have you heard of a man who lives here on the west bank and is called 'right-handed' in Arabic? He has an English name too—Adam Dexter."

Mahmoud looked at me for several seconds, forehead furrowing beneath his turban's folds. Had I offended him? Finally, he spoke.

"I do not know this name, Adam Dexter. But 'right-handed' would be *'alyad alyumnaa.'* Why do you ask?"

"I met Adam Dexter when I played my cello for a meeting of archaeologists at Metropolitan House a few weeks ago. He told me if I wanted to see him again, I should ask for him by that name meaning 'right-handed,' on the west bank of the Nile."

Mahmoud's face grew grim. "I do not know who that man was, the one who told you that. But the name *Alyad Alyumnaa* is not a good one here in Sheikh Abd el-Qurna and the other villages. A man with that name appears here sometimes, to do evil things. He goes away, but always he comes back."

"How long ago was he here? You said 'many years,' but…"

He pressed his lips together and looked up at the ceiling for a second. "It was about the time the American was here. The American and his French servant. A few years before the war started."

"This American—do you remember his name?"

Mahmoud gave me another searching look. "No, I am sorry, I do not remember."

"Thank you for telling me about *Alyad Alyumnaa.*" I began to turn away, but Mahmoud spoke urgently.

"Mademoiselle, I tell you—do not try to find this man. If he is the same as the one I told you about, he is dangerous."

"I will remember that, Sir. Thank you, and good night."

I noticed Willa and her mother heading toward the stairs to the guest rooms. "I want to say how much I enjoyed the afternoon. I probably wouldn't have seen those tombs if you hadn't asked me to join you."

"Even though you ended up in a tomb-trance?" said Willa, smiling.

"What do you mean, a 'tomb-trance'?" Mrs. Devlin stopped and looked at her daughter.

"The kind of thing that happens to you, sometimes. You lose touch with reality for a minute. France thought she saw something strange in Sennefer's tomb. A picture of Osiris, wasn't it, France?"

"Oh, that was nothing. I bumped my head about a week ago, and sometimes I still get a bit dizzy. I guess that's what happened to me there."

Mrs. Devlin grabbed my hand.

"That was lovely, the piece you played. You are a *sensitive*, France. You are susceptible to the unseen currents. Pay attention to Osiris."

Geez. I'm too tired for this. Aloud, I said, "Perhaps I am, Mrs. Devlin, but I don't know much about unseen currents."

"Ah, but you do. And you must come with us tomorrow. Mahmoud will be giving us a tour of the temples and the Colossi of Memnon. The next day we will visit the Valley of the Kings."

"I'm tempted," I said, gently withdrawing my hand, "but I'm planning to meet a friend here, so I must say no thanks."

If Mrs. D. was curious about this, she didn't show it, but Willa gave me a funny look. "All right, then. I hope you enjoy yourself. And be careful." We said our goodnights and went to our rooms.

I laid Eudora into her case, gently touching the crack. "Thank you for singing for me tonight," I said. I closed the case, daring to indulge in hope.

Going to the window, I leaned out and looked across the tumble of houses, over the cultivated land, and across the Nile to Luxor's lights. There was no moon. I remembered watching it with Adam as it rose over the river. He couldn't possibly be a man of evil. I longed to be with him again, to feel his body next to mine, his arm around me. And I wanted to experience the mysteries he had promised me.

"*Alyad Alyumnaa.* You told me I could find you by saying those words. So that's what I'll do."

11
The Chapter of Seeking the Right-Handed One

I awoke before dawn, as though summoned. The room was dark. I went to the door and opened it. No one was there. Puzzled, I peered down the steps. No one there either. I went to the railing opposite the row of doors to the guest rooms and stood there, getting a feel of the coming day. The eastern horizon was beginning to lighten and the air smelled of smoke and animal dung mingled with dust and something I couldn't identify.

I should have gone back to bed and slept until a more civilized hour, but I didn't. After washing up using the primitive jug-and-bowl setup, I got dressed and went outside again. Leaning over the railing, I took a deep breath of the cool air, relishing it despite the smells of animal and human life. Watching the brightening colours of the imminent sunrise, I remembered the ecstasy of the dawn I'd witnessed from the balloon. No wonder the ancient Egyptians were fixated on the sun's daily journey.

Muffled voices and the crunching of feet on gravel drew my attention. Four men came into view, moving purposefully. Three of them wore *galabeyas* and the fourth a shirt and pants. I must have made a sound or movement. The guy in the pants looked right at me, and I recognized him—Hank.

My first impulse was to wave and greet him, but I squashed it and ran back to my room. If Hank was here, Dr. Stanton was probably around too, since they had left the dig together. Hank would tell Stanton he'd seen me. I had to get out of here. The sooner I found Adam, the better.

Mr. Mohamed had reservations about an individual called *Alyad Alyumnaa*, and he had never heard of Adam Dexter. I had considered asking Yasmin if she knew anything about him, but now I didn't want to hang around the guest house any longer. Willa was someone I could be friends with, but I didn't want to get into explanations with Mrs. Devlin, who was an odd duck with strange notions about me.

Hoping for an approximation of the look Adam had found attractive, I re-braided my hair into the flattering French braid and applied discreet touches of makeup, using the tiny mirror in my powder compact.

I had no idea what a night's accommodation cost, along with the lunch and supper. I took a guess, doubled it, and wrote a note for Yasmin.

> *Please forgive my sudden departure. Many thanks to you and your family for your kindness and hospitality. France Leighton.*

I folded the money into the note and left it on the bed. Then I struggled into the rucksack, picked up Eudora and the beach bag, and slipped out of the house. I stood in front of the door for a few moments, listening. I wanted to avoid Hank and the other men, so I set off in a direction opposite to theirs. Otherwise, I had no idea where I was going.

Ahead of me were a couple of black-clad women, balancing clay water jars on their heads. I couldn't believe this was how the people of the village got water, but Yasmin had explained it to me the day before.

I didn't want to startle the women, so I scuffled my feet as I came up behind them. They stopped and turned regally to face me, their faces curious but watchful.

"*Sabah al-khayr*," I said, hoping I had remembered the correct words for "Good morning." The women murmured and smiled. Their expressions suggested they were suppressing giggles at my pronunciation. But I pressed on. "*Ayna Alyad Alyumnaa?*"

The smiles vanished. They shifted their eyes toward one another and said nothing. I tried again. "*Alyad Alyumnaa— ayna?* Adam Dexter?"

I guessed they couldn't shake their heads with those heavy jars on them. Or maybe head-shaking wasn't something Egyptians did. But the expressions on their faces were unmistakable, as were the movements of their hands, palms raised in a pushing-away gesture and then covering their lips. They weren't going to tell me anything. Were they afraid? Of me, or of what I had said?

One of the women muttered something. I had no idea what it meant, but it sounded like a curse.

"Excuse me," I said. "*Afwan.* I'm sorry. Goodbye." I turned around and went back toward the village. That didn't make sense, but neither did following the two women, who clearly didn't want anything to do with me.

Near the village, people were up and about—another pair of women with water jars, and an old man and a boy with a donkey pulling a cart. Considering my results with the first two women, I approached the man and boy. Smiling my friendliest, I repeated the two phrases meaning (I hoped) "Good morning," and "Where is the Right-Handed One?"

The boy didn't react, just stared at me with lazy curiosity, as though I was a new kind of bug. The old man smiled back at my greeting, but then his expression changed. "No, no, no, Miss! You go home now!" He continued with a stream of rapid-fire Arabic, all the time shaking his turbaned head.

So I guess head-shaking is an Egyptian thing.

"Now you go!" the old man finished, pointing behind me, toward the Nile. I didn't think he was saying "Yankee go home," but repeating the warning Mr. Mohamed had given me the night before. I debated with myself about offering him cash in the hope of changing his mind, but gave up when he started up again with, "No, no. Not for you! You go!"

"*Shukran. Ma'a as-salaama.* Thank you, Sir. Goodbye."

On the road leading toward the Nile—surely the one followed by the lurching donkey cart the day before—marched two military-looking figures, maybe the policemen doing a foot patrol?

Before I could get going, the man waved his arm, indicating I should get into his cart, and pointed again toward the river. Or maybe toward the policemen? Was he offering me a lift, to make sure I actually departed? He was getting a little agitated, jabbering a torrent of words I had no way of understanding.

Now it was my turn to shake my head. "No, thanks. *Laa shukran.* Goodbye." I pointed toward the village and walked quickly in that direction. Even though that wasn't where I wanted to go, it might reassure the old fellow I would be safe.

I still didn't know how to find Adam. Clearly, I hadn't connected with whoever he thought would direct me to him. The policemen were an obvious possibility, but if they decided I had no business looking for "*Alyad Alyumnaa*," I'd be sunk.

Avoiding the centre of the village, I found myself in a narrow alley with mud-brick walls on either side. Houses loomed above the wall on my right, but no one looked out any of the small windows as I went by. Roosters crowed, goats baaed, children screamed and chattered, but I could see none of them. The houses and walls ended, turning the alley into a steep little road that seemed to be heading for the uninhabited hills. From up there, I might be able to get a better idea of where to go next.

The sun leaned hot on my back. After a quarter-hour of steady walking, I stopped to take a breath and turned around. Village rooftops lay beneath me; ahead, the ground rose to a ridge, with cliffs behind it.

Adam wasn't here. Why would he be? But then, had he actually told me to look for him in this place? There were other villages. A familiar tide of dizziness filled my head, bringing with it weariness and disorientation. The brutal glare of the sunlight bouncing off the stones made me squint. I rummaged in my bag for sunglasses, failed to find them in the jumble of stuff, gave up, felt like crying.

Here I was, in a situation I'd been warned against many times since I set foot on Egyptian soil: Don't go wandering around alone. Stay away from lonely places.

What should I do? Go back to the dig and plead to be readmitted? Not likely. Go back to the guest house and look like a silly tourist? What would be the point, especially if I ran into Dr. Stanton? I might as well go back to Luxor, treat myself to a night or two at the Winter Palace, and arrange my return to Providence. Alma would gladly welcome me back.

But that felt like a defeat. I had come to Egypt eager to study its secrets, scientifically or otherwise. Adam had offered to show me those secrets, and I wasn't about to give up on that opportunity, dizziness be damned.

Could I find Adam by following this little road? By now, it was just a path, and a stony one at that. At least I would have a look at whatever lay on the other side of the ridge.

The path climbed higher, as did the temperature. My feet slipped on loose gravel and I banged my toes on potato-sized rocks. Thoughts of water reminded me I had no idea where to find any.

I stopped for another rest. The knapsack dragged on my shoulders, and the handle of Eudora's case was slick with sweat. The intense heat beat down on my head, and the intense light assaulted my unprotected eyes. Where were those goddamned sunglasses? I was beginning to think I'd left them at the guest house, along with my hat. An ache bloomed behind my eyes, as though it had caught up with me and was eager to make the most of our reunion.

Okay, I thought. I give up. I'll see what's on the other side of the ridge and then I'll go back. Yasmin won't mind since I've already paid for yesterday and last night. Overpaid, most likely. And maybe she can tell me something about Adam.

But then I remembered Yasmin saying she was going back to Luxor today. And her father would be taking Mrs. Devlin and Willa on their tour. There were probably no other English speakers at the guest house, and I wasn't feeling well enough to struggle along with my limited Arabic.

"Shit!"

Squinting at the white road behind me I saw two dark figures—the policemen I'd seen before? Were they looking for me? What else would they be doing here? Something about the way they moved made me nervous.

I forced my legs into motion, leaning into the ever-steepening slope, wishing I had a hand free to pull myself up, or to break a fall, if it came to that.

I was almost at the top. A few more steps and I would see the valley. Valley? My imagination had created an oasis, with palm trees clustered around a clear pool of water, and cool, blessed shade.

I made a final push for the top, which proved to be a narrow saddle with an even steeper slope on the other side, dropping to a boulder-strewn chasm, and on its far side, a wall of unyielding stone.

I threw back my head and howled at the sky. "*Alyad Alyumnaa! Alyad Alyumnaa! Alyad Alyumnaa!*"

Stones rattled behind me, and a voice spoke, deep and commanding. I turned, panic choking off my breath. The air vibrated and sizzled in my ears like the hum of a giant mosquito. My right foot slipped as gravel gave way. I fell sideways, landed on stones and slid downhill.

****

How did I get back on the balloon? I didn't want to, and now it's crashed again. Cap'n Hawes really has to brush up on his technique. Why did I bring Eudora with me?

I dozed off again.

Such strange dreams… Shit, I must be late! Jack'll kill me. Come on, France, wake up! Ugh, my mouth tastes bad. Orange juice. I wonder if there's any left.

I managed to pry my eyelids halfway open and tried to focus. Where was I? The ceiling was way too high. High and white, like heaven's supposed to be.

Well, I've been a good girl, haven't I? I deserve to sleep in, and anyway, I'm someplace else, so they'll never find me.

Where?

I opened my eyes again, wide this time, and turned my head. To the left, a pink princess-style telephone. To the right, a chair, and someone sitting on it.

Adam.

I stared at him. He stared back, with a still, unwavering gaze that might have been held for hours, frozen. Then, everything changed. His eyes came alive, his eyelids flickered. The room grew brighter, as though someone had flipped a switch. I looked around for the person who had done that, but there was no one else in the room. It must be a hospital room. Maybe pink princess phones were part of the décor. But how did I get here, and how did Adam find me?

"France," he said. "At last. I'm glad to see you're awake."

"I'm glad to see you too." My voice was rusty, matching the taste in my mouth. "I was trying to find you, but… something happened."

"You got lost," he said, "and then you fell." He leaned toward me. "Word reached me that you had been asking about me in Sheikh Abd el-Qurna. I sent my servants to search for you, and they brought you here."

"Where's 'here'?" I tried to sit up but felt like a small boat in a rough sea. I gave up and subsided back onto the pillow.

"'Here' is my home," Adam said, with a smile. "My villa. It's not far from the village, but not easy to find. When you are well enough, I will show you its wonders. And other wonders too, as I promised you. But now you should sleep, until you have recovered from your fall."

My first impulse was to protest wellness, to sit up and look eager for action. I wanted to ask him why people had warned me against him, and who had told him about me. But my head felt stagnant and my mouth unclean.

Adam stood. "My servants will bring you refreshment, and your possessions have been dealt with. I will see you when you are ready."

I'll bet he thinks I'm disgusting. Because I am.

He smiled and departed, leaving a faint aroma of resin and aromatic herbs, of mysteries and wonders.

I don't know how long I slept. When I awoke, I had no idea if it was early or late, but golden light seeped in through the room's high windows.

On the table by my bed stood a pitcher and a glass. The pitcher held fruit juice, bright red in colour. Pomegranate juice? I remembered how good it tasted, but I also remembered it coming back up later. Desperately thirsty. I poured myself a glass and drank it in three delicious gulps. The pleasant astringency cut through the nasty taste in my mouth. I refilled the glass and sat back to drink it more slowly than the first one.

What had happened to me? Where was I, exactly? Somehow, I had found Adam, but maybe "found" wasn't the right word. I had been carried here in an unconscious state. Wherever "here" was.

I had to find out, and that meant getting up and out of this bland, white room. Now that I was fully awake, I was aware of pains here and there, no doubt caused by the fall I'd taken. Wondering how bad my injuries were, I swung my legs off the bed, set my feet on the cool stone floor, and stood up.

So far, so good.

Except I was naked. Totally naked. I had been lying in that bed, with nothing but a sheet between my bare body and Adam Dexter. Good thing I hadn't managed to sit up while he was still here.

Who undressed me?

Disturbed and excited at the same time, I padded around the room. My knapsack slouched in a corner, with the beach bag and Eudora's case next to it. Remembering my camera emptied of film, I snapped open the latches and lifted the lid. I ran my fingers over Eudora, searching for the deadly crack. It was still there; it hadn't gone away like a bad dream.

"Eudora," I murmured, "we're still together. Whatever happens."

The bathroom was modern, with a better shower than I'd seen since leaving Providence, but no mirror. Maybe mirrors were considered unlucky in Egypt. But then, what about the ones used to light up the tombs for tourists? Even without a mirror, I could see purple bruises on my arms and legs. While shampooing, I searched for a fresh lump on my head and was reassured not to find one.

Clean and refreshed, I wrapped myself in a towel and rummaged in the knapsack for clean underwear. The blouse and skirt I had worn the day I left the guest house lay neatly folded on a wooden chest. These were the nicest clothes I had brought with me, so they were the obvious choice.

I was ravenously hungry, a sure sign of restored health. I hoped breakfast, or lunch, or both, were forthcoming. And I wanted to find out exactly where I was, how long I had been out of my senses, and what Adam meant by "wonders."

The room's door consisted of a central panel, surrounded by several rows of hieroglyphs framed in pale blue. Above it was a rectangle with pale gold and white vertical stripes. There was no sign of a latch. I searched without success for a catch or spring. My hands scrabbled over the central panel, the frame, the top and bottom, searching, pressing, scratching. Finally, panicked, I banged on it with my fists.

"Hello! Adam, can you hear me? I can't open the door! Help!" My breath pumped in and out of lungs that seemed to be shrinking. Desperate, I was sucking in a breath to shriek when a hand touched my back.

I shrieked.

"France, what's wrong?" Adam bent over me, his face full of concern.

"Oh, you scared me," I gasped, trembling. "I couldn't open the door. Hey, how did you get in here?"

"It's simple," Adam said, a small smile playing about his lips. "This door is only an ornament, meant to give the room a touch of ancient Egypt. The real one is over there. Come, I'll show you." He put his arm around my shoulders and led me to a doorway concealed by a short wall projecting from a corner of the room. Why hadn't I noticed it?

"I feel silly," I said. "That other door, or whatever it is, it looks so real. Where does it go?"

"Nowhere, as I've already told you. Come along." He took my hand and led me through the newly-revealed door. We followed a hallway leading to rooms that opened to other rooms. Large, spacious rooms, with polished stone floors, carved wooden pillars, and sparse but elegant furnishings. I was impressed beyond words, totally mystified, and weak from hunger. Finally, we came to a smaller room that opened onto a terrace, with reeds and palms in the background.

"Adam, please, I have to sit down." I collapsed onto a bench upholstered in a satiny fabric of dark blue and silver stripes, with curled arms and lion feet. "Your house is gorgeous, truly. I'm sorry not to be more appreciative, but I'm still kind of shaky, and hungry too. I'm sorry."

Oh France, don't be abject.

Adam sank down on one knee before me. For a wild second, I thought he was about to propose, and my heart did a double-thump.

His brows drew together. "I'm the one who should be sorry," he said, taking my hand. "I should have realized you would be hungry. You haven't had a meal since you arrived."

"When was that?" I asked. "How long have I been here?"

"A day or so." He reached for my other hand. "Oh, have you lost your beautiful ring?" He looked up at me, concern changing to something else. Consternation? Anger? Surely not.

"I haven't lost it. I'm just not wearing it right now." Where had I put the ring? I couldn't remember when I had worn it last. Was it with the stuff I had brought with me, or had I left it at the dig house? And why would Adam care?

"I'm glad to hear that," he said. "That's good, very good. All right, now for breakfast, or brunch, actually." He sprang to his feet and helped me up. "Come out to the terrace, and I will speak to my servants about a meal."

It was lovely on the terrace. Reclining on a cushioned settee, I watched palm fronds swaying in a warm breeze. I must have dozed off, because I awoke suddenly to see two men in dark blue *galabeyas* and black turbans setting a table and chairs in place nearby. They went away without looking at or speaking to me, and returned soon after with trays and platters, followed by Adam.

The meal was delicious. There was strong coffee, fruit, eggs, warm bread, flaky pastries. Adam sat, a cup in his hand and a look of satisfaction on his face, as though watching me eat gave him pleasure.

When I finally slowed down, he refilled my coffee cup yet again. "So, France, tell me everything that's happened to you since we dined together."

I swallowed a final bite. "Everything, really?"

Adam nodded, coppery eyes holding mine steadily.

"All right." I wiped my lips and fingers with my napkin. "I'll try."

He cradled the translucent cup in his brown hands and gazed at the liquid held in its curve, occasionally glancing up at me with an expression of sympathetic interest.

"Well," I began, wishing my thoughts were better organized, "I flew in a balloon. About a week ago. That was exciting."

"What did you see?"

"Everything! Well, everything around Luxor and the Valley of the Kings. In one place I saw something really strange—a red glow in deep in the stone. It was amazing, almost worth the crash-landing."

Adam put his cup on the table and leaned toward me. "Where was this place, exactly?"

"I don't know. It was another valley—I mean, wadi— behind the Valley of the Kings. There was a big round rock in the side of the cliff, like an eyeball. I hit my head when we crashed, so I might have forgotten some details."

"Were you injured?"

"I had a mild concussion, but I'm all right now. Almost. I get a bit dizzy sometimes."

Adam leaned back in his chair. "Are you on leave from your dig?"

How much should I tell him? "Oh, I've left the dig."

Adam tilted his head. "Really? Why?" He picked up the cup again and swirled the remaining coffee around.

"Things got a little awkward," I said. "The director, Dr. Stanton, made some... unwelcome requests. All in all, I thought, I'd better leave. But I wanted to see more of the area before going home. And I wanted to see you again."

"I'm happy you did," he said, smiling.

"So am I." My hands shook slightly, and I hoped he didn't notice.

He was silent for a while, long enough for me to wonder at the complete silence around us. I heard no birds, no insects, not even a breeze in the palm fronds.

He's beautiful. And not old at all. Why did I think he was old? The contrast between his brown skin and white shirt, the strands of black hair falling over his forehead, the long lashes hiding his eyes...

Adam looked up and gazed at me intently. "Of course, you want revenge."

"Revenge? On whom?"

"This Dr. Stanton, of course."

"No, not at all!" *Really? Come on, France!* "I just wanted to get away, and to... find you."

He smiled. "Well, you've done that."

"This place is beautiful," I said, "and so quiet. Is this where you and your parents spent vacations when you were young?"

He frowned and set the cup down again, this time with a distinct click. Raising his eyes to a spot above my head, he seemed to be consulting a god of patience. "No, they had a house in Alexandria. I came to this place later, alone."

"Oh, when was that?"

"Later. As I've said already. Do you think you can manage a walk in the garden?"

Reluctant to annoy him again, I roused myself and we strolled along meandering paths through lush thickets of plants I didn't recognize, overshadowed by tall date palms, and musical with birdcalls, the hum of insects, and a murmur of unseen water. Why hadn't I heard that before? The sun's glare was muted by foliage. I felt like I had been transported from Egypt to another place entirely.

"Where are we?" I asked, stopping near a pool backed by tall papyrus stalks that reminded me of their giant stone counterparts in the pillars of Karnak.

"You know where we are. In my garden."

"Yes, but where *exactly*?"

He gave me a look of fond exasperation. "On the west bank of the Nile, opposite Luxor, or, as the oldest Egyptians called it, Wa-set, the City of the Sceptre."

"All right, but the last place I remember is a village, called Sheikh something or other. Where are we relative to that?"

"The village is Sheikh Abd el-Qurna, Miss Persistent." Adam smiled, looking at me through half-closed eyes. "Its name honours a local holy man whose tomb is nearby."

"Okay, but it was a dry, stony place, with hardly any plants. Nothing like this. We must be closer to the Nile."

"You're partly right. But actually, we're closer to that village than to the Nile. The river has been persuaded inland by means of a canal. You're not that far from where you started."

"But I can't see any landmarks." I looked in every direction, but all I could see were palms and water, and behind us, the walls and domes of the house, misty and ephemeral in the rich, golden light. "Where's el-Qurn, for example?"

Adam waved a hand toward the house. "This place is where a wadi meets an ancient canal, so it's lower-lying than its surroundings. *Ta Dehent* is over there. That's what they called it, 'the Peak.' We will go there one day, if you wish, you and I."

"Well, sure. That would be great. Not today, though."

"No, it's not time yet. I mean, you must recover your strength first. Never fear, the Peak does not vanish because one falls and hurts one's head. You should have another rest, and then join me for dinner." He took my hand. "Wear your emerald ring, please. For me."

I did feel drowsy, despite the coffee I had absorbed along with the brunch. The idea of stretching out in a cool, dim room with a pillow under my head was infinitely seductive. It wouldn't matter if I got dizzy. I'd let myself be swept into the vortex of sleep. Yes.

I sleep in his house, as though the world has ceased to exist.

Rooms become other rooms, become narrow passages leading to more rooms. Light and dark, dark and light, colours like a kaleidoscope gone mad. I am the only thing that doesn't move.

Someone summons me. All right, except I don't know where I am.

Concentrate, France! You must concentrate if you want to achieve anything worthwhile.

Oh, that sounds like my old cello teacher. Maestro Whatever-His-Name-Was. But he isn't here. There's no one here but me.

And the faces on the walls. Faces and bodies. Eyes outlined in black, staring into the distance. This one—so still he sits, gazing into forever, holding his crook and flail. By hook or by crook. Ha, ha!

What's his name? I've seen him before. He wanted to tell me something, but I got scared of his green face. Green face, green hands. White mummy-bandaged body. Tall crown with plumes. The dead one who lives and gives life.

Hail, Osiris! I've found you. Or you've found me.

He turns his head and looks at me. What have I done, to deserve such regard? Now that I see him better, he reminds me of someone I know, or knew. Who can it be?

I open my mouth to ask, but he's gone. I'm the middle of whirling rooms and winking lights. I'm lost beyond lost unless I can find him again.

"There is a door," says a voice.

"With a bird painted on it," says another.

"Ask Eudora," I tell myself.

I awoke to dusk. The high windows of my room were faint patches of ashen light. I had no idea what time it was; my watch would have run down long ago, and anyway, I didn't know where it was.

I shook myself awake. I wasn't dizzy and didn't have a headache. Even the bruises from my recent fall didn't hurt as much. It was time I got up and dressed, but I wished I had brought nicer clothes.

I went over to the wooden chest and lifted its lid, releasing a faint scent of aromatic wood. The folded garment within proved to be a gorgeous gown of pleated white linen, richly embroidered with gold *ankh* symbols. I spent only a few seconds admiring it before dropping the lovely thing over my head.

It took me a few minutes to figure out what to do with the gold sash. I wrapped and tied it below my breasts, leaving the ends to dangle almost to the floor. One thing was clear—I couldn't wear a bra with this dress. But there was a kind of shawl in transparent linen to protect my modesty.

I turned back to the chest. A dainty necklace of blue and gold beads and a pair of stunning gold sandals lay on the dark red cloth of another garment. Next to them were two slender gold bracelets—no, they were arm rings—shaped like snakes. Cobras. Bizarre but beautiful. Needless to say, I put them on too. They clasped my arms like old friends.

I wished there was a mirror in the room. Despite my reservations about modesty, I wasn't about to change back into my wrinkled Ship 'n' Shore blouse and khaki skirt. Adam must have arranged to make these garments and accessories available to me, so I was practically obliged to wear them.

Besides, they made me feel glamorous.

The emerald ring. Adam wanted me to wear it. Was it in my beach bag or the knapsack? I must have brought it with me. Rummaging through the knapsack's many pockets, I finally found the ring, knotted into a handkerchief.

And here was the turquoise scarf I'd bought at the *souk*, intending to mail it to Alma. I'd forgotten to do that and couldn't remember why I'd brought it with me. Meg must have put it in the knapsack. How was Alma? The thought triggered another wave of loneliness for my old, normal life. I slipped the ring onto the fourth finger of my left hand and turned the emerald inward, clenching the hand into a fist. For a second, I felt a reassuring warmth from the green stone. "I'm thinking of you too, Uncle Charles," I whispered.

I had no trouble finding the door of my room this time. The hallway was dimly lit, with hieroglyphs on the walls and decorative motifs above. While I hesitated in the doorway, Adam's twin servants padded silently around the corner to my right. "Please come with us, Miss Leighton," one of them said. Relieved but nervous, I complied.

The servants conducted me to a room whose floor was made of alternating squares of black and white stone, like a giant chessboard. Against one wall stood a metal object I assumed to be a sculpture, possibly a modern interpretation of the sacred *djed* pillar, which was supposed to represent the spinal column of Osiris. I had seen it depicted in ancient Egyptian art and discussed in books. It was a powerful symbol, representing the triumph of life over death.

A closer look at the object revealed a subtle violet glow emanating from the horizontal projections near its top. I couldn't be certain, but I thought I detected a kind of pulsation. I was trying to decide if it also emitted a low humming sound when I heard Adam's voice. Startled, I whirled around, making the white and gold dress swirl around me.

"Lovely," said Adam. "You are lovely, France." He looked me up and down as though I was a work of art.

"What's this?" I asked, pointing at the *djed*-like object.

Was I mistaken, or did his forehead crease with annoyance? "Nothing you need to concern yourself with," he said, taking my right hand and steering me away from the thing. "Let me look at you again." He made a circling gesture, and I twirled around obligingly, soaking in his admiration.

"Where did you get all that—the dress, the jewelry?" he asked.

I was surprised at the question, and even more at the frown on his face. "I found them in the chest in my room. I thought you would want me to wear them."

"Indeed." He stood as though listening. "Perhaps. Come along now. We will dine."

What had I done wrong? Maybe he didn't want me to wear the dress, even though he said I looked lovely in it.

I followed him to what was obviously a dining room, where the two servants awaited us, wearing uniforms like those I remembered seeing on the waiters in the restaurant that wasn't. Less dazed than I'd been earlier, I intended to make intelligent conversation during the meal.

"What do you do here all day?"

"What do you think I do?"

I couldn't imagine. Did he admire his surroundings, wandering from room to room? Read? Sleep? I shook my head.

"Recently, France, I've been thinking about you, and wondering when you would appear."

He sat around all day wondering when I would show up? This made me uncomfortable and prompted another question.

"When I mentioned the name you said you're known by—*Alyad Alyumnaa*—people in the village were reluctant to tell me anything. I got the impression they didn't want me to look for you. Do you know why?"

Adam waved the question away. "Some of the villagers are ignorant and superstitious, that's all. That cello of yours—you have a name for it?"

"Yes, I call her Eudora."

"'Her.'" He smiled.

"She was a gift from my grandfather."

Adam gave me a hard look, his eyes narrowing. "I thought you said you never knew him."

"Oh, not Francis Dexter, but a man I've always thought of as my grandfather, even though I called him Uncle Charles. He came up with the name 'Eudora.' It means 'precious gift' in Greek."

"And she is precious to you."

I nodded, hoping my face was less pink than it felt. "I talk to her. She helps me think about things and make decisions. That's why I was so upset to find a crack in her wood. It's as though I'm killing her by staying in Egypt. A dry climate is bad for cellos."

"I think I can help," said Adam. "I have a storage room here—my wine cellar, actually—where the humidity is sufficiently high to prevent further damage. You may store Eudora there for the rest of your stay in Luxor."

"That would be wonderful. Thank you, Adam. How long will you be in Egypt?" I asked.

"As long as I am needed." There was almost nothing on his plate, but he watched me pick up knife and fork as though studying my table manners. "I see you are wearing your beautiful ring."

"Yes. I found it in my luggage. Won't you be busy meeting with people from the Egyptian government? To discuss nuclear energy?"

He smiled. A lazy, promising smile. "In time, yes. But right now, I have other concerns. Tell me about your studies."

"Oh, I can't imagine you want to hear about undergraduate courses in ancient history. Your life must be much more interesting than mine."

"Your life interests me because it's yours, France," he said, reaching across the table and touching my hand.

Our conversation after that was more entertaining than informative. Which was fine with me.

After the meal, Adam led me to a room I didn't remember seeing earlier, and motioned toward a *chaise longue* upholstered in dark blue. He offered me a glass of brandy and seated himself in a chair with gilded lions' heads on the arms.

I sipped the amber liquid and admired Adam. The soft light of the room suited him, shadowing his eyes and enhancing his air of mystery. A mystery I was eager to explore.

He might have been reading my thoughts. "How long can you stay? Is anyone expecting you back in Luxor, or anywhere else?"

"I have no schedule. No one knows I'm here, and I'm sure no one cares. I'm completely at your disposal." A feeling of delicious recklessness enclosed me.

"Well, in that case, our adventure can start tomorrow."

"Or even right now," I said, hoping he understood my meaning.

"You must be well rested before we undertake what I have in mind. France, are you ready to do what no one has done in three thousand years—enter an unopened tomb?"

"What?" I nearly spilled my drink—not good, either on the beautiful dress or the beautiful upholstery. Surely Adam was a little tipsy, even though I hadn't seen him drink anything. I sat up and put my feet on the floor, along with my glass. *These sandals are so beautiful. And my feet look good in them, but I sure as heck never put on gold toenail polish.*

"You're surprised?"

It took me a couple of seconds to realize he wasn't talking about my gilded toenails. I looked up. "Well, yes, I am. How would the two of us find a tomb no one else has, over thousands of years?"

He gazed into my eyes, a smile emerging on his lips. "By magic."

"Magic! But you're a scientist!"

The smile widened. "To those without understanding, science is the same as magic. Here, I'll show you."

Adam helped me to my feet and led me over to a tall mirror, framed in gilt and blue enamel. He turned me to face it and stood behind me, his left hand on my shoulder and the right at my waist.

He must be at least six feet two. Maybe more. And if I was a cello, or a double bass, he'd be playing me.

"Look at yourself, my golden girl."

I *was* golden—my blond hair, the gold in my necklace and arm rings, the embroidery on my dress, the sandals. But my skin was golden too, metallic, gleaming. *It's the mirror, it has to be!* I held up my hand and looked at it directly. Golden skin, golden fingernails. And yet, in my reflection, the fabric of the dress was white, some of the beads in my necklace were blue, and my grey eyes were startling amid all that gold.

I twirled around and faced Adam. "How did you do this?"

He laughed. "An experiment. No, don't panic! All I've done is bring you here and observe. You don't know what you are, the power you have. But you will discover it, with my help."

Overwhelmed with wonder and strangeness, I flung away the last scraps of caution. I pressed my body against his and wrapped my golden arms around him.

"Yes! Show me what you want me to do, and I'll do it."

I expected him to gather me in his arms and kiss my waiting—and no doubt golden—lips. I desired his kiss and was eager to respond passionately. I was ready for a mad adventure—tomb-finding, sure, but before that, I wanted to explore *him*.

Adam just stood there, a puzzled look on his face. Puzzled and—could it be?—fearful. Maybe he was worried about the difference in our ages.

"It's all right, Adam. I'm happy to be here with you and… I want you to kiss me."

Five seconds went by. I knew that because I counted my heartbeats. Then Adam bent his head and carefully pressed his lips to mine. His body was tense; the muscles of his back quivered under my hands.

I wanted to comfort and encourage him. I stroked his back and responded to his kiss, showing him I wanted more. For a moment he kissed me back with urgency and passion, pulling me close against him.

Then he twisted and backed away, his features creased. With distaste? Pain? Definitely not passion. With three feet of empty air between us, he tilted his head like the RCA Victor dog listening for his master's voice.

"No, France," he said, after a moment. "Not now. Not yet. In fact, I think it's time we ended this evening. I will call my servants to conduct you back to your room."

I stood there alone, throbbing like a plucked string and feeling stupid.

12
The Chapter of a Passage in Darkness

They appeared before I could think. This time, Adam's two servants wore dark blue suits whose jackets buttoned right up to their chins, reminding me of the Mao suits worn by some radical socialists in a couple of my college classes. They also sported little red *tarboosh* hats, complete with black tassels, which would have struck me as funny if I hadn't been so embarrassed.

"This way, Miss France," said one of them. Arriving at my room, the other said, "Good night, Miss," and they left me alone.

Alone. I sat down on my bed and put my face in my hands. I wanted to cry, and to be anywhere but here. Unfastening the necklace, I let it slide onto the bed and slipped off the arm rings to join it. I felt lighter, but empty and scared.

What had happened? I replayed the events of the evening in my memory, searching for something I might have done to repel Adam. He had called me his golden girl and promised me an adventure. Whereupon I turned around and hugged him—no, more than hugged. I had pressed myself against him, like Dr. Stanton had against me. Maybe that was it—my forwardness had repelled Adam, as Dr. Stanton's had me. After those few ecstatic seconds, he had pulled away, as though someone tapped him on the shoulder. I could have sworn his face had twisted with repugnance. Or fear, which was even weirder.

I remembered a plastic boy-doll Alma had bought as a Christmas present for one of my half-sisters. Its name was "Ken," and it was supposed to be the boyfriend of a plastic female called "Barbie," that had been the previous year's gift.

"No other kid in England will have one of these," Alma said, as we wrapped and packed Ken for his trip across the Atlantic. What struck me about him was his smooth, pinky-beige body, plain as a stick. I'd had enough experience at dances and on dates to know about male anatomy. Of course, it was a child's toy, so anatomical correctness was out, but Barbie, as I recalled, had two bumps in the right spots. Was Adam like Ken? I blurted a sad giggle and wiped my eyes with my fingers.

My fingers! They were back to their normal suntanned brown colour. I stood, making the dress rustle faintly. The embroidered *ankhs* were gold, the sandals were gold, the discarded jewelry on the bed was gold, but I—France Leighton—had returned to my normal colour. Golden brown, maybe, but definitely not metallic gold.

I hoisted Meg's rucksack onto the bed and extracted my pyjamas. Wrinkled, cold and clammy, they smelled strangely musty. But they were familiar, and mine. I disengaged myself from the Egyptian dress and slipped into them. The peculiar smell vanished as my body warmed the fabrics.

Eudora. I snapped open the latches of her case and lifted her out. My hollow wooden friend. I felt for the slight irregularity of the crack in her wood. It was still there but hadn't grown.

"How are you, dear?" I sat on the bed and stood her up before me, turned her around and ran my hands over her planes and contours. No other cracks, thankfully. "Tell me you're all right." I laid her on my knees and gently plucked her strings, drawing forth an anguished throb.

France, you have to start using your head. First, think about how strange this place is.

"Strange? Sure, okay, it is kind of strange. But there's no harm in staying here for a few days. Adam is no Dr. Stanton. More the opposite, actually."

Exactly! You've been thinking—or hoping—that he's a young man, not much more than thirty. Right? And you're a young woman, a reasonably attractive one. So why would he reject you when you showed him you wanted him?

"Because he just didn't want to. He wasn't ready. Oh, I don't know!"

Think—if it isn't sex he wants, it's something else. He's dazzled you with glamour. Glamour in the original sense of the word, meaning enchantment. He needs you for something he doesn't want to tell you about. Something to do with opening a tomb.

"That's stupid! What could I possibly do for him? He could get into any tomb he wants without me. Well, maybe the Egyptian Antiquities Department would have something to say about it, but that's all. Listen, I've been thinking, and here's my theory. Adam is involved with the movies. You know, that movie *Cleopatra*. Maybe they're going to shoot some of it here, and Adam has something to do with it."

Silly, France! Why would a nuclear physicist be involved in making movies?

"Not so silly. He could be doing special effects. That thing I saw, the one like a *djed* pillar, I'll bet it's some kind of scientific... thing."

It may be scientific, but you have no idea what it's for, and he got all prickly when you asked about it.

"That's because the movie people wouldn't want anyone to know about the special effects."

You and your silly notions! Forget that movie idea and consider this—there are no lamps in this house. Haven't you noticed that? No lamps, no light bulbs, but there is light. Where does it come from?

"That's my point. It's a new invention. Adam says nuclear power can do things that look miraculous."

"Adam says," and you believe him. But you still don't know where this place is. You could have been transported anywhere while you were unconscious.

"Okay, Smarty-Pants, what do you think I should do? Leave?"

Great idea, except it's too late. I'm betting you'll find you can't just pick up your luggage and walk out the door. Where is the door? You have to ask yourself questions. "What am I seeing here? Does it make sense?"

"But when I told him about your wood drying out and cracking, he said he has a room with higher humidity where you could stay for a few days. It might help, and anyway, that shows he's being considerate."

How would it help? As soon as we leave this place, my wood will dry out again. That would be worse than keeping things the way they are. And do you really want him to hide me in some cellar?

"Okay, you're right. It's best if we stay together. Let's play. How about *Après un rêve*? Only it'll be before *un rêve*. I'm getting sleepy."

I played and she sang for me, one more time. The dreamy, languid melody relaxed and reassured me, until I thought about the poem behind the music. My cello teacher had insisted I read it, both in French and in translation. It was about a beautiful love that turned out to be an illusion, a dream.

As I prepared to put Eudora back into her case, she emitted a gruff tone. "What's up?" I said.

Think about that music, France. There's a reason you picked that piece. Illusions can look real, until they don't.

"Are you referring to Adam?"

Those wonders and secrets he keeps promising you. Finding an intact tomb no one else knows about. How likely is that? He looks young, but he isn't. People in that village say he's dangerous and evil. You heard Mr. Mohamed. And what about Andre? He said this person comes and goes. Why has he come now, if he hasn't been here since 1935? Because you're here, that's why.

"Oh, rubbish! I'm too tired to deal with this."

Sleep, then. But take care of that ring. Remember how it helped you play the Beethoven trio. You need to keep it safe, because I think it's part of what he needs from you. He keeps asking you about it, doesn't he?

I closed the lid of the cello case and snapped down the latches. That's what I got for letting Eudora loose when I was tired, and a little drunk too. Despite my weariness, I started to fret, which brought back my anxiety and loneliness.

That pink telephone... Would Adam mind if I made a long-distance call to Providence? Or at least phoned the dig house and talked to Meg? I picked up the receiver. Silence, followed by the sound of wind. No dial tone, no operator's voice, only the sibilance of air moving over a bleak place. I jiggled the hook button without result. I dialed zero. Silence again. I was about to hang up, when I heard a tiny chattering, like a mouse laughing. "Hello, hello?" I said.

"Hello, hello?" The tiny voice mocked. A jumble of other voices followed, with only a few words I could understand. "Five." "Guile." "*Patrimoine.*" Voices from somewhere else, followed by a dark silence.

Phone service was probably shaky here, wherever "here" was. But the sounds and voices were creepy, especially when I noticed there was no wire connecting the phone to the wall. It was a toy, an artifact, a fake. *So what made those sounds? Special effects?*

Now I couldn't sleep. My mind churned and ground. Here I was in this house removed from the real world, inhabited only by Adam Dexter and his twin servants. Did the moon ever shine onto this house? I got up and went over to the wall with windows near the ceiling. They were too high for me to see out of, and there wasn't a piece of furniture tall enough to climb on. There was just enough light in the room—that weird, sourceless light—to see the clothes chest, the doorway to the bathroom, and the dark shapes of my knapsack, beach bag and Eudora. But the windows were black rectangles. I saw no stars.

What about the dress and jewels? Why was Adam surprised to see them? Who undressed me when I was first brought here? Adam? Considering his reaction to my display of desire, that idea shouldn't have disturbed me, but it did.

I imagined falling asleep and waking to the sound of footsteps, hearing the rattle of the latch, seeing a shape enter the room and approach the bed. What kind of shape would it be?

A dreamy terror stole over me, freezing my resolve and paralyzing my limbs. I had to get out of here, but I didn't know how. The prospect of wandering around the house terrified me. I hoisted Eudora onto the bed, case and all, and cuddled up to her unyielding contours. It was sort of like hugging Adam. The thought almost made me giggle and drove back the fear enough that I dozed off.

And dreamed of wandering through the passages and chambers of a tomb and entering the burial chamber, where a lidless stone sarcophagus gaped obscenely. A linen-wrapped shape lay within. Something mummified but not dead...

Silence returns, as it has for three thousand years. Nothing moves in the passages and chambers delved into solid stone. Inks and pigments maintain static shapes. Dust retains the marks of sandals made by those who brought the Osiris-one to the tomb, along with the gold and the jewels. Echoes of breaking and making have died away. A scorpion scrabbles through limestone fragments, and a colony of ants busies itself near a fissure that leads to the outer world. Masses of stone flex and stretch, limestones and shales expressing their essential rhythms. Poised between earth and air, the Peak stands, holds, and dreams.

I wanted to wake but sleep held me down like a slab of stone. My neck was gripped in paralysis, aching, rigid. Unable to move my head, I gave up and slept again.

Finally waking to ache and sickness, I rolled out of bed, lurched to the toilet, puked and shuddered. When that was over, I washed out my mouth with water, spat, splashed my face and groaned. My head throbbed and my eyeballs felt a size too big. How much brandy had I drunk, anyway?

The light beyond the slit-like windows suggested morning had come. Lying down again, I made a mental list of Things to Do. Simple: get dressed, pack up, find Adam and tell him thanks and goodbye. That's where it stopped being simple. Unless things had changed, I would need his help, or at least his cooperation, to find my way back to somewhere familiar.

Just in case, I tried the pink phone again. It was dead and silent—no desert wind, no chattering laugh, no disconnected voices. *What did you think, France? That it would have grown a cord and started to work?*

I had to repack all the clothes I'd pulled out of the knapsack while looking for my ring. The white and gold dress lay on the chest where I had tossed it the night before. I folded it up and opened the chest to put it back in, but I couldn't resist a peek at what else was in there. Another dress, of dark red linen, with many pleats and a bodice trimmed with black, white and yellow beads, in a complicated pattern of lines and squares. And matching red sandals. Pretty nice, I thought, but it's too late. I'm getting out of here.

Take the red dress.

The dress was mine. I was as sure of that as I could be. The conviction had nothing to do with Adam. It came from somewhere else. I rolled up the dress and stuffed it and the sandals into the knapsack.

Deciding on practicality instead of glamour, I put on a blouse and Bermuda shorts. And the emerald ring. Wearing it was the best way to keep it safe.

I was about to sling the knapsack onto my back when someone knocked at the door. Startled, I dropped the knapsack as the door opened. The two servants stood there, still wearing their blue Mao suits and *tarbooshes*.

"Miss Leighton," they said. Both of them spoke, tonelessly and in perfect unison. "Come with us now."

They glided toward me, one to each side, and took my arms. Their hands felt strangely cold. I suppressed an impulse to break away and run. Where would I go? And anyway, I had to talk to Adam, but I didn't like being conducted to him like a prisoner.

In the room with the black and white floor, the *djed*-like lamp—or whatever it was—glowed a rich gold. Adam stood waiting for me, looking like a photo of an old-fashioned archaeologist, in a khaki linen suit. I wondered if he had a pith helmet standing by to complete his outfit.

"Good morning, Adam," I said. "I'm sorry, but I've decided I don't really want to be involved in hunting for tombs. I'd rather go back to—"

"It's too late for second thoughts, France."

He came close enough that I smelled his incense-like cologne, and took both my hands in his. Only for a second, though. He dropped my left hand as though it had burned him and stepped back.

"We will begin today," he said.

I pulled my right hand free. "No. I'm not feeling well, and I still don't understand how we could find a tomb that real archaeologists haven't found already. And anyway, it's all fake, isn't it? You're involved with the movies, aren't you?" I waved my hand at the *djed* pillar instrument. "Special effects, right? Maybe you thought I'd be thrilled to see a fake tomb, but I'm not."

"Fake? Movies? I know nothing of such nonsense. I'm offering you the experience of a lifetime, and you want to throw away the chance. I see I must take a different approach before it's too late."

Geez, he sounds like Peter Cushing in The Curse of Frankenstein!

Adam made circling motions with his hands and struck his palms together. The light emitted by the *djed*-like instrument dimmed, casting the room into an eerie dusk. Instead of the suit, Adam now wore an Egyptian kilt, a jeweled pectoral necklace, and the striped headcloth of a pharaoh. On his forehead was neither the cobra nor the vulture, but something with tentacles. His eyes were orbs of hot copper.

How did he do that? Special effects, for sure.

"Now do you see who I am? Do you still refuse to do my will?" His voice boomed and echoed. "You cannot escape. My servants answer to me. They will follow you and yours, to the ends of the earth, forever."

I turned and fled. Where? Anywhere! No—I had to get Eudora. Back to my room! I ran for the hallway with the hieroglyphic walls, but there seemed to be more twists and turns than I remembered. The dimness didn't help, but at least I heard no one following me, neither Adam nor his servants. I heard his voice, though, chanting, intoning. Commands to the servants? Or a curse?

A wall loomed on my right. I dodged left, bounced off another moving wall and raced down a straight corridor that looked like the right one. Here was the doorway, here was the door. I darted in and shut it behind me, cursing the lack of a bolt or lock.

Well, it didn't matter. I was going to get my stuff and run. The knapsack sat where I'd left it, with my beach bag slumped next to it, but the cello case was missing. Eudora was gone.

"Oh, where *is* she?" A spasm of intense vertigo nearly threw me to the floor. I closed my eyes and concentrated on regaining stability before running back to the door. "He can't *do* this! I'll *make* him give her back!"

The door was locked. Locked from the outside or stuck, but in any case, immovable. I screamed and pounded on it, to no avail. My next impulse was to collapse in near-hysterical tears, but I didn't indulge it. Adam was insane and dangerous. He had devices at his disposal, not to mention servants who obeyed him unquestioningly. I had to get out.

The windows were impossible, but wasn't there another door? The one Adam said didn't go anywhere, was just an ornament. I approached it carefully, afraid to find it was indeed a fake, and not a means of escape.

It looked fake, like that phone. Painted plaster or wood? I laid my palms against it. It *was* wood. I pushed against the panel, and it yielded, creaking open slowly, revealing thick darkness.

My flashlight! I raced for my beach bag, digging around in it on my way back to the door, fingers seeking its cylindrical shape. *Yes!* I turned it on and aimed its beam into the black aperture. A passage led beyond the range of my light. I had no idea where it went, but it was a way out of this room, and maybe the house.

I rushed for the knapsack and was about to pick it up when I heard the bedroom door's latch click open. At the same time, my escape door started to close. The narrow panel swung slowly toward me.

"No!" I lunged for it and stuck out my arm, just in time. The flashlight lay on the floor a couple feet away, next to the knapsack. "Shit!" I jammed the beach bag into the doorway to keep it open while I scrambled back for the torch and knapsack. As I grabbed them, the bedroom door opened and Adam's servants entered, moving toward me with menacing intent.

I dived for the escape door and forced myself through it, tripping over the beach bag and landing on the knapsack. The door slammed shut behind me as the flashlight slipped out of my hand and went out, entombing me in utter darkness.

I heard nothing from behind me, and the door stayed shut. I groped around for ages before I found the flashlight. Switched on, it revealed walls and floor of greyish-white, irregular stone. Shining the light to where the escape door should have been showed only rough stone, as though the door had ceased to exist. I couldn't go back, even if I wanted to. But surely there was a way forward.

I struggled to my feet, slung on the knapsack, and got going. After a few yards, the passage narrowed and lowered considerably, forcing me to crouch and then crawl. The knapsack scraped the ceiling and my bare knees felt bruised and raw.

The flashlight's batteries must have been running down; the light dimmed and flickered. To save it for dire need, I made a hard decision and turned it off, invoking darkness thick as molasses. I put the flashlight back into the bag and concentrated on crawling forward. Surely this tunnel led somewhere, and at its end I would do whatever it took to recover my cello.

After what felt like miles, although it was probably less than a hundred feet, I bumped into a solid wall. Despair nearly engulfed me. Now what? I couldn't go back, and if this tunnel came to a dead end here, so would I. But the floor felt smoother, and there were no walls on either side of me. I dug out the flashlight again, hoping it would work. I pressed the switch.

Nothing happened. Desperate, I jiggled the damned thing, producing a faint, jittering light. Not good enough. A harder thump brightened things up enough to show me a corridor leading both right and left.

I closed my eyes and thought hard. I didn't have enough battery power to make the wrong choice. I wanted to find Eudora and get away from this hellish place. Which was more important? The exit, of course. Once I escaped, I could come back for Eudora with reinforcements—someone from the village or police from the station near the ferry landing. But right now, I had to get away from Adam's house.

During the walk Adam and I had taken around the garden, he had indicated that el-Qurn lay beyond his house and to the left, so I decided to proceed in that direction. I could be hopelessly wrong, but I had made my decision using the data I had to work with.

At least I could walk upright again, and I was heartened by the fact that the passage seemed to slope ever so slightly upward. I pointed my light straight ahead and marched on.

Maybe that's why I almost missed the opening on my right. I was nearly past it before the absence of a wall registered on my awareness.

It was a chamber, not another tunnel or cross-passage. I played my light around it, picking out a jumble of hieroglyphs, horizontal lines, and painted figures. Dim as it was, my light showed me scenes similar to the ones in the Tombs of the Nobles. Was this a tomb? Instead of harvesting grain or grapes, here the busy brown men were engaged in slaughter, or maybe torture. Blood ran in rivulets. Human figures writhed in agony. Gape-jawed crocodiles awaited grisly meals.

I didn't want to see these sights. I swept the light toward the floor, illuminating clay vessels and a pile of unidentifiable wooden objects, but I didn't bother to look at them. My full attention was taken up with the body right in front of me.

In the circle of light, Dr. Stanton's eyes stared blankly at the ceiling. The lips he had pressed to mine hung open, matching the gaping grin of the wound in his throat.

I stood frozen, noting how the light jittered as my hand shook. After an unknown interval, I became aware of the brain-alarm clanging away in my skull.

Let's go, France, he's dead, let's go, France, he's dead, let's go, France, he's dead! Let's go, goddamn it! He's dead.

Except I couldn't move, like a machine that had blown a fuse. I couldn't move, but I really didn't want to keep looking at Dr. Stanton's dead face, and especially that grinning gash under his chin.

"Of course, you want revenge." I heard Adam's words in my head.

"Oh no. Not like this." My lips shaped the words, but no sound came out.

Then I heard something—a slow, gritty shuffle and drag, coming closer. I flicked off my light, dropped to the floor and scrambled sideways, pressing myself close to the wall near the doorway. I saw no light in the passageway, but the noises grew louder.

What was it, out there in the dark? An animal? A snake?

The sound stopped, replaced by a low mumbling. Two voices or one? I held my breath. The dragging resumed briefly, followed by a thump close to me. Really close. I took quick, shallow breaths as my heartbeats grew louder and louder. What lurked nearby, watching me with huge, mirrored eyes, sniffing with a nose sensitive enough to distinguish the scent of a living person lying near a dead one? And did its ears, pointed and flared, catch every beat and breath?

Nothing. And nothing. And nothing.

I finally dared to move, gradually uncurled, stretched out legs and arms, got on all fours. I stayed that way for another long minute, listening. Silence. It was time to get out of here. I switched the flashlight back on. Nothing happened, no matter how much I jiggled it or how hard I thumped. Like Dr. Stanton, it was dead, finally and forever.

Okay, France, you'll just have to do the rest of this in the dark. Unless you want to stay here with Dr. Stanton, until whatever that was comes back. No? First, find the doorway and turn right.

Except that wasn't so easy. I felt the wall, but it went on and on without turning a corner, taking me farther into the chamber. I tried to remember if Dr. Stanton's body lay close to the back wall or in the centre of the room. I definitely didn't want to come into contact with it.

I stopped and thought. Okay, if moving to my right wasn't working, the only thing to do was go left. The main thing was to stay with the wall. I shuffled backwards, dragging my hand along its base. Something shifted under my fingers. Pieces of stiff paper. I slipped them into a pocket and went back to feeling my way out.

My feet nudged an obstacle. Not stone, something softer. *Shit! It's the body!* But at the same time my hand felt an outward corner—the doorway.

That didn't make sense. Dr. Stanton's body was well inside the room. Whatever I had bumped with my feet lay close to the doorway. Could Dr. Stanton still be alive? Had I heard his struggles to move, to breathe?

"Dr. Stanton?" My voice sounded weak and silly, swallowed by the darkness. There was no reply, not a groan, not a breath. Part of me wanted to give up, roll into a ball and wait. For what? Daylight? Help? Neither of those would come, but something else might.

Come on, France! Let's get out of here!

I struggled to my feet, holding onto that all-important doorway corner. "Turn right," I muttered, as though it mattered. It didn't, though. I was hopelessly lost. I leaned against the wall, clenched my hands together and pressed them to my lips.

"Oh, please help me! Someone, help! God—gods—if you can hear me, show me how to leave this place!" I was lousy at praying. I had never learned how.

I am with you, and I will show you the way.

"What? Who?"

The voice had spoken from inside me, but it sure didn't sound like me.

I am with you, and I will show you the way.

It sounded amused this time, as though whoever spoke was smiling at my confusion. I opened my eyes. A faint green light illuminated my hands. The emerald in my ring glowed and felt warm, like a living thing. While too faint to light my way, it gave me hope and a reason to keep going.

"All right, Beach Bag and Rucksack, let's hit the road and find Eudora." My voice was harsh but alive. "Rest in peace, Dr. Stanton."

I got moving, shuffling my feet in case of debris or irregularities. *It's simple. Just put one foot in front of the other and keep doing it until you get to the end.*

The end. Whatever it was.

For a while, I counted steps but kept losing track. I got to somewhere around 700 before I gave up. By then, the tunnel was definitely going upward, and I thought the air smelled fresher. And it was a tunnel, not a passage with vertical walls and level floor. I kept bashing my toes on rough spots and wished I had worn sneakers instead of sandals. My toenails were ragged and a couple of toes were oozing blood.

I could see!

I stopped, lifted my head and blinked. I could see the bumps and irregularities in the rough stone of the tunnel. Far ahead gleamed a slice of dazzling light.

"Aah!" I croaked, and started to run, but caught my foot on a projecting stone and almost fell. "Slow down, France. Don't fall on your face when you're almost out."

The tunnel ended at a vertical crack in the stone, so narrow I had to take off the knapsack and work it through ahead of me. The light bounced off rocks and gravel with a stinging glare. It had to be early morning. Ra, newly risen, shone fresh and hot. I leaned against the rock wall, shading my eyes with my hand until they adjusted to the brightness. *Blessed light. Blessed sun. Thanks for getting me out of there.*

Below me was a wadi, sloping down to the Nile, obviously. I could follow it to the river, but did I want to do that? At best, I would end up in the farmlands. In their currently flooded state, they weren't being worked, so there wouldn't be many people around, and any that were probably wouldn't speak English. I couldn't possibly explain my situation or report Dr. Stanton's murder in Arabic. I had to find my way back to Sheikh Abd el-Qurna, and then to Luxor.

The slope opposite me, on the far side of the wadi, looked familiar. But then, any slope around here looked much like another. From the top I would surely get a better view of my surroundings, which was precisely what I had thought just before the fall that landed me in Adam's house.

Watch your step, France!

Down the short, steep, slope I half-walked, half-slid, circumventing boulders at the bottom, where I paused to look down the wadi. Was Adam's villa visible from here? I saw no palm trees; that eerie tropical paradise seemed a million miles away. I started up the slope in front of me.

Come on — up, up, up!

Reaching the top, I was sure I'd found the place where I fell — a narrow saddle of rock, covered with loose gravel that had given way, pitching me over. And yes, beyond the rising slope to my right I could see the Peak, el-Qurn. The village, therefore, was just behind and below a bluff a couple of hundred yards to my left.

I glanced behind me. Two figures moved along the wadi, identical in dark *galabeyas* and turbans. Adam's servants, looking for me. Hot terror leaped in my chest. I turned and ran, knapsack bouncing and jolting. My feet slipped on loose gravel and bumped into rocks. Panic spurred me on, breath wheezing, legs pumping, until I crested the bluff and saw the nearest buildings of the village.

The Kid Alarm announced my return to the guest house. Several children who had been playing near the door ran toward me, yelling. The door banged open and Yasmin ran out.

"Miss France!" She came toward me, hands extended. "Come in, come in, we all worried about you. Are you well?"

I could barely speak. "Let's. Go. Inside. Please." I grabbed Yasmin's arm and dragged her toward the house.

Inside, I dropped my bag and started to laugh, winded
and a little hysterical. Yasmin stared at me, rubbing her arm.

"Oh, I'm sorry, Yasmin. Please. Just wait. A minute." I
bent over, hands on knees, until I caught my breath. "I'm all
right. I think. Oh, I'm so glad to be here! I didn't hurt your arm,
did I?"

"It is all right. Please, let us go into salon. I will bring
tea."

"Wait a second." I ran back to the door—thick and solid,
studded with copper—and opened it a crack. No one was there.
Could they have given up and left? "Okay, let's go."

Soon I was sitting in the guest parlour with a glass of tea
wafting its minty aroma, and—yes!—a plate of date-filled
pastries reminding me I was ravenous. I barely managed a poor
imitation of polite restraint.

"What happened to you?" Yasmin asked, after what she
must have considered a decent interval. My appearance—
dusty, bruised and weary—had surely alarmed her.

"Well, I... Yasmin, there's something... I have to talk to
the police."

"Police! Why? Did someone hurt you? Is that why you
run?"

"No, no one did anything to me. Not really. What I mean
is, I found a... dead person. One of the archaeologists I worked
for in Luxor. He was murdered." Saying it out loud loosened
something inside me, and I started crying.

Yasmin came over and sat next to me. She put an arm
around my shoulders and held one of my hands until I got to
the snuffling stage and excused myself to find a handkerchief.
Searching my pockets, I felt the pieces of stiff paper I had found
near Dr. Stanton and decided to look at them later.

275

Yasmin sat for a few seconds, chewing her lip. "Wait a moment, Miss France. There is a person you must see. I will find him." She ran out of the room, calling out in Arabic. Moments later, she was back. "Two days now, they are searching for a man. An archaeologist. I am thinking it might be the same one." She paused, looking behind her.

Feet clattered nearby and Hank came into the room. He looked tired and frazzled, but he cracked a wide smile on seeing me.

"France! At least one of our missing persons has turned up. Where've you been?"

"Hi, Hank." I didn't want to continue, but I had to. "I know where Dr. Stanton is. At least, sort of where. And... he's dead, murdered. I'm sorry." I was starting to shake again and clasped my arms together to stop it.

Hank dropped onto the settee as though his legs had given way. "Murdered?"

Yasmin poured a glass of tea and offered it to him, but he shook his head. She set it down on the nearby table.

Hank turned toward me. "Where is he?"

"In a... tomb, maybe. A place that looks like a tomb, anyway. A room opening off a passage, and a tunnel too. I think I could find it again. It's on the other side of a ridge, over there." I waved my arm in what I thought was the right direction.

"What were you doing there?"

Well, that was the question, wasn't it? "Oh, I was... exploring." I forced a silly smile. "That talk about undiscovered tombs we had. I thought while I was over here I'd look around a bit. I was going down into a gully—no, I guess it's called a wadi here, isn't it? Anyway, I slipped and fell, and eventually I ended up in that cave. But shouldn't we tell the police?"

Hank and Yasmin glanced at each other. "No," said Hank, turning back to me. "That police station down by the ferry landing is just for giving directions to tourists. They don't do investigations. I organized a search party of the locals to look for Bill. I'd better tell them he's been found. Say, was there only one body?"

"Yes. Why would there be more than one?"

Hank swiped a hand across his forehead. "Well, my Uncle Jim's missing too. Remember him? The geologist?" He reached for the tea and drank it down in three large gulps. "Okay, I'm going to find my searchers, and then we'll go look for your tunnel."

"Do you want me to come along?" Weariness pressed me into the cushions.

Hank must have noticed. "You're pretty beat, aren't you? No, I don't think you need to come, not yet. The fellows know the area pretty well, but we hadn't worked our way to that wadi yet. Okay, we'll see what we can find."

I supplied precise details of the route I had taken. "Do you remember seeing me here that morning? I was staying in one of the rooms upstairs and saw you talking to some men."

"Oh yeah, I guess I did see you. That was at least two days ago, I think. I was getting the search party together. It's all starting to blur. Well, I'd better get going. Thanks for the tea, Yasmin."

Hank left, and Yasmin looked at me. "I am sorry that our guest rooms are all occupied today. I will make you a bed in spare room."

I almost said, "Oh, no thank you, I'll be fine," until I realized I wasn't fine, and I needed a place to hide from Adam's relentless servants. If there was to be a murder investigation, I might have to stay in the area for a while. And I was going to get Eudora back, even though I had no idea how.

"I'm sure the spare room will be fine," I said. "Thank you, Yasmin."

She picked up the tea things and led me through the kitchen to the back of the house, into the part cut into the rock of the hillside. The "spare room" turned out to be a workshop where someone carved and painted wooden reproductions of ancient Egyptian artifacts, presumably for sale to tourists. Tools cluttered a workbench, with a drift of wood shavings on the floor around it. Yasmin pulled a folded cot from a corner and set it up. She vanished for a few moments, returning with a mattress and bedding. I helped her make up the bed and started unpacking my knapsack.

"Where is your music?" asked Yasmin.

"My cello? I... lost it. Actually, someone stole it, but I'm going to get it back."

"Someone stole it?" Yasmin's face creased with concern. "I am sorry."

"Well, it's not your fault." I shook out the red linen dress I had taken from Adam's house. The linen looked brittle. Some of the beads were missing and others were cracked. I hadn't realized the dress was so old. It looked like part of a museum exhibit.

"Oh, so beautiful." Yasmin gently felt the fabric. "Where did you get it?"

"It was... a gift." Except I didn't know from whom.

She looked at me curiously, and then back at the dress. "My sister makes dresses in old Egyptian style, for sale in *souk*. She would like to see."

"Sure," I said. "I'm not planning to wear it right now, but I would appreciate washing up and changing my clothes." What I really wanted was a hot shower, but knowing how water was supplied to the village, that wasn't possible.

"Of course. I will show you washing place."

After as thorough a wash as I could manage, I sorted through my sorry wardrobe and changed into a reasonably clean blouse and skirt. I had no more pretensions to glamour. Remembering the gold-embroidered dress and my attempt to entice Adam, I shuddered. Was he a murderer, or had someone else killed Dr. Stanton? Was the underground room part of Adam's house? Or had I imagined the house? I couldn't shake the feeling I had barely escaped a weird and dangerous situation. Did I have the guts to go back there for Eudora?

The emerald ring looked quite ordinary now. Had it really shone down there in the dark, or had I been hallucinating out of sheer terror? I decided to keep wearing it, for morale if nothing else.

I was growing accustomed to getting dressed and combed *sans* mirror. This room, being a workshop and storage room, lacked any such amenity. I was tucking stray strands of hair into my braid when I noticed an image of Osiris painted on the wall. I remembered catching a glimpse of pictures and hieroglyphs when Yasmin had showed Willa and me around the guest house. Someone must have painted this Osiris in imitation of the ancient Egyptian style. To my inexpert eye, it looked just like the one I had seen in the tomb of Sennefer. The one that stared at me.

While rolling up the Bermudas I had worn in the tunnels, I found the pieces of paper from the tomb. They *were* photographs, with drops and smears of what looked like blood.

I took them closer to the light. One had a white area in a corner. I figured out it was the sky above the edge of a cliff. The other showed cracked and layered rock, with a vaguely spherical formation embedded in it, like a bulging eye. Suddenly, I knew. These were two of the pictures I had taken from the balloon. They were prints from my stolen film.

13
The Chapter of the Red Dress and the Sharp Blade

A few hours later, Hank returned, accompanied by several men from the village. I had spent the time helping Yasmin and her mother in the kitchen, not very capably, but the activity served to distract me from my churning thoughts and apprehensions. Yasmin set a table in the dining room for the searchers, just outside the kitchen door, as distant as possible from those occupied by guests and tourists.

Mr. Mohamed invited us to join the group. Yasmin had to keep jumping up to serve the guests, so wasn't always available to translate. Too bad for me, as most of the conversation was in Arabic.

Hank was glum and dispirited, his usual smile and easy-going humour completely absent. I sat at the opposite end of the table from him, so couldn't ask him questions, and I didn't dare to intrude on Mr. Mohamed. He was too busy and important.

Yasmin came back to the table just as the tone of the conversation took on an especially serious tone. "What are they saying?" I asked her.

She frowned. "A moment, please." Mr. Mohamed was saying something to Hank. To my surprise, he put a hand on Hank's shoulder and gave it a little shake.

Yasmin turned to me. "Yes, they found the cave... the tunnel you told about, and the man you saw there dead. The professor. But there is another dead man."

I was about to say no, there couldn't be. I had seen only one corpse, that of Dr. Stanton. But then I remembered the dragging sounds, and my feet bumping against something as I felt my way out of the underground chamber. I remembered wondering if Dr. Stanton wasn't really dead and had managed to move.

"Who is he? Did anyone recognize him?"

My question fell into one of those sudden silences, and Hank heard it. He turned his tired face toward me. "It's my Uncle Jim, France. He's dead too, just like Bill Stanton."

I felt like someone had thumped me on the back hard enough to knock all the air from my lungs. "Oh, that's terrible," I muttered, even while I recognized what a useless remark this was. I didn't think Hank heard me; he had turned away and was listening to Mr. Mohamed.

When the meal was over and everyone started to disperse, I touched Hank's arm as he went by.

"Hank, wait. I'm so sorry about your uncle. I couldn't understand what everyone was saying. Can you tell me what happened?"

He sighed. "What do you want to know? Gory details?"

"Hey, that's not fair! Don't forget, I was the one who found Dr. Stanton, and that place they were in."

"Okay, you're right," he said. "But I have a shitload of things to deal with now, so I can't take a lot of time to talk."

"Just the basics," I said. We stood near the table, by the forlorn and messy remains of the meal. "Was your uncle killed... the same way as Dr. Stanton?"

Hank shook his head. "No. His neck was broken. Maybe he fell. I don't know. But someone must have moved his body to that tomb chamber. There was all kinds of stuff in there. It looked like a thieves' cache. I have to go to Luxor right away, to tell Adele and get an official investigation going." He gave a fractured laugh. "I guess this'll put the kibosh on Adele's plans to do an end run around Bill. She'll be too busy dealing with the police and other authorities."

"What end run? What was she doing?"

"Looking for Bill's intact tomb, what else? Why do you suppose she went to Cairo last week? To finalize plans with her pal from the Antiquities Department."

Mr. Purple-and-Gold-Necktie. "Oh, I didn't figure that out." I picked up the last date from a platter of fruit and nibbled it.

"Well, I did. That's why Bill and I got things rolling sooner than we'd planned."

I hastily swallowed the rest of the date. "I think I have some evidence—a couple of photos I found near Dr. Stanton."

Hank pressed his lips together and didn't say anything.

I put the date pit on a nearby plate. "The thing is, I'm pretty sure those are pictures I took from the balloon."

"Yeah, okay, they are," he said, looking at the floor. "I took your film, France. I'm sorry. You see, Uncle Jim's camera was smashed in the balloon crash. The gas tank landed right on it and crushed it. We needed photos of the wadi where we figured the tomb might be, and Jim told me you were taking snaps of the same spots as he did. So I developed yours. I should have told you though."

"You got me fired, Hank. You and your pal Bill."

"Fired? How did that happen?"

"It's a long story. Ask Adele. How did Dr. Stanton and your uncle go missing in the first place?" I wiped my date-sticky fingers on my handkerchief.

Hank sighed again and rubbed his face. "Well, I'll be telling this story a lot, so this'll be practice. Okay, Bill was sure he'd figured out where to find his Unbroken Tomb, or at least an undisturbed and undocumented one. Talking it over with Jim after the balloon reconnaissance, he decided the entrance must have been buried by flash flood deposits, just like Tut's. A wadi behind the Valley of the Kings was perfect geologically, according to Uncle Jim. Without the photos, finding the exact spot was going to take too long, so when his film was destroyed, I pinched yours. I'll give you back the prints right now if you like."

"Okay, and I'll give you the two I found. There's something that might be bloodstains on them. What happened next?"

"All three of us went up the wadi soon after sunrise. I went on ahead, looking for a landmark Uncle Jim had noted — a big concretion with iron stains."

"The eyeball! I took at least two pictures of it. And I found one of them by Dr. Stanton's body."

"Yeah, it did look like an eyeball. A bloodshot one. Anyway, I was working my way up this narrow path — well, it wasn't really a path anymore — when I looked back for Jim and Bill. Jim was climbing up some rocks, probably taking samples. Bill was quite a way behind him. I thought I saw two other men, a long way behind us but coming closer. They might have been locals, but we didn't want company, so I figured I'd better backtrack and head them off. I lost sight of everyone for a couple minutes while I climbed down and back through a narrow gap into the main wadi."

Hank puffed out a breath. "I wish we'd stayed together. By the time I got through the gap, there was no one there. No Bill, no Uncle Jim, no men with turbans. I ran around for ages, looking for them, yelling my head off."

"Those two men you saw—was there anything special about them?"

"'Special'? Geez, France, I just caught a glimpse of them, from a couple hundred yards away."

"Well, did they look alike? I mean, identical."

Hank looked at me curiously. "Guys wearing *galabeyas* and turbans tend to look alike, especially from a distance. But now you mention it, those two were both wearing dark colours—black or dark blue. That's kind of unusual. Look, I've got to get going. Where are those photos?"

I hurried back to the spare room and got the two pictures. Hank took a grubby envelope held together with a rubber band out of his shirt pocket and handed it to me. "Okay. I figure I'll be back tomorrow. How much longer are you staying here?"

"I don't know. Another day for sure. I'm pretty tired."

"Well, when you get back to Luxor, I hope you'll stop in at the police station and make a statement. It might help them take the investigation seriously."

"Okay, I'll do that."

"I'd appreciate it. Well, I'm off. Oh, do you have any messages for Adele or anyone else over there?"

"Messages?" I thought for a moment. "Please give Adele my condolences. Say hi to Meg. And Hank, I'm really sorry about your uncle."

The puzzle pieces had been given a good shake, and enough of them had interlocked to show an emerging pattern. I needed to think. The "spare room" in which I was staying was the only place where I would have a hope of privacy. Of course, it was really someone's workshop, occupied by a stack of unshaped wood, a foot-powered lathe, chisels and carving knives, pots of paint, and dozens of figurines intended for sale to tourists. They looked familiar, although brand new and shiny—seated pharaohs, standing pharaohs, Anubises, cats wearing earrings, Nefertiti's bust, scarabs, *djed* pillars, obelisks, and pyramids.

There was a small army of *shabtis*, their hands crossed over their chests, each one with a painted hoe clutched to its chest and a painted basket slung over its shoulder, ready to labour for his dead master. The craftsman, whoever he was, had done a good job on them. Their painted features showed a kind of blank determination that made me a bit uneasy.

Otherwise, the cave-like room was peaceful. The sweet smell of cedar wood mingled with whiffs of turpentine, lamp oil, and ancient stone. I sat on the cot, elbows on knees and my chin in my hands. I missed Eudora. Whenever I had a problem to figure out, I'd been able to see a way through it after a session of plucking and bowing, and listening to her responses.

My problem was getting her back. But I was beginning to think I had a bigger one.

Osiris on the wall opposite me gazed into the distance. Had this image been painted by the person who made the figurines? The paint was faded and pockmarked with nicks and stains, and the proportions and details of the figure were consistent with the ancient tradition. Might this have once been part of a tomb?

Green-skinned Osiris, god of the dead. I remembered reading that deceased persons were endowed with his name in the spells intended to ensure their welfare in the afterlife. Dr. Stanton would be Osiris Dr. William Stanton, archaeologist. And Uncle Jim would be Osiris Dr. James Dykstra, professor of geology.

Click, click, click. More puzzle pieces fell into place, whether I wanted them to or not. Dr. Stanton and Uncle Jim were most likely murdered. The underground chamber in which their bodies were found was close to Adam Dexter's house. Two sinister figures, who were most likely Adam's servants, had followed me ever since I had arrived in Luxor. I had seen them—always two, always identical—as I moved around the streets of Luxor and the dusty roads near the Theban Necropolis. Sometimes they looked like ordinary Egyptians, other times like policemen. Hank had seen them shortly before Dr. Stanton and Uncle Jim vanished.

I thought of the last thing I'd heard Adam say, before I ran from him.

"You cannot escape your fate. My servants answer to me. They will follow you and yours, to the ends of the earth, forever."

These things happened because of *me*. Because I was here. Because Adam needed me for something. He stole Eudora and I had to get her back, but now I was scared of him. Who could help me? Mrs. Devlin might have ideas, but would they make any sense? And associating with me might be dangerous for her and Willa.

I couldn't go home to Providence. If what Adam said was true, his servants would follow me. "To the ends of the earth" certainly included Providence, Rhode Island. I didn't want them anywhere near Alma and Andre and Lucy. Should I beg my way back into the Stanton dig? No—the Stanton dig was probably finished, one way or another. But Adele and the others might need help. Fine, except I'd be bringing my two shadows with me. I couldn't stay here either. Mr. Mohamed and his family didn't need my problems.

I sat and stared at the floor. Dust and wood shavings. My feet in their scuffed sandals. A bug crawling along. It stopped at a wood shaving, went around it, moved on.

"Child of my child."

Great. Now I'm hearing voices.

"Child of my child, look up."

I snapped my head up. Osiris was looking right at me, just like in the tomb of Sennefer. The eyes, outlined in black, gazed with purpose and intention. The nose was straight and long, the lips closed in a secret smile. Weird. Even weirder, he looked sort of familiar, despite the stylized beard.

Did I really hear a voice? I sat frozen, as though keeping still would maintain normalcy.

"You are afraid."

Darn right I am. I swallowed, my throat making a dry click. "Is someone talking to me?" I stood, ready to run, hoping this was something I could escape. Or was I going crazy?

"Wait! Do not be afraid. You are in peril, but not from me."

I heard the voice, but Osiris's painted lips remained closed. If I talked back to it did that mean I was crazier than if I didn't?

"Where are you? Are you really here?" My own voice sounded strange, husky and faint.

"'Here' means nothing to me. I am nowhere and everywhere."

"Okay, so *who* are you?"

"Once, I was Francis Dexter."

"My... grandfather?" No, this couldn't be real.

There was a long pause. *Okay, it's gone.* I was starting to relax when the voice spoke again. "You are my descendant. Child of my child."

"Why should I believe you?"

"Skepticism is useful, but right now you can't afford it. Since you need proof, I will supply it. Listen."

I sat down on the cot again.

"In 1935, I came to Luxor with my friend and servant Andre Boudreau."

"Andre and Lucy are still with Alma," I said. *This is so weird.* Just when I thought I had returned to solid reality after escaping from Adam, here I was, talking with an illusion or hallucination. Osiris Francis Dexter, disembodied voice.

"Andre and I climbed up el-Qurn because I wanted to see the view from the top. Along the way, I experienced a vision of the Goddess of the Peak, Meretseger. She appeared to me in the form of a cobra. On the way back, we were waylaid by robbers in collusion with our guide, a young man named Mahmoud."

"Mr. Mohamed!"

"Perhaps. I don't recall his surname. While the robbers were engaged in rifling our pockets and deciding what to do with us, another individual arrived, the one you know as 'Adam Dexter,' although he used another name then. Under the guise of rescue, he spirited us to what appeared to be a house or villa."

I paid closer attention.

"He offered us food and drink. I took nothing, but Andre tasted a little and became disoriented. He told me later it was like being trapped in a whirlwind of rooms and flashing lights. Only when I called upon Meretseger did we manage to escape. Mahmoud had a change of heart in the meantime and helped us get back to Luxor. I believe the goddess rewarded him, through me."

I slapped my hands together. "You're the American who gave him gold! He used it to build a guest house. This house where we are—where I am now."

"May I assume my tale is proof enough for you?"

His story was pretty much the same as Andre's. I looked at the floor again. The bug—or was it a different one?—was trundling toward the wall. *Dead end, my friend.*

"All right, I guess I have to believe you."

"We are of one blood," he continued, "but more than that, we share knowledge of matters removed from the ordinary concerns of the world, yet with potentially enormous effects."

"Effects like murder?"

"Murder, certainly," said the voice that called itself Francis Dexter, "but even more than that. There are powers seeking to enter our sphere, unknown except to those I call the Company of Outsiders—individuals such as I was, and you are. We have abilities that are hidden and irrelevant, until they aren't."

"That sounds like Mrs. Devlin." I wasn't sure if I was talking to him or myself.

"Amelia Devlin?" he asked. "You've met her?"

"Yes. She's here in Luxor. Or was, a few days ago. She says I have special abilities. But then, Adam Dexter told me the same thing. Is he also of your blood?"

I must have offended him, because a long moment of disapproving silence passed before he replied. "The thing that calls itself Adam Dexter is of no one's blood. It is a manufactured entity, an avatar representing a force from Outside."

An avatar? From Outside? Give me a break. "He did seem rather bloodless."

I must have rolled my eyes or given some other sign of what I was thinking, because the voice got all stern and solemn. "France, listen to me. I am not here for casual chit-chat, however amusing you may find it. I have violated laws of the world beyond to speak with you."

"I'm sorry. All right, I'm listening."

"Good. Because there is something else you must know. When I was in Luxor in 1935, I did not have with me the emerald ring I see on your left hand."

I looked at the ring. The stone glowed a faint green, as it had when I was lost in the tunnels. "Uncle Charles gave it to me when I turned twenty-one."

"Charles." If a voice could smile, his did. "I trusted him to choose the next person to have the ring. He chose you."

"Did he know I was your granddaughter?"

"I don't know. I think he must have. But without that ring—which was in Charles's keeping at the time—I was of no use to the thing that calls itself Adam Dexter. I suspect that's why he let Andre and me escape."

"But you said that cobra goddess saved you."

"She did, but he didn't find it worthwhile to pursue us. You see, France, he wants—needs—both you and the ring to attain his objectives. To that end, I suspect he's created illusions to amuse and delight you."

He paused, as though waiting for me to say something. *Well, I wasn't exactly delighted, but you don't need to know about that.* "Yes, I suppose he did. In a way."

"He intends to discover the nature of the force you carry within yourself. And then to extract that force, by whatever means are necessary, and use it for his purposes."

"What are his purposes? Do you know?"

"I can guess. What did he promise you?"

"Adventures and secrets. He said we would enter a tomb that's never been opened."

"He is an avatar of the Nameless One, assuming whatever form is expedient to do his bidding. The tomb in question contains the heart of the Black Pharaoh, Nephren-Ka. If the dispersed parts of his soul are reunited, he will come forth. That would bring about a catastrophic convergence of forces."

I thought about what I knew of the ancient Egyptian concept of the soul. The body, the ghost, the spirit, the name, the essence, the heart. The heart, in which resided will and intention. "So Adam wasn't just going to take me on a treasure hunt."

"No, not at all. Once he attains his objective, he will dispatch you without mercy."

"So what am I supposed to do? He said I can't escape. His servants will follow me anywhere I go. And they've already killed Dr. Stanton and Dr. Dykstra, I'm sure of that."

"Two deaths are less than nothing to him." He paused for a moment. "What should you do now? Surrender."

"What? Surrender to Adam? But you said—"

"Not *to* him. Never to him. You must surrender to the powers that course through you as air through a hollow reed. You will not be alone. Greater forces will make you their instrument, especially that which is called the goddess Meretseger, she of silence and the Peak above the tombs. Listen for her voice and act as she directs you."

"How do you know all this stuff? Why should I believe you?"

"Because I learned these things from Death. I had no other teacher. You do."

"Alma, my grandmother—did you love her?"

Another long silence, and then, "Yes. I loved her. Go forth now, child of my child, and meet your fate."

"Wait! I need to know more about you."

"You don't need to know more about me. Not now. I've told you all you need to know. But if you survive, ask Alma. Goodbye."

Francis Dexter was gone. The chipped and faded profile of Osiris gazed away from me, into eternity.

I laid my hands on my thighs and took a deep breath. "Okay," I said, "let me get this straight. Adam is an avatar, representing a monstrous force from Outside. So is a pharaoh called Nephren-Ka, except he's missing part of his soul. Adam wants to find that piece so he can bring Nephren-Ka back to life and the two of them can team up to... destroy the world. Right—Adam can make a great big bomb. If the monstrous force wants him to. And little France Leighton can stop it, according to my Grandpa's ghost. Oh, and maybe while I'm at it, I can get my cello back. But first I have to surrender."

I choked down a hysterical laugh and sat with my face in my hands, letting all this soak in. My complete lack of ideas about what to do had summoned Francis Dexter. He had given me advice. Without any better options, I'd better consider it.

I had to engage with Adam to recover Eudora. The question was how. I closed my eyes and let my mind drift until the shape of a plan emerged.

I wouldn't approach him as a supplicant. He needed me for a reason I still didn't understand, but that gave me power over him. I would wear the red dress. It was a dress of ancient Egypt, and I liked the colours. Black, white, yellow and red — colours of earth, air, gold, and blood. They had power. And the dress hadn't been given to me by Adam, even though it came from his house.

I couldn't find the dress, and then I remembered Yasmin had asked if she could show it to her sister. The two of them were on the rooftop area that served as the family's dining area and living room, chatting and sewing. My dress hung on the clothesline along with a few other garments. After the usual greetings, I explained that I needed the dress.

"It is very lovely," said Yasmin's sister, whose name, I think, was Samia. "Thank you for let me look at."

"You are going to wear to supper?" asked Yasmin, handing me the garment.

"I'll wear it this evening." I didn't explain that my plans did not include supper at the guest house. Turning to go back downstairs, I noticed two figures standing in the alley below. They were of identical height and build, wearing dark blue *galabeyas* and black turbans. They were waiting for me.

Back in my room, I stripped myself naked and put on the red dress, careful not to damage the fragile fabric. I was pretty sure ancient Egyptian women didn't wear panties or bras, so neither did I. Sneakers were the logical choice for the terrain I would be crossing, but right now logic was suspended. I fastened on the red sandals that went with the dress, hoping they and my feet would survive whatever would happen to them.

Is this surrender?

Looking through the photos Hank had given me, I found one that showed a grey blur, as though poorly focussed. On closer scrutiny I made out clear details of rock formations around the edges. I was sure the blur was in fact the red glow I had seen from the balloon. I saw it right after the eyeball rock, didn't I? I found the photo of the concretion and examined it closely. That was my destination. How I reached it, and what would happen there was in the hands of the gods.

Is this surrender?

I hoped that cobra goddess was listening. What was her name?

Meretseger. She who loves silence. *Dehenet Imentet.* The Lady of the Western Peak.

Over the dress, I put on the useful *galabeya,* disguising the ancient Egyptian woman as a modern Egyptian man. I hoped it and the turban would give me a better chance to get where I was going without being questioned or helped in ways I didn't appreciate.

I was tucking in the last folds of the turban when I heard a slapping of feet on the stone floor of the passage. Yasmin went by, carrying a big water jar. Glancing into the room, she shouted something in Arabic.

She thought I was a man! Probably the one who used the room as a workshop, but not while the room was occupied by "Miss France," of course. Yasmin would be back as soon as she got rid of the water jar, to straighten "him" out.

I raced for the door. Once outside, I took off at a run, along the road leading up the lower slopes toward Deir el-Bahari and the temple of Hatshepsut. I didn't look back until I had to stop and catch my breath.

There they were—those two determined shapes I had seen so many times, but whose significance I had failed to comprehend until now. No one else was following me, though. I set off again, toward the Valley of the Kings.

The eastern slopes of el-Qurn darkened as the sun slipped lower, soon to vanish behind the Theban Hills. A coachload of tourists passed me, heading toward the river and the ferries, to their hotels, to convivial meals and conversations about sights seen and plans for the next day. I had no such plans.

The two dark figures stayed a hundred feet behind me, but once past the signposted entrance to the Valley of the Kings, they drew nearer. The road narrowed to a path. This place had probably changed little since the days of the pharaohs.

I decided to stop and wait for my pursuers. Escorts? Captors? The warm brown colour of the stony slopes became ashen grey. A vulture glided overhead and a small, chilly breeze wafted down the wadi. Gravel gritted beneath my feet as I turned to meet my guides.

They did not hurry, maintaining their relentless progress, legs and arms moving in mechanical unison, until they stopped a few feet away from me.

"Good evening." I thought a certain formality was in order. "I assume you are here to conduct me to Adam Dexter. Or do you call him *Alyad Alyumnaa*?"

"We do not call," said the figure on the left. "Pharaoh calls us," said the other. "We answer to him," they chorused in unison.

"'Pharaoh'? Well, that's interesting. Would you be willing to answer a few questions?"

They stood and stared at me, eyes sharp and narrow. Their other features were rudimentary, as though pinched and squeezed out of clay—shallow ridges of nose, horizontal mouth-slits between minimal lips. Each of them carried a coiled whip and a long knife in a sheath on a shoulder strap.

"We answer to Pharaoh. Miss Leighton, come with us. He is waiting." They moved, one to either side of me.

"Wait a minute." I unwrapped the turban and rolled up the cloth. Bending over, I grasped the hem of the *galabeya* and pulled it up and off. I folded it roughly and set it on a nearby boulder, placing the turban cloth on top and weighing them down with a rock. I shook out my hair. "All right, let's go." I started up the path, toward the place where the valley sides steepened and converged to a black "V," with the burning sunset beyond.

After a few steps, I had to confess a certain gratitude for the presence of my two guides. They knew exactly where we were going. Head-sized rocks studded the slope, along with stretches of gravel, treacherous underfoot as the path steepened. Scattered potsherds were the only other signs of human activity.

We reached the top of the slope at the full glory of sunset, the moment when Ra's barque teeters on the brink before entering the nether regions. The ground leveled out and cliffs loomed on either hand. Erosion had created column-like structures resembling tall figures with bulbous heads, sagging bellies, skinny legs, bony knees, and multiple dangling arms. They stood on a thick layer of jumbled rocks and dirt that reminded me of the bound and crushed enemies trodden upon by triumphant pharaohs in Egyptian art. Fan-shaped deposits of loose sand and gravel formed a scalloped fringe at the cliff bottom.

Trudging along, I imagined the sights the grotesque figures must have witnessed three thousand years ago. A funeral procession of mourners, priests, officials and burden-bearers, carrying a mummified being to her final resting place…

Sistrums shake and rattle, a drum sounds single notes. Wailing voices blend with the chanting of Amun's priestesses. "Courage, my sisters! I have done my part, now you must do yours. My fingers clasp the black heart-stone. I wrapped them around it as I drew my final breaths, and I will never give it up. Take me into the rock and seal me within it, that I may begin my task of millions of years."

My toes bumped a rock and I came back to myself. Had I been sleepwalking? The cliffs were higher here, the path narrower, a faint groove worn into the dirt. Uncle Jim had said floods washed these sediments into the wadis. I was seeing them now, up close and personal. It was strange to think of water thundering down the narrow valley, a brown river of mud and stones filling it, hiding its secrets forever…

My head jerked up again. This wouldn't do. I had to pay attention to my surroundings and find that bulging stone eyeball, because it marked my destination. Whatever was going to happen would happen there, because that was the place of the tomb. Her tomb. The tomb of…

Meresamun. Beloved of the god.

Just ahead, two huge rock masses leaned together. *That's the place. In there.* Adam's servants drew closer, each clasping one of my arms above the elbow. My stomach grew cold. What was Adam like, now that he was no longer trying to charm me?

We passed through the gap and entered a narrow, cliff-enclosed valley. Scree slopes nearly met in the bottom, and more of the human-like formations looked down as though with regret at something lost or broken. The sky glowed dull orange above their lumpy heads.

The tomb had to be here. Where else could it be? Clasping my hands together, I rubbed the emerald with the fingers of my right hand. For luck. And then I saw it between two of the grotesque shapes—a rough, iron-stained sphere. The eyeball.

A tall shape detached itself from the shadows. Adam. Gone was the nuclear physicist, the imitation archaeologist. He was a pharaoh now. The tall double crown increased his height to freakish proportions. His body was lean, corded with ropy muscles. A broad collar of gold and gems covered the upper part of his chest, and a kilt of black linen was bound around his loins with a wide jeweled belt.

Adam Dexter or Nephren-Ka?

He stepped forward. "Good evening, France. You haven't escaped me after all." His voice, deeper than I remembered, echoed among the enclosing cliffs.

"No, I haven't escaped. And neither have you. I have business with you, Adam."

"I am no longer 'Adam.' Haven't you guessed my true name by now, Francesca Leighton?"

"*Alyad Alyumnaa*? No? Well, how about Murderer of the Innocent?"

"Those are epithets, not names," he said, with a smile. "I am Nephren-Ka. And what's that about the innocent? The word doesn't describe William Stanton, from what you told me about him."

"I never desired his death," I said. *Well, only for a minute or two.* "And Dr. James Dykstra—why him?"

Adam shrugged. "He was getting in the way, trying to find out more about his supposed colleague 'Adam Dexter,' and poking around here with his friend Stanton. If you had cooperated with me sooner, those deaths could have been avoided, so don't consider yourself blameless."

"I didn't cut anyone's throat," I said, eyeing the long, sheathed knife hanging over the shoulder of the figure standing on my left. The one on my right was similarly equipped.

"Never mind that," said Adam. "We have business together, as you've admitted. The time for it has come." He stepped closer. "Show me your hands."

I held them out, palms up. I knew what he wanted, but I wasn't going to make it easy for him.

Frowning, Adam took hold of my left hand and turned it over. The emerald gleamed faintly in the fading light. I thrust it toward him. The gem sparked a hot green and he snatched his hand back with a suppressed gasp.

"Well, Adam, I guess you want this ring—and me—but you're afraid of it. With reason—it's dangerous. Your servants took my cello. If you give her back, I might be more cooperative."

He stepped back a few paces, reached for something, and turned to me, holding Eudora by her neck. "It's fortunate, then, that I brought her along." He struck her strings, making an agonized strangle of notes.

My throat constricted and a red bolt of rage shot through my head. My eyeballs felt like hot marbles. "Give her to me," I said, wishing my voice didn't tremble. "Give her back."

"I could point out that you decided to run away, abandoning her." His closed lips stretched in a smug smile. "Now she's here to help me."

He raised Eudora over his head. "She's old and fragile, isn't she? If you don't give me your full cooperation, I will reduce your cello to a pile of splinters."

"No!" I whipped out my left hand, the emerald tracing a blur of green, and seized from its sheath the knife of the minion on my left.

Don't go for Adam. He'll smash her. There's only one thing to do.

I strode over to Adam, the blade held to my throat.

"You need both me—alive—and this ring, right? Destroy Eudora, and I'll destroy myself." The shock in his eyes sent a fountain of fierce joy from my feet to my head. *Would you, would you really? Yes! Yes! Yes!*

Adam stood there, holding Eudora like a weapon. Charged with resolve, I steeled myself for the death-stroke, but as heartbeats marked off passing seconds, my bowels turned to leaden jelly and my leg muscles to rubber. *Why did I start this? What if I can't do it? But what else, what else, what else? Oh shit, shit, shit!*

Adam slowly lowered Eudora and set her base on the ground. "All right, we're even. Let me tell you what I need from you. One favour and we're done. You may take your cello and go back to Providence."

I brought the hand with the knife to my side, hoping he couldn't see how it shook. "All right, Adam, what do you want me to do?"

"It's simple. The tomb I told you about is here somewhere." He waved a hand around the narrow wadi. "You will find it and open it for me."

"You think I can dig through that?" I pointed at the compacted mass of rocks, gravel, and dirt around us.

"Don't play at ignorance! We both know you can pass through solid matter."

"We do? That's news to me."

"How did you escape from my house?"

"Through that door in my bedroom. The one with all the carvings around it."

"Exactly." Adam shook Eudora, making me wince. "I was testing you, and you passed the test brilliantly. That is a false door, a facsimile. It goes nowhere."

"But I just pushed on it and it opened. Into a tunnel."

"The sort of tunnel you will open here, by making a small effort. Do whatever you did to open that false door, and then you may take your Eudora and leave."

"You and I both know you're lying. This is bigger than any small desire or curiosity." I brought the knife blade back to my throat. "Tell me the truth. What do you want from that tomb?"

Adam sighed. "I need only one thing from it. A thing that is my property, stolen by my enemies. When it's restored to me, there will be a glorious manifestation. You will witness it with me—the ineffable light of annihilation and creation, the earth cleared for a new beginning." He lifted his eyes like one experiencing a vision.

I remembered Francis Dexter's voice, telling me that if Adam obtained his desire, the result would be "a catastrophic convergence of forces." That certainly sounded like annihilation. But could I prevent it? I pressed the cold edge of the blade against my flesh.

Goddess of the Peak, guardian of the tombs, help me now!

Adam brought his gaze back to me. "I admire your resolve," he said, "but you have only two choices. Are you certain that knife is sharp enough to do the job? Keep your throat intact and do the only thing that makes sense."

He needs me, I reminded myself, not only alive but conscious, capable of making choices and exerting my will. But it hasn't occurred to him that includes the choice to surrender.

I thought of the emerald on the hand that held the knife. *Green fire, cold metal, secret signs, hidden strength.*

I raised my eyes to the cliffs. Deep red light lanced through a notch in the rim. Light of the setting sun, about to vanish, but so like the red glow I had seen in this very place from the balloon. I was certain now. I was here for a purpose greater than recovering Eudora, greater than myself. But was I willing to die for it? Nephren-Ka would have his minions remove the ring from my hand. He had time—millions of years—to search for another member of what Francis Dexter called the Company of Outsiders. Someone he would beguile or force to do his bidding. Unless I used my abilities, whatever they were, right now.

I stood on the cliff edge of my life, an abyss yawning at my feet. I had only to jump.

This is surrender.

I held out my arms and twirled, making the red dress swirl around me. Turning back to Nephren-Ka, who was frowning like a thundercloud, I said, "All right. I'll find the tomb and open it. But I'll enter it first, with Eudora. Give her to me, or I will make myself useless to you." I brandished the knife.

He handed her over without a word. I returned the knife to its owner, slotting the blade into its sheath and patting the shoulder of the servant attached to it. "Thanks."

I welcomed back my instrument, running my hands down her neck and gently stroking her strings. She emitted a sad little twang. Out of tune, of course. I didn't know if the crack had grown, and this wasn't the time or place to investigate. But at least we were together.

I turned my attention back to Adam. "The bow, please," I held out my hand.

"Do you intend to play?" he asked.

"Music has power."

He grimaced, but placed the bow in my hand.

Clasping Eudora to my side, I paced along the bottom of the debris slopes, as though seeking a lost article, but not with my eyes or any ordinary sense. I set myself aside. France Leighton was in the background, behind the instrument created by my body and the emerald ring. Nephren-Ka and his minions stood nearby, but I ignored them.

The stones hummed. A dark, low vibration reverberated from the columned cliffs, a brighter buzz from the boulders, chirps from the gravels, a sibilant susurrus from the sands. But this was only the eternal humming of the earth. I sought something newer, distinct, hollow, *red*. The red of the glow I saw from the balloon, the final glare of the sun through the notch in the cliff-top. I closed my eyes and stood still, imagining myself into an antenna, a divining-rod, a probe into unseen realms.

I am, I am, I am, I am she, I am she. I am she who holds, who holds the darkness, who splits the darkness and the light. I am Meresamun, servant of the god.

"Hmm, humm, hmh, hum, hmm, hum," Eudora sang through me, translating the music of earth and stone. Then, a single, thrumming chord, as though someone had applied the bow to her strings with power, with authority. At the same time, I was flooded with a current of warm electricity, a stream of feeling that began in my feet and rose to my head. I opened my eyes and pointed with Eudora's bow at the place where I stood. "There," I said. "That's where it is."

Nephren-Ka was immediately at my side.

"Open it!" he said.

I turned toward him. "Patience." I laid Eudora on the ground and placed the bow next to her. Then I dropped to my knees at the place that throbbed and glowed around and through me, and laid my hands on the earth, bedding my palms into the dust of eternity.

Nothing happened.

Whatnowwhatnowwhatnow? A plaintive scream from my suppressed self.

Patience!

I pressed and focussed, made myself sharp, made myself strong, a shaft of iron. The stones yielded, rolling aside as though weightless, to expose a sealed door.

14
The Chapter of the Heart and the Egg

The door hadn't been opened since the guardians of the necropolis pressed their seals into clay smeared over the plastered seam where stone met stone. This was the Unbroken Tomb.

I had to get us in there.

The entrance to the tomb had revealed itself to me. The tomb of a priestess, in a mountain sacred to a goddess. This was a place of women and their female powers. Nephren-Ka had his automata pressing me to do his will, but I had my woman's power. The pulsing of the earth surged through my body, and the voice of the goddess told me what to do and how to do it.

"Bring him within, to me, and I will deal with him. Be as the fertile earth, the place of death in life and life in death. Use him to make energy. You are a vessel and a weapon."

The narrow passage led into the earth, into a sacred realm which received the dead and created life. The seed enters the darkness so that new life may emerge. The last time living persons had entered this portal was to deposit a corpse. The dead went in and the living came out, as though newly born. In and out. Female and male. Nephren-Ka wanted to enter the tomb, but to accomplish that, he needed me.

And I needed to engage with Adam the man, not Nephren-Ka the dead pharaoh. I had failed completely on my first attempt to entice Adam. What was left of his humanity, his manhood? And would it respond to me?

I stood and faced him. "This is the tomb. We'll go inside, but only if you do as I tell you." I picked up Eudora and her bow, and went close to Adam, close enough to see that his face looked gaunt and haggard. He smelled of dry dust and stale incense. I reached out my right hand to stroke his cheek, running it down his neck and sliding it upward under the heavy pectoral he wore, laying my palm on his bare chest. He flinched and then relaxed with a sigh and a shudder.

"Adam, the way into this tomb is through me. I am the entrance. Do you understand that?"

"I knew there was something about you, that I needed you with me." His heart thudded under my hand.

"Do you remember when we made music together? *Salut d'amour?* It wasn't so long ago."

His lips formed a smile. "I remember."

I moved my hand in small circles on his chest. "Did you guess why I chose that piece?"

Such a strange look on his face, a distant longing overlaid with sorrow. "I guessed," he whispered. "But I wasn't..."

"Let's go inside now. Together."

"All right. Show me the way."

I turned my back toward him. "Put your arms around me and press your body to mine."

His arms encircled my waist, but he avoided touching my left hand and its ring. The fabric of the dress I wore was thin, and there was nothing between it and my skin. I felt him hesitate.

"All right, Adam?"

"Open the tomb for me."

"Have patience. I am the lock and you are the key. Each of us must do our part." The imminent conjunction of our bodies was like a giant electrical charge. I buzzed and thrummed, like Eudora in the throes of performance.

I pushed my buttocks against him, wiggling from side to side. He stirred slightly in response—not cold and lifeless after all. Warm flesh pressed back and grew rigid.

He lifted the back of my dress and stroked my hips and buttocks. My body responded to him without asking my permission, becoming hollow and wet, preparing to receive him. I bent forward slightly as his fingers opened me. Then he entered, piston into cylinder. His weight pressed me to my knees, and I let go of Eudora, scraping her against the rough ground, but not caring, not caring as I received a force that melded with me to create something I could use. I pushed against him, responding to and encouraging his thrusts, and at the same time pressed my hands against the solid stone that sealed the entrance to the tomb.

The gems of the necklace he wore ground into my back. His breaths grew harsh, he groaned and shuddered as I received the hot gush of his climax. The stone yielded under my hands. It swung inward and upward, tumbling the two of us into the Unbroken Tomb.

This was the moment, while he was weakened from his efforts. I got my feet under me and heaved myself up, leaving Adam sprawled. Picking up Eudora, I scrambled for the bow and backed into the narrow passage. Liquids ran down my legs. My body sang with pain and triumph.

Nephren-Ka got to his feet and strode toward me, obviously intending to push me aside. Behind him, the stone descended, enclosing us in utter darkness. I held Eudora in my left hand, like a shield, and brandished my bow in his face.

"No. You will come no farther."

He snarled and muttered words I didn't comprehend.

I had to create an invocation, and I knew only one way to do it. Giving myself up to the brute energy generated by taking in Adam's substance, I dropped to one knee and braced Eudora against the other.

"Come, Eudora, let's sing!"

Braying, droning dark notes and thrumming chords, meditative, deliberate and unhurried, reverberated through the earth and echoed in the hollow vessel of the tomb. I joined my voice to Eudora's, the vibration in my throat matching that in her hollow body. With long ululations in a language I did not know, primal sounds rising from the place I had invited him to violate, I sang an elegy for whatever he had been in youth and manhood, before he was enticed into serving something from beyond.

I sawed at Eudora's strings, wringing from her sounds that entwined those I dredged up from my depths. Our combined music rang through the hollows of the Peak, spaces created by dripping water and the tomb builders' patient delving. Together, we drilled and built, made a structure of curved bars, caging the avatar.

The emerald in my ring flamed and brought forth an answering glow from the walls of the tomb. With every stroke, with every note, light grew around us, revealing images — a line of goddesses, cow-headed, hippo-headed, lion-headed, and one with a rearing cobra issuing from her neck.

"Meretseger, Meretseger," I shrieked, "you who rule the Peak, I call upon you!"

Adam—or Nephren-Ka—stood frozen in the cage of sound. His skull shone through his skin, eyes like caves with copper-coloured fire in their depths, teeth gleaming diamond-bright in a naked grin. Clawed hands ready to do me violence, but unable to breach the wall of music.

If I can hold him off until— Until what? Until she comes. But how do I know whether, and when? I don't know.

Eudora brayed in agony as I dragged the bow across her trembling strings, making deep red groans that stabbed my heart. Heart-rending, world-ending. "Goddess, goddess, goddess, save, save, save!"

Only this can hold him, only this, a little longer, a little longer. Is he weakening?

He wasn't. He grew taller, menacing. His mouth moved, emitting a judder of sounds. I shouted, I howled to drown his voice. To hear him was to fear, to fail. I worked the bow over the strings, executing a fusillade of notes, sharp like knives, strong like steel, projecting, projecting—

Eudora shattered. The wood of her body split and fell apart with a final deep groan, and her strings grew slack under my fingers. I dropped the bow to my side and shrieked a last entreaty to the cobra goddess, as the bars of my sound-cage dissolved and Nephren-Ka gloated in triumph.

Into the silence that swallowed up the last echoes, the goddess detached from the wall and took living shape. Her hood, spread wide, reared up behind Nephren-Ka. Her arms encircled him. Her jaws opened in a world-swallowing gape, exposing venom-dripping fangs. His mouth opened almost as wide in a scream that faded away, along with the rest of him. For an instant, I saw the actual man he must have been before his body was appropriated by an unknown entity. The body I had used for my own purposes, one of which was his destruction. A look of lostness, of confusion, of longing, passed across his face. My last thought of Adam, before the coils wrapped around him and bore him away, was one of compassion.

Around me, the tomb hummed, as though el-Qurn, the Peak, was a struck bell, reverberating. The walls shone dull gold, and on my hand the emerald throbbed and pulsed like a living thing. My entry into the tomb, using Adam as my tool, and his removal by the Goddess of the Peak, had stirred its very depths.

Eudora lay shattered at my feet. Her front panel had split in two along the crack I had noticed days ago, and detached completely from the curved sides. Her neck swung loose, held to the rest of her only by the limp strings. I gathered her in my arms, inhaling an aroma of ancient wood that had grown as a living tree hundreds of years ago, on a sunny hillside of Italy. Shaped by hands of one long dead, played by hands of many long dead, finally by my hands. At the last, played harshly, but with power and for a valiant cause. I laid her beneath the image of Hathor, the horned goddess of music and the dance. For an unknown time, I knelt beside the fragments, feeling ebbing echoes of violence and sorrow.

Come within.

The words didn't reach me by way of my ears but vibrated through me, as though I was a plucked string.

Come within.

No foot had trod these stones in three thousand years. The invitation was an opportunity beyond belief. To see, to touch, to experience.

I ventured a few paces along the passage. On either side of me, hieroglyphs rippled and sang, expressing spells and invocations, quivering with magic. Not far ahead was another sealed door, a stone block barring the way. I took several steps closer and stopped short, my heart hammering. Between me and the doorway, right under my toes, was a pit, six feet wide and deep enough that I could not see the bottom.

"Come within." I heard the voice now. Was it tinged with amusement?

"I can't. I can't jump over this pit. There's nowhere to land, only a solid door."

"You entered my antechamber through a door just as solid."

"I can't do that again, though."

"You have power at your disposal. Believe and act, as you did when you entrained the raw force of the avatar."

"Surrender?"

"Surrender." Definitely a smile in the voice.

I couldn't go back. I knew that. The way out was not the way in. Behind me were solid stone and tons of rubble. I had to go forward or lie down and die right here.

"If you die here, if you surrender to that dark desire, your body will be taken up by the one from Outside. It will seize the thin thread of your wandering spirit and follow it to where your flesh lies, with the stench upon you of the failed avatar. This is *heka*, the magic done underground. You used it well, but you must continue."

Who was it that spoke? Not Francis Dexter. He was a faded ghost, who had used up his little strength to speak to me through the Osiris image in the guest house. And this was a woman's voice.

"Who are you?" I asked.

"I am Meresamun, priestess and guardian. Enter my chamber or become a tool in the hand of the Nameless."

The emerald tugged at my hand, making it thrill and vibrate, pulled it up and forward.

You can do it, do it, do it! Don't think, act!

I stepped back several paces, close to Eudora's shattered body. My skull felt tight, my ears rang with a high-pitched, urgent hum. I took a deep breath—my last?

Now. A step, two, three, four. I pushed off against the edge of the chasm and hurled myself toward the stone, right hand clasped around left wrist, left hand become a blade, its edge an emerald flame.

Go, Supergirl!

Fly!

Strike!

Land.

My eyes didn't want to open. They didn't need to open. Behind my eyelids pulsed and flickered a red-gold shimmer, like a small fire seen through gauzy veils. I lay wrapped in comfort, safe in a place as enclosed and perfect as an egg.

Voices surrounded me, murmuring, sonorous, like warm blue water. I didn't know how many, or whose they were, and it didn't matter. When I paid attention, the meaning of their words seeped into my consciousness. I absorbed it, as linen fibres absorb the colour in a vat of dye, as a boat made of reeds marries the water on which it floats.

"There is no division here, of body, soul, spirit, ghost, and name. It is all one. The heart beats within and does not plead. How, then, can we weigh it and render judgment?"

"This is not the place for her. She has intruded."

"No, she is a visitor. An invited guest. One who comes of necessity."

"However she comes to be here, we must judge her fitness. The Scales stand ready."

"Rouse her then, that we may proceed."

The light behind my eyelids brightened to gold. A hand, or perhaps a wing, brushed my brow, touched my eyes, and I saw.

Tall shapes stood in a circle around me. Shapes I knew only as pictures and lifeless statues. These lived. Their limbs and faces gleamed golden, their heads were jeweled, their eyes luminous. Far above them, silver stars glittered in an indigo sky.

"Speak your name," said the ibis-headed scribe.

I spoke. Was the name I uttered "France Leighton?" Perhaps, but I knew it was the last of many names.

"You have come to this place by device and guile," intoned another, from behind me.

"That has not been determined," said a bright form to my right, shaking her plumed head.

"Speak," said the deep voice of the one I could not see. "Speak from your heart. Why are you here?"

"To bring *him* here," I said. "The avatar, Nephren-Ka, whom I knew as Adam Dexter. I brought him here to remove him from the world in which I live."

"This was the place of his desire. Did you know that?" The voice of the scribe, smooth and quiet.

"I knew that. He needed me to enter. Me, and *this*." I held out the hand that bore the ring.

They leaned closer. Their heads—plumed, scaled, horned, and crowned—drew together. Over me wafted perfumes of eternity, ancient incense, fragrant wood, cloven stone. They murmured to one another words I could not understand.

"It is an artifact of power," said the deep voice, as the figures withdrew.

A slender shape came forward, wearing a single nodding plume of luminous blue. "This thing is not of our world. It is a perilous intrusion."

"How came you by it?" asked the deep voice.

"It is an inheritance."

More murmuring, and then, "Continue."

"I used myself and the ring, and his desire to violate the tomb, as tools to enter within. I used music to hold him powerless, and I called upon the Goddess of the Peak."

"So it was." This voice, soft and sibilant, belonged to the cobra-headed goddess. "So it is. The intruder has been expelled and the tomb remains sealed."

"We must weigh this heart, nevertheless."

They drew aside, and I saw behind them the tall Balance and its attendant Ape. Behind it a squat figure with the head of a crocodile snapped its jaws. The jackal-headed one extracted from my chest the red vessel, a little jar glowing with rosy light, filled with the ineffable liquid. Showing white teeth in a grinning mouth, he placed it in the Balance's left-hand pan. Another figure took from her head the single plume, blue as sapphire, and laid it in the right-hand pan.

Anubis watched. Tehuti inscribed. Osiris spoke.

"Of anger, there is none. Of making others to weep, none. Of violence, none. Of impurity, none, except from necessity. Of deceit, likewise. Of wickedness, none. Of disruption, none. Of intent to steal from the dead, none. The one who names herself France Leighton, now among us, may abide here or go forth by day, as does the Bennu Bird."

The figure of Ma'at, once again wearing the Plume of Truth, laid her hand upon my brow. "Have a care, France Leighton, for you carry a thing of peril. Beware of temptation." She touched the emerald ring. "Be vigilant."

The company breathed a sigh. The Devourer of Hearts smacked her jaws in defeat. The figures faded into the golden light, which dulled in turn, assuming its previous ruddy hue.

I closed my eyes and gave myself up to blissful thoughts.

May my heart be within me, for my two legs walked me here and my two hands and arms overthrew my foe. My eyes are opened, my legs are firm, the goddess gave me courage. I understand with my heart. I have gained mastery over my heart, over my hands, over my legs. I have gained the power to do whatsoever pleases my body and soul. I have entered in peace and I shall go forth in peace.

I was alone, in a chamber hewn into the heart of *Dehenet Imentet*, the Peak of the West, el-Qurn. The walls were painted with hieroglyphs and images of deities, winged or striding. The dark blue ceiling was studded with a dense network of silver stars. In the centre stood a sarcophagus of alabaster.

Rosy light emanated from the sarcophagus, shining through the translucent stone carved with enfolding wings. On its lid was the likeness of a woman, arms clasped over her chest. A row of hieroglyphs ran from hands to feet.

Everything was perfect. There was no dust, no peeling or chipping of the painted images. Along the walls stood stoppered clay jars. On a small table rested a delicate lamp of alabaster and dishes painted with lotus flowers. Against the opposite wall was a wooden chest adorned with scenes of festivity. I raised the lid, releasing the fragrance of sandalwood. Inside lay folded garments. The topmost one was white with gold embroidery. Beneath it, dark red linen. Shivering, I closed the chest.

Near the head of the sarcophagus stood a harp with lotus flower motifs painted in blue and green touched with gold. Its strings were intact. Struck with sorrow for Eudora, forever lost to me, I gently touched a string. Plucked. A soft, warm note filled the chamber. I stroked my fingers over the strings, as I had done so many times with Eudora's. A ripple of notes danced through the still and waiting air.

I moved to the foot of the sarcophagus. The wingtips met here, as though enfolding the occupant in a feathered embrace. I could not read the line of hieroglyphs, but I touched the characters, placing the tips of my fingers into the shallow grooves.

The ring responded, its emerald glowing a deep green and the engraving on the metal intensely bright. And I knew what the inscription said. "Meresamun, Singer in the Interior of the Temple of Amun, beloved. She who maintains Ma'at for millions of years."

I laid my hands on the sarcophagus, sliding them from the foot end to the middle. The stone was almost warm, like living flesh, and the wings felt like wave-rippled sand under my palms. The red glow intensified, as if in response to my presence. I had seen it from the balloon, like a message, an invitation, responding to the artifact I carried on my hand, the thing "not of this earth." Its presence and mine, so near this place, had set up invisible vibrations and summoned the avatar Nephren-Ka, who was also Adam Dexter.

Now I was here. Here in the pulse-point of power. I bent over the sarcophagus, my arms clasped around it, my face nearly touching the sculptured features of its occupant.

"Meresamun," I whispered. "I'm here. Tell me, show me what I need to know."

An electrical current pulsed through my fingers, palms and wrists, claiming my body as an instrument of revelation. The stone grew transparent as glass, revealing the inner coffin painted with the priestess's face and symbols of respect and honour. This too grew transparent, revealing the swathed form that lay within. Over the linen bands that covered the head was a diadem of small blue flowers; around her neck lay a wreath of acacia blooms, their yellow as vivid as on the day they were picked.

Through the mummy-wrappings, I saw her face. Not the carved features on the sarcophagus lid, nor the painted ones on the inner coffin, but the face of Meresamun, singer in the temple of Amun. Brown skin drawn tight against the bones, lips forever sealed in a smile or spasm.

And then I saw her hands. Thin, delicate bones encased in desiccated skin clasped an object the size of an egg, many-sided, jet black, with points of red light gleaming within. This was the object of Adam's desire, which had inflamed his mind and heart. For its sake, he had mustered his manhood and joined with me to force an entry into this place.

Meresamun's fingers enclosed the black stone as the pale metal gripped the emerald in my ring. She had accepted it, laid it upon her heart before she died, to preserve it for all eternity.

"For all eternity," I murmured. My body hummed with the earth-energy concentrated in this place, this artifact, this millennia-dead body. The body was dead, but not the soul, the spirit, the ghost, the name. They were here, present and united. Not wandering the underworld, not haunting the nights, not partaking of the delights of paradise and its lake of flowers. Meresamun was *here,* and I knew her thought.

I am here. I lie within the stone of the Peak, stone from the sea that was. I am rooted in this land. The river flows through my belly, my arms embrace the furrowed slopes, my fingers burrow into the black soil that brings forth life. My feet touch the place where the river finds the sea. Reeds wave above me, fish swim through me, the waters flood and depart, but I remain. My head is pillowed on the stones of the south, where the rain is gathered. The land is. The river is. They ebb and flow, bring forth and gather in, make and remake, as the wheel of the sun rolls through eternity. I lie here. I am. I hold. I hold this thing. Willingly I took it upon me, and gave my life to be its guardian, so this will endure. This river. This land. This flesh and blood. That which breaks me, breaks the world.

Her eyelids hid sunken pits where the eyeballs had withered away. Her body was dead, had been dead for millennia, but through its eyes, I saw…

A dead land under a dead sky. Smoke and ash drift over dead cities and expanses of riven rock. This is Earth, upon which no living thing remains.

Now I knew. I knew what Adam sought, and why. I knew why he became a nuclear physicist. I knew what would happen if he or another broke the seals, rolled aside the stones, wrestled the lid from the sarcophagus, tore away the flowers, unwrapped the linen bands, laid bare the slight body, wrenched apart the fragile hands to seize the black stone. In the name of knowledge. In the name of science. In the name of need and greed.

The knowledge was mine now. I could not un-know it. I, France Leighton, would go forth by day into the world of the living, holding the key to its destruction or preservation.

Except I was trapped. I could not possibly leave the burial chamber the way I had entered it. Even if I could pass through the sealed door, there was the pit, and then the outer door, the one I had opened with sex-magic. And then the tons of overburden. I was deep under el-Qurn, and no one knew that. No living person, anyway.

There had to be another way out. If there wasn't, I had to prepare for a slow death.

With the fading red light showing the way, I circled the burial chamber once more. Its entrance door was at the foot end of the sarcophagus. On the wall to my right was another door, narrow, with hieroglyph texts on either side. It looked like the door through which I escaped from Adam's house. Something small lay on the floor near it. I picked it up. An image of a cobra, made of pale blue, glassy material.

"Meretseger, you protected those who made this place, you removed the unworthy intruder, please help me." I clutched the amulet in my right hand and pushed on the centre panel of the door with my left. It didn't move.

That was it, then. I would die here. My legs turned to rubber and my resolve failed. Maybe my ghost would go forth, but not the rest of me. I hammered the lying, false door with my fists. I raised my face to the starry ceiling and howled, until I slumped exhausted against the unyielding stone.

"You must be as the Bennu Bird, who cracks the shell of each day's dawning," said the calm voice that had invited me into the sealed chamber. "The exit is not the entrance, but the spirit is the same."

The spirit. I had to surrender again, this time to the goddess and her mountain. To the stone of which it was made, remnant of vanished seas.

I placed a palm on the central panel of the painted door, touched the emerald with my lips and expelled a breath, sending with it the words "Let me go forth by day."

I leaned into the stone and gave myself to it, drawing its dry dust into my lungs. Fragments of small lives encased me, forming a carapace that pressed on my head, hands, belly, legs and back. The Peak of the West held me fast. I became a seed, a thing of earth. Like the Bennu Bird, I had to break the stony egg that encased me to go forth into the light of day.

Blood pulsed within me, my heart trembled. Essence of stone, release me. Water of life, flow within me, a river of red. Give me air and light and life.

Could I raise my arms? No. The stone held me, wanted me, kept me inert. Desire wasn't enough.

Rage and despair swelled inside me, heart to head. Heat boiled my brain. I could not break the stone. Not I alone. Summon the elemental forces! Unify, unify! Make me into the seed that cracks the stone, the root that breaks it, the tree that seeks the air, the lightning that strikes the tree, the flame that burns the wood. Red flame, red blood, red, red, *red*.

My arms shot up. I shrieked in joyous agony. The emerald ring dragged me upward. I burned, I stretched, I split the stone, burst forth into air and light.

****

A little breeze rippled my hair. Loose sand and gravel gritted under me. Light filtered through my eyelids. Red light, of course, but brighter. I opened my eyes. I lay on stone, my back against an unyielding wall, a pale sky above.

What happened? Oh, I hurt! Everything hurt, from top to bottom, inside and out. Moving was agony, so I lay still and looked at what I could see. Columnar rock formations nearby, and above me the bulk of el-Qurn, black against the sky.

I was alive. I was outside. The fingers of my left hand were folded around a small object. A little cobra, made of light blue glassy stuff. It had come with me. Carefully, I levered myself to a sitting position and realized I was on a narrow shelf of rock. What was below it? More rocks, what else? I rolled onto my knees and pulled myself up, clutching at whatever handholds I could find. From here I saw the main wadi opening out from the pinch-point formed by the two piers of stone. Now all I had to do was find a way down there.

I am coming forth by day. If I was a bennu bird, I could fly all the way to Luxor. But I'm not, so I'll have to walk. Lord, I hurt!

The rocky shelf continued all the way to the head of the wadi, although it grew perilously narrow at one point. I could see a faint path, possibly made by animals. Before venturing along it, I leaned against the solid cliffside to make sure I was really ready. A dizzy spell or shakiness at the wrong moment could be fatal.

Beside me gaped a deep fissure. It looked fresh, its edges sharp and the exposed stone on its inner surfaces whiter than that of the cliff face. When had it opened, and why? Uncle Jim would probably know.

But Uncle Jim was dead. So was Dr. Stanton. And Adam? Dead, or just gone? I was weary beyond words. I ought to be dead too. Even my wonderful ring looked tired, like a cheap piece of junk jewelry. Leaning my head against the stone, I cried, my tears absorbed by the millennial detritus of oceans.

The weeping fit over, I blinked and rubbed my eyes with the backs of my dirty hands, careful not to drop the cobra amulet. Then I saw it—blood red light deep within the crack, as though el-Qurn harboured a secret fire, like a volcano. Except it wasn't one; even I knew limestone wasn't created by volcanism.

But I knew where that red light came from. I had been down there, in the tomb. My substance had been expelled from it through this fissure. Now that I was on the surface, would it close again? Did it matter? It was time for me to go.

"Goodbye, Meresamun. Goodbye, Eudora." Clutching the cobra amulet, I picked my way along the rocky shelf, careful not to slip.

The hardest part was the steep downward path from the head of the wadi. Twice I landed on my rear end when loose gravel slid under my feet. I almost didn't care any more. I had learned to endure—pain, hunger, thirst, fear. *And to surrender, let's not forget that. Rocks and gravel, I give up. Do your worst.*

At the bottom, I paused. In the light of morning, the place looked like any other combination of cliffs, scree slopes, and boulders. It was hard to believe what lay beneath this dusty exterior—an untouched tomb anchoring an enormous power. And Eudora, a broken cello made in eighteenth century Italy.

Flood-borne sediments lay undisturbed many feet thick over the spot where I had uncovered the tomb's entrance. I thought I recognized my footprints and the marks made by my hands as I sought the subtle vibrations. Something blue caught my eye. Among the stones lay two of the figurines called *shabtis* that were placed in tombs to serve the dead. I picked them up, wondering where they'd come from.

The figurines were made of the blue-green, glassy substance called faience, like the cobra amulet, but darker in colour. They were pretty much identical—black-painted wigs on their heads, arms crossed over their chests, black hieroglyphs on their bodies. Their facial features, though rudimentary, conveyed a kind of focussed determination.

I recognized them.

"Well, well. Tweedledum and Tweedledee. Although I guess since you're ancient Egyptians, something like 'Ta-de-thum' and 'Ta-de-te' would be more appropriate. Sure."

The figures, now a mere six or seven inches tall, had to be my former relentless pursuers. Adam's departure must have rendered them inanimate. The tools they carried were knives and whips, not the traditional hoes and baskets. These two *shabtis* hadn't been made for agricultural tasks.

I debated with myself as to what I should do with them. Smash them to dust, was my first impulse.

We will answer to you.

Where did that idea come from? I shook my head. I was tired of hearing voices. Hunger, dehydration and injuries were beginning to take their toll. I had to get back to the guest house, to Luxor, to Providence. I was finished with this Egyptian adventure, which had nearly finished me.

But I'd better take the *shabtis* with me. Leaving them here would attract the attention of tomb-hunters, legitimate or otherwise. The Unbroken Tomb must remain unbroken. I didn't want to go back to the guest house visibly carrying the figurines. If I could find the *galabeya* I'd left behind the night before, I would hide them in its pockets.

Soon after I passed through the narrow place between the upper and lower parts of the wadi, I saw two figures approaching. Even though I knew they couldn't be Adam's servants, I felt a jolt of fear. Then I recognized one of them — Hank. A few moments later, I realized the other one was Willa Devlin.

I had to hide the *shabtis* before they reached me. There were two large boulders not far from the path. I tucked the figurines behind the lower one, covering them with sand. After a moment's hesitation, I added the cobra figurine.

"Keep them safe, Lady Meretseger," I said, "until I come back for them." I noted landmarks to help me find the place again and hurried back to the path.

Willa ran up to me, leaving Hank behind. "France? I almost didn't recognize you. Oh, you poor thing! What happened to you?"

Poor thing? Me? I've been inside the Unbroken Tomb and escaped from it with my life. I'm lucky, not poor. Then I realized how I must look. The red linen dress hung in tatters, its fragile fabric no match for everything I had subjected it to. It barely covered the essentials. My arms and legs were streaked with dirt, blood, and who knew what else. My knees and elbows were skinned raw.

"Willa! Yes, it's me. I'm all right, really. What're you doing here?" I crossed my arms in front of me, trying to cover myself.

"I'll tell you later. The first thing is to get you looked after. Here, put this on." She took off her cardigan. "No, better wrap it around your waist."

I didn't have much of a choice. "Thanks. I am kind of a mess." I made the cardigan into a kind of loincloth, tying the sleeves together on my hip just as Hank arrived.

"Found again, France!" he said. "Can't escape, even though you keep trying."

"Hi, Hank." Smiling made my cracked lips hurt. "I'm sure glad to see you guys. I've been wandering in the wilderness, I guess."

"How did you get all those scratches and scrapes?" asked Hank. "Did someone hurt you?"

"No one hurt me. I had an encounter… with some rocks. The wilderness is kind of harsh, you know?" I smiled again to show I was okay.

They exchanged anxious glances. "Well, it's time we got you back to Mr. Mohamed's place," said Willa. "You could use some first aid."

"If she fell, she might have another concussion," said Hank. "Did you hit your head, France? Does it ache? Are you dizzy?"

"I didn't hit my head, just my rear end," I said. "I'm not dizzy. Not right now. And everything hurts except my head. What happened in Luxor, Hank? Did you talk to the police? And Adele?"

"Yes, to both. The police might send someone over in a few days, they said." He shook his head. "The wheels of bureaucracy turn slowly. Adele is applying some grease to create a sense of urgency."

"How is she? And how're you doing?"

"Oh, I'm holding up. One thing at a time. And Adele's tough as an old boot, or knows how to fake it, anyway."

As we trudged along, I kept an eye out for my old friend the *galabeya*. Sure enough, it was right where I'd left it, making the boulder it sat on into a mushroom shape.

"Just a second," I said, interrupting Hank, who was talking about that morning's ferry crossing. I unrolled the *galabeya*, struggled into it and handed Willa's cardigan back to her. "So you came over with Hank this morning, Willa?"

Hank watched my performance with amusement, but Willa stared at me wide-eyed. "That's *yours*? We saw it on the way up but figured it belonged to one of the locals."

"Nope, it's mine. I left it here last night. What brought you back over here?"

"Oh, I may as well tell you now. Mother and I went back to Luxor two days after you left the guest house. The first time you left. Our plan was to start for Aswan the next day, but then Mother got a premonition and decided we'd better stay on, so I found us a suite in a nice little hotel. The Winter Palace was full up. Sometimes her premonitions blow over, other times they develop into something bigger. Well, this time..." She gave me another doubtful look.

"'This time'?" I prompted, winding the turban cloth around my neck.

"Well, it was about you," Willa said. "'That young France is in some kind of trouble,' Mother told me. 'We can't leave without making sure she comes out of it alive. She'll need our help.' So I thought I'd start by asking about you at that dig you were working on."

Uh-oh. "And how did that work out?"

"Well, I didn't know they'd be dealing with the death of… Dr. Stanton, was that his name? Things seemed a bit confused, but Hank said he'd seen you over here. The two of us came over first thing this morning."

I thought for a few steps. "How did you know where to look for me?"

"Those photos of yours," said Hank. "You left them in your room, with the one of the eyeball concretion on top, so I figured you might be here. Mahmoud and everyone at the guest house are wondering what happened to you."

"I see," I said. "Just like that eyeball." My laugh felt a little hysterical. "And your mother, Willa? Did she come over too?"

"Oh no, she's still in Luxor, but she gave me strict orders to bring you back so she can fuss over you." Willa laughed. "She really does mean well, and you've had a pretty rough time, by the looks of things."

"I'd love to come," I said, to my surprise.

I was welcomed back to Mahmoud Mohamed's guest house like a long-lost daughter. It was almost embarrassing, but I was grateful for the warm bath contrived by Yasmin and her mother. The cuts and scrapes that covered me from shoulders to knees stung like burns on contact with soap and water, but washing my hair was a delight. Wrapping myself in a towel, I felt newly born.

Mrs. Mohamed handed me a jar of dark green salve and mimed applying it to my skin. "It is very good for hurt," she said. The ointment smelled of pungent herbs and something I couldn't identify, but I gave it the benefit of the doubt and daubed it on. The stuff cooled the stinging of my abraded skin and reduced its redness from angry to merely annoyed.

My belongings had been moved to one of the guest rooms, and someone had laundered my clothes. I was almost presentable when I joined the family in the dining room, where I forced myself to eat politely, instead of devouring everything in sight.

After the meal, Yasmin asked if she could speak to me privately in my room. A little puzzled, I agreed, thanking her again for her family's kindness and hospitality. "I can't express how much better I feel."

"You are welcome." Her expression turned serious. "Miss France, forgive me, but I must ask you questions. I hope you are not offended."

"Not at all," I said, hoping it would be true.

"When you were outside last night, at the *Wadi Biban el-Muluk*, the Valley of the Kings, did someone—a man—do some injury to you?" She pressed her fingers to her lips, but not to cover a cough.

"You mean, was I raped?"

She looked at the floor, and then at me. "Yes."

"No, I wasn't. I got lost and ended up somewhere else, not the Valley of the Kings. And I... fell down a few times. That's all. There was nobody there but me."

"But I must ask—why did you go there, in the evening time, wearing that dress?" She pointed at the ruin of the red dress, where it lay on the bed. "I wondered, were you meeting some... person?"

"No! I was being silly. I wanted to experience the Valley of the Kings as an ancient Egyptian would have, so it had to be after all the tourists had left. But I got lost somehow." I had trouble looking Yasmin in the eye as I said this. The road to the Valley was pretty hard to miss. She knew I was lying, but not why, and she was too polite to ask.

There was a tap on the door, and Willa came in. "Oh, there you are. I just wanted to make sure you're okay. Hi, Yasmin. Your Dad asked me to remind you that he wants to talk to France. I guess he wants to find out more about what happened."

"Yes, my father asked me to invite you." Yasmin looked a little annoyed that Willa should have upstaged her.

As we trooped downstairs, Willa touched my shoulder. "Want me to be there? I'm sure Mr. Mohamed won't mind."

"That would be nice." I was beginning to figure things out. Mr. Mo was in the tourist business, wasn't he? The last thing he and the other people who lived here wanted was rumours of attacks on women tourists. Two dead foreigners, one of whom had certainly been murdered, were bad enough.

As it turned out, no one objected to Willa's presence. Hank was there too, and two older men from the village. We all sat around a table in the cool, dim room. Yasmin's sister Samia served tea. Yasmin whispered into her father's ear before sitting down. He nodded gravely, looking at me.

"Miss Leighton," Mr. Mohamed said, "I understand you were not injured by any person during your absence from my house last night."

"No, I was not injured by anyone. These scrapes and bruises are because of my clumsiness."

His dark eyes gazed at me steadily from under bushy brows and precisely wrapped turban. "Miss France, I wonder. Some days ago, you inquired me how to find a certain person, a man you said called himself *Alyad Alyumnaa,* and another name as well."

"Adam Dexter." My mouth felt dry. I swallowed some tea.

"Did you find this person?"

Yasmin was busy translating for the two old men. Hank was looking at me. So was Willa. I made up my mind. "In a way, but not exactly…"

I looked down at my hands, clasped together on the edge of the table. Now I did feel dizzy. Good thing I was sitting down. The emerald winked at me from inside my palm. I raised my head and spoke directly to Mr. Mo.

"Mr. Mohamed, you told me about an American who came here many years ago. That man, Francis Dexter, was my grandfather. He was here in 1935." I stopped to let this soak in, and to wet my parched mouth again, raising the glass carefully as the room swayed and yawed.

"I never knew my grandfather," I continued. "He died before I was born. When I met the man who called himself Adam Dexter, at Metropolitan House, I wondered if we were related, so I was curious about him. He told me to look for him here on the west bank. I remembered what my grandmother told me, about Francis Dexter's visit here, and what he and his servant experienced all those years ago. Something strange happened to them. And something strange happened to me. But I'm all right now, truly."

Mr. Mo smiled, a warm, kind smile. "Miss Leighton, I am not surprised to hear of this. I knew you reminded me of someone. Yes, I remember your grandfather, with gratitude. And this 'Adam Dexter,' he is the one we called *Alyad Alyumnaa* when I was young."

"He was," I said.

Mr. Mo's eyebrows tangled with his turban's edge. "'Was'?"

"What happened to him?" asked Hank.

"I don't really know, but I'm pretty sure he's gone for good." Like I'm gonna be soon, I thought, clutching at the table's edge.

"How can you be sure about that?" Hank again.

"Because a cobra bit him," I said, and slumped to the floor.

15
The Chapter of Speaking the Truth and Hiding It

That night and the twenty-four hours following it were a blur. I didn't even realize I was sharing a room with Willa until I woke up and saw her in the other bed.

But before that were the dreams. Dreams of a small stone room that shrank around me. I awoke with a jolt, sweating and shaking, only to fall back into the tomb, where Meresamun's mummified face split open to reveal a boil of writhing worms, and Adam's skull-like head grew a cobra's hood, rearing above me in horrific triumph. A figure I knew to be Francis Dexter rose from a table that bore something bloody and indescribable, his lips dripping scarlet in a dead white face.

I shuddered to near-waking and then sank into another sleep full of horrors. Followed by the whole sequence again. And again.

I finally came fully awake and lay in pre-dawn darkness assessing my state. My bruises and scrapes had retreated into their own realms of pain, instead of joining forces to torture me like they had earlier. My brain was working again. It was time I got up.

I had to retrieve the *shabtis*. Leaving them in their casually chosen hiding place was dangerous. Anyone who found them would suspect there was a tomb close by. Without Adam, they had reverted to inanimate little figurines, but was that a permanent state? I didn't know how he had made them work. Could I make them answer to me? Did I want to? In any case, they were my responsibility.

I slipped out of bed and got dressed. Underpants, bra, shirt, Bermudas. Each garment rustled louder than the last one, but Willa didn't stir. Finally, I eased my feet into my sandals, scuffed but holding together, like me. At the last second, I grabbed the turban cloth. It would come in handy to hide the figurines from the curious. Being suspected of antiquities theft wasn't part of my plan. Willa was still sleeping when I left the room and sneaked down the stairs.

Someone was clanking around in the kitchen, but I got in and out of the bathroom and escaped the house unnoticed. I was congratulating myself on my neat departure while I wrapped the turban cloth around my head and neck like a scarf, when I heard a voice behind me.

"Sneaking out?" said Willa. "Not without me. We spent enough time looking for you the other day. I'm coming with you." She was dressed like me, except her Bermudas weren't as wrinkled and her sandals looked new.

I almost told her to leave me to my business, but didn't think she'd do it, and arguing on the doorstep would attract attention. "Oh, all right, but let's get away before anyone sees us."

The light was growing fast, rolling the night up into the Theban Hills. It was too early for tourists. We stepped along without talking until the village vanished behind a hill and Hatshepsut's temple came into view on our left. The crowing of roosters, fading with distance, was the only accompaniment to our footfalls. No one followed us; I looked back several times to make sure.

"So we're just going for a brisk morning walk?" said Willa.

"Sure." I thought it was better to say too little than too much.

"Just what you need after passing out the other day."

I couldn't ignore her sarcasm. "I left something up there."

"Parts of that dress you were wearing?"

"Not exactly." I kept my eyes on the path.

"What were you doing out here anyway, dressed like that?"

I stopped and Willa almost walked into me. Turning to her, I said, "If you must know, I was trying to have an authentic ancient Egyptian experience. No guide, no tourists, nothing modern." *And no one bothering me.*

"No guide?" Willa's voice rose like the sun would soon. "Not even the mysterious Adam Dexter?"

"No. I just kept walking until the sun went down. Ra descending into the underworld, you know. Once it got dark, I got lost, and I was scared to go wandering around because of snakes and scorpions. You don't have to tell me it was a stupid idea." I turned around and got going again, and after a moment or two she followed me.

Our footsteps crunched along together for half a dozen yards.

"And did you have your authentic experience?"

I felt my lips forming a smile and hoped she couldn't see it. "In a way."

We reached the Wadi of the Eyeball much faster than I had the other evening. Such a contrast between those two journeys—fresh morning air and the light increasing, rather

Audrey Driscoll

than the flaming sunset and sense of doom. Not to mention Willa's company, instead of those two sinister figures.

The two figures that were the objective of this expedition.

"What're we looking for?" Willa's question exactly matched my thoughts.

"A big boulder with a smaller one above it, lining up with the top of el-Qurn. On the left side of the path, just about where those two cliffs lean together up there."

Willa laughed. "A big boulder and a little one? France, there's nothing here *but* boulders."

"Trust me. I'll know the place when I see it."

It took a while. One boulder does look much like another, and quite a few boulder combos could be made to line up with el-Qurn by moving a few steps this way or that. Knowing we'd be missed at the guest house if we stayed away too long, I felt flutters of panic.

Willa said nothing, just stood with arms folded, watching while I scrambled around, peered up at the horizon and felt behind various rocks. I thought she might be hiding a smile, but at least she didn't ask stupid questions or make useless suggestions.

Finally—there were the two boulders. The light must have reached the same angle and brightness as on that other morning. I slid a hand behind the biggest stone and felt the smooth shapes of the faience figurines.

They were unchanged. Same painted features, same hieroglyphs. *What did you expect? We are steadfast.*

I shook my head to clear out those thoughts. "Would you hold these for a minute, please, Willa?"

Willa held out her hands. "What are they? Where did they come from?"

I handed them over with a twinge of unease. Surely they were harmless. They were inanimate, for God's sake.

"They're called *shabtis*," I went back to the boulder and felt around behind it for the cobra amulet. "The ancient Egyptians made millions of them, to be servants of the dead in the afterlife. Some tombs had hundreds." There was my cobra! I slipped it into a pocket.

"Okay, so where did these two come from?" Willa turned the figures over, rubbing her thumbs over their contours. "They look like pals."

Yeah, they're pals all right. "Oh, *shabti* figures all look pretty much the same. You could call them mass-produced products."

"And where did they come from?"

That was the third time she'd asked. "I bought them. And that dress, too."

"Where? In the Luxor *souk*? You'll have to show me the shop."

"No, not there. Yasmin's sister makes replicas of ancient Egyptian dresses."

"Oh, okay. But what about these figurines?"

She hadn't been diverted. "Well, they're fakes. A man in the village was selling what he called 'genuine antiquities.' They looked genuine enough to suit me, but I've forgotten the guy's name."

Willa stared at me, a *shabti* in each hand. "Why'd you bring them up here?"

She's so persistent! "I wanted them to rest in genuine Egyptian dirt before I took them home to the States."

Willa laughed. "Soaking up ancientness. You think overnight was long enough?"

"It'll have to be, won't it? We'd better get back before Mr. Mohamed sends out a search party."

"You're right," Willa said. "We've probably been missed already. Do you want me to carry these guys?"

"No, I'd better." I unwound the turban cloth from my neck and wrapped the figurines in it. Then we began gravel-crunching our way back to the guest house.

The place was in a flurry of excitement. A group of men huddled in serious conference with Mr. Mo in a corner of the dining room. Hank had gone back to Luxor, but I was able to extract some hints about what was going on from Yasmin, as she served us breakfast.

"They found a man," she said, setting down a platter of figs and slices of melon. "He was blind." She made a circling motion near her temple. "And not in his mind."

"Did anyone recognize him?"

"He was not a man of our village," said Yasmin, refilling our coffee cups. I noted the past tense, but she hurried back to the kitchen before I could ask what had happened to the blind man.

Willa looked at me over the rim of her cup. "Do you think that could have been Adam Dexter, that man you were looking for?"

I shrugged, thinking hard. "I doubt it," I said, after swallowing another delicious bite of flaky *feteer meshaltet*. "We'll have to thank Mrs. Mohamed specially for all this yummy food."

"But the guy they were talking about was blind," Willa said. "Isn't that an effect of cobra venom?"

"Egyptian cobras don't spit their venom." *But Meretseger was said to punish criminals with blindness.* Suddenly I wasn't hungry anymore. The idea of Adam—the human part of him—wandering around blind pretty much killed my appetite.

Willa said nothing but gave me a searching look before returning to her breakfast.

Later that day, Willa and I left for Luxor, amid a flurry of thanks and good-byes and promises to return to the guest house some day. Mrs. Mohamed and two of her daughters waved from the doorstep as Willa, Yasmin, and I climbed into one of Mr. Mo's taxis for the trip to the ferry landing.

"This is better than the donkey cart, is it not?" Yasmin asked me. Remembering my arrival in the village, I had to agree.

We exchanged final goodbyes while Willa paid our fare. "Be well, Miss France," Yasmin said. She pressed a small jar of the green salve into my hand. "My country hurt you, so I give this for healing."

Her father came up to me after unloading our bags, with good wishes and a warm handshake.

"Thank you again for putting up with me," I said. "I'm sorry I caused you all so much trouble."

"It was nothing, Miss Leighton. I wish you good travels in our land."

"Mr. Mohamed, can you tell me anything about that blind man? Is he... dead?"

Mr. Mo's smile vanished and his eyes narrowed. "No, Miss. I cannot tell you anything. That man is not your concern. Goodbye."

The river crossing took longer than I remembered, probably because the Nile was near its full flood. I was mindlessly enjoying the boat's motion when Willa spoke up.

"What happened to your cello?"

I'd been anticipating this question and had an answer ready. "I traded it for those two shabtis, actually."

"No kidding. But wasn't it a real antique?"

I shrugged. "Sure, but it developed a crack that couldn't be fixed. I thought it was a fair exchange."

Willa mulled this over for a while. "So did you ever see Adam Dexter over there?" She gestured toward the receding shore.

"Why do you keep asking about him? I stayed at Mr. Mo's place for a few days, wandered around in the desert, got lost twice, and found poor Dr. Stanton. That was enough, believe me."

"Okay, but what about that stuff you told Mr. Mo? About your grandfather. Did you just make that up?"

"No. My grandmother told me that story. Maybe she made it up. And Mr. Mo believed it, didn't he? You should have asked him about Adam Dexter, since you're so interested in him. Maybe he would have told you more than he did me."

"Oh, really?" She looked like she was getting ready to laugh, until she frowned.

"Yes, really. Just drop it, okay?"

The streets of Luxor were incredibly busy and crowded compared to the west bank. I was grateful that Willa took charge, finding a taxi and giving the driver an address.

"Where's the rest of your stuff?" Willa asked, as we were whisked along the narrow streets, past pedestrians and burdened donkeys. "I can't believe everything you own is in that knapsack."

"I left my suitcases at the dig house." I hadn't told her I'd been fired. "I'll collect them tomorrow. And I have to go to the police station and make a statement about finding Dr. Stanton's body. I promised Hank." I leaned back and closed my eyes.

"Tomorrow will be soon enough. You look beat, France. Oh, here we are."

The taxi driver carried our bags up the stairs to the third floor. Mrs. Devlin was waiting for us at the door of the suite, and rushed to greet us, trying to embrace us both at once. The combination of worry and happy relief on her wrinkled face hit me harder than I expected, and I found myself blinking back tears as we gathered in the suite's tiny foyer.

"Come in, girls, come in. France, you look exhausted. Here's your room. You don't mind sharing with Willa, I hope. I'm so glad you're safe. You need some tea and a rest. Come along, Willa. Oh, I'm so glad to see you both."

The next morning, I telephoned the dig house, having found the number in a notebook among the jumbled contents of my beach bag. The phone rang and rang. I was about to give up when I heard Meg's voice, out of breath.

"Stanton Temple Project Office. Hello."

"Hi, Meg. It's France Leighton."

"France! Hi! Hank said he'd seen you. Are you back in town?"

She sounded glad to hear from me, which was encouraging. I wondered what, if anything, Hank had told her about my adventures.

"I got back yesterday," I said. "I'm staying with some friends here, and I'd like to come and pick up my suitcases, if that's okay."

"Sure. In fact, today's perfect. Adele's not here."

"How is she doing?"

"Soldiering on," said Meg. "She's got a lot to deal with. You know—her kids, the police, and getting Bill's body back to the States. All that stuff. Right now, she's meeting with someone from the Antiquities Department. Did you want to see her?"

"Well, not really. I mean, I probably should, but…"

"I get it. Don't worry, you won't bump into her today."

At the police station, I was ready to write out my statement, but of course there was a formal procedure. I told my tale to a serious young officer who transcribed it in what looked like shorthand, and then typed it, using an enormous old typewriter. I avoided any mention of Adam or his house. The last thing I wanted was to get the police interested in me. I said I had found a cave or tunnel and unwisely decided to explore it. Paintings and inscriptions inside made me think it was a tomb, so I kept exploring, and soon after that I found Dr. Stanton's body. I was deliberately vague as to dates and times, saying I had recently sustained a concussion.

After reading it over and specifying corrections—which meant re-typing the whole thing—I signed the document. The police officer rubber-stamped it in three different ink colours and that was that.

The business took more than an hour, at the end of which I ventured a few questions. Was it common for visitors to the Theban Necropolis, either tourists or scholars, to meet with mishaps?

The young officer looked uneasy, but since I had not asked for specifics about any particular case, he replied to the effect that accidents happen. "And of course, there are bandits in the area," he added.

"These bandits, do they often harm visitors?"

"Sometimes, Mademoiselle. Especially if visitors become involved with illegal activities. We advise you hire guides and do not go outside of the tourist areas. Your explorations by yourself were unwise. That is why we say visitors must return to Luxor before the evening."

"But there's a guest house in Sheikh Abd el-Qurna that caters to visitors."

He looked annoyed. "Yes, we are aware of Mr. Mahmoud Mohamed's establishment. It is understood that if visitors remain there overnight, Mr. Mohamed must guarantee their safety." He paused for a moment. "The people of those villages do not often report matters to us, Mademoiselle. They manage their own affairs."

"I understand," I said. I understood a great deal more, of course, but felt no need to discuss it. And I suspected no word would come to Luxor of a blind man found wandering on the stony slopes of el-Qurn. If I wanted to find out what really happened to Adam, I'd be on my own.

It felt strange, walking up to the gate in the wall around the Stanton Project's dig house. Strange but familiar. I even remembered the lifting motion needed to avoid scraping the bottom of the gate on the paving stones.

The workroom was messy and Meg frazzled, with a pen behind her ear and a pencil stuck into her hair. She gave me a quick hug. "You look like you've been through the wringer, France."

"Well, you could say so. But I lived to tell about it." I handed her the knapsack. "Thanks for lending me this. I'm sorry I got it all banged up."

"Don't worry about it. It's nicely broken in now. Come on, let's get your stuff. Then how about lunch at the Bennu Bird?" She led the way to the Girls' Dorm and hauled my suitcases and overnight case from the closet and under one of the beds.

"You still have the whole place to yourself," I said.

"Solitary splendour—for now," Meg said. "Do you want to change into anything?"

Considering she didn't care about fashion, I figured that meant I looked even worse than I thought. "No, I'm okay. What you see is what you get."

"Okay, then. Your cases can stay here until you get a taxi after lunch."

"Where's Hank?" I asked.

"He had an errand somewhere. He might meet us at the Bird if he gets done in time. Oh, before I forget—I have some mail for you." She hurried back to the workroom and came back with a postcard and several envelopes, which I stuffed into my purse.

I pulled out a cloth-wrapped cylindrical shape. "Say, Meg, would you mind having a look at this?" I asked, unwinding the turquoise scarf I'd wrapped around the *shabti*. I'd brought just one of the pair. By itself it was inert and harmless, but the two of them together made me nervous.

Meg looked at the figurine and then at me. "What about it?"

"Well, I thought you might be able to tell me something about it. It's a *shabti*, I know that, but I can't read the inscription, of course. Anything you can tell me would be a plus."

"Come in here and let's have a look." She led the way back to the workroom, switched on a desk lamp and put on her glasses. "Where did you get this, France?"

"I'll tell you after you check it over, if you don't mind."

Meg gave me a hard look and bent over the *shabti*. After a minute or two, she pushed her glasses up onto her forehead. "Okay, here's what I can tell you. It looks like a better-quality faience *shabti* with features and text in black paint, New Kingdom style. Pretty standard, but there are a few things…" She pulled her glasses back down. "It's an overseer *shabti*, meaning it was meant to supervise others. That's why it has a whip, right here." She pointed at black lines on the blue figurine. "But—and this is really strange—it also has what looks like a dagger in a sheath worn over the shoulder. I've never seen that before."

"Okay," I said. "What else?"

"Well, the text. It's usually parts of Chapter 6 of the *Book of the Dead*, a spell to make the *shabti* work for the Osiris-person, you know, the deceased. But this one…" She looked at me again. "Where *did* you get this thing, France?"

"Why? I mean, is it a fake or something?"

"That's actually a tempting explanation, considering the totally weird text. It follows the usual pattern, but, well, here's what it says: 'O thou *shabti* figure of the priest and king Nephren-Ka, victorious, if there be a matter of removing those who hinder the purposes of the Great Old Ones and the messenger who speaks for them to men, let the judgment fall upon thee in the matter of stalking and slaying and concealment of the remains thereof.' The name of Osiris has been omitted, and there's an extra line that says… Wait a sec." She peered at the figurine. "It says, 'Call upon my brother, for we act as one.' That suggests it's one of a pair. I've seen a lot of *shabtis*, but never one with an inscription anything like that." Meg pushed the object away from her. "Okay, France, your turn now—where did you get it?"

"Well, I bought it."

"Where?"

"In that village on the west bank, Sheikh Abd el-Qurna. There was a man selling 'antiquities.' I assumed they were fakes. That guest house I stayed in—they had a workshop to make souvenirs out of wood."

"Well this isn't wood. Making faience is quite a process. I don't know if anyone still does it."

"You mean this *shabti* might actually be the real thing? Ancient?"

Meg took off her glasses and rubbed the bridge of her nose. "It looks real, but that text just isn't right. I'd like to think it's a really good fake. That name, Nephren-Ka. I'm sure I've seen it somewhere, but not in academic literature. More your lunatic fringe."

I didn't want to take that up. "So, the *shabti* spell was supposed to make them come to life?"

"That was the idea," Meg said. "The dead person in the afterlife would speak the words and the shabtis would become life-size and get to work. Most of them were supposed to do agricultural work or manufacturing, but this one and its brother"—she flicked a finger at the *shabti*—"maybe they were meant to be assassins."

"Well, let's hope it doesn't turn into one right here," I said. "But I guess you'd have to recite the spell in ancient Egyptian, wouldn't you?"

"That would help." Meg stood and handed me the *shabti*. "Plus you'd have to have the other one *and* you'd have to be Nephren-Ka, whoever he is. Or was. Okay, wrap this guy up again and let's get going. We don't want Hank to beat us to the Bird."

The Bennu Bird welcomed us into its atmosphere of coffee, spices, and tobacco. Once we were settled with plates and cups, Meg lost no time in quizzing me.

"What happened to you over there? How did you find Dr. Stanton?"

I thanked the gods for a mouthful of food to be chewed and swallowed, and took another second to wash it down with coffee before I spoke. How many versions of this story had I told by now?

"Well, I went looking for Adam Dexter. You remember, that guy I had dinner with. But it was all so strange. I ended up in a tunnel connected to a tomb, sort of like the way some of the houses in that village are connected to the Tombs of the Nobles. That's where I found Dr. Stanton—in that tomb."

"Who do you think killed him?" Meg was sliding chunks of grilled lamb and eggplant from a skewer, and alternated glances between her plate and my face.

"I have no idea. Well, actually, I have ideas but nothing to back them up."

Meg looked like she was about to say something but changed her mind. After a few moments of silent chewing, she said, "Did you ever play your cello over there? Requiem for a dead pharaoh or something?"

The question took me by surprise and I didn't think before answering. "Oh, I played her, all right. But it was a requiem for a dead cello."

"What? I was just kidding." Meg stared at me.

"Eudora. My cello. She broke. Split, fell apart. Her wood dried out, you see. There was a crack..."

"Oh, I'm sorry, France. That must have been awful. Can it be repaired?"

"No. Not a chance. I left her there, in the tomb."

"You found Dr. Stanton and lost your cello in the same place. Wow. Oh, here's Hank."

Not a moment too soon. I hoped like hell Meg wouldn't mention the *shabti*.

"Greetings, ladies," Hank said, pulling out a chair and dropping into it. "Glad to see you back in the land of the living, France."

"Thank you."

"And it looks like the world might live to fight—or hopefully not fight—another day. Kennedy and Khrushchev have agreed on a missile removal deal, so we're not on the brink any more. We can make plans for tomorrow. For next week, even."

"On the brink?" I asked.

"Where've you been?" Meg slapped her forehead. "Okay, I guess you didn't get much news over there on the west bank. It's all anybody's been talking about the last week. Kennedy, Khrushchev and Castro. And nuclear war."

"Someone at the guest house mentioned a speech by President Kennedy."

"That was more than a week ago," said Hank, and went on to tell me about recent developments.

I decided to change the subject. "How are things at the dig?"

Hank and Meg looked at each other. "You go first." Hank nodded at Meg and turned to catch the waiter's attention.

"Well, work goes on, but Adele's pretty busy dealing with everything. She had to go up to Cairo to tell her kids about their dad and make arrangements. And Hank's had his hands full too, of course. So I've been running the dig." She turned to Hank. "Have you made up your mind about staying?"

Hank stirred his coffee, swirling the brown foam on its surface. "Well, job one for me right now is dealing with Uncle Jim's death. I have to go home for a couple weeks, of course, but I'll be back."

"Great," said Meg. "I'm glad to hear it. I have to say, I'm not sure what Adele's planning, but we really need you on board to keep things going here. My thesis is riding on this dig. Too bad she went and fired you, France. We could use your help now."

"Maybe you can persuade Adele to re-hire her," said Hank.

"Don't bother. I'm going back to the States soon." I turned to Hank. "How's the investigation into Dr. Stanton's death going?"

"I'm beginning to wonder if there is an investigation," said Hank. "According to the police, bandits killed Bill and Uncle Jim fell and broke his neck running away from them. The bandits hid both bodies in a tomb they used as a cache for looted archaeological items. Bandits are a convenient explanation for all kinds of bad things on the west bank. It lets the police off the hook. By the way, France, did you get a chance to make a statement with the police?"

"This morning. The police officer I gave my statement to said visitors who aren't careful might be harmed by bandits and the villagers won't report them."

Hank looked annoyed. "I know the people over there, and most of them are perfectly honest. Well, okay, some of them are in the antiquities trade—mostly fakes—but they need the business that comes from tourists and archaeological projects. If there were any bandits, they'd deal with them themselves. France, you were there when Mr. Mohamed was talking to those two old fellows."

"I was, but I didn't get everything they were saying. I think Yasmin left out some details in her translations."

Hank unfolded a napkin. "Well, she used some polite euphemisms. They were worried about the area getting a bad reputation. Murder and rape are bad for business." He turned his attention to his plate.

"There was no rape," I said, and immediately wished I hadn't. Here we were, back to Whatever Happened to Poor France. "Okay, I can't explain everything that happened to me. I don't know who Adam Dexter is. Or was. I'm sure he's gone, but I can't explain that either." I stopped talking. My throat was closing up and my eyes threatened to overflow.

"It's okay, France." Meg reached across the table and patted my hand. "No one's accusing you of anything. You don't have to explain." But I was pretty sure they both thought they had me figured out—silly girl fooled by fast-talking creep.

"Hank," I said, setting down the napkin I'd used to blot my eyes, "when you were looking for that tunnel I told you about, where I found Dr. Stanton, did you see a villa? Or did you go down that far? It must be pretty close to the Nile. There were these tall palm trees, and papyrus, and a canal..."

They were both staring at me, just like Hank and Uncle Jim had when I told them about my dinner date with Adam. "What's the matter?"

"There is no villa," said Hank. "Not anywhere near that place. There are date palms, but otherwise it's farmland, and pretty much flooded right now. Definitely no villa." He went back to eating.

"Well, I stayed in a villa, for at least two nights. It was a pretty fancy one too, with really nice furniture. There was a pink phone in my room. Except it didn't work." I looked at Meg. "I wanted to phone you one night, but the phone just made weird noises. It didn't even have a cord." I felt like crying again.

Meg wiped her lips and pushed her plate aside. "Let's go back to the beginning. How did you get to this villa?"

"Well, that's the problem." I drank the last of my coffee. "I walked out behind the village, and when I got to the top of a ridge I slipped and fell. I must have hit my head again, because when I came to, I was in that house. In a bed, and Adam Dexter was sitting there next to me. Don't look at me like that! He was sitting on a *chair*."

"Well, there are all those dig houses on the west bank, aren't there?" said Meg. "Some of them might be described as villas."

"Sure, but we know all those—Carter's house, Met House, Marsam House, the German one—I forget its name. It couldn't have been any of them, and what others are there?" Hank looked from Meg back to me.

"Well, I guess I have to say I can't explain it," I said. "And I did think the place was pretty strange, but I figured it was because he was a nuclear physicist. You know, modern science.

I even thought he might be working on special effects for the movies..." I trailed off, realizing how silly that idea sounded.

"It seems to me you were abducted," said Meg. "You're lucky you got away unharmed." I could tell by her expression she didn't believe that. She thought I'd been "harmed," but was too embarrassed to admit it.

"How did you get away, exactly?" Hank waved for the waiter and asked for a fresh pot of coffee.

"Well, my room had this funny little door. It was narrow, with rows of hieroglyphs on either side. I thought it was just a decoration, but the room's real door was locked. So I got desperate and pushed on that one. It opened into a tunnel, and eventually I found my way out. But first I found Dr. Stanton."

"Geez, France, that must have been horrible," Meg said.

"Well, it was, but I kept moving, you know, until I saw daylight ahead. The light at the end of the tunnel." I let out a choked little laugh.

"Sounds like a spirit door, doesn't it?" said Hank to Meg. Turning to me, he continued, "Egyptian tombs often had false doors carved or painted on the west wall of the offering chapel, to allow the dead person's spirit a way to exit and enter. To 'go forth by day,' if you remember that phrase from the *Book of the Dead*."

"Which is actually called 'the book of coming forth by day,'" said Meg. "Say, do you think France might have ended up in part of that tomb complex northeast of the Tombs of the Nobles? The suburbs."

"Maybe." Hank stared at the ceiling for a second. "This Adam Dexter, though. What do you think he wanted with you, France?"

Well, that was a question I wasn't going to answer. "I think he wanted to impress me," I said.

Meg rolled her eyes. "By kidnapping you? That's a really—"

Hank interrupted. "What you said back at the guest house, about your grandfather, and that this Adam Dexter is gone, or dead of snakebite? Were you serious, or... trying to impress someone?"

"You mean, was I lying? No, I wasn't. My grandfather really was called Francis Dexter, which is one of the reasons I was interested in Adam Dexter. I don't think we're related, by the way. As for the cobra bite, I couldn't explain what happened to Adam, so I said something that sounded like it might have happened. That's all."

"You have to understand, France. This is serious stuff. I want whoever murdered Dr. Stanton, and maybe Uncle Jim too, to be brought to justice, to know they won't kill anyone else. Mr. Mohamed and the other people who live over there, they don't want their area to be labelled 'dangerous.' Do you get what I'm saying?"

"I get it, Hank." I reached out and put my hand on his. "But if the police aren't taking the investigation seriously, who's going to figure all that out?"

He slid his hand from under mine and tucked it under his chin, elbow on table. "I guess I'll have to," he said. "Jim was an old bachelor, but his students and colleagues will miss him. Heck, I'll miss him. Bill Stanton had his faults, but he's done important work. And there are his two young kids. Adele's pretty tough, but she's hurting." He sighed. "That's part of the reason I'm coming back. I figure I owe her." He flashed a brief smile. "I wouldn't put it past her to get an excavation permit for that tomb you found. So I'll likely be spending time on the west bank and eventually I'll find out what happened to Jim and Bill."

For a moment, I thought he meant the second tomb, the one that must remain forever unbroken. Then I realized he was talking about the place where I'd found Dr. Stanton.

"But shouldn't the police be looking for a missing nuclear physicist?" Meg chased crumbs around her plate with a finger and licked them off.

"Thinking about it," said Hank, "it might be better if they went searching for a snake-bitten American or a nonexistent villa instead of bothering the people in the villages over there about bandits." He shook a teaspoon at me. "It was drugs, I'll bet. This Adam, whoever he was, probably found you when you knocked yourself out and gave you a hallucinogen. And when he'd had his fun, he left you in that wadi where we found you. Does that sound likely?"

"Maybe," I said. If Hank wanted to believe this, I wasn't going to argue with him. And maybe Adam was in Rome, having cocktails with Elizabeth Taylor and Richard Burton.

Back at the hotel, I found a note from Willa saying she and her mother had gone to the *souk* and would be back for supper. I decided to have another shower, just because I could. And to my great relief, my period had started right on schedule. I soaped and lathered, the words "womb," "tomb," and "bomb" running through my mind.

Hosed down and dried off, I slipped into lounging PJs and propped myself on my bed with the mail Meg had given me. First was a postcard with a picture of the Brooklyn Bridge.

Greetings, France. I'm back in the States. Been playing a lot with different musical colleagues. Thought of you and Beethoven. Maybe we'll get a chance to share a stage again??

Signed by Jack Stark, with an address in New York City. Well, well! I thought. Who knows? It depends on what you mean by "stage."

Next was a square envelope, cream-coloured fine stationery with insides to match, a single sheet with the letterhead of Nicholas St. George Leighton, MBChB, FRCS. My father.

Dear Francesca, I hope your Egyptian adventure is proving successful. I also hope you have given thought to your future. Are you planning to undertake an advanced degree, perhaps in Egyptology? Should you be in London after the field season ends, please telephone for an appointment with me, so that we may discuss possibilities.

Followed by an appropriately illegible signature.

"Please"—well, that was nice. And what did he mean by "possibilities?" Maybe we'd finally get to know each other. Smiling, I tucked the note back into its envelope.

Finally, I turned my attention to Alma's bulky envelope, which contained the usual typewritten letter, along with several newspaper clippings and extra pages with notes in Alma's scrawl.

After the usual Providence gossip and household news, there was this:

Got interested in that fellow you
mentioned in your last letter—Adam
Dexter—so put on my old reporter's hat
and did some digging.
He was born in Providence in
1905. Father: Albert Rowland Dexter
(no relation to Francis, I'm pretty
sure). Mother: Fatima el-Hassan
(Egyptian!) Family moved a lot. Albert
in WWI as Engineer.

If Adam was born in 1905, he was fifty-seven! I blushed,
remembering how I'd aroused his body.

Adam studied medicine but never
practiced, except for assisting the
coroner's physician. Maintained a
residence in Providence but left
abruptly soon after a post-mortem on a
young man who was found dead at his
desk after a lightning storm. There
were rumors relating to an artifact
discovered in a derelict church once
used by a group of occultists. No
further mention in local newspapers.
(But see below!)

He hadn't told me he was from Providence! Had I
passed him on the street without noticing him? Or had he left
the city before I arrived there? I shook my head. As for
occultists, the only one I knew was Mrs. Devlin.

After leaving Providence, Adam
obtained a PhD in Physics from

Princeton. 1940s, several references
in publications and scientific
meetings relating to nuclear physics
research. Adam Dexter mentioned as an
"investigator in the field of nuclear
physics," and in 1949 he is named in
article relating to work on H-bomb.

So much for peaceful uses of his knowledge, the hypocrite. Jumping to my feet, I paced around the room, the letter pressed to my thigh. I didn't want to read any more. But I did.

According to a source who must
remain nameless, Dexter was eased away
from research into nuclear weaponry
because of "extreme views and bizarre
beliefs." Possible fears of defection,
I suppose; rumors put him in Moscow in
the late '50s. Reappeared on lecture
circuit about 1960, touting nuclear
power and weapons as "modern solutions
to modern problems." Sept. 1962 (see
clipping) went to Egypt by gov't
invitation as advisor on energy.

So Adam *had* arrived in Egypt just about when I had. While not surprising, this confirmation of my suspicions disturbed me.

Finally (saved best for last!):
found an engagement notice in the
society pages from the '30s for Adam
Dexter and a lady who must remain
anonymous. I managed to track down a

relative of hers, who told me they met
through "some sort of secret cult." The
relative clearly disapproved and was
pleased when Dexter broke off the
engagement and left town. This must
have been about the time of that post-
mortem (see above). Whatever it
revealed had a profound effect on
Dexter. "He was like a different person
after that," my source told me, "like
someone had taken the heart and soul
out of him."

That sounded like the Adam I knew, all right. A man whose heart and soul had been removed. I went back to the bed and sat down. I put my thoughts on hold as I sorted through the rest of the papers.

The newspaper clippings and notes copied from a variety of other sources pretty much said the same things as Alma's letter, only in more detail. The last thing in the packet was a photograph of Adam torn from a magazine.

I didn't want to look at it and shuffled it under the other pages. Then I changed my mind and shuffled it back out. Then I turned it face-down on the bedspread and sat there staring at an advertisement for orthopedic shoes on the reverse.

Don't be silly, France! It's only a piece of paper.

I picked it up and turned it over. Adam smiled at me. Same smile, same precisely sculpted, pharaoh-like lips, same intense gaze. Except there was no way this was a young man. Middle-aged, for sure. No—old. Older than he'd looked in person.

I remembered him inside the tomb, how he had turned into a grotesque caricature of a man, his skull and teeth shining through his flesh before the cobra devoured him. Him? Or "it?" Was the Adam Dexter I had known a human being, or just a human body inhabited and manipulated by something else? What had the men of Qurna found in the dry wadis leading from el-Qurn? A human husk, blind and mindless, wandering among the stones? And did it still exist in some form?

What had I allowed inside my body? I pushed that thought away almost before I finished thinking it. At least my sexual act with Adam had produced no result. Not the usual kind, anyway, but what about other kinds? Like those dreams I'd been having, for instance.

The queasy mixture of lies and unanswered questions got to the point where I had to tell someone the truth. Sort of like throwing up. That evening, when we returned from supper at a nearby restaurant, I had an announcement.

"I need to talk about what happened to me in the Theban Necropolis."

Willa, standing behind her mother, mimed applause, but Mrs. D. said, "Of course you do, dear. Let's get comfortable and meet in the sitting room."

Once we were settled on the rather lumpy sofa and chairs, I started telling my story. Whatever Happened to Poor France, Take 3, beginning with my conversation with Francis Dexter in the guest house. Willa tried to interrupt a couple of times but stopped when her mother raised a hand. After that, she sat and listened with a look on her face that said, "Is this stuff for real or are you making it up?"

By the time I got to the part about entering the Wadi of the Eyeball wearing the Red Dress of Fate, I realized something. "I'm sorry, Willa. I think I'd be more comfortable if I could tell your mother the rest alone."

Mrs. Devlin gave me a slow, searching look and nodded. "Willa, I agree with France. She and I must talk in confidence. You'll excuse us, please? Or rather, would you allow us to excuse you?"

For once, Willa's easy compliance with her mother's whims deserted her. "Oh, Mother, can't you tell when someone's spinning you a story? Do you actually believe all this stuff she's been telling us?"

Mrs. Devlin's face crumpled, but her voice was steely. "Please do as I ask, Willa. We'll talk more about this later."

For a few seconds, I thought Willa would refuse to budge, but she got up and left the sitting room. The precise click of the door closing had the resonance of a slam.

"Mrs. Devlin, it's okay. I don't want to cause any trouble between you and Willa."

She ignored that. "All right, France. Tell me everything."

I took a breath and started again. Take 4. Mrs. D. listened without comment, her gaze fixed on her slippered feet propped up on an ottoman, as I related how I found and opened the tomb.

"Mrs. Devlin, you're a psychic, aren't you? You can communicate with the dead?"

She focussed her amber eyes on me. They looked tired, the lids wrinkled and drooping. "Under certain circumstances, yes. Why do you ask?"

I spoke to my hands, fingers knotted in my lap. "I wonder if you could reach Adam. And Dr. Dykstra."

Mrs. D. smiled wearily. "Tell me why you want to reach these individuals."

"I want to apologise to Dr. Dykstra. I feel responsible for his death. And I need to know what made Adam the way he was—not really human. I feel guilty for the way I used him to get into the tomb and then called for his destruction."

"But you say he was a murderer, if only through his servants."

"Yes, but I think he was a victim too. Something took over his body and used it. Just like I did. My coming to Luxor drew Adam here and caused the deaths of both Dr. Stanton and Dr. Dykstra. They'd still be alive if not for me."

"But you didn't come to Luxor knowing that, nor intending to harm anyone," said Mrs. D.

"No, of course not. I haven't been able to talk about all this until now. And I've told so many lies." I covered my face with my hands. "I don't know what to think anymore."

"France, coming here was your fate. You were an instrument in the hand of an unknown power."

She sounded just like Grandpa Francis, but I managed to suppress the laugh her words provoked. "Maybe so, but that doesn't really help me."

Mrs. Devlin shifted in her chair. She spread her hands in a dismissive gesture and then put them together as though she was about to pray. "You're descended from Francis Dexter. He had great gifts and overcame great flaws. You have different gifts. And different flaws to overcome, no doubt."

Why was she fixated on Francis Dexter? He was dead and gone, a ghost. "I just need to know what I'm supposed to do now."

Mrs. D. moved her feet from ottoman to floor and sat up straight. I thought she was about to get up and leave, but she didn't.

"I think you have more to tell me. If I am to help you, I must know everything. And please call me Amelia."

My face grew hot. I looked at my hands again. "Okay...
Amelia. Yes, there's more, but I don't know if you'll believe me."
Really? After the way I opened the tomb? After the cobra?

She sat on the edge of her chair while I spoke, eyes fixed
on my face, lips moving silently at times. Her intensity made
me nervous, and I rushed through the rest of my tale.

"Does that mean I'm a guardian, like that priestess,
except in the living world?"

"Yes!" Mrs. D. was tense with excitement.

"That frightens me. I don't know if I can do it."

"What makes you think you have to do anything? All
you need to do is *be*. Be yourself, be aware. When you need to
act, you will be shown what to do. The priestess in that tomb
sacrificed her life at need. I think you sacrificed something too,
didn't you?"

"Eudora, of course."

"I think you made another sacrifice as well," said
Amelia, patting my hand and smiling knowingly.

I shrugged. If Amelia thought my tattered virginity was
a sacrifice, I wasn't going to argue with her. "If I'm shown what
to do, like you said, how will I know if it's good or evil? At first
I thought Adam was a wonderful man who wanted to show me
wonders."

"Adam Dexter was an agent of chaos. He gave his
physical body to it, in exchange for knowledge and power. But
it used him as a tool."

"So did I. What does that make me?"

"That's up to you. All of us are threads in a great
tapestry. Each thread has strands of strength and weakness,
perfection and flaws, that contribute to the whole.

"You, like Francis, have an affinity for the world of the dead. I perceived it the day we visited the Tombs of the Nobles."

"But I've been having horrible dreams. I can't describe how awful they are. I feel something inviting me, telling me I can overcome the awfulness if I go with it." I thought for a moment, chewing on the end of my braid. "It's as though I'm being asked to take Adam's place."

Amelia nodded. "I'm not surprised. The outer entities seek entry to this world through people like us. But you're young and strong. You have tools at your disposal, and you have allies, both in this world and the one beyond. You will learn how to recognize them and see through their allure."

"I don't know anything about that stuff." I hid my face in my hands again.

"Don't worry. I'll put you in touch with people who can teach and advise you. Some of them live in England and met Francis when he was there in the thirties. Others are in the States."

"Do you know any occultists in Providence?"

"'Occultists'? Is that what you think I am?" Amelia frowned. "I'll write down the addresses for you and send letters of introduction. But where's Francis's emerald ring? I haven't seen it since you came back here."

"Don't worry, it's safe. Wearing it made me tired. And I think it gives me nightmares."

"Perhaps, but I think you should keep it close to you." She got to her feet and gave my shoulder a quick squeeze. "Believe me, all is well."

I didn't believe her but saw no point in saying so. "Thank you, Amelia."

"You're welcome. Right now, I'd better have a talk with Willa. She can be a little impulsive. Good night, France."

She turned away, covering a yawn, and padded into the bedroom I shared with Willa. The two of them went into Amelia's room, and she shut the door. I retreated to the bathroom and ran water to drown out any raised voices. My teeth got an extra thorough brushing, and the rest of me got yet another shower.

Returning to the bedroom, I was greeted by Willa, not asleep as I'd hoped, but sitting on her bed, wide awake and waiting for me.

"Well, France," she said. "Talking paintings. You certainly have a good imagination. And you lied to me about Adam Dexter."

"Okay, I lied." I fluffed my pillow, trying to nerve myself up to argue with her and wishing I didn't have to. "But not about what I saw in that Osiris painting. Something like that happened to me in one of the Tombs of the Nobles, remember? You were there."

"All I saw was you putting on an act. I sure never saw any talking picture."

"Well, I did. You never said you thought I was acting then. And I would have expected you to be open to supernatural phenomena, given your mother's interests."

She sighed. "It's *because* of Mother's interests that I have to be a skeptic. She's so sincere, and I think she does have a sixth sense, but that makes her vulnerable, you know?"

"Vulnerable to fraudulent types. Like me?"

"You said it. I'm not accusing you of anything."

"You just did!" I almost shouted.

It was impossible to argue quietly, so we sat and glared at each other for several seconds. Finally, I said, "Okay, you can believe me or not. Maybe I was hallucinating. Maybe Adam and I took drugs and had sex and then he dumped me in that wadi. Does that explanation make you happy?"

"Oh, don't be so dramatic!" A pause, and then, "Did you really... you know, have sex with him?"

"Yes. That part was true." I realized how that sounded and rushed to fix it. "Well, as far as I know, it was all true, but I haven't felt normal since that balloon crash I told you about. Falling and hitting my head again didn't help any. Maybe that's what caused those visions, or whatever they were. I don't know. But I'm not trying to take advantage of your mother in any way. She's been kind to me and I appreciate it. I hope you can believe that, and just let the rest go."

Willa sat and looked at me, her amber eyes staring from under her straight black fringe. "All right," she said, finally. "Okay, I can accept that. I'm sorry for accusing you just now."

"Okay. Apology accepted. And now let's call it a night."

16
The Chapter of Going Forth

That's where we left things. Until she and her mother left for Aswan two days later, Willa and I were polite, but only that. Mrs. Devlin (somehow I couldn't keep calling her Amelia) gave me a page of names and addresses I dutifully filed away with my passport and other papers. I saw the two of them off with a mixture of regret and relief.

After waving at Mrs. D. and Willa as their boat pulled away from the corniche, I went to a café in one of the big hotels. Along with coffee, I bought several newspapers. It was time I caught up with the rest of the world.

Kennedy, Khrushchev and Castro. Arguments among nations about missiles, accusations and denials, threats and counter-threats. The weapons Adam had been involved with developing were being prepared for use. Many thoughtful people warned of imminent annihilation, complete with references to *Hiroshima*, a book I'd had to read in high school. The soundless flash, the mushroom cloud, bodies reduced to shadows on walls... I remembered the vision I'd had in the tomb, of a dead and blasted world.

I put the newspapers aside and leaned back in my chair, gazing at the emerald in my ring. I thought about the ancient Egyptians' concept of cosmic order embodied in the goddess Ma'at. And the principle of chaos and violence. What was its name? *Isfet*. The Egyptian religion was all about maintaining a balance between the two. Their civilization had receded into the past, but the eternal struggle went on, and right now it looked like chaos might win.

Was a connection between an international crisis and an artifact in an ancient Egyptian tomb even remotely possible? And what was my role in all this?

I returned to the room I'd taken for the remainder of my stay in Luxor and made a start on sorting and repacking my belongings for the trip home. In my big suitcase was the turquoise scarf containing the *shabti* I'd shown to Meg and the blue cloth bundle with the other one. Thinking about what Meg had told me, I unwrapped them and sat on the edge of my bed, a *shabti* in each hand. They hadn't changed in size, shape or colour since the last time I'd seen them, but surely their painted faces looked different, alert and receptive. I could have sworn they exchanged glances and smirked.

We will answer to you. If you choose. We will help you. These weren't my thoughts. Where did they come from? Closing my eyes, I stilled my mind, holding it watchful, waiting, waiting...

The noise of traffic outside and the steady "whup-whup" of the fan above my head faded away. I would need help to deal with my recent experiences. I would need companions who understood me...

In the stillness, something stirred. Not a shape in darkness, but the darkness itself. A vortex into which I could fall, in which I would *become*. All I had to do was yield my will and speak the right words. The darkness tensed, waiting. My lips and tongue moved to shape unfamiliar words. "*I ushbity ipn Nefren—*"

Something landed on my left foot, returning me to Luxor, to my hotel room, to myself. The *shabti* from my left hand lay on the floor. I picked it up and laid both of them on the bedspread.

"Nope. No thanks. Not now. Maybe not ever. You guys are coming to America with me. We'll see how you like it there." I refolded the turban cloth and stretched it out to its full length. I put a *shabti* at one end and rolled it up to the halfway point. Then I did the same with the other one and tied the scarf around the bundle to secure it.

That night, I dreamed of a tremendous city under the sea. Pillars like those of the Karnak temple rose into sun-shot emerald waters. Seaweeds flourished and humanoid forms floated past me unseeing. And again, I heard, or felt, an invitation. *Come, France. Yield your will to me and live forever with knowledge and power.* I got up and walked around my room in an effort to shake off the strangeness. Then I slept again, and dreamed I stood on the summit of el-Qurn. Below me was not Luxor, but Wa-set, ancient Thebes, its temples shining in the sun. Near me stood a man. A human figure in the guise of a Pharaoh, like Adam the last time I saw him, except slender and youthful. Adam, alive again? He smiled at me and gestured enigmatically. *Come, France. I will make it easy for you. One moment of pain, and then endless bliss.*

I awoke exhausted, pulled off the emerald ring and put it back in my overnight case. As I tucked it away, my fingers found the cobra amulet from the Unbroken Tomb. Clasping it, I lay down again and fell into a dreamless sleep.

The day before I left Luxor for Cairo, I went once more to the Karnak temple, as a tourist. Strolling among the giant columns of the Hypostyle Hall, I recognized the place where I sat and played Eudora only a month before. The thought of her lying shattered in the Unbroken Tomb brought a shiver of sorrow.

I placed my palms on one of the columns and felt the roughness of the stone. Sandstone. Stone made of sand grains pressed together for millions of years. It was immeasurably ancient when the Egyptians quarried it and floated it down the Nile to Wa-set, this place, once called Thebes, now al-Usqur, or Luxor. My mind reeled through centuries, millennia, aeons. Here I stood, touching sand grains that once drifted in the currents of a vanished sea. Before that, they had formed the substance of some other stone in a world beyond knowing.

Now, in this temple that was new when Meresamun served here, its roof intact, its paint fresh and bright, I was at a crossroads. I tilted my head to look at the flared tops of the columns, sixty feet above me, supporting only the sky and the golden light of late afternoon. I imagined their former painted glory and felt the immense weight and mystery of time.

Time to make up your mind, France.

I had come to Egypt for thrills and adventures. What did these pillars tell me? *Stand firm, rise high.* I knew things no one else did. But what if I didn't want that knowledge? I was twenty-one years old. I wanted friends, and love, and *fun*. Why did I have to guard the legacy of a priestess dead for three thousand years?

Because I carried the knowledge to destroy the Unbroken Tomb, or to preserve it. What would happen if it were opened and violated? I remembered my vision of a blasted Earth. Who would be left to blow its dust away?

Surrender.

My fingers sought the little cobra figure I had brought with me from the tomb, a gift from the goddess of the Peak. A parting gift, because I was leaving tomorrow. Its colour was pale blue with a tinge of green. The tight curves of the tail were smooth and shiny, except for a few small nicks. The flared head and neck bore horizontal markings like those of the real creature. The face—two eye-pits and an incised mouth—was benign, almost cheerful. Would she help me keep watch over the *shabtis*? To resist the terror and allure of the dreams?

All right then, I thought, slipping the amulet back into my pocket. I had a lot to learn and do. To Cairo tomorrow, and then to London. I would accept my father's invitation. Maybe we would talk about my further education. I just had to decide on a subject to prepare me for the task I had accepted. Egyptology? Medicine? Geology? Maybe nuclear physics? Something that would bring me back to Egypt.

And I had to have a talk with Alma, about her health and my elusive grandfather, and my future. Standing half in a column's shadow and half in golden sunlight, I found myself smiling.

I left the temple complex and joined groups of tourists straggling along the avenue of sphinxes toward the Nile. Modern-day pilgrims, all of us seeking something. By the time I reached the corniche, the sun had set, flushing the turquoise sky with remnant gold. Lights winked on in windows and on boats.

El-Qurn stood solid and black between the busy scene around me and the silence of the West. Above the peak, in the radiant blue of coming night, shone a silver planet. Isis or Hathor?

Once more, I touched the little cobra—for luck, and courage and wisdom. I would need all three.

Eudora,
My wooden box of air and singing strings,
You lay against my heart
And sang my thoughts to me.
Now, broken,
You lie in state beneath the Peak,
Hidden from all but me.
I whisper your name,
So you know I do not forget
That you sleep in the place
Where one keeps watch
For millions of years.

Author's Notes

Readers who know Luxor will have realized I've never set foot there. In writing *She Who Comes Forth*, I made use of a variety of resources to remedy my ignorance. Notable among them is *River in the Desert*, an excellent account of travels in Egypt by Paul William Roberts. *Tutankhamen: life and death of a pharaoh* by Christiane Desroches-Noblecourt, in particular Chapter 3, "The world of the dead and life west of Thebes," was inspiring and informative, especially as it was published in 1963 and so is contemporary with the events of the novel. I must also mention Tim Cooper's blog, thegreatbelzoni, for vivid accounts of explorations on the west bank and life in its villages; and Bernard M. Adams' website "My Luxor," for its descriptions and photographs of the Hatshepsut Cliff Tomb at Sikket Taqet Zeid Wadi. Other internet resources are too numerous to mention individually, but Wikipedia and Google Maps were endlessly helpful. All extrapolations, misinterpretations, and errors are my own, and I take full responsibility for them.

My story "A Visit to Luxor" (Herbert West Series supplement no. 3) is a "prequel" to *She Who Comes Forth*.

Audrey Driscoll

Acknowledgements

My sincere thanks to members of the Victoria Writers' Society's Tuesday night novel critique group, who provided valuable suggestions for the work in progress: Éva Arros, Judith Berman, Diana Jones, Edeana Malcolm, and Emillie Parrish. To Kevin Brennan, for his thorough reading and insightful comments, my gratitude.

About the Author

Audrey Driscoll lives, writes and gardens far from Egypt, in the city of Victoria, British Columbia. She is the author of The Herbert West Series. More information on her books, thoughts, and opinions may be found on her blog at
audreydriscoll.com

THE HERBERT WEST SERIES

Book 1. The Friendship of Mortals
Herbert West can revivify the dead – after a fashion. Librarian Charles Milburn agrees to help him, compromising his principles and his romance with Alma Halsey, daughter of the Dean of Medicine. West's experiments become increasingly dangerous, but when he prepares to cross the ultimate border, only Charles can save his life – if his conscience lets him.

Book 2. Islands of the Gulf Volume 1, The Journey
To Andre Boudreau, Herbert West is The Doctor, who saved his life in the Great War. Andre will follow him into Hell if necessary. Margaret Bellgarde knows him as Dr. Francis Dexter, attractive but mysterious. One day she will be shocked by what she is willing to do for his sake. But who is he really? She doesn't know – and the possibilities are disturbing.

Book 3. Islands of the Gulf Volume 2, The Treasure
Abandoned and abused, young Herbert West resorts to drastic measures to survive. At Miskatonic University, he becomes a scientist who commits crimes and creates monstrosities. Decades later, haunted by his past, he finds safety as Dr. Francis Dexter of Bellefleur Island, but his divided nature threatens those he loves and forces him to face the truth about his healing powers.

Book 4. Hunting the Phoenix
Journalist Alma Halsey chases the story of a lifetime to Providence, Rhode Island and finds more than she expected – an old lover, Charles Milburn, and an old adversary, renegade physician Herbert West, living under the name Francis Dexter. Fire throws her into proximity with them both, rekindling romance and completing a great transformation.

The Supplements

Supplement 1. The Nexus
Nearing the end of his long life, Miskatonic University professor Augustus Quarrington retraces the path to his entanglement with one of his most interesting – and dangerous – students: Herbert West.

Supplement 2. From the Annexe
Miskatonic University librarian Charles Milburn was Herbert West's assistant and closest friend. He has already revealed much about their association in *The Friendship of Mortals*. But not everything. This is the part he left out.

Supplement 3. A Visit to Luxor
Reformed necromancer Francis Dexter (formerly known as Herbert West) and his servant Andre Boudreau visit Luxor, Egypt in the year 1935. A climb up el-Qurn, the sacred mountain behind the Valley of the Kings, leads to an encounter with bandits, and with one who "was of the old native blood and looked like a Pharaoh."

Supplement 4. One of the Fourteen
Dr. Francis Dexter arrives in London intending to atone for wrongs committed by his former self, Herbert West. A chance meeting in a pub leads to disturbing revelations by a veteran of the Great War, and forces Dexter to relive a terrible journey in the black region between death and life.

www.ingramcontent.com/pod-product-compliance
Lightning Source LLC
Chambersburg PA
CBHW030547180626
46816CB00005B/1442